Lost In
Atlanta

Lost In
Atlanta

A Novel by

Dean McCrary

In Association with

Rahkeem Wilburn

Black Reality Publishing
Atlanta Georgia

Dean's Acknowledgements

This project has been labor of love since it was first imagined by Rahkeem and I, and my dedications are as follows:

To God for giving me the wisdom to see that his wind is always blowing, and helping me realize all I needed to do was to adjust my sails!

To my mother Ruby Robinson for always trying to get me to see that living an honest life is the only kind worth living; I will be forever proud that you are my mother.

To Tamika Braxton for always believing in me, throughout it all! By the way, you look great on the cover!

To my brothers Carlton aka (Ceez) & Sean aka (Peasey) McCrary keep your heads up, and more importantly keep the faith because God will always see you through.

To Jacqueline D. Price for your tireless dedication to our friendship; I am truly blessed to have met you.

To Brian -rushing to judgement is never a solution for true friends. I want you to know now and forever that there was never any malice in my decision. The real tradgey is that 17 years of friendship wasn't enough for you to see that on your own! I ain't mad though, and hope all is well, and much success!

Rahkeem's Acknowledgements

First and foremost I want to thank God for keeping his hand on me.

And Second only to him: My mother Aleshia Thomas, my daughter Sharay Baugh, my sister Amira Thomas, my father James Allen, my Brother Mario Allen and the entire Wilburn family from Ga. to Pa., and the Allen family as well.

As for my friends – to my man Dame; all the late night rap, …well lets just say it's been brought to life!

Special thanks to my ace Joe for holding me down mentally, through rough times.

To my man Richard Jones keep ya head up, and see you soon!

To my cousin Michael Burton you do the same.

Special thanks to my main man Jamal Hill for doing the book cover.

To all my other homies: I love ya'll the same as the first batch; Rodney, Pat, Wali, Sean, Ceez, Jay, Jeff, Pop, and last but not least my childhood homie Kashmir Goins!

A Special Acknowledgement

An extra special thank you goes to Sheila Morris; Your assistance and dedication to this project has been tremendous, and Rahkeem and I felt that you deserved your own page!

So thanks again and you are very much appreciated!

Proverbs 31:3

"Give Not Thy Strength Unto Women, Nor Thy Ways To That Which Destroyeth Kings."

Chapter One
Welcome to Atlanta

All the hype is what first brought me to the Atl. You know, the never ending stream of props coming from every corner of black America that's spewed whenever Atlanta is mentioned: "Yo nigga, 'ATL' is the shit. The sistas down there are the bomb. Brotha's is ballin' out dat bitch. I'm 'bout to go into the music bidness down there." After arriving I soon discovered I'm not too particular about the south, but there is one thing that I can say pleased me— the scores of beautiful black women!

My name is Glenn, but my close friends and family call me G.— When I first came to Atlanta, I figured it to be like any other city. I guess in a lot of ways it was, but the more familiar I became, the more I noticed it was also very different. For many Atlanta has become the new Promised Land, the new Mecca. Complete with its share of fake, superficial, and flamboyant people. When I came to Atlanta originally, I had hoped to find a new beginning, a new sense of self. I had even hoped to find a wife. I felt Atlanta would provide me with a different perspective. Man, it did that plus a whole lot more.

****

"Yo, G. I told my man you want to sell your Benz, and he wanted to know how much."

"Whateva little nigga. You don't know cats with dough like that!"

"I'm serious man. He my man and he got a couple dollars too."

As I listened to my younger brother pitch this potential business deal to me, I began to realize it was time for me to stop treating him like a "little brother" and more like a man. After all he was getting money now and that, if nothing else, demanded respect. I encouraged him by asking, "Who is this cat, and is he serious?"

Happy to be acknowledged seriously Ceez quickly said, "His name is Malik, but I call him Leek." I had a navy blue late model S500 I had gotten tired of. I had put the word out to my close friends and family that I wanted to get rid of it so I could buy a new Range Rover. It had been a long while since I put it up for sale, and I had begun to think I would be stuck with it. I had hoped

Ceez would have wanted it, but he felt it was too big for him. He had set his sights on the BMW 850 and had been on the waiting list now for about six months.

Curious to know more about this young cat who wanted to buy my car, I inquired as to who he was and what he did. I was always on the lookout for a setup, and although my brother was older now, I wasn't sure if the streets had taught him all he needed to know to keep it from happening to him. He began by telling me he knew Malik through a mutual friend and that he "checked out."

Laughingly I said, "So you got connects that can confirm that kind of info, huh?" Ceez didn't appreciate the sarcastic response I gave him, and his response confirmed it. "Look man, if you ain't interested just say so, but stop comin' at me like I'm a joke or something. I told you dude was cool, and I vouch for him. If that ain't good enough, then fuck it."

Carlton was the youngest of four boys and he had always been teased growing up because of his size. He took the nickname Ceez shortly after getting involved in the drug game, mostly to eliminate the confusion and disrespect his given name might draw. Because of his small stature Ceez was always quick to engage anyone tempted to disrespect him; his tolerance for bullshit was zero! I later found out he and Malik had become fast friends, and my jabbing at his friend's integrity was being taken personally.

It was the spring of '98 and it was already hot as a bitch! Ceez was in town visiting for the weekend from D.C. Our mother had moved to Atlanta some eight years prior and vowed never to leave. She had four boys and one daughter, and all of whom were now grown. Atlanta for her was peace, prosperity, and comfort.

I had been coming to the city for the last eight years. To me it was more a stop over, a place to come and party in a relaxed atmosphere with people who were just as relaxed. Coming from Philly, the fifth largest city in the country, Atlanta admittedly was a welcomed change from the fast-paced lifestyle I had grown accustomed to.

Starting in '94 virtually one weekend every month my man B— short for Brian—and I would hop a flight from Philly to ATL, and spend Friday thru Sunday partying at the hot spots throughout the city. It began with club Michael's, Deon's club 21, Dominique's downtown, Keith Sweats' Industry, and in later years Café Echelon, Taboo, and Vegas nights.

We would always round out the night by hitting the infamous strip club Magic City, before it closed down and re-opened. We were coming to Atlanta long before So-So Def became a household name. Jermaine Dupri was in the business, but he had yet to conquer ATL.

Yeah, Atlanta was different then; there were no music industry wannabes running around the city pretending to be producers and rappers. People weren't wearing bandanas, wife beaters, or platinum jewelry. Yellow gold was still in hot demand! Deon Sanders and Dominique Wilkins were the only name brand pro athletes you saw on a regular basis throughout the city. Atlanta Live hadn't even opened yet.

Ludachris was calling himself Chris Luva Luva, and he and his partner, Poon Daddy, would call the Ryan Cameron morning show at Atlanta hot 97.5 every day, hoping for their big break. I wonder whatever happened to Poon Daddy. Anyway, Brian and I would fly mostly, but if we came across a long holiday weekend, we would hop in either his Lexus SC 400 or my Infinity Q45 and hit the road.

The hair show was our favored attraction. Every year we would make it our business to be there when it hit. The women the function attracted were enough to blow your mind. It was as if God had cordoned off a special Eden filled with beautiful black women whose color ranged from creamy light skin to soft mocha chocolate to deep midnight black, and all equally fantastical and alluring.

Looking back I believe attending the hair shows had a hypnotizing effect on us. All of the years of visiting had been quietly building and creating a kind of dependency, a promise of feminine treasures untold. Atlanta had been touted as the new Promised Land, and black people young and old had been migrating back down south in droves. Word on the streets was that in Atlanta the women outnumbered the men ten to one, and it was true. Brian and I have always been what one might consider opportunists, and after positively exploiting numerous financial opportunities, we discovered we had made enough money to take a break and pursue new horizons. So we decided to give Atlanta a shot and make our mark in a town notorious for major players.

We had spent the bulk of our time in Philadelphia amassing all of the necessary tools to play the game. Along with fine cars we both had handsome Cartier watches. Brian's was the classic "panther" and mine an elegant "Tank Frances," pronounced Fron-says. In addition to that we both had extensive, custom-tailored wardrobes made from fine fabrics with maximum thread counts and the all important 2-inch cuff in all of our slacks. The stage was definitely set. All we needed was an audience and we found it in Atlanta.

Chapter Two
Brian & Stephanie

"Whassup kid? Whacchoo you getting into today?" Brian yawned and stretched before answering my question.

"I think I'm a get with the broad I met a while back. You know, the one I told you I had been speaking to on the phone all the time."

After about a year or two of coming to Atlanta, Brian met and started maintaining contact with a fine little cutie named Stephanie. She was a petite fly, dark-skinned sista whose only apparent problem was she happened to have a shopping habit that would have given both of them chicks from the movie Clueless a run for their money.

I never liked the way she handled Brian though. From the earliest stages of the relationship she attempted to regulate their interaction. They had been talking for about two years—strictly phone conversations because we lived in Philly and she lived in Atlanta. Whenever we would come into town, they would have lunch or dinner, and shortly afterwards he and I would take off, explore the city, and accumulate phone numbers, mostly to plan other lunch, and dinner dates we hoped would lead to late night sexcapades.

I began to notice that whenever we came to town Stephanie would ask Brian for money to get her hair and nails done but would never invite him to stay at her place or even take him out. Typically when we came to town he and I would part company during the day to pursue the various female prospects we had met during previous excursions.

Whenever we drove to Atlanta I would take my mother's car and Brian would drive whichever car we drove to town in. One particular day my mother had a few errands to run and wasn't back home before I was ready to hit the street. So I rode with Brian as he made his rounds visiting with some of the women he had met previously.

After making a few stops we rounded out our cameos at Daweed's, a popular hair salon located in Lithonia, a small suburb of Atlanta. I had a friend there whom I had met and wanted to see before I got lost in the hustle and bustle of the weekend. While I was inside visiting, Brian got a call from Stephanie. She wanted to meet him for lunch at the Tavern in Phipps Plaza. I had finished with my visit and decided to go along with him.

I had planned to do some shopping once we got there while they dined together. When we arrived Stephanie was standing waiting for us at the valet. When Brian and she first met we had driven down in his cranberry Lexus SC 400. The following visit we drove my pearl white Infinite Q45. The visit after that one we flew to town and rented a vehicle. For this visit we drove down in Brian's new Desert Taupe S500 Mercedes Benz.

From the moment we pulled up to the valet it seemed as if a green haze had fallen over Stephanie's face, and I could swear her pupils transformed into little dollar signs. All of a sudden she wasn't hungry anymore—well, at least not for food. Instead of heading down the sidewalk to the café. She took Brian by the hand and led him straight into the Gucci shop saying, "I wanted to look at this new bag real quick before we go eat."

As we entered the store we were immediately greeted by a very attractive and petite Asian woman. Her manner was pleasant and hospitable. She smiled at me familiarly; we'd both flirted with one another during a previous visit to Atlanta as she attempted to get me to purchase a pair of Gucci loafers. She spoke to Stephanie in a way that suggested they too were already familiar with one another; and as if on cue she led Stephanie to the latest handbags for the season.

Each of the featured bags she displayed were priced between four and six hundred dollars, and those were the sale prices. As Brian and Stephanie perused the shop, I decided to cross the mall and browse the latest Versace fashions—hand-painted silk shirts were still in style then. After grabbing a few items, I met back up with them just as they were leaving the store.

Stephanie had several bags in hand and was showing more teeth than the Cheshire Cat from Alice in Wonderland. Not wanting to draw attention to what had obviously been my man getting pimped by this broad, I simply asked, "I guess ya'll bout to go get some grub now?" I wasn't surprised when I heard Stephanie say, "Well, I'm not really hungry, so y'all can go eat and I'll call you later Brian."

Before I realized it I had already blurted out, "Awww wow!" That was the classic term we invoked whenever something went down that was totally off the wall and that was some off the wall shit! Unsure, I asked, "B, I know you ain't getting ready to go for no shit like that are you?" By this time Stephanie had already begun to walk to her car, but you could see the tension in her steps much like the way teenage kids try to creep past their sleeping mothers or fathers after coming home too late, praying and hoping like hell they don't get caught. Like it or not that bitch was caught and I was the police.

Brian stood there with a look that seemed to suggest he didn't really care, but I cared. For me it was a issue of principle; this cat had been dealing with this broad for approximately two years. Racking up ridiculous phone bills and sending hundreds of dollars via Money Gram and Western Union, and Stephanie hadn't so much as brushed up against his dick!

Now she stood poised to walk away with a thousand dollars worth of Gucci products—a handbag, loafers, and belt—without even so much as offering Brian a sandwich! As she headed to the car I subtly called her back and casually asked if she could give us directions to a popular restaurant I had heard of called the Sun Dial Room.

Not having much choice she naively put the bags down and proceeded to point out the directions using various hand motions and gestures, which allowed me to segue into asking her what items Brian had purchased for her. She stupidly responded with a smile and said, "A handbag, some matching loafers, and belt."

I looked over at Brian and boldly stated, "I know you fuckin' tonight!" I knew my statement would create tension and force Stephanie to respond in defense of her honor, which is what I wanted in order to raise the issue of how and why she felt she deserved what he bought. I also wanted to force her to express her true feelings, and she fell right into the trap.

She immediately began shouting, "Mutha fucka, what tha fuck you mean, 'I know you fuckin' tonight?'" I had done it. The train had not only left the station but was also out of control! As the commotion built up Brian finally chimed in, "Yo y'all need to chill." He was always very conservative and hated attracting attention of any kind.

Stephanie, overplaying her hand as if she was truly offended, went on to say, "You need to tell your boy to chill. That mutha fucka done lost his mind! I don't know what he think this is, but it's not that kind of party."

I couldn't resist interjecting, "Well, what kind of party is it? My man been coming into town for two years, looking out for you whenever you request it and you haven't even offered this man the hospitality of your home or even offered to pay for a God damned meal."

My comments finally struck a chord with Brian, prompting him to ask, "Damn, whas'up wit dat Steph? Glenn's right, I break you off nice every time I see you, and you ain't looked out once!" Stephanie stood there speechless. She had expected the focus to remain on my comment, and for her anger to continue to be fueled by my meddling. She wasn't prepared for Brian's reality check, and her response proved it.

"Brian, it's not like that." She said before looking at me with a scowl that would have lit me on fire had she had the power. It took a little jumpstart, but Brian snapped out of the haze he was in and realized Stephanie was just using him. He took it a step further, picked up the bags, and said, "You can get these later tonight. I'll be over after I come from the club."

Stephanie stood there with her mouth wide open, and I expected her to say something fly like, "Don't no nigga jus invite hisself to my house." Ahhhhh, but I forgot the power of Gucci. The effect it has on these women is mind-boggling. Stephanie was hit with a combination of forced reverence for Brian and desire for all of that Gucci shit she now realized was definitely worth fucking for.

She softly and politely said, "Okay, just call me when you're on your way." Brian didn't respond after that. He just nodded in approval as the valet pulled the car up. We got in and drove away. Shortly afterwards Brian got a call on his cell phone as we were driving down Peachtree Street.

It was Stephanie. "I just wanted to say I was sorry for making you feel uncomfortable."

Brian responded coolly and said, "My comfort level is the same. You just make sure you get ya mind right. The reason I choose to do shit for you is because I like you, but don't think for a minute it's sweet like that!"

Brian and I both knew that Stephanie didn't give a damn about what he had just said; she was more intent on effecting damage control to ensure the next bitch didn't get all of the new Gucci shit he'd just taken away from her.

The day passed and Brian and I did lunch with a few other female friends. We hung out later that night at Café Echelon and parted company. I met up with a sista I had known from New York and left with her. Brian followed through with his plan and arrived at Stephanie's house, which was only a few blocks from the club. The next morning we both had stories to tell.

He apparently left his mark because all throughout the day he received numerous calls from Stephanie. It took a while, but I soon realized that she meant a lot more to B than he had originally expressed. In fact, he hadn't spoken on it, but his actions revealed everything his lack of words didn't. When he and I came to Atlanta on that particular occasion, we decided to stay longer than usual. The plan was to be there for about two weeks. Well, two weeks came and went, and then it turned into three.

We had traveled back to Philly a few times to tie up some loose ends, and for me to drive one of my cars down, the blue Mercedes. Brian it seemed had truly established himself with Stephanie after the episode at Phipps Plaza. She no longer predicated his visitations with her on whether or not he was passing off dough. They became inseparable.

He and I were staying at my mother's house initially. Then, all of a sudden he woke up one morning and said he was going to spend the rest of his time in Atlanta staying over at Stephanie's. "G, check this out. I think I am going to go stay with the broad for a couple weeks."

I looked at him sideways and sarcastically said, "What you mean, you think? Nigga, if that's what you trying to do, then handle your business, but I'm telling you, it's a bad move. You know how these broads get when you put yourself under their roof. They get too familiar and familiarity breeds contempt! So all I'm telling you is dig whatchoo doing." Brian started to respond, but I interrupted him and said, "And damn, since when you start taking that broad personal anyway?"

He didn't acknowledge my question, and instead chose to say, "Naw, man. I just don't want to be on your mom like that." Brian knew that was a lame ass excuse. He had known me since the tenth grade. He also knew my mother, and she was probably the coolest mom anyone could ever have. She treated him like one of her sons, and he and I both had been giving her two hundred dollars a week since we had been there, and I knew my mother was especially cool with that!

Not to mention the fact that she had an empty three-bedroom house, but I didn't ride him about it. I figured I did my part by telling him to be careful in understanding the dangers of his decision. I had always assumed Stephanie to be a marginally attractive and otherwise worldly girl. Little did I know that my assumption was dead on. For as big as Atlanta is, it is also very small.

Many of the sistas that I had met and got acquainted with knew of each other. It was as if they were all jockeying for the same cats. I would quietly sit and observe the reactions they each would display whenever another popular Atlanta chick was sighted or mentioned. After Brian moved in with Stephanie, I decided to do a background check on her and I knew just who to ask. The sista from the salon I stopped in on a few weeks prior knew all there was to know about any and everybody in the city.

She was touted as one of the best stylists in Atlanta. Her appointment book proved it. It was always filled to the brim with famous female clients or the girlfriends and wives of Atlanta's elite, both famous and infamous alike. Lynnette and I would kick it whenever I came to town.

Her face was soft and had a dark hue similar to the way coffee looks with just a splash of cream. She was tall and shapely with soulful piercing eyes that were dark and slanted just slightly. Her hair was jet black and always meticulously styled in a short cut tapered at the nape of her neck. She was beautiful, and Brian had often remarked that she was by far the finest woman he had ever seen me with.

Although she and I did have a brief sexual encounter, we both discovered our personalities mandated we remain friends rather than lovers. When I asked her if she knew Stephanie, her jaw dropped. "Please don't tell me you fuck with that bitch! Cause she try to get at every paid nigga she sees."

I immediately corrected Lynnette's assumption by saying, "No, baby. My man met her not too long ago and they are already staying together."

Relieved Lynnette sighed and said, "Oh, well just tell your boy to be careful 'cause she be having a lot of niggas running in and out her house. She likes guys in the industry mostly, but she was messing with this one dude who played her out. You probably heard of him; his name is Toby."

I didn't know any of those Atlanta cats, but the dude's name came up a lot in different conversations. Word on the street was he was getting much paper and had the check-writing game sewed up. I listened to Lynnette give me dude's bio and quietly wondered what would he do if he knew these chicks were putting his business out there like that.

It was funny though because I had met another sista on my last trip to Atlanta who was from Canada. She was in the country illegally and was desperately trying to stay by any means necessary. We hooked up early on, but she needed more shit than I was prepared to do for her, identification, birth certificates, etc. I recalled a pillow conversation we had where she dropped Toby's name too; and here it was again coming out of the mouth of someone else. I was torn between having respect for the cat and believing he was really sloppy with his shit 'cause everybody knew his business.

By the time Lynnette was finished telling her story, I had found out that Stephanie had stepped on her toes because Toby was a former friend of hers. She went on to tell me that he and Stephanie did date and he supposedly had keys to her place and kept a lot of his shit there. Thinking out loud I said, "Damn, B fuck around and get caught up in some shit fucking with that broad." I know niggas well, and I knew once word got out that Brian was staying at her place, one if not all of her former cut buddies would be popping over soon.

Chapter Three
Played

"He who would sleep with the Tigress must also beware of her sharp claws." I have always liked that proverb. I never thought it would ever apply to me. Oh, how wrong I was.

It was April 3, 1998. Brian and I were at a private party at the Georgian Terrace Hotel. Stephanie had told us about it and suggested we attend, especially since I had yet to meet anyone who I wanted to spend time with consistently. When we arrived we were the center of attention. The buzz we created pulling up in back-to-back big body Mercedes Benzes had everybody pointing and staring.

As we entered the function I had a feeling of déja vu, and then I saw her walk in. She was a petite 5' 3" size four with a soft brown complexion. Her eyes were deep brown and slanted just slightly, giving one the impression she may have been mixed. She also had slightly bowed legs that connected to the phatest round ass you could imagine. I was immediately awe struck.

She was wearing a sixties-style silver mini skirt and jacket. The sleeves were cropped at her forearms and the skirt was tightly fitted. She looked so sexy that I immediately imagined lifting her skirt and bending her over the hotel balcony railing and sexing her right there. I leaned over to Brian pointing at her saying, "That's the one I want."

As she passed I reached out and gently grabbed her arm and said, "Excuse me miss, but do you have a minute?" She smiled and politely stopped and I began my conversation. I was admittedly nervous because I didn't expect it to be so easy. I had forgotten how sharply dressed I was.

I introduced myself by saying, "Thanks for stopping and letting me get a closer look." She smiled, apparently appreciating my dialogue, and then said, "You're welcome, but you didn't tell me your name." She was right. I was so intent on getting a closer look that I didn't remember to add that part when I requested she stop. "Oh damn, you're right. I'm sorry. My name is Glenn. What's yours?"

She smiled again and said, "Tina." She then asked, "So who are you here with?"

I pointed over to Brian and said, "Me and my man are here together."

She looked over to B and looked him up and down and asked, "So how did you hear about this party?" Tina asked the question as if she were gathering intelligence or something. I answered her question and told her that a female friend had suggested we come and check it out.

As we stood there I had this feeling that I had found the one, and my search was over. During our conversation I never let on that I was the least bit uneasy. As Eddie Murphy said, "I was giving off my Mack daddy vibe!" I wasn't able to tell at that point, but I would later realize Tina was a professional. "Do you know Troy and them?" Her question was more deliberate than casual, and I realized she was very concerned from her tone. Then it hit me. Whoever Troy was, if I wanted to get to know Tina then I shouldn't know him.

Curiously I asked, "Why you ask me if I knew the dude?" Before she could respond I said, "I don't know anybody in this jawn."

She responded hesitantly and said, "Cause he's my boyfriend, and he and his friends are throwing this party. Plus he be always trying to set me up by putting his boys on me to see if I am going to go for it."

I know. I know. That should have been all I needed to hear to make my dumb ass walk away, but all I saw was a big butt and a smile. What I should have seen was the fact this girl was visibly flirting with me at her boyfriend's party, entertaining my innuendos about the possibility of she and I getting together. No, not me. I was too caught up in my own feeling of superiority, thinking, "I'm about to take this nigga's bitch."

Tina and I talked extensively about everything; she having been the military, and me having been military. We fantasized about moving away to Europe, specifically London. She'd even mentioned that she'd been married once, usually an instant red flag, but she was so alluring I ignored my usual protocol. As the evening went on we were both enraptured with each other and in the midst of our conversation I paused and asked, "Are you happy?" Before she could answer I said, "If you are I can make you happier."

Tina looked at me so intensely that I was immediately at a loss for words. She smiled and told me to write down my phone number, promising to come back to get it from me provided that I was able to pass to her discreetly. I had done it. I leaned over and whispered to Brian, "I told you I was going get her!"

As the night went on I found that I wasn't interested in meeting anyone else. Several women passed by and gave me subtle hints that they were interested, but I was content. After a while Tina approached me again and asked what I was drinking. I looked over to Brian in complete and utter astonishment because I had never had a woman offer to buy me a drink. That was it; I decided that she was the one.

"I-I'm drinking beefeater and orange juice." I stammered nervously, not because it was my drink of choice, but because their selection was limited. As Tina motioned to refresh my drink, protocol demanded I immediately ask her what she was drinking. She promptly responded "Moet. Would you like a glass?" Overwhelmed again I said yes. I naively thought, "Not only is this woman sexy, she also has class."

As she walked away Brian looked at me and began to laugh. I curiously responded by asking, "Whasso funny nigga? You heard her; she bringing me a glass of Shamp." No sooner had I finished questioning Brian than Tina returned empty handed. Not only did she not have my glass, but her glass was gone too.

Brian said laughingly, "And so it begins."

Curious to know the deal I asked, "What happened?" Tina looked up at me with the deep, sorrowful eyes and said, "Sorry, but there's none left." Brian was right. At precise moment it had begun.

Now let it be known that I pride myself on being a man of the streets, able to smell a con from a thousand yards out, but this one caught me with my pants down. Not only was it smooth, it put me on the horns of a dilemma. If I didn't offer to buy another bottle, I was going to play myself. And if I did buy it, I played right into her hands.

That was nothing compared to the real problem. You see, that particular night I hadn't brought any money with me. Well, at least none to speak of. There I was, the second most fly dude at the function, with no money. I had rushed to get dressed and in my huff had forgotten my money. I had even forgot to put on my watch. Meanwhile Brian was tickled to death. Although he had money, he got a kick out of seeing me in a pinch.

So there I was, standing there with what I thought was the best thing to ever happen to me right before my eyes. I was not going to falter. I immediately told her to go and get another bottle. She walked away with a self-assured look of seductive charm on her face. I turned to B and said, "Yo, how much is Moet?" I was screwed because all I had on me was $50.00. I still didn't panic because worst come to worst I would have left the party and rushed home to get more. I stopped one of the wait staff and asked him how much for the bottle and he said $45.00. Whew! I was straight with $5.00 to spare.

By the time Tina came back I had the champagne there waiting. She was thrilled. Probably more so because her little con had worked. I gave her my number in a way that suggested we were merely shaking hands, and she walked away. She didn't even offer me a glass of champagne.

Brian erupted into uncontrolled laughter, then turned to me and said, "You a mufuckin sucker buying that bitch a bottle of champagne, and with your last at that!" I didn't care. To me it was worth it. After all, I put myself in the situation by saying that I could make her happy. As the night went on, I waited for an opportunity to dance with her but it never came.

Her boyfriend had found out that someone had bought her a bottle of bubbly. For the rest of the night he kept a close eye on her, as well as making it known to all present that she was with him by randomly kissing and groping her at his leisure. All of his subsequent actions didn't change the fact that he had already been secretly humiliated; his broad had been booked.

The day after the party I was sure Tina would call, and I had every intention of showing her just how fortunate she was to have met me. As expected, she called and we talked of how nice it was to meet one another. She also told me about what she went through to keep my phone number and began by saying, "Right after you gave me your number, my boyfriend walked up and asked who you were. He saw me shake your hand and then asked me what I was holding. I dropped it on the floor and told him that it was just a napkin."

As she continued with her story I sat quietly and listened to her confirming how deceitful and dishonest she could be. She went on to say, "One of his friends walked up and spoke to him and when he looked away I covered the napkin with my foot and dragged it along when we started walking. I was hoping I didn't smear the number, and I picked it up after he walked away."

I snickered before saying, "I see you're a pro at this type of shit, huh?"

Realizing she was exposing too much of herself, she tried to down play it saying, "No, I just had to think fast." It didn't really matter much to me what her excuse was. All I wanted to do was to knock her off and send her back to the cat.

After a few engaging phone conversations we began to see each other. At first it was difficult because she and her boyfriend lived together. We would meet in hotel parking garages and secluded restaurants. Our favorite was the little back entrance circle separating the Georgian Terrace Hotel and the Days Inn on Peachtree Street.

About ten days had passed from the time we met. Since that time she had been calling and sneaking out to meet with me every day. She had given me the number to their house with instructions for me to ask for the wrong name if a dude answered the phone.

They lived near Centennial Park in the new development where the old Tech-Wood Projects used to be. The apartment faced the main thoroughfare, and I would regularly pull up right outside their balcony and call her. Tina, much to my surprise, actually encouraged me and never once opposed my behavior. It was as if she got a kick out of it.

There were even a few times when she would come out onto the balcony and look down at me while we conversed. She would do this while Troy was in the apartment watching football or doing whatever. After a while I began to notice that he really didn't pay much attention to her and that, unfortunately, was what she was yearning for. As time passed Tina became more comfortable with me. During that same time things became really strained between her and her boyfriend. I suppose she was becoming more secure in her belief that I was going to become a suitable replacement.

An old man once told me, "Women are like monkeys: they won't let go of one branch until they have a firm grip on the other." A firm grip was an understatement. Tina had gotten into an ugly fight with her boyfriend somewhere around our tenth day of knowing one another and decided she was going to move out. She'd mentioned she had been apartment hunting and had been

17

asking me for money almost every day. Usually no more than a hundred or so, and I would give it to her.

When it started it had only been about a week or more since we met, but she justified her requests by saying that she wanted to spend time with me and the only way to get out the house was by telling Troy she was going to the mall with her girlfriends. At first giving her money so frequently made me uneasy, but like I said in the beginning I found out that Tina was a professional who knew how to express her gratitude.

Whenever we would hang out we were always careful to go to the remote areas in the city to ensure no one familiar would see us, especially because Troy was well known throughout Atlanta. On one particular date we happened to be in Stone Mountain and decided to stop and grab something quick to eat at Cap'n D's on Wesley Chapel Road.

I had no idea Tina planned to include me on the menu. Shortly after eating Tina got up to go to the bathroom. After a minute or two she peered out the door and motioned for me to come to her. I looked around making sure that no one was watching and slid in the door. She immediately pushed my back against the door, dropped to her knees, and proceeded to put in some of the best work I have ever experienced.

Tina's performance was interrupted when a woman and her young daughter began banging on the door. Startled and nervous I scrambled to pull up my pants as Tina unlocked the door. We walked out with me embarrassed and looking down o n the floor. As we exited I heard the little girl ask, "Mommy, why was that man in the girl's bathroom?" Tina seemed oblivious to what had just transpired, evidenced by the way she had already begun to fix her hair and makeup. Then it hit me. She was trying to shore up her resources and planned to use me as her dipping well.

Her timing couldn't have been better. Her birthday was the next day, April 14th. I knew she was expecting something nice, especially after her bathroom performance, and given the dizzying pace at which we had started, I couldn't justify slowing it down. After the episode in Cap'n D's, I was both shocked and pleased— and wanted more. Surprisingly we hadn't yet been intimate with each other, although blowing me in the bathroom of a fast food restaurant should qualify.

I decided the real deal was going to go down the day before her birthday. She sensed what was going on and just as I had done not long before, I made her choose between the lesser of two evils. If her performance wasn't up to par, it would undoubtedly have an effect on the caliber of gift she received. If she satisfied me, I planned on making her birthday very special. Either way I benefited.

I was not about to spend any more money on her without sampling the goods. The day came for the deed to go down, and I decided that it would be best to take her to my mother's house in case she was on her period or something—at least that way I wouldn't waste any money. I talked to my mother thirty minutes prior to arriving, and she told me that she was on her way out to the mall to do some shopping so I had plenty of time before she returned.

When we got there I pretended to be tired and wanted to take a nap. It was obvious I was faking, but Tina knew the drill. She played along and followed my lead. Still it was an admittedly awkward situation that I tried to ignore by imagining her bedroom manner. I knew that if it was anything like her showing at Cap'n D's, I was in for a treat. As I prepared myself for our first complete sexual encounter, I didn't consider the effect the anxiety of being at my mother's home, during the day, in my little brother's bed would have on us.

As we undressed I noticed that she was very hesitant. Undeterred, I put on a condom but soon discovered my dick would not stay hard. I could not fucking believe it. Nothing like that had ever happened to me before. I stood there fighting with the thing and finally got it on. Tina by the way was as turned on as Seely from The Color Purple whenever Mister climbed on top of her to do his business. I didn't give a damn. As far as I was concerned, as long as I got my nut it could all have ended that day.

I wish I could have been so lucky. No sooner had I gotten started than I got soft again. Time was passing by so fast that I was sure my mother would be coming home soon. Meanwhile Tina was waiting quietly in the doggy style position, face buried in the pillow, tee-shirt on, no panties, and rump in the air. Finally, I was able to get myself erect long enough to stroke a few times, unfortunately too few to matter. After about the tenth stroke my mother pulled up in the driveway. Tina was thrilled—so much so that she laughed before saying we could try again in about two weeks. I guess long enough to see if the money was going to stop.

After my stellar bedroom performance I decided Tina and I should see a little more of each other, mostly to ensure I would have the opportunity to redeem myself and experience the full scope of her sexual pleasures. The way she rationed out her goodies to me made it obvious she was still sexing her ex-boyfriend, but it didn't really matter to me. If she wanted to screw the whole city of Atlanta it wouldn't have made a difference to me.

Chapter Four
The Introduction

"Brian, did you see the new CLK Benz? Brian, did you hear me? I asked you if you had seen the new CLK yet?" Stephanie had been trying to get Brian's attention now for about five minutes, and Brian was totally ignoring her. He knew that it was leading to something—something major!

It was no secret that Brian was very generous when it came to his treatment of his women. He'd never admit to it, but I knew it was because of a lack of self-esteem and the fact that he knew when it came to looks he wasn't quite the looker his attitude suggested. Surprisingly, it didn't prevent him from connecting with a bevy of attractive women. I guess money has a way of making people adjust to what they'd otherwise ignore.

Rumor was he had put his last girlfriend Dionne into a brand new white SL500 convertible. Stephanie had asked me about it a few times, but I never confirmed it one way or the other. The truth was it wasn't an SL-model but a pricey E-class. Unfortunately for him it didn't matter to Stephanie what kind it was. All she knew was that it was a Mercedes Benz! And she'd made up her mind whatever was good for Dionne was also going to be good for her!

A month had passed since Brian and I had come to town, and it looked as if we were in Atlanta to stay. Stephanie and Brian were living together, and according to him things were great. If you ask me, it depended on who you asked. One Saturday Brian decided that he wanted to take Stephanie to lunch at the Sun Dial room. Coincidentally, Tina and I were on our way to lunch as well and happened to pass Brian and Stephanie as we drove down Peachtree Street headed to Mick's—Tina's suggestion. Brian called me and invited us to join him and Stephanie at the Sun Dial. I was all too happy to accept. Tina didn't know it, but I hated Mick's. Not that it was beneath me, I was just used to nicer places, and up till that point all of Tina's dining suggestions had been Red Lobster, the Outback, and the ever-popular Waffle House.

It surprised me after having lived in Atlanta almost ten years that Tina had no idea of places like the Sun Dial Room, Pano's & Paul's, or Villa Christina's—all upper echelon dining establishments. I was quickly discovering Tina wasn't quite as polished as she appeared to be the night we met. I assumed Troy must have mandated she dress for the occasion and sanctioned the purchase of a new outfit for that night.

The more time we spent together the more I noticed that Tina's style was more like that of a country girl in the big city. All of that was confirmed when we arrived at the Sun Dial and Tina was immediately impressed. The restaurant was located inside the Westin Peachtree Hotel. The Sun-Dial room sat atop the 72nd floor of the hotel and was enclosed by glass walls with a rotating view of the city. We arrived in time for our reservation and were seated at a table along side the outer portion of the restaurant, which enabled us to see the spectacular view. Brian and Stephanie had gotten there before us and were already seated.

Tina was so excited that she seemed to forget herself and blurted out, "Oh my God, I wish I had brought my camera so I could have taken a picture." I smiled and grabbed her by her hand and gently pulled her into her seat and cut my eye up to Brian, who was fighting back his laughter. He and I had just recently had a conversation about how inner city young black women are rarely exposed to exquisite places, typically because of dealing with young, unexposed brothas whose idea of fine dining consists of Piccadilly's for lunch.

Stephanie had been to the Sun Dial room once or twice courtesy of Brian, and the thrill of being there had long since vanished. As she sat there pretending to be regal, and privileged she had no idea that Brian had already filled me in on her first experience at the Sun Dial. An experience not much different than Tina's, except that Stephanie did have a camera with her.

Our waiter introduced himself and informed us of the special for the day. As he did so Brian introduced Stephanie to Tina for the first time. They exchanged hollow pleasantries, and shortly afterwards Stephanie strategically placed the new red-piped gray Gucci handbag directly in Tina's line of sight. Tina shifted in her seat, and I could tell that she was a little uncomfortable at Stephanie's blatant display and snobbish attitude.

Tina's purse was a plain brown Coach leather bag. She also wore a simple brown linen dress along with a cute little summer straw hat and a pair of slides by Nine-West. In stark contrast to Tina, Stephanie was dolled up in a white linen tie-breast sleeveless shirt and a soft, red wrap-around skirt with matching red-piped Gucci slides.

Along with the killer outfit, Stephanie was also sporting a white gold ladies Pasha chronograph by Cartier —all courtesy of Brian. The way he spoiled Stephanie was enough to make you sick. Tina's only saving grace was that she was more attractive than Stephanie. Unfortunately, that distinction didn't seem to matter much to her. All she saw was this girl who wore the adornments of a budding princess.

I really didn't know how inferior Tina felt until she ordered a one hundred fifty dollar bottle of Dom Pérignon. I didn't want to embarrass her further so I didn't say anything. Inside I was seething with anger and Brian knew it.

He looked at me and sarcastically said, "Damn, play boy. I ain't know you was doing it like dat! I guess it's "champagne wishes and Caviar dreams" for everybody, huh?" I knew that was his get back for the incident with me and Stephanie at Phipps.

I just laughed it off and said, "You know how it is, Nigga; you the one with the superstar over there sitting next to you. Gucci should be sold out by now the way y'all two get down."

Brian and I were always busting each others balls. From the outside looking in, it might have seemed adversarial, but we never took it to mean anything more than just harmless fun. For some reason neither Brian nor myself approved of the manner in which we chose to treat our respective women. I realized later that it was because neither of us felt the other's woman was worth it.

Once lunch was over, I dropped Tina off at home and told her that I would be back later in the evening, and then drove over to Brian and Stephanie's. When I got there the first thing Stephanie said to me as I walked in the door was, "Your girl is cute Glenn, but she is corny as hell." Tina was in no way corny; she just wasn't fly. But no matter what she was or wasn't, I wasn't about to let Stephanie degrade her like that and especially without her being there to defend herself.

I smirked before saying, "Yeah, you might be right, but I'd rather have a girl who's corny and cute, over a broad who's stylish and ugly. Cause you can change from being corny, but an ugly bitch is stuck that way forever!" I left the statement open ended so as to poke at Stephanie's ego. She wasn't entirely sure if I was referring to her directly or speaking in general.

I was never attracted to Stephanie despite the fact that she had an incredible body. Her look just didn't appeal to me. She had very large teeth and gums that protruded from her mouth when she laughed or smiled. As unattractive as she was I couldn't believe she had the nerve to speak about any one else. Especially considering the fact that all of the highline items she broke her neck to purchase every few weeks were a dead giveaway for her attempts to overcompensate for an obvious lack of beauty.

It's a funny thing about unattractive black women. Many confuse being sharp or stylish for pretty, not realizing if you strip them of all of their material possessions and weaves, all that's left is who they truly are. If I had a dollar for every weave I've seen I'd be a rich man by now; and if they're not done right they look stupid. Particularly the old ones where the new growth is so abundant that it lifts the tracks and gives their heads a bumpy appearance, making the hair sit on top of the head like a hat.

Stephanie didn't know it, but her snobbery exposed Tina to a side of life that she had never experienced, a life that she vowed to have from that point on. After that day, that is all she would talk about. She questioned me incessantly about what Brian had bought for Stephanie and why he did so much for her. She even mentioned overhearing Stephanie during lunch ask Brian about helping her get the new Mercedes CLK. I knew then that Tina was searching for a way to convince me to sponsor her in the same manner Brian had signed on for with Stephanie. I didn't mind the thought, provided Tina played her cards right. Although I couldn't rectify the problem immediately I felt that I was going to make Stephanie rue the day she tried to show up my girl!

Chapter Five
Tina's Jackpot

"Guuurrrlll, you are not going to believe this, but I met this guy a couple of weeks ago at Troy's party, and that nigga was fly as hell! Erica and me had just came in the hotel, and I saw him and his man standing in front of the bar. He was wearing a chocolate brown pinstriped suit, and the pin stripes were woven into the fabric. I know that it was Armani because I had just seen the same suit in a GQ magazine layout last week when I was in the doctor's office."

Before I could go on Ranay said, "Oooh, bitch. I hope you ain't caught some shit out there fucking around with these dirty dick niggas." Ranay made me sick with that kind of shit. She was a thirty-five year old hag who looked like she might have been cute in her early twenties but who was now desperately trying to hold on to any vestige of youth that she could.

The problem was she was tacky. You know. The kind of chick who will wear a hooded leather coat with open-toed shoes tacky. She had bad feet, old looking hands, and brown fingertips that looked as if she had been smoking weed forever. She barely kept her hair done and constantly tried to get away with the typical "kitchen do" like she was from the projects or something! Whenever she did get it done she always chose some corny ghetto style like braids with deep burgundy highlights.

I didn't really like her, but I enjoyed hanging out with her and the rest of her old ass friends—Denise, Evangeline, and Lisa— because I always got all the attention as they all looked so beat down. Ranay knew her best years were behind her and would always try to get one up on me whenever she found an inroad to do it.

I ignored her and finished my story. "Bitch, shut up you are talking too loud. Troy is in the other room and you know he be picking up the phone and like he "I spy" or something. Anyway, let me finish telling you what happened. As I was walking by the dude, he gently grabbed my arm and asked me if I had a minute. He didn't know he was the reason I walked in that direction in the first place. I had seen him and his man pull up outside, and they was both driving Mercedes Benzes."

Ranay squeaked excitedly, "What he look like? He sound like he was fine as hell."

Frustrated I said, "If your chicken head ass would stop cutting me off I'll tell you. Anyway girl, the one I met was definitely tight. He was about 6 feet tall and dark skinned with a full manicured six o'clock shadow beard. He was kind of thick and his facial hair gave him that Gerald Lavert look. He ain't big like Gerald but looks more like a cuddly teddy-bear and is sexy as hell. By the time he stopped me I had already given him the two second look over. He never even knew it had happened.

"He was wearing these brown square-toe boots, and his suit was tailored to the tee. I could tell he was paid 'cause his accessories were coordinated perfectly. He had on a beige, ribbed, high drop V-neck pullover. Girl, he even had on a Cartier belt, and you could see the "C" from across the room."

Ranay, sounding jealous, paused before saying, "Damn bitch, you sound like you hit the jack pot. What kind of watch was he wearing?" I don't think that he was wearing one, but his friend standing right next to him had on a Cartier. You know, the one with the little screws all over it. And his shit was tight too! I could tell by their hair cuts and the way they both were dressed that they wasn't from Atlanta."

Sounding desperate and not wanting to be left out, Ranay blurted, "Was his boy as cute as he was?"

I acknowledged her reluctantly saying, "He was okay but not as cute as Glenn, just a little slimmer and taller."

Ranay said, "Guuurl shiiiit, that's cool with me as bad as I need a sponsor. That nigga could look like a frog and be as short as a dwarf if his money was long! I want you to hook me up with him."

I knew the minute I mentioned Glenn's friend Ranay was going to plug for me to hook her up. Ranay was notorious for running her mouth, and if I did decide to introduce them I had to be extra careful and make sure she wouldn't blow my cover.

Glenn didn't know that I was a stripper at the Cheetah—not many people did. The Cheetah was a white strip club. I decided to work there after I got kicked out of the army. I figured working at an all-white club I wouldn't run into as many niggas as I would working in a black one. Black men have an eye for that kind of shit and would definitely recognize my ass on the streets of Atlanta whenever I wasn't at work.

"Ranay, I don't know about all that 'cause you run your mouth too much. I didn't tell Glenn I danced and he definitely seems like the type that would give me walking papers if he knew."

Ranay sighed and said, "Awe bitch, stop being so scary. Once you give him some booty it won't matter to him if you worked in a donut shop as long as you keep him creamin'!"

I couldn't bring myself to mention that I had already fucked and sucked Glenn so I just let Ranay continue to ramble. "Besides I know he had to ask you what you did for a living, didn't he?" Ranay was really picking my brain, and I hated the thought of admitting I had started lying to Glenn already, but I answered anyway.

"Yeah, and I told him that I worked for the post office on the 8 pm to 2 am shift. But that don't have nothing to do with you putting me out there like that. Cause bitch, if I hook you up with his boy and he find out I dance, I ain't fucking with you no more. I been waiting to leave Troy's broke ass, and I think this dude is going to be my ticket to do it."

Ranay could tell I was beginning to get irritated by all of her questions about my personal shit, so she initiated the goodbyes saying, "I have to get ready to go to bed, but call me when you go out with Glenn next time so I can ask him about his boy."

I couldn't figure out why she thought Glenn's friend would have ever been interested in her funny-looking ass. I guess ugly people never think they're ugly. I don't know why I even entertained Ranay's request because I knew I wasn't going to hook her up. I really didn't want to mess things up with Glenn. He seemed to be the real deal, and I was really tired of Troy's bullshit dreams of being the hype man. He had one bullshit rap act and the artist's name was "agent 106." He didn't think that I knew, but that rap bullshit and him trying to promote parties was responsible for us being broke.

If it wasn't for me dancing the rent would have stopped getting paid months ago. I knew Troy didn't really care about me because when he found out I was dancing, all he said was, "I knew you was getting money from somewhere." No arguments, no "Baby, please don't do this, or even "Bitch, you better not go back." All he cared about was screwing other women, rap music, hustling credit cards, and making counterfeit checks. Whenever he did come up all he would do with the money is buy clothes, jewelry, and throw wack ass parties.

Glenn, on the other hand, had it all. I could tell from his style, clothes, and car he was doing the damn thing. Shit, even if I couldn't tell right off, the way his man was kicking it with Stephanie proved that Glenn had to be the same way. I wasn't worried about getting my piece 'cause once I really put my thing down, the shit that Brian was doing for Stephanie would seem like bubble gum to the way Glenn was going to be breaking me off!

Chapter Six
Show Me The Money

The components that make up dynamite are some pretty serious shit. The explosive capacity that shit has results in chaos! Stephanie and Tina together had a similar effect. "Glenn, I saw the new fall Gucci bag yesterday while I was at Phipps Plaza, and it's only $565." Tina was about as subtle as an elephant walking on a bag of potato chips. She didn't care either. She had been pestering me about buying her a Gucci bag for what seemed like forever.

When her birthday came I got away without having to buy anything because of an emergency back in Philadelphia I had to tend to. I left her with a few hundred dollars. I figured that would have been sufficient, but I had another thing coming. She was determined to get something more out of me.

She'd finally left Troy and moved out. She'd found a nice little apartment in downtown Atlanta called the Gables at Cityscape Plaza. It wasn't too far from her and Troy's old apartment, which was about three miles away, and I remembered thinking, "What was the point in moving out if you were still only going to be living right down the street?"

At any rate, I had begun to spend most of my time over there and was playing house like Brian and Stephanie had been doing. I guess because my presence was so visible Tina felt my financial support should have been equally visible. Since the beginning she never really stopped hitting me up for cash and felt that since we were a couple and I had a key, it was now part of my duty to look out. I didn't really agree, but I went along with it to keep the peace.

Trying not to sound too receptive I asked, "How much did you say that bag was again?" Tina rushed into the living room where I was sitting, smiling from ear to ear, and said, "It's only five hundred sixty five dollars. Can I get it? Pleeeeaaaasssse."

It was a Saturday afternoon and I had planned to go pick up some new underwear, tee shirts, socks, and stuff. I hated going to the mall to shop for anything. I didn't buy clothes off the rack so there was never any real reason for me to go except when I took my nieces and nephew shopping. I figured if I gave her the money to buy the bag she could also pick up all of the other little odds and ends that I wanted to get too.

Tina was hard headed and I knew from experience I had to be very specific with what she could and couldn't buy with my dough. If I wasn't careful she would come back with a bunch of extra shit and pawn it off as things "we" needed for the apartment, even though there was no "we" on the lease. I gave her my credit card and told her that she couldn't spend more than a thousand dollars. I figured it would be enough to cover her bag, and most of the things I wanted her to pickup for me.

I had promised my nephew that I would get him a few Sega games for his PlayStation, which were typically fifty to sixty dollars—for the good ones anyway. Just before Tina got dressed to go out the door Brian called. He sounded cheerful as he spoke.

"What's up, ock? What you over there doing? Probably playing house, huh? You bitch ass Nigga!" He started laughing, realizing he'd just described his daily routine. He'd been stuck in Stephanie's ass for months. He had even stopped wanting to go out and would only do so if I bitched about it. I was cool with his jokes; I'm all for anybody who was happy with the person they're with.

Happiness is hard to find, and when you do get it, you better hold on to it. I kept the joke running saying, "Nigga, I got the blueprint from you. Whassup though?" He said, "Nothing man. I told Stephanie I would take her to Shoemaker Warehouse to pick up some shoes. She asked me if Tina had ever been there and told me to call and ask if she wanted to go."

I knew what Stephanie really wanted was another opportunity to show Tina up and gloat over the new 1998 Mercedes CLK Brian had just helped her buy. I warned him against it, and his answer to my warning was, "Man, Ima just give her the down payment money. It's only five thousand so if she tries to get fly at least I won't be out the whole forty grand!"

What he said didn't make no sense to me. I mean, she wasn't his girl, and I had got word that some dude was taking her to lunch every day at work. I figured it must've been that cat named Toby, but since I didn't have proof I didn't see the need in mentioning it.

I was surprised to hear he was home. He had gotten locked up on fraud charges and had been sitting in jail for about six months. The last time I spoke to Lynnette she mentioned he was supposed to be getting out 'cause the charges didn't stick. I probably should have told Brian, but I didn't want to ruin whatever he had going on over there. For all I knew maybe Stephanie was feeling him like that. Whatever the case, I didn't want to be responsible for bringing bad news.

I didn't mind the thought of going to Shoemaker Warehouse with Brian and Stephanie. I would finally have the opportunity to go all out and buy up the whole fucking store if need be just to let Stephanie see how I really could get down if I chose too. I decided to go with them and yelled to Tina to ask if she wanted to go.

"Tina, Brian and Stephanie wanted to know if you have ever been to Shoemaker Warehouse, and whether or not you wanted to go?" Tina popped her head out of the bathroom door and smiled again with a look on her face that suggested, this must be my lucky day." She anxiously responded, "Yeah, I go almost every weekend."

I sat there silently thinking, "She obviously never buys much." Aside from one or two pairs of nice shoes I'd seen in her closet, Tina otherwise was seriously lacking when it came to decent footwear. I had contemplated taking her to Head-Start on 18th and Sampson Streets in Philadelphia. It was the end all to be all for women's shoes in Philly. Every woman in the city of Philadelphia hit that place like it was going out of style.

It was nothing to go in there and spend six hundred dollars on shoes and that would only get you two pairs—maybe. Head-Start would come later, if she proved herself worthy. Shoemaker would do for now. I had been to Shoemaker Warehouse quite often in my travels to and from Atlanta, and when we got there it was just like it had always been—packed with wall-to-wall women.

Secretly I loved going to that place, whether you caught the women coming in or got them going out. You were always guaranteed to come up with at least two phone numbers if you paced yourself, allowing the first sista to leave before you attempted propositioning the second.

When we walked into the store I saw and said hello to Tracey. She was the store manager. She was a tall, classy looking sista and had always been cordial whenever I patronized the store. We had exchanged numbers once, but neither of us followed up on it. I suppose my constant appearances in the store with different women contributed to her reason for not calling, and here I was yet again showing up with someone different.

Tina noticed us speak to each other in a familiar manner and asked, "What was that about? I didn't know you knew about this store."

I responded, "There's a lot of things I know that you don't. I thought we were here to get shoes, so if you see something you like then I suggest you hurry up and pick it out."

Tina sensed the connotation behind my statement and realized she was rocking the boat. By this time Stephanie had already made her way to the Via Spiga section and had two boxes tucked under her arm. Tina was tracking her every move and mysteriously appeared right next to her, picking out the same shoes but in different colors. I knew from the episode at the Sun Dial Room that Tina had begun to idolize Stephanie.

After a while I noticed the two of them were engrossed in deep conversation, laughing and enjoying the outing. Brian and I had gone over to the men's section of the store and picked out a few pairs of shoes each but did so hurriedly because that part of the store is typically infested with members of Atlanta's massive gay male community, who oftentimes would try their hand with straight dudes, looking at them seductively as they pass by or even appearing next to them and pretending to be interested in whatever shoe they looked at. In the past whenever I was in the store alone I would deliberately approach as many women as I could to ensure that no one mistook me for being homosexual.

By the time we all finished browsing and perusing the store, we had a total of ten pairs of shoes. When we got to the check-out line Tracey motioned to us as we were next and rung up my purchase. She didn't say anything but shook her head—barely noticeably—and smirked as she cut her eyes at me. She finished totaling the sale and smiled before saying, "Have a nice day," as we walked out the store. After leaving the store Tina suggested we all go to Phipps. Brian and Stephanie didn't know it but that stop was part of my and Tina's original plan.

We had taken separate cars and Stephanie surprised everybody when she said, "Tina you should ride with me." Tina was elated by the idea of riding with Stephanie, not realizing Stephanie's motivation was to have an opportunity to show off her new toy. Tina kissed me on the cheek, threw her bags in the back seat, and laughingly said, "I hope y'all can keep up," as she got into the car and fastened her seatbelt.

They sped off before Brian and I could get out of our parking spot. Brian looked over to me ominously and said, "You know, you started something letting them two ride together."

I said, "Nigga, you the one who called and invited us to come to the store together." Brian didn't say anything after that and sat back in his seat staring out into the parking lot.

It was a nice day and I decided we should take our time getting to Phipps and use the opportunity to push up on a few stragglers in the parking lot. I had seen this one chick in the store buying shoes but couldn't approach her because Tina was there with me. Now that Tina was gone, I decided I would capitalize on the situation.

The girl in the store was next in line at the check-out and I figured she would be coming out of the store soon. As if on cue she came out of the doors as I was pulling out of my parking space. I waited until she approached her car and pulled up in front of it just as she got to it, blocking her access. She stopped and shifted her weight to one leg and sighed in an expectant manner as if to say, "Alright, I'm listening."

I said, "Hi. How you doing?"

She smiled and replied, "I'm fine, but if you were so concerned why didn't you ask me inside the store while you were with your female friend and your hands were full of boxes?"

I laughed because I knew she'd seen me standing in the check-out with Tina. I didn't let it slow me down and responded, "I was trying to make sure my sister was straight."

She started laughing and said, "That's a good one, and you didn't even have to think before you responded either. You're good."

I thought to myself, "You have no idea." Before she could say anything else, I introduced myself by saying, "By the way, my name is Glenn. What's yours?" She stood there momentarily, and I could tell she was contemplating whether or not to continue her conversation with me. I coached her a little and followed up saying, "Now, I know your mother taught you better than that. What's the harm in telling me your name?"

She relented and said frustratingly, "My name is Monica White. Hello, Glenn. How are you?"

I nodded happily and responded, "Fine, thank you." She spoke in an articulate manner, prompting me to ask her where she was from. I was surprised to hear her say Georgia. She was tall and pretty. I noticed her inside the store and had even watched her walk; her gait was that of a model's.

I was never too particular about tall women, especially because I was barely 6' and that depended on the shoes I wore on a particular day. Otherwise I stood about 5'10" tall. Monica, on the other hand, was easily 6' tall in heels; her hair was shoulder length with auburn highlights peppered throughout. She was driving a very attractive Lexus ES300, and by the looks of her style, I could see right off that she was an independent woman and I had to have her.

I was certain she was interested too because of the comment she made about seeing me in the store. I knew if she was watching all of the activities, then surely she had to have been looking for a reason, not to mention the fact she could now see that I was the real deal because I was driving in some heat! I confidently stepped up my game and said, "So where we going for lunch? I haven't eaten yet, have you?"

She looked at me and smiled, then said, "Well, I probably would've eaten a long time ago if I could only get into my car."

I chimed in again and saying, "Why don't you leave it parked and hop in here with me? I'll take care of your hunger for you."

By this time she was trying hard to maintain her friendly posture, and said, "No, thank you. I have some errands to run, and Saturday is my only day to do it."

Sensing my time was running out I quickly asked, "Can I call you?"

Monica looked at me and said, "I don't think that would be a good idea."

I started to rebut but Brian nudged me and whispered, "You playin' yourself ock!"

I realized that he was right and closed out by saying, "Well, it was nice meeting you Miss Monica. Maybe I'll see you again, and if so maybe then you'll be a little nicer." I pulled back and allowed her to get into her car. As she opened her door, she looked back at me and smiled. The way she looked at me seemed to suggest she wanted to say something more but was somehow prohibited from doing so.

As she drove away I looked at B and said, "Man, I don't get these broads down here; they clock every move you make, smile at you, and even talk to you. But the minute you step to 'em, they feed you bullshit like they wasn't just on your dick! Knowing damn well they was trying to get seen!"

Brian laughed and said, "Nigga, stop trying to put shit off on them playing hard to get. She just didn't want your dumb ass." As he laughed I knew he was just playing with me. The truth was my shit was tight, and if she didn't want me she didn't want nobody!

On the other hand, I also knew she didn't have a choice because she saw me in the store with another woman who was obviously not my sister. I was both frustrated and impressed by her resolve because she was the kind of woman I'd always wanted. One who didn't care about what I had, how much money I spent, or how attractive I was.

Monica rejecting me told me she was above all of the typical shit I'd been subjected to by so many others. She seemed to stand for something and wasn't concerned with appearances. After she pulled off, Brian and me tried our hand at a few others and found reasonable success, but I was still fixated on the one who got away. About an hour passed and we were way off schedule.

We were supposed to be at Phipps, and the way my cell phone had been ringing proved it. I finally answered it, "Hello, what's up?" I knew it was Tina. She was irritated but avoided an argument so as not to mess up her daylong shopping spree.

"Baby, we been at Phipps for thirty minutes now. Where are y'all?" Tina tried to mask her frustration by leading the question with "baby." I was in a good mood and decided not to give her a hard time and acquiesced.

"My fault baby, I stopped in Brazil's and picked up a few items that were on sale." Brazil's was a stylish men's boutique located on Peachtree Street a mile or so before entering Buckhead. Tina went for it because she knew I had planned on checking the place out. It was one of the only places in Atlanta that carried stylish, quality men's clothing, things that reminded me of Philly. As I didn't have a tailor in Georgia, I figured Brazil's selections would serve as suitable replacements.

Tina paused before asking, "Are you done yet?"

I stalled and said, "Give me about ten more minutes and I'll be on my way." I knew Tina would check to see if I had bought anything so I had to stop and pick up a few things to keep shit cool. By the time we got to Phipps, the two of them had already been to three stores and had even started shopping without Brian and me. I looked at Tina and saw that her hands were full of bags.

Before I could ask what, when, where, or how, Stephanie happily said, "Glenn, I let Tina get what she wanted on my American Express, so you can just give me the money."

At first I was confused, because I had given Tina my credit card earlier, until she said, "Baby, when I tried to use it, they explained that because I wasn't an authorized user I would have to have you present."

I wondered why they'd said that to her because I had let my old girlfriend Tamika use my credit cards often back in Philly, and they never gave her a problem. I later found out that crooked broads and gay boosters had burnt Atlanta up using stolen plastic. High-end stores like Gucci and Versace had cracked down and weren't having any more of it!

They didn't accept shit from you if it wasn't accompanied with legitimate ID. Even then they'd still look at you sideways. In Phipps, if you were black they damn near didn't even want your cash, 'cause so many niggas had come through passing counterfeit big faces.

Tina was looking at me in a shy sort of way, as if she didn't want to face me out of guilt. My assumption was confirmed when Stephanie hit me with the tab. I almost jumped through the roof after hearing Stephanie say, "Glenn, I hope you got twelve hundred on you 'cause I'm gone need it before the day is out."

Combined with the five hundred I had just spent at Shoemaker, the tab for the day was seventeen hundred dollars. It was just as I figured. Tina got me and got me good!

Chapter Seven
A Day At The Beach

"Delta airlines, how may we help you?"

"Yeah, I'd like to know how much a round trip ticket from Atlanta to Miami costs, please?"

"When will you be flying sir?"

"I want to leave today around 2 pm and return on Sunday on the last flight."

"Will the reservation be for one passenger or two?"

"Two adults."

"One moment please while I look up the fare schedule."

It was Saturday morning. I happened to be on the Internet browsing some of the boutiques on Miami's South Beach. I had planned to order a new patent leather Cartier backpack for Tina. I had been to South Beach a time or two and liked the selection of boutiques that were scattered all throughout the area. It had been a while since I had been anywhere new, and I wanted to take a break from Atlanta and see some different scenery. Although the summer was in full swing in Atlanta, I had been yearning to feel the cool breeze of the ocean and the crisp Miami sun.

Tina was still asleep when I called the airline and I was glad. I wanted to surprise her. We had been a few places since we started dating and would regularly hop a flight and take daylong trips to almost anywhere—Chicago to Jordan's restaurant, Philly to JW's steakhouse, and Head Start shoes. We'd even flown to Canada to gamble at the Windsor Hotel & Casino—as a gold club member, I received complimentary rooms without reservations.

The last time I went to Miami, I was there with someone else. It's a funny thing about being in a romantic place. If you're not feeling the person your with then you may as well not have been there. I remembered lying on the beach with my companion thinking how much nicer it would have been if I were there with someone I loved. The night breeze was blowing softly off of the ocean. The salty smell of the water permeated the air. It was a comfortable night, complete with the seagulls chattering in the background authenticating the entire scene.

My memory of the visit was such that I promised myself the minute I was able I would return. Only the next time I would make sure it would be with someone with whom I could enjoy it. That someone was Tina. Much to my surprise I was feeling her—despite my original plan to "stick and move."

Taking her to South Beach seemed like it would be a welcomed break from the monotony of our day-to-day lives. I had overheard her talking to her mother about wanting to go. Stephanie had told Tina all about the glamorous boutiques and shops that lined the streets of Worth Avenue in Palm Beach—Florida's version of Rodeo Drive in Beverly Hills. Brian had taken Stephanie not too long before and broke the bank doing so.

I had been doing a lot for Tina and seemed to be subconsciously competing against Brian and the things he did for Stephanie. I didn't mind doing the things I did for Tina, and it wasn't long before I had surpassed Brian's efforts with Stephanie, even going as far as co-signing for a new Grand Cherokee Limited. Tina had asked for a Mercedes like Stephanie's, but I wasn't quite ready to go there.

After getting her the truck, Brian and a few other associates started to ridicule me every now and again about it, but it didn't bother me. I was happy and comfortable with the idea that she and I were going to be that new couple everyone would envy. I also felt if I was able, then why shouldn't I spoil my woman.?

Contrary to what they believed, I wasn't doing it because I wanted to keep her around or anything like that. Hell, she was already there. The reasons for my generosity were because I was capable of doing so. I enjoyed seeing Tina's face light up whenever I surprised her with a gift, and the trip to South Beach would very likely cause her to have a permanent glow.

She told me she'd been a few places while in the army. Yeah, the army. I thought the same thing myself. How she came to join I'll never know. I can only assume she wanted to get away from Detroit. That place would make anyone want to run away screaming. Although it was an escape for Tina, I am now sure being in the army also affected her persona. She exuded a wide array of male tendencies that, fortunately, were counterbalanced by her attractiveness and sex appeal.

An hour passed since I had gotten off of the phone and made the necessary reservations. Our flight was due to leave in four hours, and I didn't want to waste a lot of time trying to remember to pack all we needed. I went into the bedroom and tapped her on her foot and said, "Wake up, baby. I have a surprise for you."

Tina jumped out of the bed immediately, smiling from ear to ear. My surprises had come to be a welcomed part of our relationship. After making her way to the bathroom to perform her morning ritual of peeing, washing her face, and brushing her teeth, she re-emerged grinning and asked, "So where is it?"

I laughed because I realized that I had become so predictable she thought I'd bought more jewelry. I don't know whether or not she realized it, but if I had she wouldn't have had anyplace left on her body to put it. She had already gotten a three-karat diamond tennis bracelet, a one-karat twisted gold diamond ring, and an eighteen-karat gold twisted necklace, and a three-quarter karat diamond pendant.

Tina stood there hopping in place with anticipation while I jokingly said, "What you hopping for? This ain't Easter and you ain't Peter Cotton tail."

Tina frowned and said, "Glenn, stop playing. What you get me?"

I hesitated before saying, "The surprise I got you can't be worn, it can only be enjoyed." Tina took a deep breadth as her eyes widened. I could tell her mind was racing, analyzing every possibility she could conceive the surprise to be.

"Oh my God, I know what it is—we going somewhere, aren't we?"

I said, "Now, if I told you, then it wouldn't be a surprise would it?" All of the excitement caused me to shortly lose track of time. I looked at the clock on the nightstand and saw thirty minutes had passed. I interrupted Tina's premature celebration by telling her to get dressed.

"What should I put on?" She said, trying to be subtle, but I knew her question was her way of trying to get an idea of where we may have been going.

I didn't have a choice and said, "Put on something light, like linen or something." Upon hearing that Tina squealed even more excitedly than she had initially and ran into the closet and came out with an all-white linen shirt and pant set. "Do you like this? I want to wear it, but I don't have any sandals to go with it."

If it wasn't for the fact that I really liked her, Tina's plug for more shopping might have upset me. All of the shit I'd been buying her over the last four months meant she had more than enough to choose from. She didn't know it, but I had planned on taking her shopping once we arrived in South Beach and didn't want her spoiling the surprise or my budget before we had the chance to leave Atlanta.

As I fought my impulse to chastise her for not being considerate and using everything she could as an excuse for spending money, I remembered I had a friend who owned a little boutique downtown right at the intersection of Carnegie Way and Peachtree Street. He carried a small but exclusive collection of women's shoes and handbags as an accompaniment to his primary stock of highline men's wear and ties. Tony had been in business for years, and his store, Tie World, was the only black-owned boutique that catered exclusively to corporate patrons.

Tony had often tried to persuade me to stop in and patronize his establishment, and I would always promise to do so but never seemed to find the time. I decided I would surprise him and Tina both with a visit and pick up a few things for the trip.

Tina was still waiting for me to respond to her all but subtle request for a new pair of shoes, and I responded, "Go ahead and put on that outfit and don't worry about sandals right now. I know of a nice place where we can stop and probably find everything you need."

I wasn't sure what Tony had, but I did know that going there would at least keep Tina away from the mall and prevent her from picking out and trying on everything she saw that appeared to be cute.

****

We pulled up to the store and luckily found a parking space right in front of it. Tony happened to be walking a customer to the door when he looked up and saw me. "Glenn, what's up? Man, how are you?" Tony was from Nigeria and had an accent that was a mix of British and Yoruba, the tribe he was from. Listening to him speak was an enjoyable experience because his manner was that of a well-cultured European, more like a black James Bond.

Tony and I were originally introduced by an acquaintance from Philly who had also migrated to Atlanta. I responded enthusiastically to Tony's salutation saying, "I'm cool man, just trying to shine with the sun. What's up wit-cha man Wole?" Wole was the acquaintance from Philly who originally introduced us. Protocol demanded I ask about him, considering the fact he was the reason Tony and I came to know each other.

"Oh, he's doing his thing, man. He got the new CL500 Mercedes. Every time I see him he's with a different girl." I laughed, because Tony's account sounded just like Wole.

Tony and I exchanged a few more pleasantries, and afterward I turned and grabbed Tina's hand pulled her forward and introduced her saying, "Tony, this is my baby—Tina."

He smiled and politely shook her hand and said, "Nice to meet you Tina." She in turn did the same. Tina walked in the store after that and busied herself with the various selections Tony had to choose from. Tony and I stood outside for a bit, allowing us to reacquaint ourselves. We were at an industry party when Wole introduced us, and while he was busy entertaining industry chicks, Tony and I found ourselves bored with the crowd of young industry pretenders and wannabes.

As we talked that night, we were each relieved to discover the other was thearl and resolved to get together and hang out at a function more befitting our character. Tony liked the bar scene, and after meeting him I began to see him more and more in passing at Justin's or the Martini bar. "So that's your girl, huh? She's nizze man, really nizze."

The last part of his statement slid off his tongue slow and deliberate, and I knew "nizze" meant "she looks like she's a good fuck." I didn't mind the innuendo behind Tony's comment. In fact, I rather enjoyed hearing his approval. Tony and I had the same taste and later found out that we'd even dated the same women a time or two. I respected him, and he respected me.

"Thanks man, but she ain't no joke. She be in a nigga's pockets deep!" As I spoke, I simultaneously thought to myself, "Whatever she is, G, you created her."

My thought was interrupted when Tony asked, "So what are you doing here? Don't tell me you finally came to my shop to buy something." Tony knew me well. During our first conversation we discussed clothes and fashion. Not in the way women and fags talk about it, but in a GQ kind of way. He noticed I was stylish and coordinated my suit well and thought enough of it to ask who it was made by. I told him the material was Armani, but the suit was custom made for me by my tailor in Philadelphia.

Although Tony carried nice pieces, he didn't carry larger sizes for men like me. If I did happen to find an extra-large, it was typically cut small—more for a tall man with long arms rather than one who had an extra pound or two. We had stood outside talking so long that Tina poked her head out the door and cleared her throat, signaling she'd found something she was interesting in having me buy for her.

I went into the store and Tony came in behind me asking, "Tina, did you see something you like?"

Tina looked at me and then looked back at Tony and said, "Yes, I like these a lot." She moved closer to me carrying a very sexy and expensive pair of sandals by Sergio Rossi. I knew the sandals were pricey because of the way she cuddled up to me. Sensing there was no time to argue, I told Tina to go on and get the sandals. Another half hour passed and I realized I'd spent more time in the store than originally planned.

I mentioned the surprise trip to Tony, and he gave me a good price on the sandals as a goodwill gesture. At two hundred fifty bucks I found it hard to see the good will and thought it was more of a good steal. Elated, Tina slipped them on and put her slides in the box Tony provided.

"Glenn, where did you get that shirt you're wearing?"

I was surprised to hear Tony ask about my shirt. He had more shit in his store than a little bit. "I bought it from Mark Shale at Lenux mall." The shirt I was wearing was a butterscotch split-tail linen, short sleeve shirt by PalZileri.

Tony was impressed and said, "Every time I see you, you always have on nizze shit. It's good to see there are still a few of us who care about dressing nizze and looking good. Somebody needs to school these young guys on the importance of a well-dressed man. This city is full of street guys who would rather wear bandana's and sports jerseys."

I laughed and sarcastically said, "Who? You mean, the others?"

Tony erupted into laughter because he knew the distinction was an accurate representation of how he felt. In truth, Tony and I both felt we were a dying breed. Our kind for the most part had gone the way of the dinosaur.

****

An hour and a half had passed while Tina and I were in Tony's shop. I was comfortable, though, knowing we still had plenty of time to make it to Hartsfield International. Tina still had no idea where we were headed and I wasn't going to spoil the surprise by telling her. I was pleased with her selection and nodded as I said, "Those sandals look good on you." Actually they made her look incredible.

Her toes were painted with an off-colored burnt orange polish that matched her fingernails, which contrasted perfectly against the chocolate skin peeking through the white linen she was wearing. I don't know why I didn't tell her what I really thought. I suppose I didn't want her to know I was becoming more impressed with her transformation—as if the gift buying hadn't already exposed me.

"Are you going to tell me where we going yet?" Tina's question was laced with a mild frustration. I didn't let it force me to move faster because we were only a few miles from the airport and she would know soon enough once we arrived. As we made our way down interstate 75 south, Tina was watching me with anticipation as the split for 85 south crept up. Although she didn't know where we were going, she did know that if we were going to drive there would be no reason to be headed toward the airport.

Just as we were about to hit the fork I pretended we were continuing on 75 south and veered over at the last minute to the 85 south side of the interstate headed toward the airport. "Baby, are we flying somewhere? Cause you didn't even let me pack my stuff. Where are we going? Glenn, I need to get some more stuff."

I looked over at her and using my best Tony Montana from Scarface accent said, "Whachoo talking aaybou huh? Le me tell you son-thing—we going to Miami bay-bee!" Tina screamed and grabbed me around the neck in what was supposed to be a hug but felt more like a chokehold. Not wanting to crash, I pulled her off of me and said, "Chill baby. It's cool. Just relax."

Miami South Beach was a fantasyland that virtually all young, fly inner-city black women wanted to visit, and Tina was about to get her first taste of the good life. The life all the major players and rappers led. Only this episode was being brought to her by me—a man of means and one who didn't consider himself a baller, but who was more than capable of spending a few dollars and showing her a nice time. I could hardly contain my own excitement as we pulled into the airport parking deck. This trip was going to make my last trip to South Beach a forgotten memory.

"Did you bring your birth certificate like I asked you? 'cause we don't have time to turn around and go back. If you don't have it, I'll be going to Miami alone."

Tina looked at me half smiling and asked, "Why would I need my birth certificate?"

I responded, "Because we are going to take a day cruise to the Bahamas, and they won't let you off the ship if you don't have it with you."

Tina coyly said, "Oops. I didn't know it was that important so I didn't really bother to look for it."

I replied, "No problem. You'll just be staying on the boat when we get there."

Tina quipped, "Nigga, you ain't going nowhere without me. We'll just be catching another flight 'cause we can go back and get it now."

I laughed before saying, "Don't worry about it. I think that it might not be required as long as you have legitimate identification.

Tina paused before saying, "Are you sure, Glenn? Cause when we get there you better not try and leave me on that boat 'cause I will make a scene!"

I laughed again and said, "Yeah, I'm sure. Just come on so we can check in

We walked up to the Delta side of the concourse and noticed the line for the domestic flights was wrapped around several times, and it looked as if it hadn't moved for hours. Tina frantically looked at her watch and said, "Don't we have to check in at least two hours before flight time?"

I said, "Yeah," and chuckled. I liked the idea of being the first to expose Tina to all that I did. Before she had a chance to get herself worked into frenzy I said, "Don't worry, baby. Just follow me." I grabbed her hand and led her to an empty aisle way with a sign posted that read, "First class and medallion members only."

Tina elbowed me in my side and said, "You play too much. Why didn't you tell me we were going first class?"

I laughed and said, "Everything ain't for everybody," and led her up to the counter to check in.

"Good morning sir, how can I help yo... it's good to see you again. Do you own this airline yet?" Joe the Delta rep was pleased to see me. He'd remembered me from the early days of coming to Atlanta so frequently from Philly. "Where you going? Don't tell me; let me guess... Philly right?"

I appreciated his friendly manner. It's always good when people take time and personalize their treatment of you. "No, not this time buddy, I'm going to Miami South Beach for some fun in the sun and sightseeing."

He smiled and said, "Well, let me make sure that you two still have seats so you can get there. I remember faces, but not names; Give me your last name again, please." "I can come one better. I have the actual reservation number. Just tell me when you're ready for it."

"That would be great. Go ahead. I can take it now." I pulled out the piece of paper I had written the information on and proceeded to give it to him.

"Q4T893. Okay. I have it here. Glenn and Tina right? And would the lady like a window or aisle seat?"

Tina smiled at him and said, "I think I'll take the window. I hear they're bigger in first class." We all laughed at Tina's humorous remark, but somehow I couldn't help thinking she may have been serious. The flight was nice and Tina settled in and fell fast asleep—she always did whenever we went anywhere. Stepping off the plane was an enchanting experience. The whole place like an exotic island with palm trees inside and out. Because we didn't have any bags, we made our way easily to curbside transportation.

The sun had just begun to set, and the cool night air conjured up a breeze that flirted with us as it swirled about. We hailed a taxi and had him take us to Ocean Drive to the Delano Hotel and Resort. I'd called ahead and made a reservation, thinking it would save me a few coins. I quickly found out it didn't. The rep quoted me two hundred seventy five per night.

If it wasn't for the fact that we were only staying for a day I would've been tempted to stay at the Days Inn or something like it. I didn't really care where we slept, but Tina was particular and I wanted her experience to be magnificent. No sooner had we checked in and settled into our suite than Tina wanted to shop. She had remembered all of the posh boutiques and shops

Stephanie told her about and wondered if it were all-true. It was.

Since we arrived around 7:30 pm and the day was over, I figured it would be better to put off the shopping spree until the following day. Now that we had free time on our hands, we decided to take a walk along ocean drive. As we walked we realized that we were both hungry. We'd forgotten to stop and eat as we rushed out that morning and only stopped to buy the sandals from Tony.

Now that we were in Miami I thought it would be nice to eat at an exclusive place to satisfy our palette. The only restaurant I had visited when I was there last was Joe's Stone Crabs. I liked the place but wanted to experience something that Tina and I both could enjoy for the first time. I had no clue as to what other places were considered nice. On South Beach there were a lot of the usual dives we passed by walking along the strip, but we wanted something posh, something befitting our first real vacation together in an exotic environment.

We saw and stopped a passerby and asked him to direct us to a nice restaurant. He was Caucasian and told us of a nice place called A Fish Called Avalon. The funny thing about it, though, was as soon as he finished giving directions on how to get there, he somehow felt it necessary to tell us it was pricey.

His words were, "Be careful what you order. Those prices can catch you off guard." I smirked and shook my head slightly, trying to be both grateful for the info and project my financial ability without cursing him. Tina noticed my irritation and tugged at my arm trying to avert an angry outburst. She thanked him as she pulled me in the direction of the restaurant.

She knew I was on the brink of blasting him for his condescending attitude. I was sure had we been white he wouldn't have felt it necessary to attach a warning to our dining possibilities. The restaurant was classy and elegant. I could hardly enjoy it because I was still irritated by the white man's comments. I decided I would eliminate any subsequent doubt in our white waiter's eyes by selecting the most expensive item on the menu. It didn't matter if I liked the dish or not.

The place had a live fish tank filled with oversized lobsters and Dungeness crabs. I went over and selected the largest lobster in the tank! It was in excess of 10lbs. When they brought it to our table, Tina was immediately embarrassed. The entire restaurant seemed to stop and stare at us. I sat there feeling regal and vindicated. Naively believing it somehow made a difference—as if those crackers gave a damn about my financial ability to afford a meal like the one I was about to indulge on.

After dinner we decided to walk back to the hotel and took the long way along the beach. We took our shoes off and walked along barefoot, burying our toes in the surf at every step. The soft breeze was still blowing as we stopped to look out over the ocean. We saw a few luxury ocean liners off on the horizon, and we both silently wished we were on one. Tina found a stick and drew an image of a heart in the sand and put both our names inside it. I grabbed the stick and drew an arrow through it just before the tide washed it away. The air was crisp and salty just as I'd remembered it. The moon was full and its reflection seemed to illuminate the entire ocean, giving it a dark, shadowy glow.

Staring at it brought back memories of being in the navy. I stood there entranced by my memories of all of the fascinating things I used to see while out at sea, like watching dolphins swim and frolic alongside the ship under the glow of a moonlit night.

"I'm cold, baby."

I was so wrapped in my thoughts that I had almost forgotten Tina was there. "Here take my shirt." We started walking again as she wrapped herself in my shirt and passed another couple lying on a blanket listening to a portable radio and could hear the sound of Intro singing "*Like the First Time*." The music filled the night air, causing me to drift into thoughts of love and companionship.

We found a stack of reclining beach chairs about fifty feet from the other couple, and climbed on top of them and laid down. As we lay there, Tina straddled on top of me and slid down on the side just slightly but still in my grasp. I held her close and gazed up at the stars. It felt like the moment would last forever.

She must have sensed my completion and added to it by unzipping my pants and blowing me. I closed my eyes, feeling as if I was truly in heaven, and reasoned, "This has to be what it feels like." After she finished I looked up again at the starry moonlit sky and heard the faint cry of a seagull off in the distance but only briefly. It was quickly swallowed by the sound of the rolling tide.

I fell in love with Tina that night, and the next day I showed her. We awoke early the next morning on a mission. We rented a car and hit South Beach and the surrounding area malls with a vengeance. We finished by mid afternoon and embarked upon the hour, and a half journey to fabulous Palm Beach. We hit just about every store that lined Worth Ave. Cartier, Neiman's, Louis Vuitton's, Hermés, and last but not least the Queen mother of them all—Gucci.

By the time we finished shopping and drove back to South Beach it was well into the evening and we had long since missed the boat to the Bahamas. None of that mattered to Tina though —she was high on the days events and had forgotten all about the day cruise. Only a day had passed and I had already spent roughly three thousand dollars, not including the money I spent on the sandals the previous day.

Chapter Eight
"C" is for Crazy

"Glenn, close your eyes and don't peek." We'd been back from Miami a week, and Tina still hadn't finished showing me everything I'd bought for her, and was having a field day modeling it all. She had been at it for hours, trying on different combinations and mixing and matching different sets. I wasn't paying much attention to what she was doing and threw out an occasional, "Yeah, looks nice. That one does, too. Oh yeah, definitely." I was in a zone.

We had just come from the bedroom where she'd just finished thanking me again, and I was ready to take a nap. It was a lazy Sunday afternoon, and I wanted to watch television but couldn't because Tina kept interrupting me every three minutes with a different outfit to display. When she was picking out the stuff, I was usually off in some other part of the store and didn't see much of what she had selected. I was surprised to notice she really picked out some nice things.

Tina hurried in and out of the bedroom, anxiously showing me all sorts of outfits, seemingly satisfied at having been taken on her first shopping spree. On the flight back she leaned over, kissed me on the cheek, and said, "Thank you for a dream come true." She seemed at peace with herself and I was happy because of it. I was still sitting in the living room of the apartment when Tina burst in wearing a tight Versace tee shirt, Gloria Vanderbilt jeans and Louis Vuitton mules—all courtesy of Palm Beach and me.

"Glenn, look at the way this tee shirt fits. I hate it." Tina pouted like a sixteen year old who just found out she couldn't go to the movies and stormed into the bedroom and took the shirt off. She re-emerged into the living room without a shirt or bra examining herself saying, "Look at 'em. They so little. I can't even wear dresses cut for cleavage 'cause I ain't got enough chest to fill them out."

Tina was right; her chest was little. Her bra size was an A cup but looked more like an A minus. She'd always worn padded bras and bustiers to give the illusion of voluptuousness. She looked at me trying to detect to see if I was paying attention to what she was saying. I was, but I didn't care about all that. Breasts were never a concern for me, I didn't like 'em, never made time for 'em, and couldn't care less about them! As far as I was concerned, as long as a woman had a phat ass, her chest could be as flat as a twelve-year-old girl's! Even when I ate chicken all I liked were legs and thighs! I never understood the significance of tits. They couldn't bring me pleasure, so I didn't see the use for 'em.

"Glenn, are you listening to me?"

"Yeah, I heard you, but I don't know why you care. Baby, I like what you got, and God made you that way for a reason."

"Well, I don't know what His reason was, but it sure wasn't so I could put on a halter-top! I went to see a plastic surgeon and priced some implants. I got as far as the work up, but couldn't decide if I should've gotten the saline or silicone ones. He said it would only cost $4,000." I sat up and looked at her, thinking why on earth would anyone be so foolish as to want to put something foreign in his or her body, not to mention some shit that had already been reported as dangerous.

I had heard of thousands of women who'd developed cancer fucking with those implants, and I couldn't believe Tina was even entertaining the thought, and all because of vanity. I was always critical of people who demonstrated a lack of common sense, and I was beginning to see that Tina was a master at it. Her stupidity on the subject made me want to blast her. I decided instead to think about what was I going to say and how to say it. Out of curiosity I asked, "What size you trying to get, anyway?"

She smiled and said, "C cup." Her enthusiasm resonated so completely that it almost made me want to get 'em done for her—almost.

I responded, "You ain't got to worry about having bigger titties, baby. You got the perfect size, a mouthful. Anything more would be a waste." Tina wasn't feeling my attempt at encouragement. I suppose it's the same for men who have little dicks—no amount of encouragement in the world would make me feel better if mine was small. Still I reassured her by telling her that I was okay with what she had, but it didn't seem to matter.

It was almost as if she wanted bigger breasts so she could draw the attention of other men. I was surprised to discover Tina had such large self-esteem issues, issues that I needed to pay closer attention to.

We'd talked extensively about her past, where she mentioned she had been diagnosed as a manic depressive, been in therapy for anger outbursts, and had even once been prescribed medication for it.

I never bothered to ask what other problems her disorder might create. I didn't care as long as none of them would interfere with our sex life. Now that she had expressed dissatisfaction with her God-given appearance, I was beginning to realize each day spent with Tina brought about a new issue containing some hidden riddle that, once cracked, bade me to run away now and do it quickly!

Chapter Nine
The Follow up

"I'm *looking for Riki, and all her Freaky friends,/ We're searching for Tanya, hoping like hell she'll let us in, / We're looking for loving any and everywhere we can,/ When it comes to freakin' ain't nothing like her friends.*"

I reached to turn up the radio. I loved Looking For Riki, even though it was a local favorite. It was a song about a stripper and a bunch of her friends and the freaky things they liked to do. Whenever I heard it I daydreamed about how nice it would be to know a girl like that who had a bunch of nasty girl friends who were down for whatever.

It was a late Saturday afternoon and I was riding with Brian. We had been out all day roaming streets of Atlanta as part of our usual weekend routine. We were nearing the Memorial Drive exit on our way to the Covington intersection when Brian tapped me on my arm and said, "Yo, G ain't dat sis you tried to get at a while back?"

I looked and noticed a burgundy Lexus ES300 speeding along in the inside lane. "Yeah, that is her." It was Monica from the parking lot at Shoemaker Warehouse. I put on my left blinker and pulled in the lane next to her. She was in a zone and didn't notice us for about ten seconds or more. I tapped the horn and she looked over at us.

She smiled once she recognized who I was. I lifted both my hands from the steering momentarily wheel as if to say "What's up?" She smiled and put one of her hands up and hunched her shoulder as if to respond "You tell me." We both smiled before B interrupted the moment saying, "Nigga, just get the bitch's number before you have a fucking accident and kill all of us!"

I laughed and said, "Yeah how bout dat." I rolled down the window and yelled across the lane, "Can I call you?" Monica wasn't a good driver, and I noticed she swerved a time or two as she tried to acknowledge me. I didn't want to cause a pile up so I grabbed my cell phone and held it in the air so she could see what I wanted from her. She nodded and began to sign the digits of her phone number with her fingers.

It took about a minute and a half, but by the time she finished I had dialed 770-555-8455 on the keypad to my phone and pushed send. "Hello," she said.

I'd remembered the way her voice sounded from that day at Shoemaker's. I was surprised to see it had the same effect over the phone. I said, "I guess it was meant for us, huh?"

She laughed and responded, "What do you mean?" She knew what I meant and I began to realize Monica was the playful type as she tried to hide the obvious. I played along, sensing her upbringing wouldn't permit her to acknowledge she was just as happy to get acquainted as I was.

"I must be a lucky man running into you twice, and the second time getting your number."

Monica laughed and said, "I only gave it to you to keep you from running me off the highway." I knew better but decided not to comment on it and instead thanked her.

"I appreciate your concern, but what I want to know is how do I go about getting to know a woman like you." Monica was tickled. I realized it was because she'd never heard that request put quite that way.

"I don't know what to tell you, but I do have a question for you. What's your name?" I wasn't sure if she was pretending or didn't really remember my name; nevertheless, I decided to tell her again anyway. "My name is Glenn."

She replied, "I knew it began with a G, but I didn't want to guess and say the wrong thing." Monica sounded sincere, and I wasn't concerned about her not remembering my name. I was just happy to have run into her again and to have gotten her number.

We drove side-by-side for about a mile or two and then parted ways. I had missed my exit early on trying to get her attention. "What are you doing later?" I asked. "I hope you're free because I'd like to do dinner and a movie." I gave Monica the benefit of the doubt and offered her both. Any other female would have been hard pressed to make it to the nearest wing spot to grab some hot-wings and a beer.

If looks were the judge, Monica was definitely something special, and I knew without knowing I had to play my cards right with her. "Well Glenn, I don't know. I had a few things to do. It's Saturday you know. I think I told you before that Saturdays are my only days to take care of my personal matters."

I did remember her telling me that when we first met, and I was happy to hear it again because it proved she didn't just make it up the last time. I said, "That's cool. Just call me if you find yourself free later." I had remembered Brian's words the last time and didn't want to apply too much pressure. Besides, I had her number and she had mine, and I knew she wouldn't have given it to me if she didn't want me to have it.

There was a brief pause after my last statement, and I wondered if it was because I didn't push the issue about getting together. Whatever it was she kept her thoughts to herself and said, "Be careful" before hanging up. Brian had been on his cell phone the entire time that Monica and I were talking. I looked at him and raised my head as if to ask who he was talking to. He bent his mouth downwards and motioned his hand in a cutting gesture across his neck to let me know it wasn't anybody special.

I whispered, "Yo, tell her you'll call her back." As Brian got off the phone I awaited his adulation, especially after his last remark about how Monica "didn't want my dumb ass." Now that I had gotten her number, I was anxious to hear what his response would be this time and couldn't wait to gloat for fear of the moment being lost.

"Man, I told you she was on my dick! She just had to play it off 'cause she knew I was there with another woman."

Brian looked up at the ceiling sighing before reluctantly acknowledging, "Alright Nigga. What you want? A cookie?"

I laughed and said, "Damn right, mufucka, and make it butter-crunch!"

Chapter Ten
When the Well runs Dry

A couple months had passed since the daylong shopping spree, but the fun continued. I would regularly surprise Tina with small gifts and tokens designed to show her how much I thought of her. She was satisfied because she could now compete with Stephanie. I had proven my point as I had vowed to do.

Now that Tina's social status had been elevated, I was able to relax knowing Stephanie was forced to acknowledge her as a potential equal. Brian it seems had made the biggest mistake he could possibly have made when he assisted Stephanie with the purchase of that new CLK 320 Mercedes. Prior to that she was driving a beat up black Acura Integra.

I guess she knew it didn't accurately represent the image she was trying to portray. It also seemed as if she had only played her part with Brian until he helped her with the mother lode. Now that she had it she became this whole other person. I didn't give it much thought that day when Brian said I started something, letting Stephanie and Tina hang out together, but I was beginning to realize maybe there was something to it.

Stephanie and Tina became fast friends after that daylong shopping excursion. The nature of their friendship was strange though. I mentioned to Tina what Stephanie said about her being corny, thinking it would make her apprehensive toward Stephanie, an automatic reaction for most people. But it didn't stop Tina. It was almost as if she turned up the heat and started brown-nosing Stephanie even more.

The average person wouldn't have had any more to do with someone who viewed them as inferior and would've been angered by the revelation. Tina was smarter than that. She knew what Stephanie said about her was true, and instead of being angry, she chose to pal up with Stephanie and learn all she needed about how to be high maintenance on a low budget.

****

It had been a while since Brian surprised Stephanie with a nice gift—about a month to be exact. Aside from buying her a pair of shoes now and again and going to nice restaurants, the high-end purchases stopped.

Things had gotten a little shaky for Brian back in Philly, and he had to go back almost every weekend to tend to business there. I was still in a position to do a few things and would have gladly given him whatever he needed had he asked, but he didn't ask. Brian was prideful that way.

During his various departures to and from Philly, Tina and Stephanie had started making habit of hanging out together, mostly on the weekends. During the day they would drive all throughout Atlanta in Stephanie's new CLK, stopping at Phipps and Lenux to shop and doing lunch at various spots. I remember Stephanie as being one of the first young black women to have that car, and the attention she received while in it was ridiculous.

Every time I turned around Tina was on her way to Stephanie's house, or Stephanie was picking her up. I always gave Tina free rein to do whatever she wanted and rarely clocked her movements or asked about her whereabouts. Although I was giving her money when she asked, I noticed at the end of each weekend she would appear with items that were more expensive than the money she received from me legitimized.

I would quietly observe, being ever careful not to make her aware of my suspicions. I also noticed Stephanie had a whole lot going on. Knowing Brian's financial situation for what it was, I realized those two were up to something. What it was, I didn't know, but I decided to keep a closer eye on their actions from that point. I felt bad because Brian had to go out of town so much, and I knew how much he liked Stephanie. He would never admit it, but I think his like was more like love.

Whatever it was, it was apparent that it was giving Stephanie massive confidence. She was beginning to lose respect for the relationship now that she had dudes coming at her in droves. One particular day, Brian was on his way back from one of his many excursions to Philly and I had to pick him up from the airport. I thought it strange he asked me to pick him up, knowing Stephanie was able to do it and it was a Sunday and she wasn't at church or work. I didn't mention my thoughts and did as he asked and arrived there at the requested time.

When I picked him up I could tell he was angry about something. Knowing him, I figured it had to do with her. I never pried into his personal business with her and waited until he decided to share it with me. It seemed as if he wasn't going to say a word until I said, "Yo, Tina called me and said she and Stephanie are going to Spa Sydell for the day."

Brian looked at me surprised and asked, "What? You gave Tina some dough for that shit? I heard it cost like two or three hundred for a daylong treatment."

I looked at him puzzled because I hadn't given Tina anything and had no idea a day spa cost that much. "Man, that shit can't cost that much—can it?" I responded nervously because if Brian was right, it meant those two were about to spend upwards of six hundred dollars for something, according to their budget, they definitely couldn't afford. I reasoned it away saying, "I ain't got Tina spending no three hundred on no massage. They must have a gift certificate or something." My comment seemed to cool Brian's angst for the moment.

I shifted the conversation to Philly and started asking him about the latest in the city of brotherly love. "What's happening up top?"

B let out a big sigh and said, "Man, ain't shit going on up there, but a bunch of bitches begging for money. Niggas still on the block hustling and shit. Oh yeah, I seen Tammy too."

The way Brian casually mentioned seeing Tammy prompted me to ask, "Tammy who?" I figured he couldn't possibly be talking about my ex-girlfriend Tamika. I hadn't seen her since I came down to Atlanta, and I hadn't spoken to her in the months I'd been here.

Brian looked at me and said, "Your old girl Tammy, nigga! What that bitch Tina got your head so fucked up you don't know who Tammy is now?"

Agitated I said, "Nigga, you said her name so casually I thought you was talking about somebody else." Half afraid to know, I hesitated before asking, "What she say?" I knew she had to have had something to say because of the way we parted. The mere mention of her name made me feel ashamed because I knew I went out like a coward when we broke up.

Instead of telling her face-to-face, I pretended I was going to Atlanta temporarily to visit my mother and never came back. I never mentioned it to Brian but part of my decision to leave Philly was because I found out Tammy cheated on me.

"She told me to tell you she thought ya'll was better than that, and she was okay now that everything was over."

Trying my best to remain indifferent I said, "Yeah, I bet she is okay. I heard she up there doing her thing with some cat in the NBA." I felt uncomfortable talking about Tamika for a lot of reasons and switched the subject back to Tina and Stephanie.

Talking about Tammy made me anxious, and in a momentary lapse of judgment I went outside of protocol and asked, "So what's up with you and Steph, and don't feed me no bullshit either!"

When Brian started talking it seemed as if he had been waiting for me to ask him. He took a deep breath and exhaled like he was about to unload—and he did. "G, for real-for real, I think the bitch on some bullshit!" Ever since she got that car her attitude changed. She be coming in the crib late; when I call her, the cell phone go straight to voice mail; and when she finally do come in the house she don't even be trying to break-bread wit me. I be going at her, and she still be acting like she ain't wit it."

I sat there listening to B run everything down. He paused briefly, and I remembered Lynnette telling me about that dude Toby. I wondered if Stephanie was frontin' on B now that dude was home from jail. In the midst of my thoughts Brian's voice came back into focus.

I was surprised when I heard him say, "I think it's time for me to rollout. My money ain't right and running back and forth to Philly every other week ain't cutting it." Hearing Brian say what he said made me realize that shit was worse than I originally imagined. He was actually stressing. Although I knew he would refuse me, I decided to offer him a loan. "What's up man, you know I got you if you need anything. All you got to do is let me know."

Brian paused and thought to himself. I gather it was because he didn't really want to leave Atlanta. After about ten seconds he responded, "Naw, man. I'm cool."

Chapter Eleven
Coach Bitches

I didn't like seeing B stressed out like he was and decided to give Lynnette a call to see if I could get some inside scoop on Toby. "Hey baby, what's up? What happened to you? I thought we were supposed to be getting together for lunch or something?"

Lynnette saw right through my vain attempt to pacify her for not being in touch with her since I had been in Atlanta. It didn't really matter much. After all we were only friends. She had someone who she was feeling real strong about and hadn't bothered to call me either.

"Glenn, please don't go there with all that B-S you trying to sell me. What's on your mind, or better yet what do you want to know this time?"

I paused for a moment trying to recover from being read so thoroughly. Lynnette was no dummy, and I should've known better than to come at her with something as transparent as that. Awkwardly I said, "You got me. I was calling to pump you for some information about that dude Toby. What's the deal with him? Did he get back at Stephanie or what?"

Lynnette laughed and said, "Dang, you really pressed. What happened? Stephanie started flaking on Brian?" I didn't respond because I didn't want people to look at my man sideways like his game wasn't tight, especially after he had broke Stephanie off the way he did. If word got out that she played him, it would make him look like a sucker, and me as well since I was his man.

I deflected Lynnette's suspicions by saying, "Ain't nothing wrong. I was just asking because he's thinking about taking things to the next level with her, and I remembered you telling me she was still feeling the dude. I figured I owed it to B to find out if she had any skeletons in her closet before I let him jump out the window."

The lie was pretty good. Still I don't think Lynnette went for it, but she didn't comment one way or the other after that. She opened up and told me everything she knew about that dude. "Yeah, he came home about two weeks ago, and he even called me. When I talked to him I asked him was he still messing with the backup team. He lied and said he wasn't. I told him to let me know when he was ready to resign his star player, but made sure he knew not to come around until he got his money right and his shit together."

I was happy to hear the dude was home because I didn't wish jail on no black man, but Lynnette wasn't telling me what I wanted to know. Frustrated I asked again, "So what's his story? Is he trying to get at Stephanie or what?"

Lynnette responded, "I heard he came home and went right back to the same hustle that got him put in jail in the first place. He asked me to help him with some of the stuff, but I told him I was cool on all that. Plus, my dude ain't having it. I asked him about his backup team again, and he said he wasn't dealing any of them anymore, but a few of them were still in pocket and were handling some business for him. He wouldn't say who though."

Lynnette had hit the nail on the head. I figured both Stephanie and Tina had to be down with the dude 'cause they had been shopping an awful lot and bringing home new bags almost every weekend. The money B was giving Stephanie wasn't enough to do it like she was doing it! Lynnette finished telling me little odds and ends about what she thought might have been going on with Toby and surprised me in the end when she said, "Even if he is using her to do some of his dirt, I don't think they dealing with each other though. Stephanie is supposed to be messing with some guy up at her job. At least that's what she told Toby."

I paused for a minute trying to figure out how in the world she would have been able to pull off dealing with anyone given the fact she and Brian were always together. Then it hit me. It was easy now that B had was going out of town so much lately.

****

A week or so had passed since I last spoke to Lynnette, and I still hadn't mentioned to Brian what I heard. I was confused because I didn't want to create any additional tension in their relationship and would have felt horrible if the information I passed was wrong.

On the other hand, I felt like I had a responsibility to tell him what I knew. After I got the scoop, I wished that I had never asked. At least that way I couldn't be held accountable for any negative outcome stemming from Stephanie's escapades.

It had also been a week since I last spoke to Brian after picking him up from the airport. He mentioned that he would be flying right back out again, and since he would only be gone for a day he was going to drive his car to the airport so he wouldn't have to wait on me again once he got back. I gathered his lack of contact with me during the previous week and him making his own provisions for his return flight was his way of taking a break and falling back in order to get his thoughts together.

The shit he was going through with Stephanie was beginning to overwhelm him. Although he didn't say it, I knew it was. In truth, I was as surprised as he was. He and Stephanie had been an item for a good six months, and if you counted all of the time they logged on the phone prior to us moving to Atlanta then it was more like two years. Whatever Brian's faults may have been, he definitely wasn't guilty of neglect. He did everything he could to make sure Stephanie was cared for. Maybe that was where he went wrong. Now that the money had slowed down and she was in her new car, she obviously felt he was of no further use to her.

Just as I was about to pick up the phone and give him a call, my phone rang. It was B. "G, whachoo doing man?"

I responded, "Nothing. Just about to go to Waffle House and get a grub. What's up wit you?"

"Man, I got rap for you." Brian sounded serious and I knew from his tone that whatever he wanted to talk to me about was definitely heavy on his chest. I also knew it had to be about Stephanie.

He started off saying, "I flew in town this morning, but I told Stephanie I wouldn't be back until tomorrow and decided to surprise her for lunch. I went to the house and freshened up and got dressed around 11:00 am and left out a half hour later so I would have time to make it to Alpharetta."

I interrupted him and asked, "Why you drive all the way out there?"

Brian responded, "Oh, that's right. You ain't know, but Stephanie don't work downtown no more. She got a new job working for MCI and it's in Alpharetta. She been working there for about six months now. When I got out there, I was pulling up in the parking lot just before noon and was about to call to tell her to come outside, and I see her walking out the door."

I almost didn't want to hear the rest of what I knew he was

about to say. And said, "Awww wow, don't tell me what I think you about to say."

Brian pressed his mouth against the phone making his words sound muffled and said, "Nigga, you know what I'm 'bout to say, don't you?" The question was rhetorical and he continued with his story. "G, I see the bitch coming out of the building smiling and shit at some nigga walking next to her. I wouldn't have had a problem with it if I didn't see her holding his hand!"

I could hear the hurt in his voice as he struggled to finish his story. He wasn't struggling the way people do when they are trying to fight back tears or anything like that. He was struggling to maintain his composure. As he spoke I noticed his voice kept fluctuating between two different octaves from his usual monotone manner of speaking. He was pissed! I was waiting for him to tell me he ran up on her and smacked the bullshit out of her, but he didn't. He told me a different version.

"I started to drive up on them and yoke the bitch up, but I didn't. Instead I did an "Oran Juice Jones" move and went back to the condo. When I got there, I gathered up all of my shit. I went room to room to make sure I wouldn't overlook anything. After I got all of my stuff out, I went back in and sat on the couch and thought about what to do next."

By this time I was sitting on the other end of the phone with bated breath. Brian had always been a rational-minded person. In the thirteen years we had known each other I had never seen him lose his composure, nor had I known him to be violent. I wondered what was on his mind as he sat there and if he was going to say he burnt the house down or something.

"G, as I sat on the couch I thought about how the bitch had played me and how I had been nothing but nice the whole time I had known her. She had some Tanqueray in the kitchen. I grabbed a glass and poured some with some orange juice and took a strong gulp of the shit and leaned up against the refrigerator." I didn't want to hear him tell me he started crying. If he had I wouldn't have judged him for it, but it would have confirmed my biggest fear— he really did love her.

He paused for a minute and I am sure that he was about to reveal his emotional state. I chimed in just as he was about to and said, "Nigga, I know you ain't shed no tears over the broad?" That was my way of coaching him and a way of letting him know I didn't need to know everything. I already knew he was going through a major heartache, and his pain was evident. I owed it to him to help him keep his dignity by preventing him from revealing his innermost feelings.

My macho attitude put him back on track and let him know I was only interested in knowing how he played Stephanie and nothing more. "Fuck no, I ain't cry over that bitch!" His overaggressive response indicated that I was right, and I knew what he saw up at her job broke him down. I didn't say anything and let him continue. "While I was leaning on the frig, I noticed the door to the pantry was open and I saw a big ass bottle of bleach sitting on the washing machine."

I tensed up in anticipation and said, "Awww don't tell me yo…"

Brian cut me off mid sentence saying, "Main man, you might want to grab a seat for this one." And then continued, "Nigga, I took bleach and poured it on top of everything she had in her closet. I started from the left to right, and then splashed it on the shit that I thought I might have missed." I flopped down in my seat after that because that was a coup de gras.

Stephanie's whole world revolved around her clothes, and in one fell swoop Brian had taken away everything that mattered to her. Her identity was destroyed. Unbeknownst to her, the pomp and arrogance that had become part and parcel of her character was now a thing of the past. Brian was uncharacteristically amused by his own story and would break into laughter in an almost maniacal manner.

I was speechless and sat there on the other end so quietly that he stopped mid-story and asked, "Yo kid, you there?"

I sighed and said, "Yeah, man. I'm still here. Whachoo do after dat?"

He laughed again and said, "Nigga, that was just the beginning. After I finished dousing all her clothes, I went to the living room closet and poured the bleach on all of her coats, too."

Stephanie was a fly broad and was known to have a mink or two in her closet, one of which Brian had bought personally. I quickly asked, "You poured bleach on the minks, too?"

Brian paused before saying, "Come on now G, I was mad. I ain't saying I went crazy. I grabbed the stuff I bought and doused the rest of it. The feeling got so good to me that after a while I couldn't stop. I emptied the bleach bottle and went back in the kitchen and grabbed a butcher's knife. I went back to the bedroom closet, sat on the floor, grabbed one shoe out of each box, and sliced each one through the side, and popped all of the straps off of the sandals, and then did the same to all of those Gucci and Louis bags, too!"

I said, "God damnnnnn! You went all out."

Brian said, "Nigga, you fucking right I did. I bought damn near all that shit. That's why I couldn't believe she had the nerve to try and act funny now that she got that new car, but I wasn't about to let her floss with the next cat in some shit I paid for! The bitch must have thought that I was sweet like that."

She wasn't the only one. The way Brian had been spoiling her made me think something had to be wrong with his ass. But then I remembered he was quiet and unassuming, the kind people always say are the ones who you need to watch out for 'cause if you push them too far they will snap!"

Just when I thought the story couldn't get any better Brian said, "Oh yeah, and I really got my Oran Juice Jones on when I stuck her up for every piece of jewelry I ever bought her. She only wear her nice stuff when she go out. Other than that she leaves everything on top of her dresser. I grabbed the Cartier and half-karat diamond earrings!"

I was surprised to hear about the earrings and said, "You a funny cat. Why you ain't tell me you broke her off like that?" I couldn't resist busting his balls for that one because he hadn't told me about that purchase. Feeling half embarrassed and half justified, he responded, "G, she let me get that asshole one night, and while I was up in it she made me promise to take her to the Shane company the next day. The bitch could've got the Hope diamond as good as that ass was!"

Brian was a freak and would often brag about his deviant sexual exploits. I didn't blame him 'cause Stephanie did have the kind of ass that would make any man want to stick his dick in it. Brian had always been secretive about everything. Secret or no secret I now knew why his funds were so low. I asked, "So what's next? You know you got to get the fuck up out of there before she get home today, 'cause Dekalb County is going to snatch your ass up when she find out what you did."

Brian laughed and said, "I know. I got my shit all packed up in my car, but I ain't done yet. I'm 'bout to call the bitch now and let her know I saw her today."

I would've never thought in a million years I would have ever hear Brian tell me something like he was telling me. I figured since he had done all that he had and was obviously finished with Stephanie, it was safe to tell him some of the things Lynnette had told me about her.

"I ain't want to get involved man, but I had been doing a little recon on your behalf and spoke to Lynnette about Stephanie's background. She told me she was dealing with some cat up at her job. Maybe he was the cat you saw her holding hands with earlier."

Brian didn't say anything after except, "Hold on a minute while I three way the call, and don't say nothing 'cause I don't want her hanging up before I can get a chance to lower the boom."

The phone rang about two times before Stephanie answered. "Hello, thank you for choosing MCI. How may I help you today?"

Brian said, "Hey baby, how you doing?"

Stephanie responded, "I'm fine, how are you? And why haven't I heard from you?"

Brian knew Stephanie's question was bullshit; she had his number and hadn't bothered to call in the day and a half he had been gone. But he played along saying, "I just been busy handling my business that's all. But whassup wit-choo?"

Stephanie paused before responding, "I ain't been doing nothing. Me and Tina been hanging out a little bit."

Brian's tone changed as he said, "What you mean, been hanging out? I see that bitch Tina been dragging you out in the street like a little whore *too*, huh?" Brian had gotten anxious and didn't realize how abrupt his accusatory segue was.

He also must have forgotten that I was on the phone because his comment about Stephanie being a whore too caught me by surprise. Sure, I had begun to have my doubts about Tina, but that was for me to speak on and definitely not anyone else. Brian continued with his accusations, "I know all about you two, running around the city flirting with every nigga that steps to y'all."

Stephanie broke her silence after that and said, "Ima call you right back." She was at work and couldn't fire back at Brian the way she wanted to. She took a break, went outside, and called him back from her cell phone. Brian had barely answered his phone before Stephanie said, "Let me tell you something Nigga, you don't do enough for me for you to think you can talk to me like you crazy. I don't care what you think I do when I hang out with my friend, you need to worry about Brian, and what Brian needs to do to make sure Brian don't get left out in the cold!"

She had done it. Stephanie's innuendo about kicking Brian out of her house confirmed she was looking for a reason. Brian stuttered after her statement but kept his game face on, "Humph, yeah, wu–well you think you slick or something, but I saw you today. And all I want to know is when did it become cool for MCI employees to be holding hands with their coworkers and shit? I know that shit has to be forbidden because it definitely isn't acceptable business protocol."

There was a long silent pause on the line. Brian had attacked Stephanie on two fronts, and she was stunned by his revelation of having seen her. She knew the jig was up and switched from defense to offense, sensing she had nothing left to lose. Had Brian played his hand right he might've been able to gather a little information before getting kicked out, but keeping your composure under pressure is damn near impossible when your angry and hurt. I know all too well. Still had he done so he would have at least been able to find out who the person was that he saw taking Stephanie to lunch.

"What was you doing up at my job any way? Don't be just popping up on me like that. That was my coworker and I don't need to explain myself to you." Stephanie was an expert liar. Although the dude was her coworker technically, she was flirting with the truth because she chose to omit the fact that they were seeing each other.

In one stroke she managed to lie to Brian and shift the tide of the argument in her favor. She did it so effortlessly that she seemed to be schooled in the art. Brian's only saving grace was that he had already gotten his get back and was on his way back to Philly. Were it not for that, the situation would have been ugly. What came next proved it.

"Brian, I think you need to get your shit together 'cause I don't think this is going to work out."

"So whatchoo sayin? You telling me I got to get outcha house now?" Brian couldn't believe what he was hearing. After thousands of dollars, gifts, a Mercedes CLK, numerous trips in and out of town, Stephanie said those words as if he was just some nigga who she had just had a one-night fling with. Worse than that, her words were casual and had no more feeling than if she'd asked him to pass the ketchup.

"Stephanie, I ain't stupid. I already know the real deal. You wasn't holding hands with that dude for nothing. I know you dealing with him like dat! I already knew that you was dealing with somebody up at your job. It was probably that Toby nigga. That's how you been getting all of that new shit you been popping up with."

Stephanie was silent again. She was completely baffled as to how Brian, being from out of town, could know so much about her personal business. "I don't know where you getting your information from, but you can tell your bitch Glenn to stay out of my business. He need to worry about what Tina doing."

Brian chuckled cynically. Stephanie's correct assumption about the source of his information was a little unnerving. I guess it was obvious; after all she knew Brian didn't know anyone in the city except for her.

Brian didn't know it, but he fucked up letting Stephanie know what he knew. Doing so helped her formulate another series of lies. "I don't fuck with Toby. That nigga is still in jail, and I don't have time for niggas that ain't got their shit together, especially niggas like you!" Brian wasn't expecting that one and it shook him a little. The contempt Stephanie expressed would've made anyone question whether they'd just spent the last three months living under the same roof.

Brian managed to compose himself before responding, "Don't worry, I'm cool with the whole thing. Whoever you fucking can have your trifling ass!" Stephanie didn't like Brian calling her trifling and blasted him.

"Fuck you, you broke mother fucker! I ain't want you anyway, and nigga, you ain't got the power to give me to nobody 'cause I was never yours!" She hung up the phone after that. Brian was stunned again by the viciousness with which Stephanie had attacked him and called me.

"G, that bitch hit me with a couple of gut blows! I'm glad you wasn't on the phone to hear that shit. If you was, I probably would've drove up there and beat that bitch's ass!"

I anxiously blurted out, "What she say?"

About five seconds passed before Brian responded to me. I knew he was thinking about which parts to tell me and I could only imagine what he was feeling at that point.

"G, that bitch said so much crazy shit I don't even feel right repeating it. All I could do while she was saying it was try to think of some fucked up shit to say that would crush her too, but all I could think of was to call her trifling."

Brian laughed because he knew his rebuttal was lame and ineffectual. I was relieved when he told me what transpired because I was afraid he'd lost it and admitted to bleaching and tearing up her shit. Stephanie lived in Dekalb County and those muthafucka's ain't got no problem locking a nigga up for some dumb shit. If you don't believe me, get in your car and drive down the road without proof of insurance. They'll make you a believer!

"So you just let it go after that?" I asked.

"No, the bitch hung up the phone before I could say anything to her. But hold on. I just thought of what I can say that will fuck her head up." Before I could say anything, Brian had already clicked the line, dialed Stephanie's number, and clicked me back in on the three-way. She answered expectantly, "What you want now?"

Brian was cool and composed when he said, "Oh I ain't want nothing much other than to tell you to memorize all of the names of the seven dwarfs 'cause when you get home all yo shit is going to be snow white!"

Stephanie sat puzzled for a moment and wondered what he meant. It wasn't long before she realized that she had played herself being so belligerent toward Brian. After all, he did have the keys to her condo. Realizing she left her flank exposed, Stephanie said, "Brian, we ain't even got to end it like this. We both need to calm down and talk about this." Gone was all the tough talk she so brazenly hurled at him less than twenty minutes prior. I sat there listening to her plea for clemency and wondered how Brian would react. I wanted to remind him that reconciliation at point was not an option, and any offer of such would just be a ploy by Stephanie to prevent him from doing any irreparable damage before she could get home and change her locks.

He impressed me when I heard him say, "Fuck you, bitch. You

think you can say all of the shit you just said to me and everything would be cool after that? The only reason I ain't come up there and beat yo ass is because the shit I did do was a thousand times better."

Upon hearing that Stephanie's words became increasingly frantic as she realized she misjudged Brian, which prompted her to ask, "What are you talking about? I didn't even do anything. Why are even acting like this?"

Brian feeling triumphant said, "Yeah, bitch. You did a lot and you been doing it ever since you got the damn car! And you damn sure ain't give a fuck about how I felt until I reminded you I had a key to your place." Brian was in rare form and was feeling good knowing he had already gotten his vindication from destroying all of her personal property.

She would learn who the real playa was the minute she got home. Nothing she said to him thereafter made any difference. "So take care of yourself, and oh yeah—it's been nice knowing you!" He disconnected Stephanie after that and said, "G, it really don't matter what you do for these broads. They ain't 'bout shit. All that matters is what a nigga can do or is going to do 'cause you can damn well forget about bringing up what you used to do!"

Brian had a quiet resolve by then and I could feel his sense of satisfaction as he relayed his newfound philosophy. "G, you need to roll with me. You wouldn't be losing shit; both of them bitches is just coach bitches trying they hardest to be Prada queens. You said yourself Tina was content with her corny ass life until she met you, me and Stephanie."

I sat silently listening to Brian go on about why I should leave with him. I thought about defending Tina, but deep down I knew he was right, and had already begun to suspect major impropriety on her part as well. "G, I'm telling you the game ain't what it used to be out here, and the minute your dough get low you gon go through the same shit. Both of them bitches think they doing something, but niggas ain't droppin' dough like they used to.

"When and if shit does start poppin' again, those two ain't gon be contenders. Both of 'em pushing thirty, but still trying to dress like they twenty. Tina don't even have a job, and the way she spend your money she act like she don't need one!"

I let Brian ramble for two reasons; the first was because I knew he needed to vent. The second was because I wanted to hear his rationale and how he felt. He made sense, but I also knew he only expressed it because his fun had stopped.

Had it not I'm sure he would have been singing a different tune. Finally I said, "Yo, kid, just be careful driving up the road. You need to get on your way now so you can at least be out of the county before Stephanie get home from work. That way you won't have to worry about these pressed-ass cops trying to pull you over with an all points bulletin on your PA plates."

Brian took a deep breadth and said, "Alright Nigga. I'm out, but don't say I didn't warn you. Peace." As I hung up my phone I had a premonition that maybe there was something to what he said but quickly dismissed the notion as the sound of my phone ringing interrupted my thoughts. It was Tina.

Chapter Twelve
Sweet Revenge

A limited imagination has prevented many people from reaching their goals in life. It has also caused others to miscalculate the extent of other people's resolve after they've been crossed. Stephanie had no idea that sweet, unassuming Brian would have ever had the capacity to do something so devastating, so complete, and so total! Many women have made the same mistake thinking, "Oh, he ain't like that," or "He would never do anything like that."

That kind of thinking has put many in the hospital and many others in their graves. In this case, it cost Stephanie an extensive and highly valuable wardrobe—not to mention several pricey jewelry items—and all because she thought that she could take advantage of a quiet, easygoing guy.

A few hours had passed since Brian hit the road. I got a call from Tina just as he and I concluded our call. She wanted me to pick her up so we could go out to dinner. I went and scooped her up, and from the time she got in the car I was lost in thought imagining Stephanie's reaction at seeing all the damage B did to all her shit!

A few hours had passed since Brian hit the road. I got a call from Tina just as he and I concluded our call. She wanted me to pick her up so we could go out to dinner. I scooped her up, and from the time she got in the car I was lost in thought imagining Stephanie's reaction at seeing all the damage B did to all her shit!

"Oh my God!" were the only words Stephanie could form her mouth to say once she walked into the bedroom and saw the chaos that resulted from Brian's anger. There was bleach everywhere. She could barely keep her fingers on the dial pad as she pushed 911.

"911 what's your emergency?"

"My ex-boyfriend poured bleach on all my clothes and cut up all my shoes!" The words came out fast and furious; Stephanie was only on the phone for less than thirty seconds before she started going room to room witnessing the damage Brian wreaked throughout her condo. He'd only told me he messed up her clothes and cut up her shoes. What Stephanie saw was much more than that.

"Oh my God! There's water on all of my electronics, too."

The 911 operator chimed in, "Ma'am, unfortunately your situation doesn't constitute an emergency, but we will dispatch an officer to your location to take a report. I have your address as 2200 Thunder fork Lane, Atlanta, Georgia. Ma'am, is that the correct address?" Stephanie had zoned out as the 911 operator repeated her question. She'd discovered more shit and the shock of it put her at a loss for words.

She hung up with the 911 dispatch and immediately called Brian. I might have never have known how bad Brian was affected by the sight of seeing Stephanie holding hands with another guy. One thing was clear; his reaction was a combination of built up frustration and confirmed suspicions, and he was through! "The number you have reached, 215-666-1403, has been disconnected." Stephanie screamed at the top of her lungs into the receiver, "You muthafucking baaaastard!" I suppose screaming brought Stephanie some kind of relief, but I'm sure nothing like the kind Brian was feeling as he made his way up I-95 north.

I chuckled to myself; fully entertained by the show my imagination had just displayed for me. Tina didn't notice; she was off in her own little world lip syncing the words to some girly song playing on the radio. We'd pulled into Houston's parking lot on Peachtree Street when my phone rang causing me snap out of my daydream. I looked down at it and saw it was Stephanie. I hadn't mentioned what Brian told me about the episode that had just transpired. I knew had I done so Tina would have gotten angry with me believing that I was somehow in on it.

I hesitated before answering the phone, because the sound of it was making me anxious. Still, I couldn't wait to hear the dejection in Stephanie's voice. I handed the phone to Tina and said, "Answer this. It's Stephanie. She must know that you're with me."

Tina lifted the lid of the phone and said, "Hello, what's up girl? How you know I was with Gle.." Tina's words were abruptly interrupted by a ranting, crying, and hysterical Stephanie.

"Put Glenn on the phone Tina. Put his black muthafucking ass on the phone now.""What's going on, Steph? Why you tripping like that?" Stephanie stopped shouting long enough to tell Tina a brief summary of what happened, the impact of the story caused Tina to exclaim, "Oh my God!" before handing me the phone looking at me with a suspicious frown on her face, as if she knew I was well aware of Brian's actions. Tina's reaction confirmed my assumption, and I was all too happy to take the phone.

In a way I was glad Stephanie was the first to tell her about it. I wanted her to hear the hysteria and frustration in Stephanie's voice. I wanted Tina to appreciate the fact that what happened to Stephanie was self inflicted because she decided to step out on my boy.

Stephanie's voice was hurried and frantic, "Glenn, what's Brian's number?"

I played dumb saying, "What you asking me for? You been sleeping with the nigga for the last six months and you ain't got his number?"

Stephanie started screaming louder, "Stop fucking with me Glenn. The police are here and I need his number. That muthafucka poured bleach on all my shit, and I need to talk to him!"

I added insult to injury saying, "don't you think he said all he needed to say when he bleached all your shit!" I chuckled as I tried to hold my composure. Knowing what I'd just said made her want to kill me. I was happy, because the slick bitch got what she deserved!

Tina was watching and listening. She chimed in "You ain't shit!"

I didn't give a fuck what Stephanie was going through, after Brian told me what he told me. Not that I would have had any sympathy otherwise.

Nothing bothered me more than the thought of a deceitful woman getting over on a man. The shit did something to me inside that I have yet to define, even the Bible says that shit ain't right! Tina grabbed the phone and started consoling her. "Don't worry about it Steph. It'll all come back on him."

Stephanie wasn't trying to hear that shit. She wanted justice and she wanted it immediately! "Tina, make Glenn give me the number. I want to call that muthafucka and tell him that my brother and my father are coming up there after his ass!"

Tina looked over at me and said, "Glenn, what is Brian's number?"

I was confused by now because they had the same number I did, and I couldn't understand what the big deal was. "Why y'all keep asking me for his number? Y'all got the same number I got."

Stephanie heard me through the phone and screamed, "He changed it or got it disconnected after he tore up my shit!"

Although I heard her, Tina repeated it anyway, but I had already started laughing my ass off; stopping long enough to say, "My nigga! Damn, that mufucka wasn't playing. He told me he was going to change his number, but I thought he would at least wait a day or so before he did it."

"Glenn, that shit ain't funny. Why didn't you say something or stop him or something?"

I stopped laughing just long enough to say, "Look, when I talked to him he mentioned he was pissed at Stephanie when he saw her wit that dude. Shit, I at least stopped him from coming up there and beating her ass. She should be thanking me for that. I guess after that he decided he was going to do what he did." I trailed off saying, "I see Nextel be on they shit though. They got right on it. Ima keep that in mind."

Tina was frustrated and said, "Glenn, Stephanie's on here crying and you making jokes."

Stephanie could hear what I said and told Tina, "I ain't even worried about it. The police is going to get his ass." Tina repeated it, telling me as if that would miraculously cause me to divulge a number I didn't have. I wanted to know the extent of the damage Brian had caused and asked Tina to ask Stephanie what all did he tear up.

She asked and Stephanie said, "He tore up everything—all my shoes, my clothes, my coats, my furniture, and even opened my drawers and poured bleach on my panties! I ain't got shit no more other than the shit I wore to work today."

Tina raised up in the seat anxiously and asked, "Did he get all new stuff, too?" Stephanie responded saying "Yeah."

Tina disingenuously said, "Damn girl that's fucked up. You can wear some of my stuff if you want."

Secretly, she was thrilled Stephanie had been dethroned and could no longer boast as the Queen bee. Her mind was already probing its deepest recesses for the bullshit she was going to offer Stephanie; surely none of the stuff I had bought recently. No, she was going to give her the very same shit Stephanie so casually dissed in the beginning as corny.

I was almost moved by Tina's gesture until I heard her say, "What he do to the car?" The way it came out was selfish and deliberate, totally devoid of the concern she'd expressed at the top of the conversation. Like the way Seely resentfully told Harpo to beat Sophia in The Color Purple.

When Stephanie said, "Nothing, I drove it to work," I could swear I saw Tina's sense of anticipation leave her, and she was noticeably disappointed.

I started to comment but instead chose to make a mental note. I was beginning to see Tina's true nature for what it was. All that mattered to her was elevating herself by whatever means possible. The whole episode was like something out of a book. Life is funny like that, though. You just never know how the road is going to turn. Tina was Batman now and poor Robin didn't even have a costume.

Chapter Thirteen
Troy Black

"Yo son, since your girl rolled out how 'bout letting a nigga move in this piece?"

"Nigga, go head wit dat shit. That bitch a be back. She always come back."

For some reason I wasn't as sure as I had been in the past. Things had gone bad between Tina and me before but never like this. Maybe she was finally tired of all my shit.

The crazy shit about it was even Hosea could tell something wasn't right. A couple months had passed and even though she called and came by from time to time, I felt something wasn't right. The last time I heard from her she had stopped by and fucked me and left rent money and apologized for leaving so abruptly the night she moved out. Before she left I asked her where she lived and she simply said, "Close," as she walked out the door.

After she left I felt like Eddie Murphy did in Boomerang when Robin Givens did the same to him. I had known her a long time and I knew that something was up with her, and I was definitely going to find out.

"Yo, Nigga. I ain't want to be the one to tell you this, but I seen your girl driving around town in a blue big body Benz with PA plates on it." Hosea didn't know it, but I had already gotten word. Tina had always been a sneaky bitch! Worst of all, the car belonged to the same cat I saw her talking to at my party, the same dude who bought her the champagne.

"Hosea, remember them two dudes that pulled up in valet at our party?"

"What dudes, nigga? You know I don't be looking at no hard legs!"

"Mufucka, you remember 'cause you was the one tapped me on the arm when they both pulled up in matching big bodies. One was blue, and the other was gold or somethin'."

"Dammmmn, yeah. I remember now, and it was PA plates on both of 'em, right? Oh shit, kid. You think that blue one she was driving is dat same nigga's?"

"Probably so son, but it's cool 'cause I ain't want that bitch no more anyway." I was honestly ready to roll from the relationship, but I wanted to be the one to do it, and I definitely wasn't cool with no bitch playing me out like that. I know a lot of people in this town, and Tina was making me look real bad. It was already bad enough Hosea's dumb ass had seen that sneaky-assed bitch driving around the city. Ain't no telling how many of other niggas peeped that shit!

"Yo, Black. I remember her and my girl talking to them niggas come to think of it. Yeah, the one dude was dark skinned and looked like Barry White or some shit; he was the one who was driving the blue car. His man had a little fro with a light-colored suit on. When I walked over to 'em I grabbed Erica by her arm and the dude gritted on me. Tina kept on talking to the other cat, and the next thing I know she was walking around with a bottle of champagne. That's when I asked you if you let her get a free bottle, 'member?"

"Yeah, nigga, I remember. You thought I had let her get a free bottle and asked me to let Erica get a bottle, too. Now that I think about it Tina started acting real funny a few days after that, and I remember a lot of hang-ups and wrong numbers to the crib, too."

"Yo son, you think she would do you dirty like dat?"

"Man, ain't no telling with these broads nowadays. All I know is about a week and a half after, the bitch started an argument with me and packed her shit and rolled out. I didn't stop her 'cause I was tired of playing house. She started coming around again after a couple of months and I ain't heard from her since. And that was a month ago!"

Whenever Tina and me went through similar shit she always came back after a few days or so and would only grab a few articles of clothes before storming out the door. The last argument we had seemed staged, and I watched as she confidently packed her things.

I knew something was up because she had her friends pull up in a pickup truck and loaded all of her furniture as if she knew this time she wasn't coming back.

The argument had caught me totally by surprise. I was still trying to recover from the party we had, which turned out to be a complete and total bust.

The highlight of the whole thing was when those two niggas came in all suited up and shit and stole the show. From the looks of things they stole my bitch, too! Hosea and them niggas didn't know it yet, but I had put my last ten thousand into that shit and didn't break even. To top it off, the rent was due, and I was in the hole so deep I couldn't see daylight. Tina knew our shit was shaky, and obviously had been planning her getaway all along. Cause the bitch rolled and didn't look back!

That was fine with me 'cause I'd always known Tina to be that way, the kind of woman who went any way the wind blew, always searching for a bigger fish than the one she already had. Tina had lied to me on numerous occasions, and whenever she got tripped up she would always claim she wasn't wrong for whatever it was that she was wrong about, claiming that she did it 'cause I didn't treat her right and never paid attention to her.

I should've known better 'cause she was married when we met and her husband was still a part of her life, even though she claimed to love me. It took months for her to finally stop going back and forth between us before her divorce was final. Mentally I knew she wasn't wrapped too tight when she let me fuck her and her best friend Palace at the same time, and then afterwards the two of them did each other. Don't get me wrong. I enjoyed it. What man wouldn't? But I knew then that she would never be the woman to raise my kids.

Marrying her would have been like suicide. She spent the bulk of her time running the street, sneaking around with other men and lying about it. The funny part of it is that she would always cry foul whenever she caught me lying. The last time it happened I said, "It's strange how someone who spends her entire life lying for a living can honestly be angry when someone lies to them. I can't believe you even have a problem with anything."

Tina had even lied to me about stripping and was even more surprised when I didn't make her stop. The truth was at that point I didn't care what she did and had long since stopped taking her personal. There were even times when I would come home after hanging out all night and come into the bedroom and find her and different girlfriends doing each other in our bed. I was cool with it because I loved freaky shit and would always lay back and enjoy the show when they turned their collective attention on me.

Knowing all the while that any woman who enjoyed sharing her man with other women wouldn't have no problem with sharing herself with other men. I also knew any man who tried to make a girl like her his woman was asking for trouble. I couldn't help feeling sorry for the next nigga she was going to go at. He wouldn't have a clue as to what he was dealing with, who he had, or the world of shit that awaited him.

That's why these dudes out here should always research a woman's background before they jump out here. I couldn't see spending my life with Tina. Being known in this town is a gift and a curse 'cause I got a call from a nigga who was cool with me but who I rarely dealt with and who I didn't really like. He had always known I didn't care for him and took great pride in calling to tell me that he had seen Tina over at Cityscape Plaza apartments.

"T-black, whassup son? What the deal nigga? What? You and ya girl moved over here now?"

I didn't know what in the hell that cat was talking about, but it got my attention immediately. I didn't want to let on that things were messed up between Tina and me so I just answered him by saying "Naw, my girl got her own shit now."

Lonnie knew I wasn't living there and just wanted a reason to have something to say, and sarcastically said, "Oh, nigga, 'cause I was bout to say damn, the nigga Troy done moved over here and ain't even come holla at a nigga. Then the nigga went and got a new big body Benz and ain't even come scoop a nigga up."

As the words rolled out of Lonnie's mouth my stomach knotted up. He knew he was jabbing at me and seemed to enjoy his strategic way of disrespecting me, knowing I couldn't address it because it wasn't direct. The only good that came out of the phone call was I had found out where Tina had moved to.

I closed out my conversation with Lonnie and exchanged more fake ass feedback. I wasn't cool with the way he called me and shitted on me with the news, but I had to take it. Had he known it affected me, it would have been even more satisfying for him. I hung up the phone and sat back in my chair and fought with myself about whether or not I should go over there.

It was a sunny Saturday afternoon and just before hanging up Lonnie slid in that he had just watched her drive off in a blue Benz. If Tina was alone when she left, then it meant that either the nigga was still in the house or she was going to pick him up from some place. Either way if I went to the complex I would be sure to catch her coming or going.

Chapter Fourteen
Caught

"Glenn, I'm on my way. I just had to stop home real quick. I left my tampons in the house and my period just came down, and oh, did you know the air conditioner in the car blows hot air when you stop at traffic lights, and then starts blowing cold again after I pick up speed?"

"Yeah, I know. It does that sometimes. I'm 'bout to get rid of it anyway so don't worry about it. But what you doing anyway? You were supposed to be back by now." I didn't quite know why, but something about Tina made me leery, and I felt I had to check up on everywhere she said she was going. She had already showed me just how sneaky she could be from the first night we met at Troy's party.

"I told you I had to run home real quick. I changed my clothes 'cause when I came on it leaked through and I had a spot in my pants. Damn, what is this? Fifty questions?"

I started to say yeah, but I knew that she couldn't have been up to much if her period was on. Little did she know that was the only time when I gave her the benefit of the doubt whenever I was unsure of her whereabouts.

It was Mother's Day, and we were supposed to be taking my mother to the Sun Dial Room for brunch. Tina and I had left early and ran around to pick up flowers and a card. She had to run home and I let her take the car because I didn't want to drive all the way back downtown. When I first introduced Tina to my mother, I could see that my mother wasn't at all pleased with my selection.

Aside from being cute, Tina had a look to her that suggested she was not to be trusted and my mother saw what good sex had prevented me from seeing—the devil in a blue dress! Shortly after brunch, Tina got up to go to the ladies' room.

My mother looked at me and said, "I see that you still dealing with this girl. I told you she's trouble. You ain't gon be satisfied until you get yourself caught up dealing with her." I didn't want to hear what my mother was saying, but I had a feeling maybe she was right, plus I could tell she resented Tina accompanying us on her special day. Even still, I felt that if Tina was a bad seed, it wouldn't have an effect on me 'cause I had a green thumb when it came to cultivating and converting women.

Every woman I had ever dealt with had always ended up loving my dirty draws by the time the relationship was in full swing. I had no reason to believe things would be any different with Tina. In Philly, a real thearl nigga never had a problem handling his broad, and my playa's membership had long since been elevated to platinum status.

By the time my mother finished admonishing me, Tina had come back. She smiled as she sat down and asked my mother, "Did you like your meal Mrs. Helen?"

My mother paused and smiled disingenuously back at her and said, "Yes, thank you. The food here is very good." The look on her face was that of a detective who suspects you are guilty of murder but doesn't have sufficient evidence to convict you. Yet.

After a while our waiter came over to the table and closed out the tab, and we all got up and left the restaurant. I went down ahead of Tina and my mother to the valet. That's when my mother took the opportunity to ask Tina some very direct questions. I was standing only a few feet away; they didn't know it but I could hear everything they were saying. "So Tina, what are your plans with my son?" Tina looked surprised, mostly because most of her other boyfriend's mothers never bothered to ask her anything. She was from Detroit, a town notorious for breeding treacherous and deceitful, money-hungry young black women.

My mom knew that and that is probably what prompted her to ask Tina the question. Tina hesitated and then responded, "What do you mean, Mrs. Helen?" Before my mom could respond, Tina continued, "Right now, me and Glenn are just kicking it. I like him, but we haven't taken it to the next level. We just coasting for now."

My mother gave her an ominous look and said, "Well, sweetie, I just want to let you know my son is very nice when he's in love, but the minute his feelings change he will turn on you, especially if he discovers you've been toying with his feelings." The valet pulled up in front of the hotel just as Tina and my mother had concluded their conversation. I tipped him, turned around and told them to come on, and opened the door for my mother then Tina.

My mother got in first, and after I closed the door, Tina scowled at me and shook her head. Up until that day she had believed that my mother liked her. The drive home was not as pleasurable as the drive there. The silence was deafening and none of us noticed the radio wasn't on, each lost in thought. My mother was obviously displeased at my choice of companionship. Tina was now feeling awkward, knowing that she was disliked. I was wondering, "What in the hell was I thinking bringing this girl with me on my mother's special day?"

When we got to the house my mom got out of the car without waiting for me to come around and open the door for her. I had to remind her to come back and get the flowers and the card I had bought for her. Whatever she sensed in Tina was enough to make her act totally out of character, a rarity with my mother.

As Tina and I drove away she waited until we were well out of my mother's development to start her tirade. No sooner had we hit Redan Road than she started with, "Why did you invite me to go with you if you knew your mother didn't want me there?" I sat there thinking, "Women are fucking crazy," because Tina knew just as well as I did I didn't invite her anywhere. She invited herself, and even went into a whole production on what we should do for her, even going as far as suggesting that we buy a cake and get it specially decorated with my mother's name on it.

To me that was overkill and I opted against it. I knew my mother well, and she would have been just as happy to receive cash and a card. I responded coolly and said, "First of all, you need to lower your voice, and secondly, you invited yourself. I don't know why you so upset anyway. Nobody told you to try your brown nose routine on my mother. I could have told you it wouldn't work. She raised five kids on her own—four of them boys. We tried everything in the book on her while growing up. That woman can see black paint on a wall in total darkness and can smell bullshit with cotton-balls stuck up her nose!"

Tina sat there silent and surprised that I had called her out on her little attempt to win over my mother. She knew she had overdone it and had no idea I too had seen through it. She thought my mother was going to fall for her little miss innocent role, but she had another thing coming.

My mother was something of a pistol herself in her younger years, being a still attractive 50-plus-year-old woman. There were probably a lot of unspoken similarities that existed between the two of them. I had heard scattered stories of my mother's youth and glory days, days that were filled with games only privileged, attractive, and desirable women were allowed to get away with.

Had Tina been her daughter, perhaps she might have turned a blind eye to the negative characteristics she sensed. But because I was her son, she had an obligation to prevent me from subjecting myself to the sneaky and deceitful nature that seemed to permeate Tina's personality.

"I just can't see why you would even let me come if you knew or had an idea your mother felt that way about me."

I laughed and said, "Personally, I was hoping she would have taken to you by now, but I guess she is still irritated by what happened at the house when you first met her." Tina's mouth dropped wide open as she recalled our first sexual encounter.

"Your mother knew we had sex that day? Why didn't she say something then?" I laughed because she did say something, but I never told Tina. When she arrived back home that day I introduced Tina to her as we were leaving. After Tina got in the car my mother came to the door and beckoned me to come back in the house. When I came in she punched me lightly in my arm and said, "This ain't no hotel. The next time you decide to lay down with one of your little hoochie mamas, you had better not bring her here!"

Since she didn't have any real proof she couldn't blast me. I knew she was really trying to feel me out to check my response, and I assured her laughingly that I didn't know what she was talking about. She knew better and slapped me in the back of my head as I turned to go back to the car.

After I told Tina the story, she erupted with the fury of a volcano. This time she was deadly serious because it was then that she realized she never stood a chance. No matter what she did or how she tried to act, my mother would always see her as some little floozy who had sex in her home, understandably every self-respecting woman's worst nightmare.

"Glenn, I can't believe you didn't tell me your mother thought that about me."

I wanted to say, "I didn't care what she thought because all you were supposed to ever be was a quick hit and run." But I didn't and instead offered a half-hearted apology and let the issue die. It was late afternoon by then and we decided to go to Piedmont Park.

There was a festival of some kind going on, and I thought it would be nice to go and take a relaxing walk through the park and see the sights. We went and had a pretty nice day. We ate at one of the many vendor stands and got full off of chicken shiskabob, sausage, peppers, and lemonade. The day wound down and we were both tired and decided to turn in early.

Tina had calmed down and had become as docile as a lamb. We stopped at Blockbuster and rented a few movies and took it in. The sun had already begun to set, and as we entered into the gate at the apartment complex, we were oblivious to any thought of danger. We rounded the corner and entered beneath the parking deck adjacent to Tina's apartment. I tapped Tina on her shoulder because she had fallen asleep on the way to the house.

She awoke as I was about to pull into a space about twenty feet from her door. All of a sudden her eyes popped wide open and her jaw dropped, "Oh my God! There goes Troy!"

I had never seen Troy before and looked around confused because I couldn't see anyone. The night sky had descended upon us and everything around us was engulfed in shadows. I strained to see a male figure but soon gave up trying because I didn't know where to look. I said, "I don't see him. Where is he? Is he at your door or what?" I said it frustratingly because I didn't like the idea of some nigga lurking in the shadows and me not knowing where he was, what he planned to do, or how he was going to do it.

Tina broke into my thoughts and said, "He's sitting over there in his car. It's the one with the parking lights on."

I looked over and saw a gold Acura TL in the cut. I was cool because now I could prepare for an attack and I knew the direction it would be coming from. I finished pulling into the parking space and looked at Tina and asked, "So how you want to handle this?"

She responded nervously, "I don't know." I got out of the car and looked over to where Troy was parked. He was already out of the car and walking up fast. I leaned back down into my car and said, "Stay in the car and lock the doors." By the time I pulled my head out of the car, Troy was less than five feet away from the passenger side. I rushed around to Tina's side of the car, headed him off and said, "What's up, nigga? You rolling up real fast. Can I help you with something?"

We looked at each other for the first time and sized each other up. He stood about 6'2" tall, had a slender build and looked like he weighed about 180 lbs. Compared to my 6', 240 lbs frame he looked like a twig. Luckily, that day I had decided to wear a tee shirt and jeans with a matching denim jacket and a 10 _ " pair of Timberland construction boots.

As long as he wasn't packing heat I was ready for whateva, and he knew it. Tina had given me his bio early on and had mentioned that he never got into skirmishes, choosing instead to talk his way out of shit. She mentioned that whenever they were out together and she was wearing something sexy, guys would regularly say whatever they wanted as they passed by and Troy wouldn't even turn around and challenge them.

It had gotten so bad that he had taken to telling her not to wear certain things so they wouldn't have to worry about dudes disrespecting him. Because of that she never felt safe with him. I took the information with a grain of salt because the game always changes when there's direct male involvement. Like Eddie Murphy said in 48 hours, "Lack of pussy make a nigga brave!"

Only in this case, the thought of another man fucking his woman can make a nigga crazy. I didn't know what to expect from the dude but felt reasonably sure he wasn't carrying a gun. In that same conversation Tina had confirmed Troy didn't own a gun and didn't like it when his friends would come to the house if they were carrying. If someone did come to his house and they were dirty, he would refuse to let him enter and demand that they leave the weapon outside.

At any rate, all of my concerns disappeared after I asked him what his business was with Tina and he responded saying, "I just want to talk to her." I couldn't believe my fucking ears. Tina had hit the nail on the head with dude! First of all, had it been me I wouldn't have had two words for any nigga who stood between me and my anger. Secondly, I definitely wouldn't have sought permission from some new cat to speak with the woman who I had just spent three years of my life with, the same woman who just left from living under my roof and who was now caught with the same nigga who I suspected her of cheating with all along!

After I confirmed his heart was pumping cherry Kool-Aid I laid down some ground rules and said, "All I'm saying is you ain't gon put your hands on her."

He stood there and looked me up and down again, seemingly trying to determine whether or not it was a no-win if he went against what I said and responded, "I ain't gon touch the bitch. All I want to do is ask her a question."

I was satisfied that I had made my point and went over to the car where Tina had been sitting and watching the entire exchange between Troy and me. I knocked on the window and motioned for her to roll it down. She did so slightly and I said, "Dude said he want to talk to you." She looked at me and waited for me to assure her that she wasn't in any danger. I said, "Don't worry about it. Ima be standing right there, and I ain't going to let nuffin happen to you. You wanna hear what he gotta say or what?"

She looked at me again, and then looked over to him, and said, "Yeah." She opened the door and got out of the car. I stood about three feet away as she walked over to Troy and asked, "What are you doing here? We're not together anymore Troy."Before she could say anything more, he erupted, "Is dat what it take? A nigga wit a Benz? Bitch, you ain't shit and you ain't ever gon be shit, but a dirty, tricking ass, stripping gay bitch!"

I inched up closer, thinking that Troy was going to follow up by punching the shit out of her. Tina noticed I had moved in closer and, feeling more secure, launched her own line of attack. "Fuck you, you broke ass mother fucker! I was tired of your young dumb ass anyway, making counterfeit checks and getting stolen credit card numbers, buying a bunch of dumb shit, trying to be a fucking hype man for a duck-ass rapper, and driving around in a fucking stolen car!"

Troy looked at her like she had just violated the Geneva Convention rules of engagement for war. I could tell his originally bruised ego was now shattered after Tina revealed his history in front of me. Before he could find the time to regroup and find the words to respond, Tina assailed him again with a gut blow saying, "Matter fact mother fucker, remember when you called me a few weeks ago, complaining about how I moved out and left you hanging with the rent, and you was six hundred short and didn't know how you were going to pay it?"

Troy looked at her in disbelief and stood there speechless as if to say, "Bitch, don't you say what I think you're going to say."

Tina didn't stop and followed up by saying, "Well that six hundred I gave your broke, beggin' ass came from this nigga," and she pointed to me. I along with Troy stood there dumbfounded as we witnessed the ferocity Tina displayed and continued to throw at him.

I had begun to sympathize with what he was going through. After all, it's a hard thing to lose your woman to another man, but an even harder thing to accept the fact that the chosen nigga is built strong enough to take your woman and support your household all in the same breath. Troy was so rattled that he began digging in his pocket.

I thought, "Aww shit, this nigga is 'bout to shoot this bitch!" Then I remembered that he wasn't carrying, at least not in the pocket he was digging in 'cause I looked at him thoroughly when he first walked up. Relieved, I went back to thinking, "What in the hell is this nigga digging for?"

And before I could react, he had pulled out a wad of money and flashed it saying, "Yeah, bitch. I ain't broke. I got three thousand right here. So you ain't saying shit! You a fucking trick; all a nigga need with you is a Benz and a couple dollars and you automatically start shaking yo ass!"

Being a man, I knew Troy was devastated by everything Tina had said, even though he initiated the attack. She wasn't supposed to respond in the way that she did. Tina violated protocol because she was supposed to be worried and concerned about having been found out. I stood there torn between enjoying the show I'd just witnessed and being angry she had used money I had given her to help her ex-boyfriend. Not to mention I was trying to dissect Troy's comments from their coded meaning.

The "shaking yo ass" part had me wondering what he meant because the minute he said it Tina seemed to go off the deep end. She wasn't concerned nor did she have any sympathy for his hurt feelings and his thoughts of losing his woman to another man. Her response was deliberate, raw, unrelenting, and definitely un-lady like.

That night I saw what my mother was trying to get me to realize earlier that day, a mean, angry, unhappy woman who seemed to get off on toying with men's feelings and shattering their egos. For an instant I found myself lost in my thoughts but was brought back to reality when Troy, finally realizing Tina was not going to react in the way he had hoped, opted to say, "You dirty bitch. That nigga don't know it, but he just did me a favor 'cause I was done with your dusty ass anyway! You the next man's problem now, you fucking dancing ass whore!"

For some reason yet unknown to me, that statement sent Tina out of control. So much so that she felt compelled to reveal how long and the manner in which she had been cheating on him. "Yeah, mother fucker. Call me what you want, but you can damn well bet I had you sucking on my pussy many a night after plenty of niggas had just came out of it!" I couldn't fucking believe what I was hearing. It was as if she had forgotten I was standing there. Or she didn't give a damn 'cause the shit she said to him was making my stomach turn—mostly 'cause I believed her.

There is a difference between saying something to get at someone and saying something that you know is going to hit home. Tina was playing for keeps, and that shit she said cut Troy off at the knees! Troy had all but turned to walk away, convinced his last words had crippled Tina. I guess he hadn't banked on Tina having a trump card, and she played it masterfully! If it wasn't for the fact that I knew it would have been impossible, I would have sworn I saw her words physically rip through him like a sling blade chopping down sugar cane. Troy stopped dead in his tracks, turned around to Tina, who was foolishly following closely behind him, and hulk spit the biggest ugliest lump of phlegm and saliva I had ever seen—right in her face.

Chapter Fifteen
Lies

I never liked the taste of bullshit. If you accept the first spoonful, people always try to feed you more. I could tell Tina was starting to sense that I was becoming suspicious of her and would always counteract my suspicions by fucking me or giving me head, typically right after I would ask a loaded question, at which point I would fade into the pleasures of sexual oblivion. I would allow her to think that I had forgotten about the issue, but in truth each inconsistency was carefully cataloged in the back of my mind.

When we met, she originally told me that she worked for the post office. As I had no reason to doubt her and had always been an arrogant son of bitch, I was confident she would never lie to me. Foolishly, I paid no attention to the fact that she would always leave for work at varying times throughout the day.

Some days she would leave at 7 pm; other times it would be at 8 pm; and other times still it would be at 9 pm. On a few occasions, I did inquire about the sporadic nature of her departure time, and she explained it away by saying her boss was very lenient and allowed her to get away with things like that.

Whether or not it was because I didn't want to know or I didn't care, I may never know, but I never asked again. I guess none of it really mattered to me because Tina and I were having a good time with each other. We were well into our fourth month, and Atlanta felt strange now that Brian was gone. I had begun to think about the warning he left me with, thoughts brought on by my witnessing Tina's explosion with Troy.

I didn't know why Brian was so sure I was heading for the same catastrophe he'd experienced with Stephanie, but I was admittedly beginning to think that maybe he was right.

Meanwhile, Tina and Stephanie became like two peas in a pod. Now that Brian was gone, Stephanie had a lot more time on her hands and she ran the street constantly, pulling Tina with her every chance she got. I didn't rain on their parade and rarely interfered with their merriment.

I had business of my own to tend to and had begun to travel out of town more frequently than I had in the past. I had to go Philly one weekend on the spur of the moment and the decision was made on such short notice that I barely had time to drive myself to the airport.

Tina volunteered to drive me and asked if she could drive the car while I was away. I saw no problem with it and naturally said yes. So I left on a Friday and returned late the following Sunday evening. She picked me up at the airport and I put my bag in the backseat. As we drove home I suggested that we go and get something to eat.

We both had a true love for gourmet food and frequented a marketplace in Atlanta called Eatzi's. Whenever we would go, we'd fill the basket with delicacies of all kinds. This night in particular we went and selected things we had never tried before. In the rear of the market there was a hot food section where the chefs prepared different entrees depending on the day of the week.

On that day the featured entrée was curried duck with squash and au gratin potatoes. We had the chef serve us a generous portion of it and proceeded to the refrigerated section where Tina wanted to try the specially made jumbo lump Maryland crab cakes as an appetizer. She had the server give her two, and she ordered an additional side of broccoli with cheese. Tina was a big eater. We topped it off by grabbing a bottle of chardonnay and a loaf of cheese Fougasse, a gourmet bread.

We anxiously drove home because eating, sexing, and sleeping had become our forte. After getting home we began to indulge ourselves on the food we'd purchased. As we began to lay out the spread we realized the crab cakes we wanted to sample were cold and needed to be reheated. Since Tina had recently moved into her apartment she didn't have many utensils, and when she placed the crab cakes into the pan, she realized there wasn't a spatula to turn them over.

I remembered having one in the trunk of my car. It was part of a set that I'd bought for the kitchen. I told her to go and get it but being the lazy, selfish person she was, she complained about having to go despite my having just returned home from a flight. Funny though, they say the Lord does work in mysterious ways because if Tina hadn't been so lazy and absentminded I am sure she would have remembered she'd left some of her personal belongings in my trunk. At any rate she didn't, and instead of arguing back and forth about who should go to the car to retrieve the spatula, I decided to go and get it.

As I went to the car, I never would have dreamed of the surprise that was waiting for me as I opened the trunk. I lifted it open and there in my face was what appeared to be an overnight bag. The funny thing about it was when she picked me up from the airport, she apparently didn't think twice about the possibility of it being discovered. I could have very easily chosen to put my bag in the trunk instead of the back seat. I don't know what was on her mind that day, obviously a lot because she completely forgot the bag was even in there.

I reached in and began to fumble through it, not wanting to jump to conclusions, while struggling to keep the lump in my throat from choking me. As I looked through it, I found a pair of thongs and a bra. I immediately thought to myself, "This bitch done went and fucked some nigga while I was gone."

I dug deeper into the bag and found another pair of matching thongs and bra, only this pair had red sequins all over them. As I looked further I found several pairs of matching strap up platform shoes and garter belts. That's when I realized Tina was a stripper.

I turned around and slumped on the lip of the trunk space and stared into the night sky, wondering, "How in the hell did I get myself caught up with a dancer?" Even worse, all I could think of was making her stop versus leaving her ass alone.

It was at that precise moment I knew I was hooked. After sitting for what probably seemed like an eternity, she came to the door and asked, "Glenn, why are taking so long?" Not wanting to engage her outside, I chose not to respond and quietly walked back into the apartment with the spatula in one hand and her bag in the other.

I came into the kitchen where she was and dropped the bag in the center of the floor at her feet. She looked at the bag first and then looked at me with a fear in eyes I'd never seen before and haven't seen since. Capitalizing on her shock, I immediately asked her, "What the hell is this?" as if I didn't know.

"It's my bag," she murmured, trying to be evasive. I lowered my voice an octave and repeated more forcefully, "What the fuck is this?" Before she could answer, I said, "You're a fucking dancer!"

She looked at me and said, "I was going to tell you but I was afraid you would have left me alone."

Tina didn't know it, but wild horses couldn't have pulled off that job. She was perhaps the best sexual partner I had ever been with and I was not prepared at that point to part with a rarity such as that. As I stood there with her looking at me with bated breath, I knew I had to maintain my position. She didn't know what to expect from me, and I took full advantage of that fact.

As I stood there all I could think about was how many of my friends knew about her dancing and how many more had actually seen her. I felt my anger quietly building inside me. "Bitch, what you think this shit is? You think I'm sweet like dat? How you going disrespect me like dat? I see you had this shit down pat too. Even down to the phony post office job and schedule."

Tina was terrified. She had never seen me like that and I never had a reason to let her see that side of me. "Glenn, I…I wanted to tell you, but I didn't know how."

"Bitch! All you had to do was open your fucking mouth. You know how to do that I'm sure, seeing as how you sucked my dick in the Cap'n D's bathroom after knowing me only a week! You fucking whore, I knew it was going to be some shit when I started dealing wit yo ass. I don't know why I didn't follow my first instinct and walk away from you then."

My thoughts kept going back to Brian telling me that I was headed for the same shit he'd gone through with Stephanie. I stood there thinking how much of a fool I must have seemed to him because he saw through all of Tina's bullshit early on. The thought of Tina keeping something so vital from me for so long and the fact she was able to do it with such ease infuriated me even more. I wanted desperately for her to lash out at me the way she had done Troy when he caught her with me.

I was looking for anything that would push me over the edge and justify knocking the bullshit out of her. I guess she sensed it too and didn't tempt the fates. There was a lull in the argument, and she went off into the living room and made a phone call. While I walked quietly into the bedroom, picked up the receiver and listened to every word. "Ranay, Glenn is over here tripping. He found out that I dance and I don't know what to expect, but if I don't call you back in fifteen minutes, call 911 okay?"

"Girl, if you think I might need to call 911 in fifteen minutes, then you need to get your ass out of there right now. Don't be taking no chances with these niggas 'cause all of 'em are crazy." Tina was smart and made the call to inform somebody—anybody—of my presence at her house in case I killed her slick ass.

Still it made me more angry especially now that I knew she was plotting to call the cops. "I know you ain't just get off the phone? Whachoo think having your girlfriend call 911 going save yo ass? After you played me like I was a nut? I ain't that kind of nigga. Shit ain't sweet with me bitch! You must really think I'm a fucking joke or something, don't you? I don't know what I was thinking about when I started fucking with you. My mother told me you was probably a whore, and Brian basically said the same thing, and ain't no telling what you was out here doing while I was out of town. And bitch, if I find out you went to see some nigga in my car, that's yo ass!"

As I continued on my maniacal tirade, I found myself recalling the way she sneaked around at Troy's party. I cursed myself for getting caught up with a woman like her and disobeying my own mother who knew better. I wanted to blame Tina and tried desperately to pretend that she deprived me the benefit of making an informed decision, but the truth was she didn't. I saw all I needed to see the first night, only I chose to ignore it.

"Glenn, I'm tired and I want to go to sleep. I'm sorry I didn't tell you, but we don't need to fight about it."

That was easy for her to say. I couldn't believe that she was being so nonchalant and said, "Bitch, you got the audacity to say that shit like this ain't no big deal. You got me looking crazy to all my friends. Everybody laughing at me for taking a dancing ass trick personal! I see now. You really do take this shit for a joke."

"Glenn, I don't think it's a joke. I-I'm sorry."

"Bitch, sorry didn't do it, you did!" I slapped Tina so hard her cell phone flew across the room, and she dropped to the floor. She balled up in a corner thinking I was going to beat her more. I didn't. "Fuck this shit and fuck you too, bitch!"

I turned to walk out the door and she grabbed my leg and said, "Glenn, it ain't like that. I was going to tell you. Don't leave like this. Just do what you need to cool off, but don't leave."

I didn't know how to take that statement. It seemed as if Tina would rather I beat her than leave, hoping it would somehow make everything better. I looked down at her as she looked up at me. It was an awkward moment. I was torn between my anger and the shame of attacking her.

Both emotions were holding equal ground, utterly refusing to be conquered by the other. Standing there, I had a flashback where I remembered Tina telling me she had witnessed her mother getting battered by the men in her life and how she swore she would never stay with a man who beat her. I quietly observed the contradiction that had become evident through Tina's request for me to stay.

Strangely, I wanted to but couldn't bring myself to do it. The thought of being humiliated by a stripper kept replaying in my head. I started having flashbacks to the night she'd argued with Troy. I remembered he called her a "dancing ass trick, who liked to shake her ass." The memory was enough to make me shake my head in disgust. I guess I was a joke. I had come all the way to Atlanta and got stuck in quicksand, searching for salvation between the thighs of a stripper.

The thought almost caused me to burst a blood vessel. I was getting a headache dealing with everything that had just transpired and decided it would be best if I left. Tina was still clutching my leg as I reached down and pulled her arms from around it. "Glenn, I'm sorry."

I didn't respond. I reached the doorway and noticed that her cell phone was lying on the floor two feet from me.

Tina didn't notice it as she had gotten up and gone into the bathroom to tend to the swelling on her cheek. I picked it up and went to the "dialed calls" section and saw Troy Black's number. It was second to last number dialed after Ranay. I backtracked and remembered that she had been with me from the time she picked me up from the airport and realized the call had to have been placed while I was away. I hit the view button and retrieved Troy's direct number. Mr. Black and I were going to have a talk.

Chapter Sixteen
Refuge

I stood there looking in the mirror wondering what just happened. Plus, I realized Ranay never called back to check on me. I called her and she answered the phone out of her sleep. She'd barely said hello before I ripped into her, "Bitch, you ain't even call back to see if I was dead, hurt, or shot!"

"Girl, I knew nothing was going to happen to you. Glenn ain't crazy like that."

I interrupted her saying, "Well, bitch, then the nigga musta had a twin 'cause he damn sure slapped the shit out of me!" I hung up the phone before she had a chance to ask what happened or apologize. I let it ring when she called back; I was through with her funny looking ass.

I leaned closer into the mirror and murmured, "I can't believe I let that nigga put his hands on me." I winced as I applied alcohol to my swollen face and gave myself a few more choice words, "Fuck Glenn. He ain't all that anyway! I'm glad that muthafucka left!"

I was lying to myself. I didn't want to be alone and needed to feel needed. I was reeling from all that had happened and couldn't believe I let Glenn talk to me the way he did. He tore me down with such ease that it felt like he'd known all along I was a stripper.

I wondered why it seemed so natural for him. I didn't have much time to reflect on the question because I had dialed Troy's number the minute I'd finished applying makeup. "Yo, what you want man? I told you don't call me no more. You wit dat nigga, ballin all over town in his Benz and shit. I know that kid would be mad if he knew his broad was hittin' some other nigga."

"Troy, I'm not his broad. I'm yours. I'll always be yours." There was a long pause on the line, prompting me to ask, "Are you there?" I didn't know how Troy would react to my comment. We hadn't spoken since the big argument we'd had. I had called him a thousand and one times, but he wouldn't answer.

I prayed that he would answer before I called him tonight, and the Lord answered. "Can I come see you? I need to see you! I miss you."

"Why you want to see me,? Ain't dude taken care of you now?" Troy's attempts to remain detached weren't working, and I knew him well. If he really didn't want to be bothered, he wouldn't have answered the phone the way he hadn't all the other times.

I was getting tired of going back and forth with all of the pettiness and said, "I'm on my way," and hung up the phone. It took me all of three minutes to get to his place. I felt myself getting wet as I walked up the steps to our old apartment. I had missed him or at least certain parts of him. I rang the bell and waited five minutes or more before he appeared at the door. I knew it was deliberate. I didn't care. I knew he had to save face somehow.

I also knew that he was still crushed by the way I jumped ship. I was going to make it up to him tonight in ways I was sure he'd remember. "So what you here for, that nigga must've checked you or something, huh?" I didn't respond, I knew if I had it would've been something flippant and would've defeated my purpose in coming.

I closed the door behind me and stepped out of the full-length raincoat I'd put on. I'd needed something to hide the matching leopard print bra and thong set I was wearing. Troy was wearing boxer briefs. I was glad to see at least one part of him was pleased I had come, despite his best efforts to pretend that he wasn't.

"What you think? You can just come over here when you want?" He grabbed me by my arms, pushing me away from him. I struggled toward him and wrangled between his arms, dropped to my knees and greeted an old friend who was always more than happy to see me. "I don't know what you think you're doing, but I…"

Troy fell silent as my mouth welcomed his erection. I pushed him against the wall and forced every inch of him into my throat. I felt his body relax and go into mild convulsions almost simultaneously. I knew him well and could tell that I was missed. He grabbed my ears and started thrusting into my mouth.

His strokes were firm and deliberate and made me yearn for the taste of his juices. Just as the thought entered my mind, his warm fluid entered my mouth and splashed against the back of my throat. I shared many nights with Glenn between my loins and my mind filled with thoughts of Troy. Nothing could compare to the extreme pleasure he guaranteed, and that night was no different.

"Damn girl, you'll have a nigga ready to climb the walls fucking witchoo you!" What I liked most about Troy was his ability to cum repeatedly without getting soft. After I'd finished quenching my thirst, he immediately grabbed my waist and led me to the balcony. It was his favorite spot.

When I moved out I'd left my patio furniture and I was happy to see that it was still there. He guided me to one of the chairs and had me climb in it facing the back support with my knees resting on the cushion. His movements were gentle but certain, and he knew how to handle me. Without losing the moment Troy grabbed the top of my thong and hooked the string with his finger and slid it down along the crack of my ass, pulling it to the side exposing my now drenched twat.

At first he toyed with me putting his finger inside me and pulling it out and then putting it in my mouth. Then he did the same with his dick. The patio chairs rotated making it easy for him to maneuver his erection from my pussy to my mouth. He smacked my ass at each turn as I eagerly licked the juices that ran the length of his nine-inch erection. I stared out over the patio railing and had a fleeting thought of what Glenn would do if he happened to drive past and see Troy and me in action.

My sense of anticipation grew as I visualized the scene In my mind. I came after that along with Troy. Since it was his second ejaculation, it took an exorbitantly long time before he released. Reaching my climax came with a price, I was sore and was happy I hadn't worn any clothes over there because my coochie would-n't have been able to handle anything touching it after that episode.

I wanted to cuddle afterwards, but Troy brushed me off saying, "I have to get up early, so just call me when you get home so I'll know you made it." I wanted to ask him to let me stay, but I knew it would have been a futile request. After an incredible session like the one we'd just had, any man would've been more than happy to spend the weekend with me.

Troy's refusal to grant me refuge was both expected and deserved, only now I had compounded the original problem. I went there hoping to get over what just happened between Glenn and I. Instead, I made things worse by fucking a man I knew I could never have anything with ever again. I had also just been caught lying by the man I'd hoped would be the one to rescue me from myself. I was beginning to see that I was the reason for all of my problems. No matter how hard I tried, I just couldn't seem to get out of my own way.

Chapter Seventeen
Close Call

"Girl, I don't know what to do with myself. I feel like a lost puppy. I just left Troy's house and he played me like a board game."

"What happened?"

I hesitated because I didn't want to relive the humiliation I had suffered through all night long, but since I had already mentioned it I saw no need to stop now. Ranay had been calling me non-stop after I hung up on her to apologize for not having my back.

Although I was still mad at her I knew she wasn't going to let me hang up without telling her. "Right after me and Glenn argued, I called Troy and invited myself to his house. All that crazy shit Glenn said left me feeling fucked up, and I ain't wanna be by myself. After I got there, Troy fucked me like an Asian whore. When we finished I went to go to his bedroom to lay down and go to sleep, but he stopped me and told me to call him when I got home so he would know that I made it there safely. That mutha fucka played me like a trick! I was only over there for all of an hour. The dick was good though. I'm sore as hell, but I needed it bad."

Ranay was silent and didn't know what to say after I told her the story. She knew what I was going through and thankfully didn't say anything that might've made things worse. "Don't worry about him or Glenn. Both of 'em frontin. I know for a fact Glenn ain't going nowhere. That nigga done spent too much money. He ain't no fool. I wouldn't be surprised if he came back over there tonight."

"I doubt that shit. He was hot when he left and I probably won't see him again for a while. Well listen, I just ran some bath water, and I'm about to get my ass in the tub and soak in some Epsom salt and go to sleep. I'll talk to you later."

"Okay, make sure you call me. Bye."

I was looking forward to soaking. My body ached and I was still a little dizzy from both Troy's sex and Glenn's violent outburst. I lit a few candles, climbed in the tub, and sunk down into the hot, soapy water. The lights were off and the glow from the candles was the only light that could be seen. I'd set the cd to repeat my favorite song by Janet Jackson, I Get So Lonely, from her Velvet Rope cd.

The sound of the music echoed throughout the apartment, and I drifted off into thought about all of the night's events.

Thirty minutes had passed and the bath water had gotten a little cold. I turned the faucet on to replenish it with a surge of freshly heated liquid and a half bottle of Victoria's secret melon body wash. After doing so I sank back into the confines of the garden tub and let the hot water envelope me once again, resting my head on the inflatable waterproof pillow Glenn had bought for me when I moved in. I dozed off for what seemed like hours and was awakened when I heard the tumblers of the front door lock.

The sound was barely audible over the sound of music playing, but it occurred just as the track was repeating itself. "Who's that?" I said only half surprised because I figured it had to be Glenn. He was the only one who had a key. If it wasn't him, then my ass was toast; and the way I was feeling, it wouldn't have mattered.

I felt like dying anyway. If it wasn't for the soothing Calgon moment I was having I might've been tempted to slash my wrists. A moment or two after I heard the door close I saw a large, dark figure appear in the bathroom doorway. I recognized the frame; it was large and the darkness made it appear ominous, but I knew it was Glenn.

He came into the bathroom and sat in the chair next to the tub and looked at me. He was silent and seemed to be deep in thought. I was lost in my own thoughts, too. The most prevalent one was: "I am so glad I came back home from Troy's house." The second was: "But what the hell am I going to do if this nigga wants some pussy?" My shit was sore, and I knew it was going to be that way for days.

I softly said, "Hey, I hope you didn't come back to fight with me. I am tired baby, and I apologize for lying to you."

Glenn stared at me for another minute before speaking. "Yeah, I knew that you was going to say you was sorry again, but it's okay. I came up with a solution to this problem." I sat up, pretending to be interested in what he was about to say. I listened to him speak and noticed that his words weren't as crisp as they normally were and he seemed mildly incoherent.

Then it hit me. Glenn was drunk! The news of me dancing must have really been more painful than I thought. Here I was thinking it wasn't that big a deal but him going out and getting drunk put things in perspective because Glenn didn't drink, at least not enough to speak of. Aside from an occasional beer or mixed drink, he rarely touched the stuff.

I stood up grabbed a towel from the rack and dried off. My body glistened in the candlelight, and Glenn broke from his conversation and said, "Come here." I knew what was coming next; he wanted to have sex. I hesitated, causing him to repeat himself " I said, 'Come over here.'" Glenn reached out and grabbed my arm. I felt a rush sweep through my body. His touch had that effect on me. I think that it was a combination of lust and fear, whatever it was it made me get wet all over again. He pulled me in close and snatched the towel, letting it drop to the floor.

I stood there looking into his dark, emotionless eyes. I knew what I needed to do and how to bring the glow back into them. I dropped down to my knees, unzipped his pants, and started breathing life into his barely erect manhood. I was surprised because he'd always gotten instantly hard whenever we were about to fuck. His limpness told me that he was truly torn, angry at me and probably at himself.

In a scene not unlike the one I'd performed at Troy's house barely two hours before I bobbed and slurped his dick back to life. My performance seemed to give him newfound strength, and he picked me up and carried me into the bedroom and laid me down on the bed. His dick was rock hard by then, and I wanted to keep it in my mouth, but he wouldn't let me, and instead spread my legs apart and buried his face between them.

I resisted, but only briefly, as I was unable to push him away. He overpowered me and sucked my clit until I let out a sound that seemed much like a fire truck passing, loud at first and then trailing off as it passed out of range. He didn't stop there. Just as I tried to catch my breath, he lifted my limp body from the bed, turned me on my side, and plunged himself deep inside me. Glenn wasn't as big as Troy was but was just as capable, and before long I was writhing and moaning with each stroke. He flipped me over, pulling out only briefly before re-inserting himself.

I flinched on his second entry; I would've flinched the first time had his entry not been so sudden. He noticed that I was having trouble accommodating him and said, "Why you flinching and shit? What? You went and got fucked after I left?" I knew that his

101

question was more theatrical than suspicious. Glenn was freaky that way and got off on asking how I fucked other guys from my past. Almost every time we had sex, he and I both would talk dirty to the other and ask questions about how we performed with other people.

The shit was exhilarating and made me gush like a hydrant in summer every time. When I get turned on I can't resist the taste of dick in my mouth, I don't care if it was pulled from my throbbing pussy or somebody else's. I just want it in my mouth. After about fifteen minutes of voracious stroking, I felt Glenn's body start to convulse and I slid off of him and turned around opened my mouth to catch his warm semen; I liked the feel of cum hitting the back of my throat.

Glenn's rarely made it there. It oozed out slow and thick. Still I liked the taste of it and sucked him dry. "You feel better now?" I asked the question, half-believing that what we'd done had made a difference and half-hoping that he would forget about my lies and fall off to sleep.

When we woke up the next day, I had breakfast ready and brought it into the bedroom. I tapped Glenn on his leg as he stirred from his deep slumber. "Wake up, baby. I made you breakfast."

Glenn was still groggy and croaked, "Thanks, but let me go pee first."

Glenn's sinus' had been a problem for him for years, and every morning he would get up go to the bathroom, piss, rinse his mouth with water, and blow his nose. The sound of his blowing and snorting was nothing short of listening to a trumpet blare on the highest note. It was so annoying I would just stare at him with a look that suggested, "Is all that really necessary?"

That morning I didn't because I was still in the doghouse for lying and was trying my best to make up for it. "Are you alright in there, baby?"

Glenn didn't answer. I walked in the doorway and saw he was washing his face and clearing his throat frantically, stopping long enough to say, "My throat is bothering me. It feels like it's sore or something."

I stood there silently thinking, "Damn, Troy came in me last night." I quickly snapped out of my thoughts and suggested, "You know, it may be your post-nasal drip bothering you. You know it affects your nasal passage and throat." Glenn looked at me and I could swear that he was looking right through me, as if he knew that I had gone and had sex last night and that was the reason for his sore throat.

Troy screwed a lot of women and I was used to sucking him off. I always knew when he'd stepped out on me because the foreign bacteria used to make my throat hurt too, and that was probably the same thing that was wreaking havoc on Glenn's unfamiliar throat tissue. I didn't know what to say but knew I had to deflect any possibility of him thinking the worst of me.

"I got some Cepacol under the cabinet. I think it's cherry flavor. Just spray some in the back of your mouth and it should make it feel better."

Glenn reached down, grabbed the bottle, and sprayed it, saying, "I don't know what the fuck is going on, but this shit ain't never happened to me before; my shit was fine last night, and it's not even cold outside. You probably need to disinfect this nasty ass bathroom for germs."

Glenn looked around before commenting again, "You got thongs and shit lying around on the floor." Glenn picked up the thongs I had just taken off last night before I got in the bath tub, I went stiff wondering if he was going to sniff them. Luckily, he didn't and just commented, "You into a lot of freaky shit. Leopard print panties and shit." He held them in the air as if examining them before throwing them in the hamper and walking out the bathroom.

His breakfast had gotten cold, and he grabbed a piece of bacon from the plate and ate it, still complaining about his throat. He cut his eyes at me a few more times. I was amazed by his perceptiveness, as it was obvious that he suspected me as the reason for the soreness in his throat. He put on his clothes and left without saying bye. I didn't know when he was going to call again and didn't want to call him and rock the boat.

We needed some time to deal with this new crisis, a crisis I had complicated by going back and dealing with Troy. Ten minutes passed after Glenn walked out the door and the phone rang. It was him and he said, "Oh yeah, the solution I was talking about last night was you ain't going back to that club, so you need to go get your shit if you got anything there 'cause you won't be back!"

103

He hung up the phone after that, and I noticed that his tone was no longer an angry one but still hard and cold, as if he didn't care how he addressed me. I went into the kitchen and started throwing away the food Glenn wasted and washed the dishes. My thoughts drifted, and I began to wonder if I had made a mistake hooking up with Glenn so soon after leaving Troy.

My thoughts were interrupted by the sound of phone ringing. It was Stephanie. "What's up, Steph?"

"I was just calling you to see if you wanted to go to Shoemakers today?"

"I ain't trying to go nowhere. I am worn out. Last night, Glenn found out that I dance."

"Oh, my god. What he do?"

"Girl, I thought he was going to slap the shit out of me, but he didn't. He just cussed a little bit and told me I had to stop."

I was lying and Stephanie knew it. She chose not to speak on it and instead played into it and said, "Bitch, you lucky as hell 'cause Brian would've knocked my head off!" Stephanie didn't know it, but not only had Glenn just done the same to me, he had also collared me up once before for mouthing off to him. I kept that to myself, though. I didn't want anyone knowing that I had gone through all I had and was still dealing with him, especially my mother.

Growing up I watched her endure one abusive relationship after another and swore that I would never deal with anything like that. Stephanie had known for a long time that I was dancing, and once we became friends I made her swear not to say anything to Brian. I figured with him gone and no-longer dealing with her, Glenn would never find out. But he did.

I didn't want to stop dancing. I was making good money and didn't know what in the hell I was going to do now that Glenn had ordered me to stop. In the midst of my thoughts, Stephanie chimed in, "Well, at least he gave enough of a damn to make you stop." She was partially right, but I had a feeling Glenn's command was done more as a power play rather than out of genuine concern.

Chapter Eighteen
Withdrawals

"When's the last time you spoke to Troy?"

"It's been a while, and the shit is killing me. When I call sometimes he answers and sometimes he doesn't." Stephanie knew what I was going through, having not spoken to Brian in the six months since he left. She also knew that I was slowly driving myself crazy.

When I moved out, all I really wanted was for Troy to pursue me. After he showed up at my new apartment I was shocked because I hadn't expected him to react so soon. In the past when we argued, I would always be the one to come running back. I tried to offset my departure from our happy home by moving less than a few miles away, mostly so I could be the one to drive by whenever I wanted to reminisce about our life together.

I hated that he ambushed me. I didn't want him knowing that I had moved out and was already playing house so soon after leaving. I wanted him to think that I got the strength to walk away on my own. But the shit blew up in my face and now he knows the truth about Glenn and me. "Steph, what you doing right now?"

"Nothing. Why?"

"Because I need you to come and pick me up so I can act like I'm out with you in case Glenn calls."

"Why you need to go through all that?"

"Because I want to drive by Troy's house."

"Well, just tell Glenn that you got some shit you trying to do, and you'll be busy for a few hours."

"Girl, that Nigga ain't going for no shit like that. The first time I don't answer my phone he'll be calling non-stop and won't quit until I pick up. If you're with me then he won't think I'm up to anything."

"Why he act like that?"

"You know ever since he found out that I lied about

dancing, he don't believe nothing I say and only trusts me as far as he can see me." I hated that Glenn didn't trust me, but when I thought about it I wouldn't trust me either. I don't know what my problem was. When we met I thought our relationship would be the perfect fairytale I had always dreamed of, but I guess the truth was I wanted a new boyfriend but never stopped being Troy's old girlfriend.

The problem with that, however, was Troy didn't want me. He never wanted me. He didn't know it, but that last argument hurt me more than him. I never thought it was possible to hurt him, but the look on his face that night proved I was wrong. I've been replaying it over and over in my mind since it happened. I even wrote him letter trying to explain what I was going through, but I never mailed it.

"Does he talk to you at all?" Stephanie didn't know it, but I saw Troy a few times after Glenn found out about me dancing, and I decided to tell her everything. "Girl, I was a wreck that night after Glenn stormed out of the house, and I hopped in my car and drove over to me and Troy's old place, and we've been sleeping together ever since." I paused for a moment, thinking about how things weren't working out the way I planned them because Troy wasn't paying me no mind. I'd expected all the sex would've made him want me back, but all he ever did was fuck me and leave ten minutes after he finished. Stephanie chimed in, "Why you so quiet? Are you all right?"

I said, "Yeah, I was just thinking about something is all. Anyway girl, after a while Troy cut me off again, and shit got so bad I started driving by our old apartment more frequently and popping up at all the spots where I knew I'd find him. Plus, I started lying to Glenn so much that I needed a wheel barrel to hold 'em all. The worst part about it was I wasn't even ashamed of it."

After I finished my run down Stephanie said,

"Oooooh bitch, you know if Glenn find out he is going to kick your ass. Why you keep chasing Troy anyway? He ain't got shit, and you say he always broke." The shit Stephanie said made me think of the movie What's Love Got to Do With It starring Angela Basset and Lawrence Fishburn, when Ike said, "You can't leave me, Anna May. I'm up here," and pointed to his head.

I said, "Stephanie, I don't know what it is. Maybe it's the sex 'cause he be fucking the lining out of me and I can't get enough. The last time we fucked I sucked his dick so hard that if it had been a piece of rice the color would have been gone!"

Stephanie said, "Um, um, um. How you be getting away from Glenn?"

"I just tell him I'm out with you or at the mall. And sometimes I even tell him I'm getting my hair and nails done." I thought about what I'd just said to Stephanie and hated being that way, but Glenn was so thorough and intrusive when it came to knowing my whereabouts, nothing slipped passed him.

When Troy and I were in a relationship, I had free rein to come and go as I pleased, mainly because he was busy running the street, fucking any and everybody he could. That kind of shit kept him busy and kept me off his mind. Glenn on the other hand wanted to know my every thought.

He even knew when I was thinking about Troy. Once when we were out having breakfast, I drifted off in thought about life with Troy and was snatched back into reality when Glenn said, "I know you ain't sitting here thinking about that nigga 'cause you can go be with him right now!" He said it with such confidence and ferocity I had to second-guess myself just to make sure I hadn't subconsciously mumbled my thoughts out loud for him to hear.

Before leaving Troy I prayed that I would find a man who gave me all of his attention and always wanted to be in my presence. I got my wish with Glenn, except his reason for being with me was for monitoring purposes and had nothing to do with love.

Chapter Nineteen
The Thoroughbred

It had been months since Ceez had asked about selling my Benz. The summer was in full swing and it was hot as a bitch! The air compressor in the car had been out for a while and I decided that I wasn't going to put any more money into it, especially not the eight hundred the dealer wanted to fix it, knowing I was going to get rid of it soon.

I remembered Ceez telling me about his boy wanting to take it off my hands so I gave him a call. He had long since left Atl to go back to DC. We didn't speak often and he was glad to hear from me. "What's up, young buck? You up in DC holding shit down?"

Ceez laughed before answering, "You know what it is. But what's up though?"

"I wanted to know if ya man still wanted to cop the Benz, and if he do give him my number and tell him to call me."

Ceez said, "i-ight, I'll do that. What's up wit mom? She cool?"

I said, "Yeah, she alright."

Ceez said, "Good. Ima call her later. Ima call my man right now and give him your number. I'll holla at you later. Peace."

The buzz of my cell phone startled me. It was sitting in my lap on vibrate while I was trying to beat the heat, sitting in traffic with the windows down trying desperately to catch a breeze. I didn't recognize the number on the display so I answered it using the semi-hostile voice I use to receive unwanted callers

"Hello, who dis?"

A male voice on the other end responded, "It's Ceez's bull Leek."

I said, "Who?" 'cause the name I remembered was Malik.

He realized it too and said, "Damn, My fault. You probably don't know everybody call me Leek."

I said, "Oh yeah," as I remembered Ceez mentioning it originally. "What's up, man? You still trying to cop this piece?"

Malik said, "Damn right. I asked Ceez what year it was and how many miles was on the jawn, but he said that he ain't know."

Right away I could see this young cat was on point, and I was not going to be able to treat him like a sucka. So I came clean and told him, "It got about 65,000 on it right now, and it's a '94 and it runs tight."

Malik didn't waste any time getting to the point. "So how much you want for it?"

"I see you ain't playing, huh? I figured you to be like the rest of these young cats out here—all talk and no action. Anyway, I want $35,000 for it cash, but if you trying to pay in installments, then - Ima charge you $40,000." There was short pause after my last statement, and I was sure I had scared him off.

But he responded by saying "So when you want to do it?"

I thought for sure he was calling my bluff and I said, "Shit, we could do it tomorrow."

Still on point, Malik said, "Before we do anything I want to check the jawn out. Is there anything wrong with it?"

Not wanting to play games due to the fact he seemed like a straight shooter, I relented and told him about the compressor problem, which fortunately wasn't a total loss.

It did work occasionally, mostly if you switched it on while driving on the highway when all of the belts were turning at a faster and more powerful rate. Other than that the car was an immaculate four-year-old machine. Malik was undeterred by my report of the malfunctioning compressor and said, "I been seeing you around town a few times, and I seen the jawn up close once when you let Ceez hold it for the weekend, and I liked it then. All I want to do is take it for a spin on the highway to see how the performance is and after that we can sign off."

I said, "That's cool with me. So what time tomorrow?"

Malik responded, "About 3 o'clock."

I figured he probably needed the better part of the day to get his money together. The following day I had written my conversation with Malik off as all talk and suspected I wouldn't hear anything else about it. I was so convinced that I hadn't bothered to remove any of my personal belongings from the car.

Around 3:30 pm my cell phone rang and it was Malik. "Yo, what's up old head? What's the deal? You ready to do dis shit?"

Fumbling through my words, I muttered, "Yeah, yeah. Tell me where to meet you?"

For a young dude I could tell Malik was a familiar with the streets 'cause he immediately said, "I want to meet you at your crib to pick the jawn up and then afterward we can drive over to my crib to get the money."

I didn't have a problem with that because I knew he stood to lose more than me if a setup was in the works. After all, I could always report the car stolen if he got fly with me whereas he would just be got if I stuck him up for his cash. I liked the way he thought and could tell that he was all about business.

When we finally met up I saw that he was a bonafide Philly dude. He was a tall, slim, light-skinned cat, who stood about 6'2"and weighed about 200lbs. His mustache and goatee were the only things that separated him from being mistaken for a kid. I don't typically judge men's looks, but if I had too I would say he was a pretty boy, -a street version of Shamar Moore. What distinguished him the most was the precision haircut he sported—a dead giveaway for cats from Philly! The outline was so crisp that it seemed like it was chiseled in his scalp.

"Yo, what's up, man? Nice to finally meet you. Ceez talk about you all the time."

I said, "Nice to meet you, too. Give me a minute while I clean this shit out the trunk and I'll follow you to your crib. Ima have my girl follow behind me." I called out for Tina and asked her if she was ready. When she walked out the door, Malik took one look at her and said, "Damn, what's up, Tina? Long time no see," as I stood there wondering how in the hell this young nigga know my girl!

They both looked at me and started laughing. I was about to go postal on both of 'em until Malik started by telling me he had met Tina a few years back and they were friends. Tina chimed in by saying, "Remember, Glenn. I told you I knew a guy from Philly, but we were just friends." I didn't remember her telling me shit, and honestly, I was very uneasy about both versions of the truth that they were giving me.

The only saving grace was it was before my time. Wanting to hear more of what Malik had to say, I decided kill two birds with one stone and ride shotgun and let him test drive Benz on the on the way to his crib. I knew once we were alone that I would get the real story. When we got into the whip he turned to me and asked, "Do you take sis personal?"

Not wanting to lose face and sensing he had the goods on the Tina, I naturally said, "Naw, man. She just a piece of ass. Why, what's the deal with her?"

Malik had no way of knowing I did take her personal or that

I was disgusted and ashamed of myself for having fallen for a woman I had just found out to be a stripper and a whore. He started his story off by saying, "Man, I met that bitch one night when I was coming out of 112. I was in the parking lot sitting in my whip. I had a pearl white Lexus SC400. She and her girl were coming out of the club at the same time and saw me go to my car. How 'bout they ain't say shit until they peeped the wheel.

"That's when Tina said, 'Can you give me and my girl a ride to our car? It's all the way on the other side of the parking lot and my feet hurt.' Glenn, the bitch's ass was so phat I said, 'Cool. Come on. Get in.' I ain't say it, but once she got up close I remembered seeing her before at this white strip club, and I knew the body was on point. I took 'em over to they whip and got her number.

"When she got out I peeped she got into this champagne colored Acura TL. I had seen the jawn before and knew that some dude named Troy be driving it. I wasn't for sure until I looked at the rims and saw that they were identical to the ones on my man's car. I capped her up and said, 'Damn, that's a nice looking vehicle you got.' How bout the bitch said, 'Thanks,' like it was really hers.

"I started to say I know the dude whose car it is, but I chilled 'cause I ain't want to fuck up before I could smash. She called me the next day wanting to meet for lunch. I told her that was cool and to meet me at my house. When she got there I came straight at her. How 'bout she had the nerve to get mad like she was offended, but ain't have no problem driving the dude's car to my crib. Now that's a dirty bitch."

As I sat there listening to Malik, I realized that he was telling the truth. First off, he didn't know me and had no reason to lie. But more importantly he confirmed many of the things I knew to be true from dealing with Tina. The car, the stripping, and the slick and deceitful way she operated. I also figured the only reason he didn't knock her off on the spot was probably because she was on her period, and rather than confirm it she pretended to be offended.

After all she had sucked my dick in the bathroom of a fast food restaurant after I had known her only a few days and all while she was still living with her boyfriend. Malik closed out the story by saying, "We lost contact after that." He explained that he had particular inhibitions about females who played dudes close like she did. Noting the fact that Tina was driving her boyfriend's car to his crib told him all he needed to know about her character, not to mention the fact she was a stripper.

He reasoned, ""If the broad didn't have enough respect for the dude who let her use his whip, then she would never have respect for nothing, including herself." He went on to say "About three months ago, I was at Lenux Mall on a Saturday and I saw the bitch with her girlfriend Erica. And she stopped me and told me she'd met some cat from Philly she was dating. I ain't pay no attention to it cause I knew none of the niggas I knew would ever take a bitch like her personal.

"So I figured she must had met some corny dude or something. I ain't even ask her what the bull's name was. The only other thearl dudes in town at the time was you and your man B, and I knew about your work from back home. And a bitch like Tina wouldn't have made the cut."

The lump in my throat was so big I was sure Malik could see it. My mouth was suddenly dry and I had to clear my throat before I could even say anything. I sat there ashamed thinking "Aw naw, hell naw, I done up and done it" Fell for a fucking trick! Not wanting too much silence to pass and reveal the emotional state I was in, I quickly responded, "Man, that bitch is just something to do, but the pussy is all that! You should probably go at her again. She'll probably go for it this time."

Who was I kidding? At that point I would have killed Malik and Tina both if some shit like that went down. But still I had to save face. This young cat looked up to me, and there was no way I would have been ever able to live down the fact that I was taking some stripper personal.

As we pulled up to his house he unknowingly added insult to injury when he said, "Man, you got to be careful down here in Atlanta. A lot of these broads come down here from wherever they from and recreate themselves with a formula. A lot of 'em was ho's and tricks where they from, and they come down ATL hoping to find a baller, and dudes be fallin' for it.

"Most of these chicks come down here and go straight to work in the strip clubs and shake they ass until they meet some cat that'll promise to take care of em." I wondered if Malik could tell that I was one of them. I couldn't believe it. I was being schooled by this young nigga, who apparently knew the Atlanta game a whole lot better than me.

As I struggled to maintain my composure, I realized that I had been uncharacteristically quiet, a sure sign I was too interested in what he was saying. Fearing he might pick up on it as well, I immediately shifted back to our original plan of business. "Damn, Nigga. I don't know what I'd do if the police stop me on the way back to the crib with all this money."

Malik was quiet, seemingly concentrating on the business at hand. When we walked into the house he had me follow him into his bedroom where he proceeded to extract several shoe boxes from his closet. He handed one of them to me and asked me to count the contents of it.

I opened it to find it packed with twenty, fifty, and hundred dollar bills. As I counted I started thinking to myself, "This young nigga is the real deal." At twenty-three, I could hardly keep my hands on fifty dollars, let alone thirty-five thousand.

Malik lived in College Park, Georgia. I wondered how on earth he was able to sleep at night knowing he kept that kind of money in his unsecured apartment. Living a life on the street causes you to observe every detail of your surroundings. And as soon as we entered into his apartment, I noticed it was not equipped with an alarm. It was also facing the rear of the complex and the back faced the open woods.

If I was a stick up kid he could have easily been got! Fortunately for him that wasn't how I got down. I had always been a gentleman hustler and actually prided myself on maintaining a good rapport with everyone I did business with regardless of the level they were on.

I had counted fifteen thousand dollars by the time I lifted my head. Malik knew what was supposed to be in the box, and I realized that he wanted to impress me with the amount he had on hand. I didn't have a problem letting him know I was indeed impressed and casually uttered, "I see you must really be getting it down out here."

I had already asked Ceez about it and he filled me in, saying Leek wasn't in the street game. In actuality, he had his own trucking company and was deeply involved in major contracts throughout Atlanta's construction scene. The shoebox thing was a way to maintain his street credibility with me and avoid Uncle Sam from getting in his personal business.

Happy I had acknowledged his production, Malik looked over to me and smiled as he said, "Man, I been getting money out here since I came down. I just be stackin' 'cause it ain't really nothing else to do here but get money and pull bitches. But I don't give these broads shit but some dick and send 'em home."

I believed him. I could tell by his manner that he was completely detached from feeling obligated to play their game. The same game that B and I, with all of our successes, couldn't seem to avoid.

By the time we emerged from the bedroom, Tina had fallen asleep watching television in the living room, the same living room that she had visited some years earlier, only she didn't know that I knew. I tapped her on her leg and motioned to her, signaling it was time to leave.

As we drove back to her place she was visibly excited. "Baby, when we get to the house I'm going to cook dinner tonight. I haven't let you see what my skills are like and I decided it's time." I sat there half listening to her as my mind drifted in and out of wondering about what else I didn't know about this girl.

I thought of this movie I saw once called Dream Lover that starred James Spader. It was about this rich man who met and married a woman he thought he knew, only to discover that her identity was manufactured and she had plotted and planned it all along.

Throughout the entire course of their courtship and marriage she had been living a lie and secretly fucking his best friend. She had even gone as far as to have her husband set up. During a heated verbal argument with her, he left the house and she had her lover come over and beat her up. She called the police and told them her husband did it.

The movie culminated with her having him committed to an insane asylum, but he beat her at her own game because he ended up killing her. He knew he could get away with it because he was already believed to be crazy!

My thoughts were interrupted by Tina's repeated questioning, "Baby. Baby, are you listening to me?"

"Yeah, I heard you." I wanted to say you decided to cook tonight so you can jocky for your piece of this 35K. But instead said, "Yeah, baby. that's cool. I want some seafood. Lobster or something." Tina returned to her babbling, and I returned to my daytime nightmare.

Neither Tina or Malik or anyone else for that matter knew part of my reason for finally getting rid of the Benz was because I had found her dance bag in the back of the trunk, and the possibility that Tina had probably been out visiting other niggas in my car while I was away. I gritted my teeth at the thought of it and recalled all of her lies—the phony post office job, phony work schedule, the lesbian encounters, and the trashy way Troy would treat her she seemed to relish—and cursed myself again for falling for her.

Chapter Twenty

Truce

Intuition is a funny thing. It pops up out of nowhere and takes up residence in your mind. No matter what the subject, person, or situation, it gives you a clear picture of a thought you haven't even seen or confirmed.

I'd been having premonitions about Tina and wondered if I should follow up on them. After finding out about her secret career, my mind was made up. The remaining time in our relationship was going to be spent doing reconnaissance on her every move. It'd been several weeks since our big fight, and I had had my doubts about how my throat had gotten sore all of a sudden.

I never mentioned my suspicions about it to her. The thought of it disgusted me, and I did all I could to keep it from coming to the forefront of my mind. I had a lot of questions I needed answers for. The kind of answers that I knew I would never get talking to Tina.

On a sunny Wednesday afternoon, I was driving down Peachtree headed to the Cheesecake Factory for lunch. My favorite meal was the chicken madeira and I could hardly wait as I pulled into the valet. My mouth was watering and I hadn't eaten breakfast. I walked up to the circular island counter and gave them my name. "Table for one please."

"Your name. sir?"

"Glenn." It was just barely noon, and the afternoon rush hadn't made its way there yet so I didn't have to wait more than five minutes before I was seated.

"Right this way, sir." I followed the hostess to my seat she directed me to a small booth that was located near the stairwell. "Your server will be with you shortly, and thank you for choosing the Cheesecake factory." She handed me a menu and returned to her station. I knew what I wanted and didn't have to look at the menu. I sat it on the table and pushed it to the side.

I didn't notice that my eating utensils were already sitting close to the edge of the table. When I pushed the menu I knocked them onto the floor at the bottom of the steps. As I bent down to pick them up I was startled to see a pair of Nike

Air-Force Ones stepping down off the steps dangerously close to my fingers. I snatched the silverware from the floor and sat upright at the table. I heard a voice say, "My fault, man. I ain't see you bend down."

Dude's apology sounded sincere and I was cool with his mistake and said, "It's all good, man. No problem." In the five seconds it took for the exchange to take place, neither of us had taken the time get a good look at the other.

Dude turned to walk away, and then stopped and turned around and said, "My man, I know you from somewhere, don't I?" I looked at him directly for the first time and realized that we were familiar to one another.

It was Troy. I realized he didn't remember me and decided it would have been best not to bring up the origin of our acquaintance. I wasn't surprised that he didn't remember me. We had only seen each other twice. The first time was back in April at his at his party, and the second was at twilight when he and Tina had argued.

I'd changed my look since then, lost a few pounds, and cut my hair short. I had a head full of waves. My hair was curly when we had our brief encounter. I finally responded, "Probably just in passing dog." As I said that I wondered if he secretly knew who I was and was just frontin' like he didn't.

It didn't matter to me though. Nothing had changed since the last time. I was still ready to engage any nigga who felt like he wanted to try me. Troy didn't give me that impression, and he had a female with him. She was bad as hell too and stood there silent as he suspiciously tried recall when and where we might've met. The vibe turned from neutral to apprehensive as Troy realized who I was.

He nodded his head upon the realization saying, "I-ight. Stay up." As he walked away I saw that he had started to comment to his female friend. Whatever he said it caused her to turn and look back at me in a curious sort of way. My server came shortly afterward and I ordered my food and ate lunch. Midway through the meal, my cell phone rang. I started to ignore the call and finish my lunch, but I looked and saw it was Tina.

"What's up?"

She paused before saying, "Nothing. Where are you?"

I responded, "I'm eating lunch." Tina paused again, wanting desperately to challenge the information I'd just given her. I knew something was fishy. The temp assignment she was on was hectic and didn't allow her to make phone calls, and on top of that they only got a half hour to eat lunch. I looked at my watch and saw it was 12:30 pm and remembered her telling me she couldn't take lunch until 1pm.

What was also strange was the fact that my phone rang not ten minutes after Troy and I spoke to each other. "So what's on your mind?" I said. That was yet another classic line I used when I wasn't in the mood for talking. It forced the other person to state their case immediately or get the hell of the phone.

Tina knew I was forcing her hand. She played it smart by not pushing the issue. I knew she thought I was at the restaurant with someone. I also knew Troy must've called and told her that. But she was stuck. If she challenged me, it would confirm she had been speaking to Troy, and if she attempted to accuse me of being with company, it would prove she'd heard it from him also, especially since he was the only person I'd seen that day.

The thought of it all must've been killing her! She sat silently, trying to think of a subtle way to get her question answered without divulging too much information. Somehow thinking I wouldn't be able to figure it all out. She was wrong. We rarely, if ever, spoke during the day, and for her to call me so soon after dude and me exchanged words was a dead giveaway! Lack of self-control is a mufucka.

"I was just calling to see what you were doing today. I was thinking about asking you to come up here so we can eat lunch together, but I see someone already—I mean you already ate." I laughed at the thought of Tina's imagination forcing her to reveal her jealousies and suspicions and was admittedly impressed by Troy's little game. I didn't blame him for trying to stir up strife between Tina and me. After all I had stolen his woman from him.

Tina's call confirmed that the two of them were still having dialogue, only I didn't know to what extent. "Yeah, I just finished it too and I'm full. I'm 'bout to leave. The valet bringing my car now. Do you want me to grab you a piece of cheesecake or something?"

Tina sighed in frustration and said, "No. I'll just go some-where out here and get something quick. I'll call you when I get off work."

I chuckled as we hung up the phone. I was glad that I'd found out that she was still dealing with Troy! I liked games and decid-ed to play one of my own. I pushed the phone book selection on my phone and scrolled down to the entry I'd saved the night of the argument—Troy. I pushed send and turned the radio down in the car and prepared my thoughts. His phone rang twice and he picked up anxiously.

"Yo, who dis?" He was hoping that I was female. I could tell by the way he sounded. I hated dashing his spirits, but I had questions.

"What's up, Troy? This is Glenn. You just saw me at the Cheesecake Factory.""Glenn who? I don't know you son, and how you get this number?"

Troy surprised me playing like he didn't know who I was. I was tempted to say, "I'm the dude you just shitted on when you told Tina that you seen me sitting in the Cheesecake with some broad."

I chose not to. I knew he would have lied and that would have just created unnecessary tension. He knew what he did wasn't cool. He also knew that as a black man, he was bound by the unwritten code of the playa's handbook. A book that, if it were real, would definitely have section on "Playa Hating" that would read, "It is forbidden to speak negatively about another man while in pursuit of a woman. To do so is blasphemy! If your nat-ural ability to win her affections is not sufficient, then you must step up your game, but never ever hate on the next man to win her over. Doing so will forever place you in the category of a sucka, and thereby taint your accomplishment!"

I gave Troy a pass and didn't judge him. I had witnessed all that he went through the night he caught Tina with me, an episode I'm sure he couldn't have fully recovered from. I didn't want to waste a lot of time playing footsy on the phone about who I was and just told him. "I'm the dude that was with Tina the day you came to her apartment."Troy paused briefly before saying, "What's up, son? Why you calling me and how you get the number?"

I answered his second question first. "I got the number from Tina." The answer wasn't entirely true, but I knew it would have a psychological effect on him. I figured if I could succeed in making him think I had her in pocket to the extent that she would willingly give up his number, then it would make him feel betrayed and cause him to want revenge. It worked.

"Oh, she did, huh? Well, when she gave it to you was it before or after she came to my crib and fucked me?"

I was unprepared for what he'd just shared with me and had expected to have to draw shit out of him. I hesitated briefly and collected my thoughts before responding, "Come on ock, I ain't call you to get into no pissing contest. I know you was fucking her. She was your girl."

Troy laughed, realizing he hadn't put his statement into the proper context. "Yo son, I just hit dat like a week ago!"

I stuttered as I tried to recover and compose myself; the news floored me! "Wa, when this happen 'cause she been on my dick ever since I met her at your party."

"I don't know nothing about all that. All I know is she showed up at my crib unannounced about a week ago, wearing nothing but a raincoat, leopard print bra and thong set and burn't orange polish on her toenails!" I had barely recovered from the initial shock of what Troy had originally said and was floored again by his revelation that my girl had showed up at his house on some pop up shit, like she was really pressed over this nigga.

I was holding my composure well as I endured the barrage of armor-piercing rounds Troy rained down on me. It was as if I was in a Tyson fight, only I didn't have no arms and weighed 90 lbs. What started as an attempt to gather information and gloat had now turned into something I wasn't sure if I could handle. I decided that I didn't want to know anymore for fear I might snap.

I was proud of myself though because I never let on that I was the least bit perturbed by what he'd said to me. "You know what, ock, I ain't really concerned about all that. What I called for was to find out if y'all was still fucking around like in the beginning, and I see that y'all are so Ima just fall back and let you have her."

Troy responded very seriously, "Yo, Dun, I'm not fucking with Tina like dat. You seem like you a thearl cat. Didn't you see how she fucked wit-choo at my party? That shit should've told you she ain't shit. I didn't even want to fuck her the night she came to my crib, but she ambushed me dude. Cause you know she got some bomb ass cock, and the head game is crazy!"

The only reason I endured listening to Troy tell me about Tina's bedside manner was because he had been with her before me. He took control of the conversation saying, "My man, listen to me. She ain't no good, and she only down wit-choo if you got dough. The minute your money go, she go too. If shit ain't right, then she ain't right! What you say your name was again?"

I answered, "Glenn."

Troy very assertively said, "Glenn, leave the bitch alone 'cause I'm telling you she ain't nothing but trouble. She can't be trusted and she only out for self. Plus, she told me she got you whipped and be getting away with all kind of shit wit-choo, and you still be buying her anything she want." Certain things Troy said confirmed that it came from Tina's mouth. Other stuff I knew were his personal attempts at getting me back for humiliating him both at his party and in front of her apartment that night he'd found out about me.

Still I listened intently to what he had to say. He'd been with her for three years, and she had been sneaking, cheating, and lying the entire time. Of everything he said, the thing that stuck out the most was her popping over to his house. It bothered me so much that I shifted back to the fact-finding portion of the conversation, although cautiously because I didn't want to hear any new shit, just the shit he'd already spoke on.

"Yo, when she came to your crib that night, how was she acting?"

"She was trying to be all loving and shit, but I ain't have no rap. I just pulled out my dick and pushed her to her knees and she started eatin' me up! She was wearing a lot of makeup too. I thought that was strange 'cause she really don't wear it all that much." I was searching for a point—any point—to humiliate her the way the news of her presence at his place humiliated me, and I'd found it.

"She had on makeup because I knocked the shit out of her when I found out she was a stripper!"

Troy laughed and said, "All you had to do was ask me and

I would've told you." Troy's comment that Tina was wearing makeup all but confirmed she'd gone there the night we'd fought. After Troy described what she was wearing, I remembered seeing a pair of leopard print thongs on the bathroom floor the following morning. The same morning my throat started bothering me and thought, "That dirty bitch!"

"Let me ask you one last question. Did you fuck her raw?"

Troy laughed hard, amused that his actions were having such an intense impact on my mental state. "Did I?! Nigga, I ain't never used a rubber with her. She called me a few nights ago wanting to come over, but I ain't answer the phone, and my neighbor be telling me she be doing drive bys in your car and shit. She even be leaving messages, offering to bring her friends and shit too."

That's what I didn't want to hear! I couldn't believe she was still on trying to see Troy like that. I found it hard to accept and couldn't believe that a Nigga who ain't have half of what I had was able to have my woman under control. It was like he was using some kind of Jedi mind trick or something.

Part of my mind rationalized that it was because she used to be his girl. The more ego-driven part of me didn't give a damn she used to be his girl! She chose me at the party, and I had been splurging on her nonstop since then. I had had enough and didn't want to hear anymore. In ten minutes all of the bravado I'd felt after meeting her at his party and the night the two of them argued had been neutralized and eliminated in one conversation.

I realized when Tina dissed Troy it was only a temporary deflection from how she really felt about him. I recalled the night and how cocky I felt, like I was the shit! Talking to Troy made me realize which of the two of us was the real mack; in Tina's eyes it was Troy. Brian said something early on about how it just don't matter what you do for these broads. Once they make up their mind to do something, no man can stop it!

I slapped the shit out of Tina that night because I found out she was a dancer, and what'd she go and do? Turn around and fucked her ex like what I said ain't mean shit! I was glad I'd called Troy, and as the conversation wound to a close I said, "Good looking out."

Troy said, "No problem," and hung up the phone. I thought about the night he and Tina argued and how I was ready to beef with him. I searched my mind for the reason and realized there wasn't one. She was his woman, and I was the outsider. They were just going through something, and now I had confirmation that all I ever had been was a rebound.

Chapter Twenty-One
The Grapevine

I hesitated as I picked up the phone and dialed her number. I'd heard Tammy had moved back home with her mother so she could finish her degree, and I knew I didn't have no business calling her mother's house, but I dialed it anyway. I needed to hear her voice.

"Hello."

I paused a minute before I spoke, it had been so long since I heard her voice that I had forgotten how sweet and innocent it was.

"Hey gweeda, what's going on?" Gweeda was Tammy's pet name—short for Tamigweeda, a playful spin from her real name. Tamika, that was given to her by Brian when they first met. Tammy was surprised at hearing my voice and paused for a moment. She sat silent so long that I thought she'd hung up on me. Thankfully, I heard her breathing and was relieved but still wasn't sure what to expect.

She had every right to curse me and slam the phone down in disgust, but she didn't. That wasn't her way. After all of the pain and anguish that I caused her, she still had love for me. "Glenn?! What do you want? You know you ain't got no business calling here. If my mother had picked up the phone, she would have had a fit."

I interrupted her by asking, "Why aren't you having a fit?"

She paused again and said, "Humph, I see you're still cocky." Tammy was right, and I chilled because she deserved better from me. "How you been?"

She responded hesitantly, "Why you asking now? You ain't been worried about it." Tammy's sarcasm was deliberate, and I knew that she was purposely being tough with me. I didn't blame her. She felt I'd abandoned her when I left Philly and went to Atlanta. I heard that She had gotten scattered reports that I was down there playing house., but didn't think enough of the rumors to give them any real attention.

Arrogant and sure that my escapades in Atlanta were a well-kept secret, I confidently proceeded to question her about rumors I'd heard that pertained to her. "I heard you messing with the dude from the Philadelphia 76ers now?"

She replied, "And I heard you down in Atlanta playing Cap'n Save-a-ho!"

I was surprised to hear Tammy say that to me and tried to deflect it by saying, "What are you talking about?" I knew exactly what she was talking about. It was the reason I called her. Black America ain't no joke. Here I was all the way in Atlanta and Tammy all the way in Philly, and through word of mouth, we both had up to the minute information about what the other was doing. It truly is a small world.

I wanted to ask her how she knew and who told her, but I knew doing so would have confirmed it as true. I held my tongue instead and shifted the conversation. My original reason for calling was because I needed someone to talk to about what had just gone down with Troy.

I was torn between kicking Tina's ass and just walking away. I was worried and didn't want to move too fast and end up doing something crazy like Brian had done with Stephanie. I was too dug in in Atlanta and couldn't just up and leave at a moment's notice like B. Whatever I decided to do was going to require some thought. Calling Tammy was just a way to nurse my bruised ego.

She had always been loving to me even when we weren't speaking. Brian mentioned that she'd asked for me when he went back to Philly. I never called because I knew that it was about something I had involved Tammy in indirectly that resulted in a big commotion that caused a lot of stress for Tammy and her family.

Tammy's mother, Mrs. Paxton, is a strong, God-fearing woman and a very forgiving one too. Throughout the entire ordeal she never made me feel unwelcome. She knew I didn't mean for things to turn out the way they did for Tammy and me. On the few occasions that I would call, although her mother preferred I didn't. She would always call to Tamika to pick up the phone, never once saying anything out of the way to me. I was grateful for that.

Still, I didn't know how to face her or her family. People often say that young black women don't stand by their men in times of trouble, but Tammy did. Her loyalty and love for me stood even when her family and friends shamed her for it. After all she went through I felt stupid whenever I remembered the original reason I left Philly.

It had been rumored Tammy had been dating Baron Mckree

from the 76ers. When I asked her about it she denied it, but I found out later they had been talking on the phone and went out a few times. The confirmation was enough to knock me off my square. Looking back I see I was on some self-righteous bullshit. She hadn't done anything different than I had done.

Before leaving Philly, I'd had my hands full with just about every hot Philly chick who had a name in that town and had been stepping out on Tammy for years. Funny though, the mere mention of her stepping out on me sent me off in a tailspin. I don't know what bothered me more: losing her or the thought of her dealing with a million-dollar nigga.

Either way I was crushed. Instead of letting her know how I felt and confronting her about it, I took the easy way out and left town on a so-called vacation. Only I never returned. I allowed everybody to think I was tired of Philly and needed a break. The truth was I was humiliated and couldn't bare the public scrutiny and embarrassment of the whole city knowing my girl was fucking around on me.

Roughly one year later, in a whole new city, the shit was happening all over again. I took a deep breath and asked, "Tammy, can I talk to you?"

Tammy quizzically responded, "You're talking to me right now. What do you mean?"

I said, "I know you been in Philly doing your thing and I been in Atlanta doing my thing, so let's not get caught up on petty details. I want your opinion about another female, and some shit I just went through. I'm feeling real crazy right now, and I think that I might do something stupid."

Tammy said, "Um, um, um. It's about that girl, ain't it? I knew it wasn't going to last. Brian told me all about you and her. He said she was a dancer or something, but you ain't know about it." I was blown away by what Tammy said. I couldn't believe Brian knew about Tina's dancing, and worse than that, he didn't tell me about it.

It became obvious that Stephanie knew and must've told Brian, and then swore him to secrecy. "What was y'all down there doing? I seen Brian a few weeks ago, looking dejected. I asked him about you and he told me he wasn't fucking with you no more 'cause you ain't tell him his girl was messing around on him, and he said you knew for a long time. I thought y'all was supposed to be friends."

I never knew that Brian had a problem with what I'd shared with him the day he left Atlanta. He never said anything about it. What Tammy told me made me realize that he did in fact have a problem. As I processed all Tammy shared with me, it dawned on me that Brian and I hadn't had a real conversation since he left. I had called him from time to time, and the few times he'd answered the phone he was always short, saying he was busy or he'd call me back.

Talking to Tammy made it all make sense. "I can't believe Brian told you all of that."

Tammy responded defensively, "Yeah, he told me about it and you better not say anything to him. He made me swear not to tell you he told me." I couldn't believe B went out on me like that. I wasn't mad at him for it. I figured he must've been venting when he saw Tammy because he believed Tina to be the reason Stephanie had started to diss him. I only wished that he would've spoken to me about it. Tammy's inside information on Brian had me a little scrambled, and I felt mildly betrayed.

Now I had two issues to deal with: the Troy and Tina shit and the realization that my so-called best friend ain't have no rap for me because of a misunderstanding. All of the emotional realities that I had been bombarded with that day were beginning to overwhelm me, and I didn't want Tammy to know so I pretended that I wasn't bothered by it.

"I don't care what Brian told you. I heard you been getting it in up there so don't come at me like your backyard ain't dirty. I just called you so we could talk. Are we friends? Or do you have some hidden issues with me, too?"

Tammy chuckled saying, "Boy, just go 'head and say what's on your mind."

I sighed a deep sigh of relief because I thought she was about to take the floor and rant about the firestorm she'd just emerged from, but she didn't. Like I said, that wasn't her way. Hers was a forgiving nature, and her lack of pettiness was a blessing.

Most people, myself included, live a lifetime and never come close to obtaining those kinds of virtues. I started my couch session by saying, "You know I don't deal with a lot of people and I didn't know who else to call." I was lying. I had called Brian, and he casually mentioned that he was busy, giving me no indication he was angry with me.

Now that I knew better it all made sense. Tammy didn't want me to know, but she was concerned over my hurt feelings. I understood her apprehension. As of yet, I still had to make amends for the trouble I caused her.

"Well, Ima go ahead and talk to you about it this time, but don't make it no habit. You still in the dog house for that slick shit you pulled."

I smiled and said, "Thank you, baby. I knew you still loved me."

Tammy hurried me along saying "Yeah, yeah, so what happened?" She had changed, and her assertiveness was clearly distinctive.

I proceeded to tell Tammy the whole story of what went down. She sat silently on the other end listening intently. I could hear her radio in the background as it played *I Heard it Through the Grapevine* by Brownstone as I finished my account. Tammy was speechless and took a minute to gather her thoughts before saying, "So let me guess. You want to kick her ass, right?"

I immaturely responded, "Damn right!"

"Well, you're not! You're going to let her do whatever she wants to do and be whatever she's going to be, but you will not degrade yourself by stooping to her level."

I interrupted Tammy in an attempt to rationalize why I felt it was important that I teach Tina a lesson for crossing me saying, "That bitch don't know who she fucking with!"

Tammy burst my bubble again, saying, "Yes, she do. I heard she had your nose open and you let her see she did. That's why she did what she did because you let her do it." For years I had been the one who would always impart knowledge and wisdom to Tammy. Now it was she who was dropping science on me, and I had to accept the validity of it. It was my fault.

How could I legitimately persecute someone for being who they are. Once again, I was reminded that Tina was who she was in the beginning, middle, and end. I was the one who ignored it. "Glenn, remember all them girls you were up here messing with? You didn't think I knew about them, but I did. I wasn't worried about what you were doing with those people because I knew none of them wanted you for you. They didn't see you for who you really are; all they saw was what you had.

"I knew sooner or later they would all be gone, and you would be right back at my doorstep. Girls like the one in Atlanta ain't about nothing. I know her type: uneducated and out of work, or if she does work, she's temping or doing telemarketing. She lives from check to check and her bills are always behind, but all she cares about is being the flyest thing on the street carrying Gucci and Prada with barely a dollar to her name."

Tammy hit the nail on the head, and I wondered if Brian had given her Tina's complete bio. Tammy's advice was what I'd needed and was enough to help me make up my mind to walk away from Tina without physically hurting her and making a fool of myself.

In a separate thought, I found it funny that Tina would never know it but she owed Tammy a debt of gratitude because I was no longer angry with her. The advice Tammy gave me was strong, sure, and couldn't be ignored. I was glad I talked to her. When we finished discussing my crisis, we reminisced about our past and acknowledged our continued love for one another.

It felt good to know we had become friends in the way former lovers sometimes do. I was impressed by Tammy's growth and was humbled by the way she was able to educate me in the way of moral character. When she was speaking, flights of fantasy entered my mind and I couldn't help thinking of what life would be like if we were back together now that she had grown up. She helped me to see that I needed to let go of my juvenile self-image. Secretly, I wondered if she would even consider the possibility. The fear of rejection prevented me from vocalizing my thoughts. I chose instead to ask, "So, are you still dating that dude from the NBA?"

Tammy laughed at me. She knew that was my way of asking if she was single and expressing my interest in the possibility of there being an "us" again.

Chapter Twenty-Two
Head's Up

"Ya nigga just called me so you better get your story straight 'cause I told him everything."

"Damn Troy, why you put me out there like that?"

"What? You think we cool or something? You left me and got wit dat nigga, plus he said he got my number from you." I paused for a moment trying to figure out how on earth Glenn could have gotten Troy's number and then I remembered that night he smacked me and explained, "I left my phone in the living room when Glenn was at my house and went to the bathroom. That must be when he got your number."

"Well, however the shit happened, tell that nigga don't be calling me. You his problem now, and both of y'all need to leave me the hell alone!" Troy's words were harsh. He was serious, and I wondered if he said the same to Glenn. The more I thought about it the more I realized probably not. Glenn was intimidating and if he had the balls to call Troy, then I knew Troy wasn't going to say anything that would have caused them to have beef later.

My biggest problem was how in the hell was I going to get out of this one. Glenn had already beat my ass the last time after he found out about me lying about dancing. I know he going to whip my ass after finding out I slept with Troy. I drove around for an hour or two because I didn't know what to do, and I didn't want to go home and find Glenn sitting there waiting for me.

I grabbed my cell phone and called Stephanie. "Steph, you ain't going believe this shit. Glenn called Troy and found out we was messing around."

"Bitch, you better go home and pack yo shit 'cause I know he gon try to kill you! And didn't I tell you that was going to happen?"

I wasn't in the mood for fifty questions and said, "Where the hell Ima go. He fucked up my chances of getting back with Troy."

Stephanie gave me a reality check saying, "Girl, you need to stop living in the clouds. You messed that up yourself the minute you cussed him out in front of Glenn. I don't care if Troy say he love you and he want you back, you better not believe it! If he did say something like that it's only because he probably want to get you back for leaving him."

Stephanie was right, and as I realized the pickle I had put myself in, I was instantly depressed and angry. That God-damned Glenn! I guess he figured he would mess me up and then leave me high and dry. Well, I had something for his ass. I'd just call his ex and mess up whatever he got going in case he try to drop me and go back to Philly to Tammy.

I had written Tammy's number down early on when Glenn and I first met. When he was still calling and talking to her frequently out of guilt for deceiving her. I knew that she was the only woman he gave a damn about, even though they hadn't been together for a while. Well, just in case he had plans to get back in good with her, I was going to make sure I eliminated that option, just as he'd just done to me with Troy.

"Hello, can I speak to Tamika please?"

"This is she. Who is this?"

"You don't know me, but I'm sure you'll be happy I called you. My name is Tina, and I have been with Glenn now for the last eight mon…"

"Listen honey, I know who you are. You're the little stripper girl in Atlanta who runs around sucking, fucking, and begging men for money right?" I was shocked Tammy knew my bio and was surprised by the directness with which she addressed me. Glenn had always mentioned how mild mannered and docile Tammy was, and this person certainly wasn't the one Glenn had talked about! This person sounded like she was a no-nonsense professional with little tolerance for bullshit!

Tammy cut me off before I could get started good. "Listen Lina, Nina, whatever your name is. Glenn and I are good friends, and there is nothing you can tell me that would change that. In fact, let me tell you something about him, since it's obvious you don't know. Glenn is very vindictive, and if you're not careful, you may find yourself assed out if you cross him. A word to the wise: do not cross him. It would behoove you to quit while you're ahead!"

Tammy's bluntness and nonchalance caught me off guard. I had expected my information to make her come unglued, but she flipped it on me. I was more unnerved that she seemed to know what was going on between Glenn and me and all of my personal business. I guess that's what I get for assuming because it was obvious that Tammy had moved on with her life and wasn't concerned with the pettiness I tried to subject her to.

Tammy's voice came across confident and strong and made me immediately envious. I had seen pictures of her and knew her to be a beautiful, young black woman with a career. I was embarrassed and irritated that I had allowed Glenn to convince me that she was back in Philly waiting on him. I was so embarrassed at having misjudged Tamika that I quietly hung up the phone. I had a new frustration now, one that was compounded by Tammy's warnings to disengage from trying to one-up Glenn. Somehow I realized I should heed the advice. Tammy's warning was delivered confidently, as if she had a crystal ball and was looking into the future, a future that wouldn't have a pleasant outcome for me if I didn't listen to her.

Chapter Twenty-Three
Community Property

Almost a whole day had passed since I got the call from Troy. The news of Glenn's awareness of our cavorting made me nervous, and I wondered why he hadn't called me and worse still, what was he up to.

I hadn't been home because I was afraid he was going to be there waiting on me to kick my ass. At the same time I wondered if he had been there and tore up all my shit like Brian had done to Stephanie. As bad as I wanted to know, I wasn't about to walk into an ass whipping. All kind of shit was going through my mind.

I assumed after our talk, Tamika must've called him and told him of my attempt to sabotage their relationship. I was a wreck and had been driving around town for hours. I finally decided to stop over at Stephanie's house and collect my thoughts. When I got there she was all too eager to get the latest details.

"So where you been, ho? Ducking that nigga all day, huh? You can run but you can't hide. He gon catch up with you, so you might as well call him and get the shit over with." Stephanie's comments seemed strangely familiar, and I realized I must have sounded just as cold when she was going through the shit she went through with Brian.

She seemed elated by the idea that Glenn and I were on the verge of collapse. She had a new man, but he didn't do it for her the way Brian used to. She compensated for the difference by going to the mall every weekend and spending his money and bragging about how she ran shit in their household!

"What you got to drink in here? I need a drink." Stephanie went into the kitchen, opened a bottle of peach schnapps and poured it in a glass with some orange juice. I grabbed the glass and went over and sat down on the couch. I had taken a large gulp and felt a vibration coming from the side of my leg. I jumped, spilling my drink all over my lap, only to discover it was my phone. But it scared me half to death.

"Oh shit! What's the matter?" Stephanie said as she watched me trying to regain my composure and clean up the mess I had just made. "Bitch, you got it bad. You must really be guilty cause you jumping and shit, telling on yourself." I grabbed the phone and looked at the screen. It was Glenn.

"Steph, turn the music down, it's Glenn. Should I answer it?"

Stephanie, desperately wanting to witness a show, said, "Yes."

I lifted the flip lid to the phone and spoke softly into the receiver. "Hel-lo." Glenn's voice was cold and hard, similar to the way it'd been the night he'd found out about me dancing. I looked out Stephanie's window to see if he was parked outside. Had he been I think I would have pissed in my pants.

"I'm sure ya nigga already told you he spoke to me, but don't worry. I ain't on no bullshit. I ain't got the energy for none of this anymore. I just got one question to ask: Why you keep going back to the dude?" Glenn was serious, and the question was a loaded one.

I never really knew why I kept going back to Troy, and now that I had to think about it all I could think to say was, "Glenn, we weren't together when I went to his house, so can we not talk about this?" I wish I had thought of something better to say 'cause the shit hit the fan after that.

"I see. Don't shit matter to you, huh? I'm over here trying to maintain my composure and you still feel the need to try my intelligence. He told me you did whatever he wanted you to do. Why you ain't tell me you was gon like that over him? You was even bringing your girlfriends and shit to join in. You definitely one for the record books!"

When Troy said he'd told Glenn everything I didn't know he meant everything.

"I need you to listen to me because Ima only say this once, and you better not lie. If you do, I will be over to Stephanie's house quicker than you can blink an eye, and when I get there the shit ain't going to be pretty." How Glenn knew I was at Steph's was beyond me, but his knowledge of it was enough to momentarily stun me because I'd thought I was safe.

I paused before I acknowledged his statement and said, "Okay."

He immediately launched another line of questions starting with, "Troy fucked you raw the other night, didn't he?" Before I could answer, Glenn said, "That's why my fucking throat was sore!" I hesitated before answering Glenn's question. Common sense demanded I tell the truth. I knew he'd already spoken to Troy and Troy had given him the goods on everything I'd done with him.

My only alternative was to answer the question and tell the truth, but put a little twist on it. "I…I haven't been dealing with him all like that Glenn. It only really happened that night after you hit me and left." I mentioned Glenn's violence as a way to deflect the attention from my infidelity. It didn't work.

"So you did fuck him that night? I can't believe this shit. You fucked that nigga and let him go up in you raw! Now I know why you was flinching and shit that night!"As Glenn's anger intensified, I thought for sure he was going to show up at Stephanie's to kick my ass. Since he knew the truth I tried to offset it saying, "Yeah, we did, but it wasn't good. He started without a condom, but I made him stop to put one on." Glenn was silent for a minute and I thought he bought it. For good measure I followed up by saying, "Troy don't satisfy me like you Glenn. I just did it 'cause I was mad at you."

The instant I finished, Glenn laughed cynically before saying, "Girl, you the best who ever did it. So let me guess: you went back to him because he got money? Or because he treat you like a queen. No, no, I got it, because he 'bout to get a record deal, right? Get the fuck out of here with that bullshit!"

"I know why you went back. Because you ain't shit but community property, and any nigga who want a piece can just put you under contract like a fucking time share!"

I choked on my drink after that comment. I had continued sipping on it, hoping it would calm my nerves. After coughing briefly I realized that I had had enough of Glenn's attacks. It didn't matter what I'd done. He didn't have the right to talk to me the way he did, and I felt like a fool sitting there taking it all, and like a scene from the movie Sybil I switched from being docile and apologetic to the bitch I'd been the night Troy showed up at my apartment.

"Well, muthafucka, if you think all that about me then why are dealing with me? Just leave me the fuck alone then!" I didn't really want to be left alone, but it was the only thing I could think to say that made any sense at the time. In truth, I was still mulling over Glenn's assessment of my reality, and it stung. It brought me face to face with the stupidity I'd consistently subscribed to for the better part of my life.

Honestly, I don't know why I kept going back to Troy. I was thirty years old and had been with him for three years and had nothing to show for my life up to that point. Lately my days were spent running the streets of Atlanta with Stephanie, hoping to attract niggas with money so we could try and convince them to take us to lunch and to the mall for the promise of conversation or, if the price was right, sexual pleasures.

I shuddered to think what Glenn would say if he knew about all of the other men Stephanie and I encountered throughout our many escapades on the streets of Atlanta. I'd told Glenn many times that I loved him. Unfortunately, it was always right after he'd taken me shopping or did something nice for me. Because of that, he'd always questioned my sincerity.

That night as I sat listening to him I realized that I did love him but somehow didn't and couldn't believe he loved me. Even before all of the nasty things he said, I questioned his devotion to me. None of the other men in my life had ever cared as much as he said he did. Not my ex-husband, Troy, or the countless others whose names I have long since forgotten.

I never knew my father and wondered if my behavior would have been different had he been around. As it stood, all of the other men in my life had toyed with me and betrayed me in ways unimaginable. Glenn might have been one of the good ones, but I wasn't prepared to take the chance to find out.

I was tired of being hurt and lied to. Having sex didn't hurt; it brought pleasure, money, and attention and that was good enough for me. Maybe I was community property. But one thing was certain—this property was well kept!

Chapter Twenty-Four
MCI.

It had been four months since I stopped dancing, and aside from a few odd temp jobs, I hadn't been able to hold down anything steady. I was determined not to go back to dancing no matter what. Glenn and I had faded. We rarely spoke anymore. Aside from an occasional hello on the phone or late night booty call initiated by me, he had all but written me off.

Stephanie had been working at MCI now for a while. Her new boyfriend Stephon originally ran the small business department and she had it good. "You know I can get you a job working for MCI if you want. Stephon got a promotion and is the senior manager for the entire long distance department, and they're hiring. Plus, you wouldn't have to worry about getting the job. I'll just tell him to hire you." Stephanie was a true friend, but a little absent-minded at times.

"I guess you forgot you were already supposed to be doing that."

"Ooooh you right. I did say that already, didn't I? Well, don't worry. I'm going to call Stephon now. I'll call you back."

My life had been a mess for a long time. I never knew which way to go, and I was tired of not knowing. I wanted Glenn back in my life on a full-time basis and figured if I walked away from dancing despite our absence from each other then he would see that I was serious about making a change for the better.

When he first ordered me to stop dancing, I secretly thought about just changing locations because I knew his demand wasn't a sign of love but more like a band-aid for his bruised ego. That idea quickly faded, though, as I realized if I ever wanted to have anything with him again, I had to walk away from dancing completely.

The thought of working a normal job was kind of scary because I was used to getting up when I wanted and used to making damn good money. I guess it was time for me to change my life for the better because all that good money came with a price: my dignity.

None of my family knew I was down in Atlanta dancing, and

if any of them ever found out, I swore I would never go back to Michigan again and instead would crawl under a rock and die. I was surprised Glenn hadn't found out sooner. There had been plenty of times when he and I were out together and he noticed strange looking white men staring at me.

That nigga paid attention to everything and even asked about it once or twice. I lied as usual, pretending I didn't know what the hell they were looking at me for but knowing all along it was because they recognized me from The Cheetah. As if being noticed as a dancer wasn't bad enough, there was a time or two where a few men who I had tricked with spotted me out too.

One of them even had the audacity to speak to me while I was with Glenn. I thought my life was going to end at precise moment. I don't know if my deceitfulness should be viewed as a blessing or a curse because although it may have hurt Glenn in the long run, in the short run it always saved my ass!

Somehow after it all came out I was relieved and content with being found out—at least I wouldn't have to lie about it any more. Now that Stephanie was putting the word in for me with her company I felt comforted by the thought of working a regular job.

Stephanie was doing well at MCI. She had been asking me to come there for a long time but I wasn't feeling her. Now that I decided to change my career, I realized it was time for me to get with the program.

✳✳✳✳✳✳✳✳✳✳✳✳✳✳✳✳✳✳✳✳✳✳✳✳✳✳✳✳✳✳✳✳✳✳✳✳✳✳

"The interview process went well, and I'm so glad they ain't have me in there all day 'cause I am hungry as hell."

"Well, come on. Let's go to Chick-Fil-A and get a sandwich."

As promised, Stephanie had it all mapped out and I was rushed through and selected. It wasn't that big of a deal because the job was in the telemarketing department. The turnover rate in that place was ridiculous.

When I first arrived there it was like a zoo. It was all the way out in Alpharetta, and the people there looked like rejects from some science fiction movie. The men wore braids in their hair, and the women always came to work in the tightest shit they could squeeze their asses into. MCI tried its best to enforce a dress code, but the way them niggas came to work they would have been better off telling them to come as you are because they did anyway.

Before my arrival and Brian's destructive outburst, Stephanie was the flyest broad there, but that all changed on my first day. There were a few other sistas there who were cool. Stephanie introduced me to a few of them. The first one was a cute girl named Shelly. She was from Baltimore. She was a tall, slim girl who was down to earth and had a little style, but her breath stunk horribly; she had a mouth full of cavities, and Stephanie and I always ducked whenever she came around.

There was one other girl there named Dawn. She was a little heavy set but cute, and she tried to come sharp, but her shape was a little bit more than her clothes could handle. I turned the whole place on its ear when I started.

"Tina, I want you to meet this guy. He used to work for Stephon, but now he runs his own department. His name is Carnegie." I was cool with meeting new people now that Glenn and me were no longer seeing each other. I am still fascinated by his abrupt 360 degree turnaround after he found out I danced.

It began with him loving me different. In the beginning, he used to take his time with me and would caress my body and pay attention to my sensitive spots. Once he discovered I was a dancer he shifted to fucking me and treating me like a slut. Like I said, we enjoyed asking about our former encounters with other people but never took it the levels he did after finding out about my dancing, talking to me dirty and calling me a nasty bitch while we had intercourse.

I liked it at first. Thinking he was trying something new I encouraged him until I noticed his face once in the mirror while we were sexing. He didn't know that I was watching him, and I saw he had an intense look on his face, one that seemed like he really believed what he was saying. One other time after that, when we were about to make love, I told him I didn't want it to be rough and forceful like the other times and asked him to take his time and make love to me.

His response was, "You ain't ask them other niggas to make love to you, so don't ask me to either. Ima do you like they do you." I was devastated by what he said, but I couldn't blame him for saying it. Talking to Troy really messed him up. I still couldn't get over the way Troy put me out there, telling Glenn things that didn't have nothing to do with he and I. Whose business was it anyway that I liked women with big breasts?

Tammy wasn't lying when she said Glenn was very vindictive. He seemed to be torturing me for my past behavior. I thought that he would have appreciated my honesty, but all he did was ensure I would never share my secrets with another man ever again. I didn't understand how he let my past upset him the way it did, but I was tired of dealing with his negativity and decided the first man who wanted to treat me nice was going to get the star treatment from me.

This Carnegie guy sounded like he at least had his shit together, and he worked for a living. Stephanie seemed to be content with Stephon, and maybe I needed someone or something similar. Aside from her constantly seeking approval about his looks, she was satisfied by the way Stephon provided for her, and I had to co-sign 'cause she damn sure knew how to find them niggas who broke her off well!

I felt a little bad for him because I knew she was only with him because of security, and he looked a lot like Brian, who she hadn't heard from in the year it had been since they fell out. I was surprised because it seemed that she had all but forgotten about what he did to her personal belongings. She'd even mentioned how she didn't blame him and the shock of seeing her holding hands with someone must have been too much for him to handle. She wanted desperately to hear from him and had even started going to therapy to get over it, and it was killing her!

I didn't expect anything from this Carnegie guy and was concerned that Stephanie might've been trying too hard. I was tired of jumping into shit and wasn't about to do it again. "What do he look like Steph? He better be cute."

Stephanie looked at me and said, "Bitch, just shut up. All you need to know is that he's the one of the top managers up in here." When Stephanie approached him, I recognized his face and realized I'd seen him when I first walked into the building. He was cool I guess, but he had an arrogant attitude when we were introduced, one that suggested he thought he was the shit.

I looked down at his shoes first before extending my hand and said, "Hi, I'm Tina."

Stephanie jumped in and said, "Remember I told you. I wanted you to meet my girl?"

Carnegie nodded and answered, "Yeah, I remember, but you didn't tell me she looked this good." He looked at me, hoping I was going to be flattered by what he said, but I wasn't. I had dealt with Glenn for a long time, and I knew the difference between the workingman's version of cool versus that of a street nigga. Carnegie was trying to force it, but it didn't come off smooth. His words seemed more rehearsed. I didn't let that prevent me from giving him the benefit of the doubt.

I stood there thinking maybe he was what I needed. Dealing with that cool nigga from Philly wasn't quite the come up I'd originally thought it would be. I learned a lot from him though, and wanted to immediately pass on some of that knowledge to Mr. Carnegie, specifically the importance of having on nice shoes and a decent pair of pants.

Stephanie saw that he was losing me as she watched me give him the once over again. I realized I was subconsciously comparing him to Glenn. I turned to Stephanie and said, "What's up with his shoes? They got a bunch of creases on the top of them like they the only pair he got."

Stephanie said, "Bitch, you don't need to be worrying about that 'cause he be making plan every cycle, so you know he be getting big bonuses."

Making plan at MCI was the equivalent of making a targeted quota for a given period for any sales job. Only at MCI it meant that you or your group sold the required amount of long distance or switched phone service and generated new or return customers. If you reached or went above the quota for a particular cycle, then you and your group received a prize in the form of a bonus or a trip, or sometimes even a new car.

After my first month working there, I discovered that there was a big competition between the various groups, and it made the days go by fast and the money pile up even faster.

Chapter Twenty-Five
No Love Intended

I suppose all people have a breaking point, a place they arrive at when they've had enough of the bullshit. On the other hand, sex has a way of making people tolerate bullshit. I suppose that's why righteous people preach against sex before marriage. They know the power it can have over a man 'cause it damn sure had power over me.

I used to tease cats I knew who got caught up. Dudes who took tricks personal, knowing they ain't have no business trying to claim public property. Thinking about all I'd endured while dealing with Tina made me realize I too had become a rest haven for ho's and all because of sex. I mean that's all it was. There was no love intended; all she wanted was a good time and I gave it to her.

It was my turn now. Going forward, that is all any woman would ever mean to me—a good time. I tried to fight the good fight but soon discovered you just can't change a ho into a housewife. You got to let a ho be a ho! Now that I had departed I couldn't help feeling sorry for the next man whose path Tina would cross. He wouldn't know her background, and she was very capable of projecting a quality image, long enough to get what she wanted that is.

Tammy pointed out something that I had never really put into perspective. Women like Tina only wanted one thing—money. And Atlanta was full of broads just like her. After Tammy mentioned it I wondered why I rarely, if ever, met women like her: strong professional black women with their own. Women who knew how to appreciate a strong black man for who he was and not what he had.

Something in the back of my mind kept telling me it was a hopeless prospect, finding a black woman who would choose you for you was a virtual impossibility. I even began to think maybe I was doing something wrong, and maybe I should just fall back and let things happen on their own. I tried that, but it took forever because all of the good ones are taken, and all that seems to be left out here are the money hungry, lazy, good-for-nothing broads that give quality sistas a bad name.

Truth is a funny thing. Depending on where you stand, your

interpretation of it can be seriously deluded. With Tina I knew I had done all the right things, and I still got shitted on! I knew leaving her was the best thing I could've done. What I didn't know was what to do afterward. The only thing I was sure about was as long as I lived I wasn't going to ever give another female the benefit of the doubt.

Being played like that did something to me, something I have yet to define. It was as if I was being consumed by the dark side, like Luke Skywalker in Star Wars. Turning the other cheek as Tammy had advised didn't eliminate the feeling of humiliation I was suffering through, and now that I was gone from the relationship, it was too late to make Tina pay. But somebody sure as hell was going to.

It was my turn to sell dreams, only I was going to be offering bulk rates and doing it wholesale. In my younger days I was something of a dog—a dirty dog—and now that that leash had been broken, I was going to show them all that every dog has his day. It started almost immediately after I walked away from Tina. I ran through no less than twenty-three broads, and I didn't discriminate. They were young, old, professional, blue-collar, skinny, fat, ugly, and pretty. It was as if I was trying to prove something to myself, maybe to see if I still had it.

The first unsuspecting casualties never knew what hit 'em: Kennedy, Sheila, Deanna, Tasha, Shanta, April, Meon, Tonya, Rejetta, Clorisa, and Thereasa, all of whom at some point believed me to be their boyfriend. None of them had the slightest clue I was on some bullshit.

There were others, but they weren't worth mentioning. Make no mistake, they too had a hard way to go; the majority of them saw me for what I was—damaged goods. My ego had been shattered; and luckily, most didn't stay around long enough to get cut by the pieces. There was one, however, who did.

Chapter Twenty-Six
Tawanna Newcomb

"Kevin, you aid you were going to be here by now."

"I know, baby, but I can't get away just yet. Just go ahead and take them into the show and by intermission I should be there with the money."

"I don't know what in the hell I was thinking about when I decided to trust you at your word! I'm so tired of you and your bullshit! I can't believe you would leave your own kids hanging like this. As I hung up my cell phone, I turned and immediately barked orders to my sons. "Preston! Taylor! Come on. The show is about to start."

Preston, the older of the two boys, looked up to me and asked, "Mom, how could you have forgotten to bring your money? Dang, we can't even get a tee-shirt or nothing." As soon as Preston finished his statement, I remembered why I left his father. The disappointment in his voice seemed to echo all of the disappointment I had suffered at his father's hand.

When I married Kevin he was as broke as a joke. I even remember times when we would lie in bed and dream about how life would be when our ship came in. When it did it was infested with rats—hood-rats. What is it about black men that makes them change the minute they get their hands on a little bit of money? Somehow they all seem to be blinded by the sudden influx of attention these money hungry, trifling-ass, broke down bitches give 'em.

The same bitches didn't give them the time of day when they were penniless. Hell, money was never an issue for me and my family. My daddy had made his fortune before me and my sister came into this world. He and my mamma had always done well.

Maybe I should have listened when my mother urged me to marry Dexter. Damn he was fine, but he just didn't have what Kevin had. Kevin was cool, and he had style, and all the women wanted him. Sadly, ten years later, two sons with me and an illegitimate child by some stripper bitch proved that he wanted them too.

Divorcing his dirty dick ass was the only solution to his lust-filled escapades. Niggas ain't shit. You give them the love and respect they ask for, and they still don't appreciate you. No matter what I did for that man it was never enough, and to think I have never even been with another man. When I think about it it's enough to make me sick!.

I saved myself for that man, and never once went outside of our marriage. And all through high school didn't even think of lying down with anyone, mostly 'cause my daddy wasn't having that shit, and the fact that I am a pure bred southern young lady.

I guess all good manners and etiquette in the world won't make a black man keep his dick in his pants. My mother knew then Kevin was a pig, and I refused to listen to her advice. I guess that's what I get—Momma knows best!

I heard through the grapevine that Dexter is a doctor now living in the lap of luxury. Word is he owns a seven-bedroom home in the Blue Ridge Mountains of Tennessee, a Porsche Carrera 911 turbo, and a brand new Silver H2 Hummer! Thank God, I got my own money. Otherwise I would feel like a complete fool.

My name is Tawanna Newcomb, and I am a self-made woman. When I discovered that my husband cheated on me I left him. I left the mink coats, the Jaguar, Range Rover, and the four-bedroom, three-car garage house that I thought was our home. I was a bonafide housewife.

All of my girlfriends told me I was crazy for not taking Kevin for all he had, but that would have showed him he mattered. The truth is he didn't. Just months prior to finding out about his newborn child and skanky love affair, I was diagnosed with breast cancer and had both of my breasts removed. I had the option to keep the one that was unaffected by the disease, but I didn't want to run the risk of the cancer spreading so I opted to remove them both.

Only God knows how I made it through ordeal, with the pain of what my ex-husband did to me and the fear of not being around for my boys. I swore that if I ever got through it,

I would never again trust another man for as long as I lived—until I met Glenn.

He was at the little Bow-Wow concert the night I'd left my money at home and rescued me and my boys. He was standing in the lobby of the Civic Center during intermission and had witnessed me ranting and raving on the phone to my ex-husband, who was giving me another excuse for not having shown up with money for the boys' souvenirs.

He smiled at me just as I slammed the lid to my cell phone down in disgust. This man was incredible. He stood about 6 feet tall, and his complexion was a soft dark chocolate, just light enough to make out the well-manicured beard he sported. Our gaze was abruptly interrupted by another man who approached me to ask if I was alright. He had also apparently overheard the negative discourse between Kevin and me.

Not wanting to be rude, I entertained his conversation long enough for him to feel satisfied that he had accomplished something—all the while keeping Glenn in my sights. I could still see him in the backdrop and noticed that he was motioning his hand in a cutting gesture across his neck. So I cut my conversation short and thanked Franklin for his concern. Before I could walk away, he handed me his card and told me to give him a call if I needed anything. Without looking at it I thanked him again and stuffed it in my purse.

By this time I noticed that Glenn had received several enticing stares from a few of the other single mothers who were there. It is a rare thing indeed to see a black man out with his children without the escort of their mother. I was anxious to know who he was and why he was at the concert alone. And I wanted to mark my territory from those thirsty ass ghetto mamas searching for sponsorship.

No sooner had Franklin walked away than Glenn approached me. As he came toward me, my sense of anticipation seemed to betray me. I couldn't stop smiling. He, on the other hand, had a look of determination that suggested he had staked his claim and was about to make it known to all present. His walk was slow and sure. At our first glance I could only make out his facial features. Now that he was upon me

I noticed he was extremely fashionable. He wore an all-grey summer weight wool crepe ensemble. As he sauntered over to me the flow of his pants hypnotized me. When he stopped they came to rest atop of the nicest pair of black square toe boots I had ever seen.

It was all I could do to keep from staring him up and down. Just as I was about to open my mouth two beautiful little girls came rushing toward him. Each of them had a dark complexion and long, pretty black hair colorfully adorned in barrettes and bows. One might have mistaken them for twins were it not for the height difference between them.

"Uncle Glenn, can we get some pictures and tee-shirts?" They spoke in unison as if they'd rehearsed what they were going to ask their uncle.

Then he spoke, "Hey, hey now. You guys know it's rude to enter a conversation and not introduce yourselves. Now what do you say?"

The taller of the two girls spoke up first by excusing herself and then saying, "Hello, my name is Kennedy."

The smaller child looked up and mumbled shyly, "Hi, my name is Brooke."

I was immediately impressed because I was expecting typical ghetto names like Shamiqa or Kieshawn. I responded by saying, "And hello to you both. My name is Tawanna." They both looked at me and waved and immediately went back to asking their uncle for souvenir money. He granted their request, and they took off running to the nearest stand they could find.

Finally, we were alone and before he could utter a word I said, "Wow, Uncle Glenn, huh? But they look just like you. Are you sure you didn't coach them into saying that?"

He laughed and said, "Now, why would I do an awful thing like that? Besides I wish they were mine. Unfortunately, I don't have any children."

I looked up to the ceiling and muttered "Thank you, Jesus." Not only was this man gorgeous, he also did not have any baby mama drama. I had hit the jackpot. Recalling the earlier situation, he asked me what it was all about, and I began by telling him I had left my money at home and I was disgusted with my ex because I couldn't buy my boys anything to remember the night by.

He laughed and said, "I'll make a deal with you. If you let me call you, I'll make sure your boys are able to get all of the souvenirs they want. Deal?" What he didn't know was had he not said that I was going to ask him to sponsor their night anyway. When it came to my children I had no shame. Thankfully, chivalry is not dead and Glenn proved it.

Nervously I said, "But you don't even know my name."

He responded by saying, "I'm not deaf, you know. I think you said it was Tawanna, right?" Before I could say anything, he said, "I ain't blind either, and that cat you were speaking to earlier didn't have no business harassing you like that, and besides he wasn't your type." His voice was firm and sure, just like his walk, and I was immediately turned on.

"So, just exactly what is my type, Uncle Glenn?"

Right on cue he said, "You're looking at him."

Had any one else said that I would have thought it was the corniest line I had ever heard, but his delivery was smooth and deliberate as if he knew I'd agree. We both laughed, silently relieved that we were mutually interested, knowing all to well that good looks don't always guarantee good conversation. By this time intermission was over and the curtain call had begun. I looked over and saw Preston and Taylor, who were both leaning against the wall. Each had a dejected look on their faces. Although Glenn had bargained with me to exchange phone numbers, I didn't really expect him to follow through with what he said.

I turned to gather my guys to re-enter the show, and Glenn grabbed my arm and said, "Aren't you forgetting something?"

I said, "Oh, I'm sorry," and reached into my purse and grabbed a card and handed it to him.

He took it casually from my fingers and said, "No, no. Not that," and shook my hand and said, "Nice meeting you."

I felt something pressing the palm of my hand. I told him it was nice meeting him as well and turned to walk away. As I reached to put what I believed to be his number into my bag

I was surprised to see that it was a neatly folded fifty-dollar bill. I turned around to thank him, but he was gone and I didn't even get his phone number.

Chapter Twenty-Seven
The Call

"Hello, can I speak to Tawanna please?"

All I could think of when the phone rang was "Who in the hell could this be calling me at 9 o'clock on a Sunday night on my business line?"

"Who's calling?"

The voice on the other end came across with a rehearsed coolness. "It's Franklin, sweetie. You remember from the little Bow-Wow concert last night." Damn, I did remember. Franklin was the first guy to approach me last night when I was arguing with Kevin. The funny part was I didn't remember giving him my phone number.

"Yes, Franklin I do remember you, but I don't remember giving you my number. Do you mind telling me how you got it?" He paused momentarily. I assume because he realized his phone call was a bit forward to say the least. After all, I never gave him the number.

"Well, you remember you told me you were a real estate agent for Re/Max. Well, I went to their web site and pulled up the agent listing, and I found your virtual business card posted on their website. I was going to wait and see if you were going to call, but I decided to impress you by making the first move."

It was all I could do to keep from saying, "Nigga, please. I don't know where you from but where I come from stalking someone is considered a crime, and the only people that shit impresses are the police!" Just as I was about to dash his spirits I remembered he had approached me out of concern for me. If nothing else that warranted a polite and considerate let down.

"Well, Franklin, I really appreciate the effort, and I am flattered you thought so much of me as to track me down, but sweetie this is my business phone and I don't take personal calls on it."

Franklin interrupted me before I could continue. Sensing that rejection was imminent he said, "Tawanna, listen. Judging from the episode the other night I gathered you probably have a lot on your plate right now. I don't know what you were going through with your ex-husband last night, but I want you to know that if you give me the chance, I will always put you first. I can tell that my calling you tonight didn't sit well, but I can assure you I am not a nuisance. I only did so hoping for an opportunity to take you to dinner so you could see how nice of a guy I really am."

I sat there on the other end of the phone silently, and when he finished talking I realized I should have had a response for him, but strangely, I didn't. Although I was still uninterested, his sincerity made me feel that I at least owed him the opportunity to prove himself. The night we met, Franklin mentioned he was a pro-football player.

I didn't bother trying to remember the team because I never cared for athletes. I am a recently divorced thirty-something mother of two, who has no time for some young platinum-wearing, womanizing, Bentley-driving, sports figure who would drop me quicker than he would meatless rib bone at a barbeque the minute our sexual pleasures were finished. Franklin seemed a little different, and he was in his late twenties—well past the age of innocence and frivolity. I decided that going out with him couldn't be all bad.

"Well, Franklin, I tell you what. How 'bout you give me a call on the weekend. By then I will have decided what I am going to do. I can't make any promises, but I will at least think about it."

Franklin paused before responding, "That sounds fair. I'll call you on Friday around noon time so if you decide to see me I'll have enough time to plan the perfect evening."

I laughed because I admired his confidence; still it was funny he went through all he did to contact me. I wondered why Glenn hadn't done the same, but then I remembered only a day had passed. Remembering Glenn's manner I realized it would probably be a week or more before I could expect to hear from him, and if the nigga took that long then he could forget about ever talking to me.

****

"Mom, can I wear my Roca-Wear warm-up suit today?"

"No Preston, you know Wednesdays are uniform days. Now, stop wasting time boy and get dressed. Your breakfast is getting cold, and if you miss the bus today I'll make you walk to school!"

"How you gon make me walk? The bus drive allaway down the highway to get to the school. You want me to get hit by a car or something?"

"Shut up, boy, and sit at this table and eat. You're just like your father—always got something smart to say." Preston was beginning to sass me more than usual, and I noticed Taylor would sit and silently observe as if taking notes. I was realizing more and more that life without their father was becoming more and more noticeable. They tried things they never did when Kevin and I were together. Kevin still took them on the weekends but somehow it didn't change their behavior with me the moment he dropped them off.

I don't know how in the hell I was supposed to deal with all of the stress of raising them without their father. Kevin had been with me long enough to know me, and I knew he was expecting me to break and allow him back in my life. Well, that would never happen. The day I took him back would be the day I laid my black ass down to die.

Men are such animals they have no regard for the sanctity of marriage, no respect, no loyalty, or whateva. Whether young or old the male species should be corralled and kept for the sole purpose of breeding, and if there were a way to create detachable penises, I would be the first in line to donate money for research. At least that way I wouldn't have had to worry about what Kevin did when he was out of my sight. "Preston! Taylor! Put on your jackets, and let's go!"

"Good morning, Atlanta, and welcome to C-103 and the Hank Lee morning show, with Shonda and Spiffy 2k. And this is Morals Wednesday! Today's issue is why married men cheat."

My heart jumped into my throat as I listened intently to what the issue for Scruples Wednesday was to be. Preston and Taylor were both in the back seat and had been bickering with one another the entire ride. Preston had missed his bus again, and I was running late for work because of driving him to school. I always drove Taylor; his school was only a ten blocks from our house. Preston's school, on the other hand, was ten miles north on I-85, which took me twenty miles out of my way. I couldn't wait until I was able to drop him off because I didn't want any of what I was about to hear to cause me to break into tears, and I dreaded the thought of him seeing me cry.

"Bye honey, and make sure you eat all your lunch today. If I see another apple and half-eaten sandwich in your lunch box, I promise you I'll make you take it to school every day after that until you eat it!" Who was I kidding? I knew all he would do from point on was either give to another child or throw it in the trash.

"Hank, I don't know why you have chosen this topic for today. I can tell you all you need to know about what makes a man cheat on his wife—new poontang!" Shonda erupted into laughter at what she apparently thought was a joke.

I liked Shonda, but that issue was especially sensitive to me. Kevin cheated on me and I still hadn't gotten past it. I stifled my anger because there was nothing I could do about it and turned the volume up to listen more intently, hoping not to miss any part of what was being said.

Soon after Shonda's remark Hank asked, "Spiffy, what do you think?"

Spiffy responded, "I am a man and I know that if I ever were to cheat, it would probably be because I was bored and unhappy with my wife." Spiffy's voice was raspy and high pitched and seemed to contradict his large appearance. I thought he was a nice guy, but his response proved that he was the typical male.

I wish someone would explain to me exactly how does one become bored with someone you have vowed to love until "death do us part"? It had been about one year since Kevin cheated, and I still couldn't understand what was on his mind or why he chose to ruin our happy home for the likes of some cheap, dirty, slut stripper! I decided I would call to see if I could finally get an answer to my question.

"The phone lines are open for our first caller. Caller,

you're on the line."

"Hello, my name is Tawanna, and I have a question. My husband cheated on me and had a baby outside of our marriage. I did everything he wanted throughout the marriage. I gave him two sons and was a stay-at-home wife. I catered to his every wish, only to discover that he never appreciated my efforts.

"I was diagnosed with breast cancer shortly before I discovered he was cheating on me. The news of his gallivanting around with another woman almost destroyed me, but I had to stay strong for my boys." A tear began to run down my cheek as I recalled the story. I couldn't believe I was actually on the radio spilling my heart out for the whole city to hear, but I didn't care because I had to get it off my chest.

"After the divorce I had spent many nights alone crying in my pillow and talking to Jesus, asking Him why did all of this have to happen to me. My family and friends tried to get me to talk to them, but I didn't feel comfortable revealing that part of my pain. They all knew me to be the strong black woman I had always portrayed, and I didn't want to ruin that view." In the time it took for me to express my pain to a city full of complete strangers, I realized it made me feel better because they didn't know me, and any negative judgment wouldn't affect me.

I paused before continuing, and Hank Lee chimed in, "Caller, are you still there?

Shonda interrupted him and said, "Her name is Tawanna, Hank. Dang! Why you sound so impersonal? Can't you see the woman is choked up about what she is telling us?" I appreciated Shonda defending me and thanked her for consoling me.

"I'm sorry, guys. I should have talked about this long ago. I have had it bottled up for long time, and aside from the cancer, I never told anyone I was bothered by anything else I was going through, especially Kevin.

"I just want to know why h…h…he…he would do that to meeeeee?"

"Oh, my God. Hank, I think she's crying."

"I know Shonda. Cue for commercial."

"We'll be right back, Atlanta. One of our listeners has a

personal emergency." I could barely see the road in front of me as I pulled over. The tears were streaming down my face so fast it made it hard for me to see where I was going. I couldn't believe what I had just done, crying on the radio and after I told them what my real name was.

Chapter Twenty-Eight
Friends

I didn't go to work after the episode on the radio that morning, and instead stopped at a Starbuck's coffee shop and spent the day browsing through Ilyanna Vanzant's book Yesterday I Cried. It was two o'clock before I realized I had spent the better part of the day in the shop.

My peace was interrupted by my cell phone ringing. It was Dana.

"Hey, girl. Are you okay? I heard you on the radio this morning, and I knew it was you. I didn't tell anyone though. I have been calling you non-stop since they broke for commercial, but you weren't answering."

I sighed and said, "I'm sorry, I didn't want to talk to anyone after that." I knew Dana was unhappy that I didn't answer her calls. She believed herself to be my best friend. In truth, she was a good friend but a friend who always needed help with bills. For some reason no matter what the situation was, she always found time to ask me for a loan. Why she called it that I'll never know because she hardly ever paid me back.

"Did Lina call you? Cause she called me and asked if that was you on the radio. I just told her I didn't know."

I was glad to hear that because Dana had a mouth on her that would put a sports announcer out of business. She broadcast gossip faster than any radio show around. Dana was fishing for acknowledgement and gratitude, and I obliged, "Thank you, Dana. And yeah, I'm okay now. I just had a little breakdown is all. Lina called me a few hours ago; it seems she heard me too. I don't know what I was thinking when I told them my real name. Somebody should smack me in the back of my head." Dana and me both laughed, but I was dead serious. I must have really been losing my mind because I was smarter than that.

All I could think of was Kevin calling me and trying to be sympathetic, believing that he was the reason for my breakdown. If he had any sense he would know not to call me with his phony sympathies. I would be liable to stab his ass through the God damn phone.

"Well, Dana, let me get off of this phone. I have to go and pick up Taylor from school, and it looks like the traffic is already backing up. I'll call you later when I get settled in. Bye." Dana started to say something, but I hung up before she could get it out. I didn't care what she wanted. I was going through my own personal hell that day, and I needed a drink.

I drove home slowly, thinking of all of the signs that should have been obvious to me about Kevin's cheating, like his sudden desire to work late four nights a week. His weekend business trips out of town, not to mention his reluctance to tell me the names of the hotels where he would stay. I guess that was all water under the bridge now.

Lina, Dana, and all of my family were all appalled at my decision to file a non-contested divorce. They didn't know that my fight with breast cancer sapped every ounce of energy I had left inside, and I couldn't care less what Kevin did at that time. I had to stay alive for my boys, and taking Kevin's money would've legitimized his existence and the farce that was our marriage.

By the time I got home Preston was already there playing in front of the house. "Boy, what did I tell you about playing in your uniform? You put holes in the knee of the last two pairs of pants I bought and got grass stains in the ones before that! I tell you what—if you mess up this pair you'll be wearing them every day for the rest of the year."

Preston stopped dead in his tracks. His friends covered their mouths to hide the laughter and snickering they each couldn't contain. Preston was immediately embarrassed and stormed into the house and threw his book bag down on the floor. "Dang, mom. I didn't even do nuffin. My pants ain't even dirty. My dad let me play all the time and he don't never say nuffin."

Taylor stood there laughing at his older brother. It seemed that Preston's sudden shift to negative behavior was a welcomed respite for Taylor because he was usually the one who bore the brunt of my scolding, being the younger and more mischievous of the two. "Preston, what did I tell you about talking back to me? You have gotten a little too smart for your own good, and I am here to tell you that it stops today. And I don't care what your tired-ass father lets you do. I said you're not going to do it, and that's that!"

Up until that point I had gotten past my disaster of a day, but the mere mention of Preston's father rekindled my anger and disgust. I remembered that I'd originally wanted to have a drink, and now those plans had been crystallized in my mind. All I needed was a sitter, and I knew just who to call—Corretta.

I knew Corretta wasn't going to be busy. She and her husband Julian never did anything during the week and were just as happy staying at home tending to their children, Brandon and Hunter. Every one in our family found it interesting that my sister and me both had two boys after we were married. Preston and Taylor were older than their cousins by about two years respectively, but whenever the kids visited one another they always had a ball.

"Hey, what are you and Julian doing tonight?"

Corretta was surprised to hear from me and paused before she responded, "Well, hello to you too. Since when did you decide being polite was no longer required when speaking to your older sister?"

I laughed because Corretta was right. "I'm sorry, but I have had the worst day and I think I need to go out and relax and have a drink."

Corretta said, "Now, you know you don't need to be drinking anything. You're still undergoing chemo, aren't you?" I sighed because it had been well over a year since I had had my breasts removed and my doctor informed me that the cancer had gone into remission. I figured it had to be gone because it hadn't metastasized and I'd removed the parts of my body that originally contained it

I knew Corretta's questions were out of concern for me so I didn't sass her and instead reminded her that I informed the family a year ago about the positive outcome. I guess being the youngest child causes every one to be overly protective. I wasn't mad at her for it—at least she did care, which is more than I can say for Kevin.

"Corretta, can you just sit for me? I need a break tonight and Preston has been getting on my last nerve. I think that it's time to send him to be with his father. His mouth has gotten unbearable lately, and I don't know what to do." As I proceeded to vent to Corretta about Preston's terrible behavior I noticed that she repeated every instance of Preston's bad attitude aloud. The way people do when they are shocked and surprised.

After a barrage of "Oh no, he didn't!" and "Whaaaat? Stop lying!" I heard Julian in the background say, "Just send his little butt over here and I'll straighten him out!" Julian was a nice guy, and when he married my sister the word was that Daddy was against it because he was from the street and was raised in the projects. Ironically,

Julian proved to be more of a man than Kevin ever was.

He respected his wife and their marriage, and after Corretta gave him two healthy boys he provided her with all of the creature comforts any woman could ever wish for. He started with purchasing a four hundred thousand dollar home for them, a Mercedes Benz, and Land Rover too, not too shabby for a man who was born and raised in the projects.

Corretta never knew it but I envied her relationship with Julian. Daddy was wrong about Julian, and I wished that he had been as adamant in objecting to my marriage to Kevin as he had been about refusing his blessing to Corretta and Julian.

"I can't believe Preston has been giving you all of that trouble. Girl, if that's the truth then you do need a break. What time did you want to bring them by? I just started dinner, and it will be finished in about an hour so you don't have to feed them. Just bring them over whenever you're ready."

I never worried when I called Corretta because she was always there for me. I really wanted to tell her about this morning's episode, but I didn't want to make her worry about me. It had been a long time since the family put aside their concerns for me. During my bout with cancer everyone sat around me and worried as if in a vigil. I guess no one knew what the outcome was going to be. We had already lost our mother to the same illness, and after I came through I never wanted to subject them through that ever again.

"Where are you going on a Wednesday night anyway?" Corretta asked. She hadn't been out in the gang of years since she had been married to Julian. She didn't know that Harriston's had become the new hot spot on Wednesday nights for the thirty and older crowd. It had gotten so popular that people had started parking in the Kroger supermarket parking lot across the street because the club's lot couldn't accommodate the massive influx of people who now converged on the old school club like it was going out of style.

"You didn't know Harriston's is the new spot in Stone Mountain?"

Corretta laughed and said, "That spot hasn't been happening for years. You mean to tell me people still actually like the place?"

I said, "I don't care if people like it or not. I'm going to have a drink and relax and hopefully have a good time. I'm getting dressed right now. I will be at your house by 7:30 pm. I'm going to bring the boys' changes of clothes too so that I don't have to rush in the morning."

Corretta paused before she repeated my last word, "Morning? Since when do you make plans for the entire night?" Corretta was surprised at the way I had mapped out my potential evening. I had always been a conservative young black woman, but I had begun to feel that it was time for me to shed my conservative image and recreate myself, even if it meant shaking up a few things with my family and friends.

In the midst of our conversation my other line clicked. "Hold on, Corretta. That's my other line." I clicked the line and said, "Hello."

The voice on the other end said "Hey, I been waiting for you to call me back all day. What's up? Are you ducking me or something?" It was Dana.

"No, Dana. I haven't been ducking you. I had a long day and I just haven't made time for anyone today. Hold on I have Corretta on the other line." I clicked back to the other line and asked, "Corretta, are you still there?"

She responded hurriedly, "Yeah, I'm here but I am hanging up. I have to put dinner on the table so hurry up and bring the boys so they can eat with my boys."

"Okay, I'll be there in a minute." I clicked back over to Dana, "Hello, I'm back, but listen I am about to go to Corretta's for a minute to drop off the boys because I'm going to Harriston's tonig..."

Dana interrupted me as the last word rolled out of my mouth and said, "Oooh, I wanna go. What are you wearing? Cause I want to borrow that blue Gucci dress you have. If you're not wearing it. How much do they want to get in?" Dana strategically dropped the question because she knew that I knew whatever the cover was, and she didn't have it. I did my usual and offered to pay her way in and sponsor her drinks for the night.

Dana was the single mother of three children and had four different "baby-daddies." In her mind it was insurance in case one of them fell off of her personal welfare cycle. I don't know how she juggled all of those different men. The youngest child was the one who could claim two daddies. For some reason Dana thought it was cute. I didn't.

Women like her are what make the majority of black men resent black women. I suppose that she was already paying the price for her treachery. She was always broke despite her brilliant plan to have four different men supporting her. She never could seem to

161

hold down a job, and she constantly borrowed anything she could—money, clothes, food. She had no shame.

"Dana, now you know I am not about to let you wear that dress. I haven't even worn it yet. Besides you can't even fit in it." Dana hated when I said that because she knew it was true. She wasn't much bigger than me but her shape was square, and in truth I did her a favor because the dress was form fitting and on her it would've looked like someone stretched some fabric over a vertically erect diving board.

"Girl, I don't know what I was thinking about anyway. I have this hot new black mini skirt I bought last week from BCBG that I can wear. Can I wear that white flared cuff-link blouse?"

So many times I had been temped to scream at her and demand that she stop asking to wear my things, but I always chickened out. I just found it hard to believe that she didn't feel awkward constantly asking the way she did. "Yeah, you can wear it. As a matter of fact you can have it because I just bought a similar one the other day 'cause that one has gotten a little tight around my chest."

Dana didn't acknowledge my gesture, choosing instead to immediately ask, "What are you going to wear?" I knew that meant she was especially curious. She knew that I used to really like that blouse, and for me to give it away like that meant maybe I had something that was going to shut the house down. She was right. I was going to wear the Gucci dress she had just requested. "I think I'm going to give my new dress some out time."

In classic girlfriend form, Dana all of a sudden had something to say about the dress. "Just remember to make sure you don't show too much cleavage 'cause you still have a little discoloration from the skin graphs and radiation treatment."

I wasn't sure if she was being a true friend or just being jealous of the incredible boob job I had gotten done after my breast removal. I chose to ignore the comment. The discoloration was barely noticeable, and my experience has taught me that niggas ain't interested in what color the skin is that covers a woman's breasts as long as what they can see is impressive—and my new bosom was impressive to say the least.

Chapter Twenty-Nine
Harriston's

I always liked Harriston's because people didn't feel the need to overdo it. Rarely did you see the bulky jewelry and loud clothing that was synonymous with many of the downtown Atlanta nightclubs. Yeah, going there required that you be dressed, but in a conservative kind of way, without all the glamour and glitz.

The atmosphere there was always comfortable, and if you were going to go, Wednesday night was the night to do it because that was ladies' night. It had been a while since I had put on a suit. Ever since Brian left I rarely hung out because the thought of hanging out alone was never too appealing, but the good thing about Harriston's was whenever I went I always saw other friends of mine I could hobnob with and pass the time.

Although the club was in Stone Mountain, surprisingly it was never a disappointment. I always enhanced the odds by arriving dressed to a T and that night wasn't going to be any different. I decided to wear an almond tan, four-button, single-breasted, custom tailored Armani suit and a pair of brown Salvatore Ferragamo loafers. I'd always received massive compliments whenever I wore that suit and learned early on that clothes do make the man. It also didn't hurt if you were somewhat attractive.

When I pulled up to the parking lot I noticed that it was packed and the valet was turning just about every one away. I wondered if I would be one of the people until I recognized the valet from Café Echelon., I'd always tipped him well, and he smiled when he saw me and signaled me to pull up and drive past a few cars that were already sitting there. I got a few sneers as I passed, but the majority of the people in line knew the routine. In Atlanta, anyone who drives a fancy foreign car got the star treatment whenever he or she pulled up to a public place, and my new platinum Range Rover commanded star treatment indeed.

The old boy rushed to the driver's side, opened my door, and greeted me with much enthusiasm. I smiled because it felt good to be respected—even though he didn't know my name. He took my keys and told me to go in. I didn't get a ticket because he knew he would receive a nice tip and that way he wouldn't have to record the transaction.

As I walked up to the door I noticed the line was extended down to the other end of the club. I dreaded the thought of having to wait in that long ass line, but unfortunately, I didn't come to Harriston's frequently enough for the owners to know me personally. They didn't give me front of the line privileges they way other club owners did. No matter. I wasn't about to go to the back of that line and searched my mind for a clever ruse that would enable me to bypass it entirely. Just as I reached my wit's end I heard my name called from the distance.

"Glenn? Glenn? What's up, ma nigga? Nigga, why you ain't call me and tell me you was comin here?" It was Vic. I had met Vic a few years back at Café Echelon. I remembered we had exchanged numbers, but I never thought to call. He was one of the first cats Brian and I met when we started coming to Atlanta. Vic was a hustler, and from what I knew he did quite well at his chosen profession.

He was also very stylish and was dressed impeccably whenever I saw him. If it wasn't for the southern accent he had, it would have been easy to confuse him for a New Yorker or Philadelphian. Prior to becoming acquainted, we would regularly compliment each other whenever we saw one another in the club. The dap was always genuine because we each knew and appreciated the uniqueness of a strong outfit—it definitely set you apart from the rest of the dudes in the club.

"Damn, nigga. Where you been?"

Vic was happy I remembered him and anxiously responded, "Hey playa. I just been running these bitches, nigga. Das it. You know me. Das what I do!"

I laughed because that is what he did. I often saw Vic with some of the finest women Atlanta had to offer. He got off on parading around clubs, drinking Cristal from the bottle. I suppose he did it because he knew it attracted the women, and they knew the production meant that he was generous. Although I was never one to carry on that way, I didn't judge Vic for it. In certain Atlanta circles that's what it took. It was just part of the game. You had to pay the cost to be the boss!

Vic was anxious to rap about the latest with me and said, "Nigga, fuck dat shit. Whassup wit-choo, playa?" I smiled 'cause I knew he must've seen me pull up in the Range Rover. When I met him I was driving the blue big body. Success for the black man was often judged by what he was seen driving. So Vic's question was more or less directed at what I was into these days, not how I was doing.

I satisfied him by feeding him a watered down version of my personal goings on. "Man, you know me. I'm just out here trying to shine wit the sun. I ain't makin' no noise though."

Before I could go on Vic acknowledged what I suspected, "Nigga, you definitely shinin. That platinum Range you got out of is on fire!"

I laughed and shrugged my shoulders, and then attempted to deflect the attention he was giving to me by saying, "Nigga, that ain't shit to you. If I had your hand I'd throw mine in!" We both laughed after that but for different reasons. Vic because he knew he wasn't going to get much more out of me. And me because I knew he wanted more than I was willing to say.

It didn't dampen the enthusiasm though, and Vic placed his hand on my back and guided me through the doors into the club. Vic had a V.P pass to Harriston's. I don't really know why because everyone there knew him and it appeared they would have let him in regardless. Once we got in the club, he asked me what I was drinking, and I said, "Grand Marnier with a splash of grapefruit."

The bartender nodded to him and Vic repeated my words and added, "And a double shot of Chivas Regal on the rocks." The bartender handed us our drinks. Vic disappeared into the crowd chasing a familiar female face, looking back as he walked to say, "Ima holla at you later, playa."

I responded "i-ight," but I knew he was too far away to hear me at that point. I walked through the club and ended up in the rear near the main dining section. Whenever I went to Harriston's I always picked that area to post because it was not as busy and seemed to attract women who appeared to me more interested in friendly conversation than dancing.

I think the women liked area because it was the gathering place for men who seemed to have it going on, the laid back cats who enjoyed one-on-one conversation over bouncing around and getting all sweaty. I would always lean on the back wall in a relaxed, nonchalant kind of way, projecting a pose that was both inviting and non-threatening.

I always believed that was important in a club. Women are easily irritated by rowdy, rambunctious men. Nothing is worse than happening upon a woman who has just been accosted by some lame dude. She'll shoot you down quicker than an anti-aircraft missile, and you're left not knowing what or why it happened while the culprit is off on the other side of the club fucking shit up for the other half of unsuspecting brothas. Over-aggressive behavior should be against the law, and any dude caught perpetrating it should be taken outside and shot.

I finally positioned myself well enough to be noticeable to all of the women who found their way to the rear of the club. The DJ was playing *"One More Chance by Biggie,"* and the vibe was nice as I stood there sipping my drink, enjoying the scenery. Harriston's was unique like that. It brought out the more sophisticated sistas, real black women who were doctors, lawyers, and professionals from all walks of life, not the typical high-class low budget wannabes who frequented clubs that catered to the bling-bling crowd.

Every now and again you might find a straggler there. You know, the kind who fits the typical hoochie bill but who believes herself to be something different. I had been to Harriston's a few times in the past, and whenever I went I was always pleased with the turn out. I liked going places where the quality of women was guaranteed to be satisfying. Strangely, it seemed as if every club in Atlanta came complete with its own stock of beautiful black women.

The script for approaching a woman in Harriston's was a little different than that of younger crowds, especially if you're not adjusted to reading the signs they give off. I was always subtle whenever I spoke to someone, careful to express my interest in the most humble manner possible, so as to feel them out. Friendly conversation usually does the trick.

That way the women don't suspect you're trying to come at 'em, and shut down thinking you're just another cat with a corny line. I generally observe a woman who has already shot down several guys and strategically place myself in her field of gravity. When the moment is right, typically right after she shoots some nut out the sky like a duck, I ask, "Damn, is it hunting season?"

That usually breaks the ice and gets them to laugh, and then I follow up by saying, "I was just about to say something to you until I saw the way you sent that dude on his way with his tail stuck between his legs. Just tell me what he said so I can make sure I don't say it too." Success usually comes shortly after that, mostly because they aren't used to someone noticing and making jokes about the way they reject men.

I spent the better part of that night in Harriston's playing the background. I very rarely danced and would only do so if someone asked me or if the woman happened to be exceptionally attractive. Even then the music would have to be just right—something mellow that wouldn't require me to move a great deal. I don't know if what I do can legitimately be called dancing, but I get by with it.

My swagger is calm, cool, and collected, much like the way people wearing headphones nod their heads to a smooth beat. Put a little leg movement to that and you have a clear picture of my groove. An hour had passed since my first drink courtesy of Vic, and I was anxious to return the favor. I looked for him as I made my way over to the bar. I didn't see him and decided to order another Grand Marnier.

The bartender remembered me from earlier and didn't charge me. He and Vic seemed to have some kind of rapport, and I wasn't about to argue with him. The dude handed me my drink, and I turned to walk away but stopped after I hearing a soft voice say,

"That was rude. I thought for sure you were going to ask me what I was going to have." I looked to my left and noticed a sharply dressed young sista standing there. I looked her over and almost choked. She was stacked! I paused, smiling before speaking, and decided I would offer some friendly conversation before offering to buy her anything. That way I would be able to determine whether she was truly interested or just wanted someone to quench her thirst.

"I usually like to at least know a person's name before I spend my money on them."

She smiled seductively and said, "I didn't hear you ask, but I'll tell you anyway. My name is Alex, but you can call me Lex—all my friends do." Lex was sexy as hell but young and definitely not in league with the older, more sophisticated women in the club. I admired her style though because she was well dressed and I could see that it wasn't just for the night. She had a mystique that suggested she was no stranger to fine wears.

She wore matching diamond jewelry, carried a designer handbag, and drove a Mercedes. I knew that because she had her car keys strategically placed in plain view on the bar the way guys do when they want everyone to know what kind of car they drive. I asked her what she was having and she said, "Remy Martin VSOP." I motioned the bartender again, this time expecting to fork over some cash for sure. To my surprise he didn't charge me again.

Lex noticed and said, "I see you must have some clout in this place.

I didn't want to smother my own shine and responded, "I got a few connections here and there." I was lying through my teeth, but what the hell. I wasn't trying to marry the broad. She knew it too. We were both waiting for a spark that would allow us both to justify taking things to the next level, bypassing the all-too-familiar "let's go to breakfast" line. Because she was sexy and had surprisingly interesting conversation, I didn't mind her standing there conversing with me.

Thirty minutes had passed and I refreshed her drink for her, now sure she wasn't hiding an ulterior motive. She complimented me on my outfit and took particular interest in the shoes I was wearing, stating, "Most guys from here don't care about nice clothes and shoes. I knew you wasn't from here by the way you dressed." I laughed because she was smooth and I realized that she had been around the block by the way she perceived the difference in mannerisms between men from different regions.

I said, "Yeah, you're right. I'm not from here. I'm from Philly." She barely let me finish before she interrupted me and said, " I been there. And oh my God! Philly has this shoe store there called Head-Start that is the bomb!"

That was it. That reference confirmed what I had assumed about Lex. She was a former drug bunny, drug dealer's girlfriend. Any sista who knew about Head-Start and wasn't from Philly had only come to know about it after being sent for and taken shopping after arriving, tell-tale signs and signature of a hustler. In my earlier years I too had flown many pretty out of towners to Philly and always made it a point to stop at that spot.

It was mandatory, especially if you wanted to ensure that your female guest would reciprocate your kindness with a little specialized kindness of her own. Lex and I continued our conversation with renewed vigor after discovering we had much in common. As far as I was concerned, all I could hear was "blah, blah, blah," mixed with an occasional giggle. Although I didn't let on, I wasn't interested in anything she had to say unless it related to sex.

Ten more minutes passed and I decided it was time to swap numbers and send her on her way. There was still a lot of night left in the club, and I wanted to book at least three more before the night ended. Lex and I exchanged information, and she surprised me by asking what I was doing later. She looked up at me and said, "I haven't eaten anything today, and I shouldn't be drinking on an empty stomach."

The sound of the music faded as my mind drifted to thoughts of late night sexcapades with this woman who was obviously a natural. My daydream was interrupted by Vic who had walked up as Lex and I finished our conversation.

"Damn, nigga. I see you don't fuck around 'cause that bitch be shootin' niggas down like it ain't nuffin. I seen her standing over here wit-choo for bout thirty minutes. Whachoo say to the ho that got her all excited and smiling and shit like she 'bout to bungy jump!" Vic didn't let me answer him and went straight into saying, "All Ima tell you, playa, is watch yo back with that ho man 'cause she only mess wit ballers. I bet she ain't tell you she used to dance at Magic City did she? The ho's stage name used to be Indigo." No sooner than Vic made the comment about Lex did I remember that I had seen her there and remembered her body was slammin.

****

"Dana, just come on. I told you I was going to pay your way in." Dana was fumbling through her purse as if she was really going to pay her own way in the club. I hated dealing with her sometimes because she overdid it. We had been standing in line for the last thirty minutes, and the whole time Dana was smiling and flirting with every guy she saw pull up in a nice car.

It was so obvious that I was sure the guys knew it, but they didn't seem to care much. By the time she finished with all of her smiling and prancing around she had three different men promising to buy us drinks once we were inside the club. I didn't want to be bothered by any of them and made sure Dana knew not to include me in any blind date seeking "dynamic duo" hoping to meet "the girl friend of the girl friend."

Lina was supposed to be meeting us, but I had a feeling she wasn't going to show. She lived all the way in Douglassville, and I couldn't see anybody driving from there all the way to Stone Mountain just to have a few drinks. When we walked in the club Dana and I both went straight into the ladies' room. We had been standing in line so long that I was sure I needed to fix my hair, and makeup. Dana definitely did; her hair looked a mess.

Now, don't y'all go judging me, thinking I am one of those friends who wouldn't tell her girlfriend her shit ain't right. I did tell her that her kitchen was dirty. Dana just didn't give a damn! She had no problem coming to the club with a kitchen do. If she liked it then I loved it! Harriston's was in full swing when we emerged from the ladies' room. The whole place had a lounge feel to it. Men in suits, women wearing dresses and slacks—I felt at home.

The DJ had just started playing *"Joy and Pain"* by Maze featuring Frankie Beverly and was mixing the hell out of it. It made me want to get on the floor and dance away some of my pain. I needed a drink first. I had promised myself that I was going to loosen up, and loosen up is what I was going to do. I looked around to tell Dana I was headed to the bar, but she was not to be found.

I made my way to the nearest bar without her, feeling somewhat relieved I wouldn't have to order for two. I leaned onto the bar and beckoned the bartender to come my way. When he got to me I had already had my mind made up and ordered a glass of chardonnay. It always relaxed me, and I was all too anxious to get there. He smiled as he handed me the glass. I reached in my purse to pay for it and he extended his hand in a stopping motion, like a crossing guard preventing me from completing the attempt, and pointed to the end of the bar and said, "Compliments of the gentleman standing at the end of the counter." It was Glenn!

He stood there with his drink raised smiling ear to ear. I couldn't tell if I was smiling or not because my stomach was doing flips and my mind was in a thousand places at once. Glenn started walking in my direction. I felt like I was beginning to sweat, and I didn't want to seem nervous. Flash backs of the night we met started playing in my head, and I began to feel a pleasantness envelope me. It might have been the drink—I had all but slammed it when I saw Glenn standing at the end of the bar. Just as before he was smooth and confident, and when he spoke I almost melted.

"Hey, I didn't know that was you standing here. I thought you were just another pretty face." He smiled as he pretended to be enthralled with my looks.

I on the other hand stood there thinking, "Nigga, if you thought I was so damn pretty then why haven't I heard from you?" I knew Glenn's type, the kind that has so many women he can hardly keep up with them all. And when he does find the time, he feeds them all the same bullshit, hoping they can't see through it.

Every part of me wanted to ask him why he didn't call, and why he didn't give me his number, but I knew better and didn't dare expose my vulnerable side to him. He didn't deserve it—no man did.

Instead, I surprised him and went in my purse and handed him two twenty-dollar bills and a ten and said, "By the way, thanks for rescuing me and my boys that night. I really appreciated it." He stood there and cocked his head to one side the way most dogs do when they're confused and are trying to understand their masters. It was uncanny the way Glenn did it because he looked just as confused.

"What's this for? That money I gave you was for you to keep," he said as he tried to hand it back to me.

I stopped him and pushed his hand away and said, "No, I only took it from you that night because it was an emergency. Besides you could probably do something nice for your nieces with it."

Glenn smiled nervously and looked around. Although he didn't say it, I realized he didn't want to be seen taking money from a woman. He stuffed it in his pocket hurriedly and returned to his phony story starting with, "I was going to call you today."

I looked at him as he continued. I was thinking he must really be used to dealing with a bunch of airhead hoochies who go for crap like that, so caught up on his looks that their brains stop working at the mere sound of his words.

"So how you been anyway? It's really good to see you. Damn, you look nice in that dress."

I knew I did. I was waiting to catch him looking at my cleavage, but he didn't seem to pay it much mind. I did however notice that

171

his eyes constantly wandered down to my ass. "Thank you, Glenn. But if I look so nice in this dress then why are you only looking at the back of it?" He laughed and the only thing that stopped him from turning red was the fact he was as dark as the chocolate on a Snicker's bar. His smile was refreshing, and I was happy as hell to see him though. I wanted him to grab me on the next slow song and pull me on the floor.

Dana had made her way back over to us and stood between us and looked Glenn up and down like she wanted to eat him alive. I tapped her on the shoulder and cleared my throat and said, "Excuse me, but we were in the middle of a conversation, Dana."She stuck out her hand and said, "Hi, I'm Dana. What's your name?"

I couldn't get mad at her because before we came to the club I told her if she saw anyone talking to me to come and step between us because I was only out to have a drink and didn't want to be bothered by none of them niggas that night. Dana thought Glenn was just another nigga until he said, "Hi Dana, I'm Glenn."

Dana had just taken a sip of the white zinfandel she was holding and damn near choked as Glenn finished introducing himself. She was hacking so badly that he put his hand on her back and patted it gently and asked, "Are you okay?"

Embarrassed Dana responded, "I…I'm alright."

She turned to me and frowned and mumbled, "You could have stopped me before I made a fool of myself. Why you ain't tell me you was talking to Glenn?"

I was laughing the whole time and could barely stop to say, "I tried but you were trying to be so sexy, I just let you go on." In the midst of all that comedy, the DJ slowed things down and put on *"If This World Were Mine"* by Luther Vandross. Glenn must have read my mind when he grabbed my hand and led me to the floor. When we got there he gripped me tightly around my waist and pulled me in close to him. His breath was cool and mint fresh with a hint of orange. As he talked I leaned in closer, both to listen and to continue to smell his sweet breath.

"So what was all that about? Your girl seemed like she was trying to throw herself on me or something." Even though Dana was doing what I had asked, she was also truly attracted to Glenn. The aggression in her approach confirmed it. I shifted the focus from

Dana's overzealous action to our present circumstance.

"Don't pay her no mind. I just think she had too much to drink tonight."

Glenn accepted my explanation and leaned into me and said, "Damn if I knew that you felt this nice I would've grabbed you that night at the concert."

I said, "I'm glad you didn't because my boys would've definitely told their father."

Glenn laughed and looked in my eyes and said, "Somebody need to tell that nigga something 'cause he fucked up. Ain't no way you should be single looking this good." The song seemed to last forever. It was like we were standing still and the whole place had disappeared. I was glad I came out. In Glenn's arms I felt that I had found salvation, I and quietly drifted off into oblivion.

My dreamy haze was interrupted by some chick who came out of nowhere onto the floor and tapped Glenn on the shoulder and said, "Glenn, I'm leaving but I want you to call me when you leave so we can go to breakfast." I swear I heard the needle on the turntable do that scratch thing as if somebody bumped the turntable and all the music stopped.

I don't know if Glenn knew her personally, or if she was just some bitch trying to steal my glory, but he played her like the bitch she was saying, "Whoa, sis don't you see me out here dancing? I got your number and I know how to reach you. Dig yourself though. You disrespecting this young lady I'm dancing with."

After that he turned his back on her without giving her a chance to respond and left her standing there looking like a fool. A few people in our immediate area knew what had happened and they all snickered as the girl eased her way off the floor feeling as if she was only an inch high. Glenn danced with me for the rest of the night, and by 2:00 am I was ready to go.

I wanted to take him with me but I wasn't about to proposition him. Little did he know all he had to do was offer breakfast or whatever, and I would have instantly said yes. He didn't and I guess it was just as well. I was feeling vulnerable and the Lord only knows what would have happened had I joined him. He walked us out to the valet and waited with me until the valet brought our car, and he even paid for the service.

As he closed the door and watched us pull off, I could hardly wait before I looked over to Dana and let out a small scream and said, "I feel like Cinderella!"

Dana responded, "He was cute. Does he have any friends?"

I didn't respond and instead thought, "As if they would really be interested in you." C-103 was playing the slow version of Aaron Hall's old song *"Don't Be Afraid."* I drifted off again, back to the place where I was when I was dancing with Glenn and blissfully floated up the highway.

Chapter Thirty
One Nighter

At 2:30 am, the phone range. "Hello, is this Lex?"

"Yes, this is she. Who is this?" I knew that she knew who I was. she had just programmed my cell number in her phone and I know my name flashed when the phone rang. I played along, knowing she was probably irritated and embarrassed by what I'd said to her on the dance floor.

"This is Glenn from the club. I'm about to get some breakfast and remembered you said you wanted to get together and eat." Breakfast after hanging out at a club should be called Buttfest because that's all it is, a way to dispense with all of the customary pleasantries between two people who really want to fuck have to go through before they can officially get at it.

Lex and I both knew what we wanted, and she met me at the Waffle House at the intersection of Memorial and North-Harriston. I'd gambled when I dissed her in front of Tawanna the way I did. I didn't have a choice really and figured the only way to come out on top was to play big all the way through. Women respect confidence and arrogance—the latter in mild doses. Had I catered to Lex she would have gotten one up on Tawanna and very likely stood me up later, having been satisfied with conquering me through my acknowledgement of her.

On the other hand, I would have lost Tawanna, who would have viewed my lack of assertiveness as a sign of weakness and a window into my character. I learned a lot of hard lessons dealing with black women and was intent on mastering the game.

Lex respected my directness and didn't let it affect her choice to follow me home. When we got to 1660 Peachtree she came in and made herself comfortable. She pretended she was tired and immediately disrobed and climbed into bed. I on the other hand needed a little more time to bed down for the night. My suit needed to be hung up and my shoes put in the proper place. I cherished my wardrobe and took meticulous care not to allow my things to become worn or snagged by laying them across chairs or dropping them on the floor. When I finished hanging my things I emerged from the closet to see that Lex had dozed off clutching a pillow and lying on her stomach.

She'd grabbed one of my tee shirts and the bottom of it teased the curves of her ass and hips as it rested on the top of her rump. It was a picture of perfection! Vic mentioned that she used to dance, and I vaguely remembered her from Magic City. I thought to myself that if it were true then why in the hell wasn't she rich because her body was on point and I wanted in.

I crawled into bed beside her and tapped her gently on her back. She lifted her head, looked at me, sat up and took off her shirt, and laid back down. As she did so she leaned over to me and released my now throbbing manhood out of my boxers and greeted it with a kiss. Twenty minutes later, her thirst now quenched, she commented on my continued erectness. I was just as surprised, knowing that I had always been a one-and-done kind of cat. I guess the old saying is true, "Ain't no pussy like new pussy!"

Lex was pleased to see that I was still at attention and eagerly started to climb on top of me. I stopped her and reached in my nightstand for a condom. I wanted desperately to hit it raw, but I also liked living and was in no hurry to die. My resolve surprised her, and I could tell she was irritated by the break in momentum. I hurriedly put on the condom, as she attempted to mount me for a second time. This time her effort was successful, and she rode me until I'd had enough.

Right at the point of climax she hopped off, pulling the condom off at the same time and caught every ounce that tumbled out of me. I went to sleep after that, and awoke the next morning to see Lex up and in the mirror tending to her hair as she prepared to leave. I quickly looked around the apartment for anything that might have been missing, realizing that I didn't even know her last name. As she finished styling her hair and was about to walk out. I said, "Damn, baby, I don't even know your last name or what you do. Do you have a card or something?"

She smiled and said, "Yes. I am a mortgage broker," and handed me her card. It read Alex Whitherspoon and contained her complete contact info along with the address for her place of business. I wasn't taking any chances or being too careful in Atlanta. Years earlier at Club Michael's I got caught out by a Rolex bandit; that's what they called them back in the day—women who sized dudes up by the kind of jewelry they wore. I was no more than twenty when I got set up. It happened so fast I almost never knew what happened. She smiled at me; I bought her a few drinks; we left and went to breakfast; then we went back to a hotel, bringing my drink from the restaurant to the room. When we got there, I sat my drink down and went to the bathroom. I came out, took one sip, and woke up the next morning woozy, the way you feel when you hop off of a merry go round after it's been spinning real fast.

I looked around and the broad was gone and so was my money and jewelry. Luckily she didn't take my car, and I grabbed my keys and stumbled down the hallway of the hotel, looking much like I had cerebral palsy bumping into the walls and feeling nauseous. By the grace of God I made it to the hospital. As soon as I got there, I threw up all over the admissions counter and was rushed into emergency. They were never able to tell me what she'd put in my drink, but I never forgot the lesson—or did I? Cause here I was taking chances all over again.

I guess if Lex wanted to rob me she would've done it while I was asleep. So I guess my getting her information was just a subconscious process my mind concocted to put me at ease over dealing with something I couldn't have prevented if I'd wanted to. The thought of my recklessness frightened me and brought back memories of the past. Only this time I was lucky.

Truthfully, my constant quest for sex made it impossible to avoid the dangers of picking up stragglers. The lessons from the robbery so many years earlier made me realize that I should at least ask a few probing questions and look at their identification before bringing them home, a simple task that only required initiating a conversation about age and projecting a noticeably exaggerated response of disbelief no matter what age they claimed. It never failed, and they whipped out their driver licenses every time.

Chapter Thirty-One
Prince Charming

"Hello, Tawanna?"

"This is she. Who is this?"

"This is Glenn."

"Oh, hey Glenn. I see you finally decided to give me a call, huh?" Tawanna didn't know it, but I planned on doing a lot of calling. Seeing her at Harriston's that night reawakened my senses about her. I had forgotten how nice she looked when we met at the little Bow-Wow concert and now that I had reconfirmed what I had already knew, I was eager to embark upon a new mission, one that would include conquering her and moving on to the next one. The dress she was wearing the other night was still fresh in my mind, and I wanted to know what was inside it.

"I'm glad you called today, Glenn. My sister is having a dinner party and I told her all about you." I always liked the idea of being discussed and was eager to hear anything positive people had to say about me.

"What could you have possibly told her about me? We haven't had the opportunity to get to know each other."

Tawanna laughed as she said, "No, silly. I mean when I first met you and you helped me out that night. I told her how much of a gentleman you were and that I especially liked that you love children because you had your nieces with you that night." I smiled as I realized that I had unwittingly made a good impression. My intention that night was merely to lay the foundation for future possibilities, a way to establish credibility.

Unbeknownst to me Tawanna compared my actions to those of Prince Charming, and she likened herself to Cinderella. I was cool with that because it made my job easier, and I was happy to know one simple gesture had done the equivalent of three weeks worth of dating. Knowing the fickle nature of women, I realized it was imperative that I embark upon my mission immediately, before she had the opportunity to see me for what I was or what I had become—something far from Prince Charming. But by the time she discovered it I planned to be long gone.

"So what's the story with this dinner party? Do I have to wear a black tie and all that, or is it something I can come to in casual wear?"

Tawanna was noticeably pleased I had re-inquired about the function unsolicited, and responded excitedly, "I don't know how Corretta wants to do it, but I'll call you back later and let you know. I'm about to put on dinner for my boys right now."

I said, "Dinner, huh? Why don't you make enough for me?" Tawanna hesitated and I could see that my suggestion caught her completely off guard.

"Well, Glenn, I had only planned on making beans and franks, nothing spectacular."

I responded, "Baby, that's fine with me, I ain't picky." What I should have said was, "It don't matter what your making. All I want is a reason to come over and after that it's on!" I kept my thoughts to myself and followed up by saying. "Besides, I just want to have an opportunity to sit and talk with you face to face. After all, we never got the chance to explore each other's thoughts."

She responded, "We're doing that now, aren't we?"

I said, "Yeah, I guess you could say that, but I prefer to look you in your face while I delve into the recesses of your mind. That way I can see if your reactions are genuine and determine if you're feeling me and what I have to say." Tawanna didn't respond after that and I knew she was considering my suggestion. I wanted her to do more than consider it. I wanted her to accommodate me.

After a ten second pause she said, "Let me call my sister to see if she'll watch the boys, and we can just have the house to ourselves. I'll call you back in ten minutes. Okay?"

I responded, "Sounds like a plan. Just hit me back. I'll be waiting for your call." Tawanna tried as best she could to pretend as if she was unsure about letting me come over, but I'd remembered the way she reacted to me the night we'd seen each other at Harriston's. I knew from that night I had her in my the palm of my hands, and the only reason I didn't take her home with me was because I had plans on getting with Lex.

Tonight was her night, and I wasn't going to pussyfoot around about it. Ten minutes passed as I awaited her call, and like clockwork my phone rang. "Hello," I said. "Glenn, this is Tawanna. What time do you want to come?"

I looked at my watch and saw it was already seven. I wasn't doing anything and asked, "How long before you can have dinner ready?"

She responded, "That depends on what you want to eat. If you want something quick then you can be on your way. I did want to go to the market though."

I said, "Well, that's fine with me. Why don't you do that, and call me when you get back home, and then I'll be on my way."

Tawanna said, "Okay, I'll give you the directions when I call you back."

I smiled, happy to see that she managed to accommodate me on such short notice, and asked, "What kind of wine do you like?" I'd remembered she was drinking a chardonnay the night I saw her at Harriston's, but I didn't want to bring the wrong kind as I didn't know what she was going to make for dinner.

She must've been thinking the same thing and said, "Don't worry about bringing anything. Just let me take care of everything. All you need bring is yourself, and everything else will be taken care of."

I was happy to hear that she was a take-charge woman and relished the thought of dealing with someone who wasn't going to be dependent on my money or me. I ended up getting to her house around 10 pm, not because I was late but because she kept putting me off each time I called to be on my way. When I got there she opened the door, and I entered her place.

As I walked in the lights were dim, and candles provided the only light in the place. She grabbed my hand and led me to the dinning room where I saw the reason for her delaying my arrival. I could hardly believe my eyes. I had come expecting nothing more than baked chicken and broccoli and maybe some mac & cheese. Instead, I felt like I had just been seated at a gourmet buffet, and she was the grand hostess. From the time I got there she catered to me incessantly.

I knew I was in for a spectacular night when she brought out a platter filled with and assortment of cheeses, grapes, kiwi, slices of cantaloupe and honeydew melon topped off with jumbo chocolate-covered strawberries. She went into the kitchen and came back carrying two chilled wine glasses and filled them to the rim with Martini & Rossi Asti Spumanti. The layout was spectacular, and the colorful assortment of fruits was barely overshadowed by the beautiful flowers that adorned the center of the table.

I was surprised I'd even noticed them, but the spread was so impressive I was obligated to acknowledge them. "Damn, where'd you get these flowers from? The color in them is so robust that they look like they were dipped in paint."

Tawanna smiled, swaying side-to-side and trying to contain the euphoric feeling that was quickly bubbling inside her. "I was hoping you'd notice them. I like that you pay attention to things, Glenn. That says a lot about you." My compliment excited Tawanna so that she got up and grabbed the appetizers from the table announcing, "I'm ready to serve dinner."

She didn't seem to care I was still in the process of stuffing my face with grapes and cheese. I squirreled a few more pieces of fruit into my mouth and took a man-sized gulp of Spumanti as she carried the tray back into the kitchen. When she re-emerged I was surprised to see her carrying a large serving dish containing two gigantic lobsters garnished with deveined shrimp, Top Neck cherrystone clams, and mussels. It was a smorgasbord.

I sat up thinking, "Sis knows how to get it down!" The last time I saw a spread like the one she produced was during an excursion to Caesar's Palace in Atlantic City where they provided a complimentary, all-you-can-eat buffet and hotel room to their Caesar's club members. That night I felt as if I was a member of Tawanna's my-future-man club because I knew that was the only reason she had pulled out all the stops.

I didn't mind. I knew what I was there for, and the meal was just an added perk. I gorged myself on the lobster and filled any remaining space in my stomach with shrimp and clams. Tawanna had prepared corn on the cob as well as wild rice. I had barely touched the sides as I'm a meat eater. The taste of the lobster saturated with butter almost made me forget the real reason I'd come.

Immediately after finishing the meal I was ready to lie down and let some of the food that now occupied my belly digest. I got up from the table and wobbled over to the sofa, flopping down as my legs collapsed beneath me. Tawanna followed closely behind me, bringing yet another sampling of delicacies—german chocolate cake with coconut walnut icing and another glass of spumanti.

"Glenn, you have to try this recipe. I got it from Corretta and I want you to taste it to see if I made it right." I looked at her face and it was glowing with the kind of satisfaction one gets when all is right with the world. I didn't have the heart to tell her that I'd had enough, and instead silently told myself I would have just one bite, and that would be all.

"Just give me a little piece, baby. I don't know if I can stand much more of anything else."

She smiled and said, "Okay, whatever you don't eat, I'll wrap up for you to take with you if you lea…I…I mean when you leave." We both looked at each other and laughed, knowing exactly what she meant. After the chuckling stopped we both slumped back into the sofa. Tawanna, despite my telling her not to, continued to feed me more chocolate cake until I gently pushed her hand aside.

As if on cue she got up, gathered the plate, silverware, and now empty champagne glass from the table and took them back into the kitchen. Shortly after she returned, she sat back down and grabbed the remote control to the stereo and the lights on the receiver appeared as if by magic. I noticed the tuner was set to Magic 104.1. The sound of the Isley Brother's song *"Choosey Lover"* floated out across the room.

She leaned backward onto me and looked up into my eyes saying, "So Uncle Glenn, tell me more about you." While we were dining she had managed to get me to utter a few words here and there between the forkfuls of food that I shoveled into my mouth. I'd already told her I was single, and she knew I didn't have any children.

We talked about other things she felt it pertinent to ask, like if I was gay or bi-sexual, to which I answered, "No." My response was casual, and I noticed she looked directly into my eyes while I was answering, as if looking for certain pantomimes that would contradict my statement. I wasn't worried about it and confidently waited for the next question she directed to me.

"Have you ever been married?" I paused after that question, not because I had to think about it or anything like that, but because I didn't really understand the nature of her line of questioning.

I realized later it was because Tawanna had big plans for me. Little did she know my plans for her were just as big, only they weren't going to involve anything long term. I didn't want to sit and play fifty questions all night and instead said, "I see where this is going, and I tell you what. How 'bout I just run down everything I think you'd be interested in knowing." She smiled at me, realizing that the question and answer session was taking its toll on me.

Truthfully, I didn't mind the questions she asked. I was impressed by her concern and appreciated the quality of character she displayed in asking. We had been sitting and talking for about an hour when she stopped and very seriously said, "Glenn, I have never been with another man other than my husband. We had been married for eleven years and had been together all through high school. What do you think about that?"

My immediate thought was "Shit, if it's true then that's definitely a good thing, depending on how you look at it." I almost said what I was thinking, but I knew it would probably have put a damper on whatever route the night might take. The knowledge of it also made me uncomfortable because it meant one of two things: either she was telling me because she wasn't trying to be with anyone but her husband, or she chose me and I would now have to indoctrinate her in the ways of love with a different man.

As I pondered over what reason Tawanna had for mentioning what she did, all of my thoughts suddenly shifted to the uneasy feeling that was now present in my gut—I had got the bubblies. Out of nowhere my stomach was turning flips and making subtle noises as if an eruption was imminent. I began sweating and started shifting my weight from one side to the next trying as hard as I could to keep the pressure off of my colon.

After about ten minutes of that, I realized there was nothing I could do to prevent the impending disaster. My mind raced as I tried to figure out a way to exit gracefully and find my way to the nearest bathroom. By now my stomach was churning like I had just eaten a double scoop of butter pecan ice cream, a bite of ex-lax, and swallowed a tall glass of milk! I wondered if the sweat that I felt beading up on my forehead was visible to Tawanna.

I couldn't believe that this shit was happening and just when I had laid my plan out so perfectly. "You know what baby? I think I should go." Tawanna looked at me stunned, trying to figure out what on earth could have caused me to want to exit from her pres-ence so abruptly. If I'd known her better I would have just told her what the problem was, but I didn't and wasn't about to take the chance of turning her off so soon after we'd just gotten started. If I had used her bathroom, by the time I would've finished the people from FEMA would have come and designated it as a disaster area.

"Glenn, why are you leaving so suddenly like this? Is everything alright?" I hesitated before answering her.

"I just remembered I have a few things I have to do tonight before it gets too late."

Tawanna looked at the clock on her wall and it read 1 am. She looked back over at me in disbelief saying, "Well, okay, if you're sure everything is alright. Then just call me when you get home so I'll know you made it." I know she was really thinking, "Nigga you got some shit with you!" If she was she wouldn't have been that far off 'cause if I didn't get out of there soon the shit would've been on me.

"Listen, I really have to go, but dinner was incredible and I enjoyed the evening." The words poured out of my mouth as if I was interviewing for lead auctioneer at Sotheby's Auction house in New York. Tawanna was still standing in the doorway after I hugged her and walked to my truck clinching my butt like I knew something was about to fall out of it.

She called me on my cell once I was in the truck but I couldn't answer it. If I had I would've lost the concentration I so desper-ately needed to keep from having an accident on myself. I got home in less than ten minutes, and she lived thirty minutes away. She never knew what devilment I had planned that night; I guess it was just as well. If what she said about being a virtual virgin were true, I would have plenty of time to stake my claim as the second man to enter into uncharted territory.

I couldn't help wondering about the way things happened that night; if they were meant to turn out that way, or if it was just a fluke occurrence. Either way, Mother Nature decided that night wasn't the right night and unceremoniously postponed my planned activities indefinitely.

Chapter Thirty-Two
Choosey Lover

I spent the next several weeks playing my position with Tawanna. I didn't have a choice. Getting her to part her legs turned out to be harder than Chinese arithmetic. She had already taken to treating me as Prince Charming, and after that memorable night at her place she began to think that maybe I was the one.

She had no idea the only reason I had made a break for the door was because of the eruption that was brewing in my stomach; instead, she thought I was gentlemanlike by choosing to leave without putting the moves on her. It didn't matter anyway because she was acting as if she had no intention of breaking bread. I was confused about it, though, because the night at Harriston's I would've sworn she was feeling me and ready to do whatever I wanted had I just asked. Now she was acting like sex was the furthest thing from her mind.

She didn't seem to mind spending time though. That was her thing. I was truly thankful for a weekday, which was the only time I caught a break. She kept our weekends booked. If we weren't going to a concert at Chastain Park, then it was daylong trips to Lake Lanier, and those were the local venues. I wouldn't let her make plans for anything that required we leave town together. I wasn't about to pay for a weekend stay anywhere until I knew for sure that it was going to be an adventure.

She tried once and even offered to pay. I almost felt bad when she asked me because I knew the answer was going to be no. "Glenn, have you heard of this place called Chateau Elan? It's supposed to be very romantic. A few of my girlfriends went for a wine tasting, and they all said it was serene and relaxing. The whole place is surrounded by botanical gardens with woods and manicured shrubbery. They have horseback riding and all sorts of outdoor activities. I hear it's a very popular honeymoon spot."

Truthfully, Tawanna almost had me until she added the part about it being a popular honeymoon spot. Those words reminded me that I was no-longer playing fair, and going to Chateau Elan for the weekend would've been a serious violation and contradiction of my newly adopted credo: "Women are fickle and are not to be taken personal!" Tawanna was nice and all, but I still hadn't gotten over what Tina did to me and wasn't about to betray myself by letting myself get caught up with another fickle ass female.

Not to mention the fact that going would've meant I would also be stuck with one woman for the entire weekend, and that wasn't going to happen. Admittedly, dealing with Tawanna almost made me forget that I was in it for me and only me. I'd been giving her much of my time, and we were actually on our way back from yet another dinner date. The fact that we hadn't had sex yet didn't really bother me. I had other friends to keep me busy.

When I did stay at her place it was only because she lived so far up I-85 that after dinner, movies, or concerts, driving all the way back downtown made the whole thing seem like a marathon. I didn't know it, but spending the kind of time we were spending with one another began to have a very strong effect on Tawanna. She sprung it on me one day out of the blue.

"Glenn, I want to share something with you. Remember when I told you I had never been with another man other than my husband? Did you believe me?" I didn't know what to think or why she was asking me that question, but I decided to be honest and answered her.

"Truthfully, not initially, but after having dealt with you this long, I can see how it could be true. What made you ask me though?"

She responded, "I just wondered mostly and because I had wanted to sleep with you the night I saw you at Harriston's and was hoping you were going to offer to take me to breakfast, but you didn't." I smiled because I knew she was on me that night and was glad to see that my instincts weren't wrong. I couldn't help wondering, "If she was on me so strong that night, then why hadn't she shared the wealth by now?" I decided to ask and get it over with.

"Well, damn. If you were feeling me all like that, then why you been acting all distant since then?"

She looked at me and smiled before saying, "That night at my house, after we ate dinner—I was impressed by the way you left. At first I thought you must have had other plans, but then I gave you the benefit of the doubt because of the way you treated me at the concert."

I sat there feeling like my mouth was wide open and subtly

stroked my chin to make sure it wasn't and thought, "Ain't that a bitch!" She was following what she thought was my lead. I wanted to tell her so bad that it was all a mistake and my actions were first a strategy, and then a fluke. I almost blurted it out before realizing it wouldn't have made any difference. I was still in like Flynn. She was just trying to show me she was a good girl and I had to respect that. Deep down I believed there may very well have been some truth to her story about being a pseudo-virgin.

After I finished kicking my thoughts around in my head a few more times, I realized that I had almost forgotten that she had just admitted to wanting me. Hoping that the moment wasn't gone I said, "The way you felt that night at Harriston's, was it only for that night, or do you still feel that way?" She answered my question by leaning over and gently kissing me on my cheek. As I drove up the highway she went from my cheek to my neck, then down to my chest and stopped just long enough to unbutton my jeans.

As my foot danced on the gas pedal I wondered, "What in the world was wrong with that Kevin cat? Because Tawanna was definitely a keeper!" By the time we arrived at her house, I thought for sure we were going to be pulled over by the police after all of the swerving that I was doing. I parked the car and we both got out, only I was out of it. My knees felt like they were made of rubber and I could barely make my way to the door.

Tawanna on the other hand was as vibrant as a little girl playing double-dutch on a cool spring day. "When we get in the house I want you to stay in the living room while I go and freshen up for you. Okay?" I was fine with that and wondered if I would be able to keep from falling asleep on the couch before she even had time to do anything. I stayed up, though, because I knew that night was my night. Fifteen minutes passed before Tawanna called to me, telling me to come into the bedroom. I could barely walk as I made my way to it because all of the lights were off and I was unfamiliar with the layout of her apartment.

I finally made it after she got up and grabbed my hand and guided me to the bed. "I'm sorry. I should've lit a candle or something." I wasn't upset by it and just wanted to get out of my clothes and crawl into bed. It was dark in there and since I didn't know where anything was, I reluctantly left my things on the floor—after folding them that is.

"Glenn, come over here." Tawanna's bed was a California King size and it was huge. Finding my way over to her took all of three seconds, but once I got in range she reached out, grabbed me, and started kissing me ferociously. As she did so I began to feel on her body and noticed she was wearing a sports bra of some kind and had a scarf wrapped around her head. I reached to grab the back of her head, and she moved my hand away, but not before I had a chance to touch the top of it. It felt strange and lacked the density her hairstyle suggested. I didn't think anyhing of it and continued with my objective.

When I reached to touch her chest she did the same thing again, gently moved my hand from the area. I didn't really care and had only ventured to her breast area for her benefit. I was happy to see that I wouldn't have to waste time playing with body parts that didn't contribute to my pleasure. I didn't know what to do after all of that though and became slightly apprehensive about my next move. I didn't expect for things to go the way that they were going and didn't have a condom. So after kissing and rolling around in bed for a while, I rolled over on my back.

As soon as I did I felt Tawanna's hand reaching down between my legs. She began to fondle me. Before long I felt her fingers lifting the elastic band from my underwear as she pulled them off my body. I was rock hard but didn't allow myself to become anxious because I knew I didn't have a condom. If anything was going to happen I figured she was going to take care of that part. Otherwise, all she would be able to do would be to resume her activity from the car. She didn't. I don't know how it happened, but the next thing I knew she was sitting on top of me riding like she was a cowboy, and I was the black stallion.

I hesitated and started to stop her, but she felt so good all I could do was drift off, hypnotized by the feeling of her now twice touched pleasure box. I woke up the next morning and saw that the bedroom door was closed, and I could hear the rustling of several people in the outer rooms. I heard one adult and two children. Tawanna entered the bedroom, and I noticed the scarf was gone and her hair was styled exactly as it had been the night before. The curls hadn't dropped, it was full of body, and sat robustly on her head like a lion's mane.

I immediately flashed back to when I touched her scarf, and

realized there was no way what I touched last night was the same as what I was now looking at. I also noticed that she was wearing a sports bra, and her chest was picture perfect, and I wondered why she didn't allow me to touch her during all of the heated passion we exchanged. She walked over to my side of the bed and said, "Good morning. I fixed breakfast. Do you want something to eat?"

I didn't answer her question, and instead launched a series of my own. "What was all that noise I heard earlier?" Tawanna laughed. She could see the concern in my face as I asked the question. "That was the boys and the sitter. She was helping me get them ready for school and offered to take Taylor for me."

I sat up stretched and said, "Why didn't you tell me we weren't alone last night? I would've been a little quieter."

Tawanna smiled and said, "I was the one making all the noise, so I don't know what you talking about." We both laughed because she was right. I don't know how those boys or the sitter slept through all of rustling and moaning that went on. I even had to put my hand on her mouth a few times during intercourse.

I stretched again and stood up asking, "Is everybody gone because I have to pee?" Tawanna nodded and I stood up naked and walked to the bathroom. I came out and she was standing near the doorway smiling from ear to ear and holding a large plate of food that contained fruit, waffles, eggs, and bacon. I hesitated before taking it from her hands remembering the last time I ate here. I figured everything would be cool since it was morning and I would be on my way home within the next hour or so.

"Would you like some orange juice?" Tawanna handed me the plate and turned in a sweeping motion headed toward the kitchen to retrieve the orange juice. As she did so her arm brushed the stem of the fork, knocking it to the floor.

"Oh, my goodness, Glenn. I'm sorry. Here let me get you another one."

I said, "Don't worry about it. I'll just kiss it up to God, and it'll be all right." I reached down to grab the fork, and my eyes met up with a pair of the ugliest feet I think I have ever seen. They were large and each had a protruding bunion. I think there may have been a few corns but I turned away so quickly that I can't remember. I was scared that if I looked at them any longer I would've turned to stone.

I stood back up immediately and put the fork back on the plate and handed it to her. My appetite was gone. There was no way I could stomach anything after seeing what I had just seen. I was polite about it though. There was no need to hurt her feelings by telling her what the true problem was. After all I wasn't trying to marry her.

"Glenn, are you all right? You seem a little squeamish."

I wanted to say, "You hit the nail on the head."

Don't worry. I didn't. Instead I said, "I must've bent down too fast because my head is spinning and I feel nauseous." She pulled out one of the dining room chairs and forced me to sit down thinking that it would help. I kept my head tilted upward so as not to mistakenly glimpse her feet again. I liked Tawanna, but seeing her feet was turning me off. I don't know why, but since my breakup with Tina I had begun to physically compare virtually every woman I dated to her physical attributes. And they all were failing miserably.

Last night's episode with Tawanna was nice, and I wasn't going to let the sight of her feet prevent me from enjoying her special pleasures and decided going forward I wouldn't look down.

Chapter Thirty-Three
Secret's

"Glenn, remember the dinner party I told you my sister was having?"

I remembered Tawanna mentioning it and responded, "Yeah, but you never told me when it was."

Tawanna said, "I know because she hadn't ironed out all the details. The party is going to be at her house, and it's a surprise for her husband's birthday, and I want you to be my date, will you?"

Tawanna had been trying to get me to meet her sister for weeks. I didn't mind the thought of it. I just wasn't too keen on driving forty miles up the road to Suwanne to do it. I thought of how good Tawanna's dinner was and figured if her sister was anything like her, then dinner would be definite treat.

"Dinner sounds like it might be nice. Yeah, I'll be there, but when is it?" Tawanna smiled a big Kool-Aid smile and said, "It's Monday August 14th and don't worry, you can ride with me so you won't have to drive all the way out there by yourself."

I said, "Good because you know I hate those Henry County assholes. They act like they stuck in the 1960s the way they try to intimidate black people, especially cats they catch driving nice cars."

Tawanna was elated and opened the lid to her cell phone and immediately called Corretta, informing her to include an extra table setting for the party. After she got off the phone with her sister she gazed at me and said, "Glenn I have something I want to tell you. It;s very important that you listen to me. I've wanted to tell you for a while now. What I am about to say is something that I have never told anyone outside of my family and close friends." I could see whatever Tawanna wanted to say to me was obviously very serious. The way she prepped it made me feel awkward. I wondered why she wanted to tell me anything ultra-personal. We weren't a couple, and I wasn't feeling her like that.

It wasn't like we'd lie in bed after sex and I'd confess my feelings for her. Hell, there were none to confess. "Glenn, are you listening to me?"

I laughed and said, "Yeah, I heard you. Just make sure you don't tell me you used to be a man or something 'cause that would be a problem."

Tawanna broke into laughter at what she thought was an attempt to make her feel more comfortable about what she was about to say. Little did she know I was serious as hell.

A lot of strange people inhabit Atlanta, and you never can tell who's who, bi-sexual men and women, gay men who dress as women, some who have even had operations to make the transformation complete. I had a legitimate concern, having once encountered a transsexual during my early days in Atlanta. Luckily a friend noticed my interest and stopped me before I had an opportunity to make a fool of myself. Ever since then, whenever I see a tall, incredibly attractive female, I look first at her Adam's apple, and then at the size of her feet. After seeing Tawanna's feet I didn't know what to expect but was prepared for anything.

"Glenn, I don't know if you noticed or not, but the reason I never let you touch my breasts when you reach for them is becau..." Tawanna stopped mid-sentence and looked away. She rocked and shifted the way a bashful child does when put on the spot. I wasn't sure what the big deal was and didn't really care what she was about to say as long as it wouldn't affect our now thrice weekly sexual activities.

I sensed what she was trying to say to me was making her uneasy and asked, "Are you alright? Because if you need to sit down or something we can go in the house." We had been standing in the parking lot of my apartment complex. Why she chose that location to spring all of what she was trying to say was beyond me. The fact that I wasn't really trying to hear any of it didn't help.

Earlier that day she asked if she could come and spend the night. She'd also informed me she had picked up a few items for my apartment, offerings I'm sure she felt would grant her instant access to 1660 Peachtree, and she was right. "What's the matter with you? Why you standing there looking off into space like that Is what you have to say that important to make you trail off and zone out like that?"

"No, Glenn. I just don't know how to tell you this. I think I love you."

Now I was lost in a zone. I wasn't expecting to hear that and it floored me. I didn't want this girl feeling anything remotely close to love and not because I couldn't feel the same, but because

I didn't want to be responsible for anybody's happiness. I was lost in my thoughts thinking, "How in the hell was I going to get out of this one?" I was snatched back into reality when she followed up with another earthmoving statement.

"Glenn, I would cross the street in pouring rain with no umbrella with a new hairdo for you."

I leaned back on my truck thinking, "Aw wow, sis really got it bad!" Shit was getting serious, and I wanted to lighten the tension and said, "Stop playing. You don't love me; you love my doggy style." Tawanna laughed and I was relieved and thought maybe what she said was simply something to say. I stood stiff, hoping she didn't expect a response. I hated rejecting her love. It was nothing personal. I just didn't have it in me. I was still running around lost and wasn't sure if I ever wanted to be found.

We walked into the apartment after her heartfelt confession, and I was satisfied she told me all she wanted me to know. I was wrong again.

"Glenn, that wasn't what I wanted to tell you. I only said that to let you know what you mean to me so you could better understand why I was telling you what I'm about to tell you."

I wanted to say, "Please, no more. I can't take it." Truth is I didn't know what to say and was terrified by the thought of hearing something else I wasn't going to be able to handle. Sensing she was on a roll, I took control of the conversation and changed the subject saying, "How come whenever we have sex you always wear a scarf, and the next morning your hair never looks sweated out?" I didn't let her answer and followed my last question with, "Is that a wig?"

Tawanna's jaw dropped. She was completely taken aback by my observation. Flustered, she hesitated and started to deny it but stopped and told the truth. "Oh, my God, n... how did you know I'm wearing a wig?"

I knew it was a wig all along and laughed before saying, "I've paid for more hairdos than I care to mention. I have also dealt with a lot of women in my lifetime and know the difference between real hair, weaves, and wigs, too.

Tawanna let out a sigh of relief before saying, "Well, now that you've figured out part of my secret, I might as well tell you the rest of it. You probably noticed I always wear something to cover my chest, too." I didn't interrupt her and was actually a little irritated by my own perceptiveness, realizing that I provided her with the perfect segue to return to what she was originally trying to tell me. She looked deep into my eyes; the same way she had done the first night at dinner. She looked at me as if she was searching for refuge.

I don't know what she saw, but she hugged me tightly and buried her face in my chest saying, "Glenn, I have breast cancer and during chemotherapy and radiation treatment I lost my hair. That's why I always wear the scarf and special bra to bed." I didn't know how to react after that and felt horrible for not being able to return the feelings she had just expressed. I stood there holding her and felt her grip tighten around my waist, and I wondered what she was thinking; she no doubt was probably thinking the same about me.

There was a long silence after her second confession, and I searched my mind for the right thing to say. So many things about her attitude toward men, life, and herself instantly made sense. In that same instant I was immediately humbled by the strength that was now evident as I thought of all that she'd gone through. I wondered if I could've done the same. The thought of my motivation for dealing with her made me feel like a flea. I cursed myself for playing with her the way I had done. Here she was standing in the middle of my living room, pouring her soul out to me and all because she believed I was the one.

Chapter Thirty-Four
Silent Goodbyes

"Tawanna, are you sure your friend is going to show up? It's already seven and he was supposed to be here by six."

"I know it's seven o'clock already Corretta; I do have a watch and I know how to tell time."

I don't know what I was thinking when I expected Glenn to still be interested in coming to Corretta's dinner party. I had barely seen him in the month after I told him I had cancer. We went from seeing each other almost every day to once per week, once every two weeks, and ultimately to me calling and asking if any of our pre-planned excursions were still on schedule.

The news of my cancer must've been more than he could handle. I kind of saw the signs after he asked, "Can a person catch cancer from having unprotected sex?" I laughed when he said it. He sounded so juvenile when it came out, which was a surprise coming from him. I didn't have proof, but was pretty sure it was a virtual impossibility.

I looked at my watch to make sure it was actually 7 o'clock. I was surprised to see it was actually thirty minutes past. I had spoken to Glenn early that afternoon to confirm if we were still on, and he said yes. Just to be sure I reminded him that he was to meet me at my house so we could leave together and get there in time for dinner. I should have known he was blowing smoke when he said, "Just give me the directions now, and you go on without me and I'll meet you there."

I never thought Glenn to be the cowardly type, but I was beginning to see that he wanted to fade out of my life. I didn't have a problem with that. All he had to do was just tell me, and not play catcher's catch can. My thoughts were interrupted when I heard Corretta say, "Tawanna, I wanted to wait, but I'm going to go ahead and put dinner on the table. Julian is on his way home and I wanted all the invited guests to be present when he got here."

I took a deep breath and looked at Corretta and wondered what she thought about Glenn. I had praised everything about him, and now I was standing here with egg on my face, apparently stood up. Not long after Corretta set the table, Julian showed up and acted surprised. I could tell he knew something was up, but he played along earlier that day when Corretta sent him out on a thousand meaningless errands. I sat there with all of my friends and family pretending to be happy; in a way I was.

I loved Julian and all that he meant to my sister. I was happy that their lives had meaning. All the love that radiated between the two of them made me drift into flights of fancy, and thoughts of why things between Glenn and I hadn't materialized the way I'd planned. In the beginning everything seemed perfect. Even my boys liked him. Whenever he visited and they were there he would sit and play video games with them, and they loved it. Especially Preston. Glenn would always let him win.

My daydream faded as everyone finished dinner and gathered around Julian's birthday cake. Corretta lit the candles and instructed us all to sing happy birthday. I could barely remember the words because my mind was stuck on where Glenn was, and why he hadn't called to let me know why he wasn't here. I gave up hope as Julian blew out the last candle on the cake.

It was 9 o'clock and I had been secretly calling Glenn once every ten to fifteen minutes for the last two hours, and he wasn't answering his phone. My dejection turned to anger as I reflected on his thoughtlessness in leaving me to look foolish in front of my friends and family. If he didn't want to come, all he had to do was just say.

"What's up, baby-girl? I knew you and Corretta were up to something. Who's idea was it to send me on a wild goose chase to Home Depot looking for wild grass seeds?" Julian laughed at the thought of the mission we'd sent him on. Corretta sold him on the idea that Brandon needed to get grass seeds for a school project on the growth differences between wild grass and regular garden variety domestic grass.

"That was a good one. I would've been looking around all day if it wasn't for the attendant telling me there was no such thing and that wild grass was actually just weeds. Julian started laughing again and noticed that I didn't respond and wasn't paying attention. I was just staring out the window I a daze.

"What's wrong, baby-girl?" Julian was the only person I let call me that. He heard my Daddy call me that once back when he and Corretta first met and had been calling me that ever since.

I looked at him and didn't say anything. A tear welled up in my left eye and gently rolled down my cheek. I hurriedly brushed it away with my hand and said, "Nothing's wrong. I was just sitting here thinking how happy you and Corretta are and wondered if I was ever going to be happy again."

Part Two

Chapter Thirty-Five
Malik

Damn, I can't believe when I first got to Georgia I was only nineteen years old. I didn't have no car, no money, and no girls. The plan was to come live with my pops in Atlanta. Only thing was it wasn't Atlanta. It was some slow, country-assed town twenty-five miles east of Atlanta called Ellenwood.

Prior to arriving I had just come off of a banging Labor Day weekend at Virginia Beach that any other nineteen year old would have killed for. I went to Virginia as a kind of farewell tour with my friends who made sure I had a good time. They were all hustlas and each of 'em had been successful in the street game. They all wondered why I never wanted to be a part of the street game. Truth was, I thought about it from time to time. Who wouldn't? Fast money has a way of luring even the most straight dude into considering the fast life, but not me.

For as good as life could be when you're getting fast money, I also knew of the downside and had seen an equal number of my friends end up in jail or buried in South Philly graveyards. Going down south ensured my exclusion from the temptations the fast life exposed me to. Besides, I always believed that anything I wanted to keep would be something I had to work for. At least that way I would never have to worry about my life being turned upside down because of making the wrong choices.

In the beginning, life in Georgia was a bitch. Every day I would sit and patiently wait with my eyes glued to the clock anticipating my father's arrival. He would get home from work at 6:30 pm most days, but by 6:25 I knew he was near 'cause I could hear the rattle from the rusted exhaust pipe of his '85 Jeep Cherokee as he entered the driveway. The noise didn't bother me because no sooner as he entered the house I would speak, grab his keys, and hit the streets bound for Atl.

****

I had met Yasmine at Virginia Beach two weeks before I got to Atlanta. When we met, I told her I was moving to Atlanta and she told me she was going to be in Georgia too, attending to Spellman College. I was surprised to hear from her when I arrived in Georgia and my pop told me I had a message from a girl named Yasmine on the answering machine. I thought to myself that I would remember her forever because she was the first girl I met in Atlanta.

For some reason me and Yasmine bonded instantly. We were cool and would hang out from time to time. Since I had just arrived in Atlanta, I never really had any place to go and even less money. I would always meet Yasmine down at the campus and hang out. On days when the temperature got too hot to bear she would invite me to her dorm room to kick it and cool out.

I remember the first time I entered Yasmine's room. I noticed her walls were filled with posters of The Dr. I thought it strange that a female would be that interested in basketball, but I didn't ask no questions 'cause it wasn't my nature. As I settled in I noticed not only were there posters of the famous basketball player, she also had various photographs of him and her set throughout the room. Each photo contained him with Yasmine at different ages in her life. Then it hit me. Yasmine must be his daughter. All of a sudden her 5'11" height, her last name, and their uncanny resemblance confirmed that my assumption had to be correct. After a while she introduced me to her brother Julian. I initially wasn't interested in meeting him because I knew that he would be apprehensive about some dude dealing with his sister, but Yasmine introduced us anyway.

"J, this is Malik. He from Philly too."

I stuck out my hand and said "What's up?" Dude looked me up and down in a way that suggested he was curious about the relationship between his sister and me. Philly cats have a way of knowing without knowing who's cool vs. who's not. Julian knew I was a thoroughbred, and after what seemed like five minutes, he finally took my hand into his and acknowledged me saying, "What's up, ock?"—the Islamic word for friendship.

I could tell that he wasn't the spoiled rich kid type like most celebrity children are. He had a normal street appearance, and I found out later we knew a lot of the same people from back home. He was in Atlanta going to school as well, attending Clark University. As we stood there familiarizing ourselves with one another, I realized that meeting him was perfect for me because now I would have a reason to come to the AUC, not to mention being in the midst of all of the beautiful girls who went there.

We exchanged numbers and went our separate ways. As time went on I saw less and less of Yasmine and more of Julian. He had the inside tract on the party scene on campus and every weekend we would call each other for the scoop on the hottest party he had lined up for us to go to. And every weekend I would make it a point to plug in with him and hit as many of the parties we could. The floodgates had been flung wide open, and my social life in Atlanta had begun.

Chapter Thirty-Six
Keep on Trucking

"Wake up, Malik. Don't nothing come to a sleeper but a dream." As my pop yelled up stairs I hated thought of getting up. It was 5:30 am and cold as bitch outside. He had cosigned with me for a WesternStar Tandem dump truck. My pops was in the trucking business, hauling dirt, gravel, sand, etc. He had a lot of friends in the business and set me up nicely after I got my commercial driver's license. The only thing was I was having second thoughts about hauling dirt. I mean niggas like me don't do no shit like dat. If my homies from up top knew I was driving a dump truck, they would laugh at me every time they see me.

"Malik, get the hell up boy. I told you its time to get up!" We supposed be at the Morris Brown stadium job site by 6:30 am, and I want you to be there on time so I can show you where the truck routes are to the dump sites. Don't have me waiting there all day for you either!" By the time my pop finished ranting and raving at me to get up, I had barely rolled over. I looked at the clock and it read 6:00 am. I knew I was going to be late, and it was my first day.

By the time I got there I pulled up and parked my truck and saw my pop standing in a group of men whose ages ranged from 50 to 65 years. Each had been driving for 20 to 30 years apiece. As I approached them I began to ask myself, "What the fuck am I doing here?" I didn't see any one who was remotely close to my age and felt totally out of place. I found a position in the group and stood there as the conversation passed by several times until my pop introduced me as his son. Without missing a beat they all acknowledged me, and after a bunch of, "Hey theres, nods, and one 'howdy partner,'" they all went back to their conversation about a previous job.

Again, I felt like just leaving and going back home to Philly. Just as I had made up my mind to get in the truck and leave, my pop called to me and told me it was time to start. I followed him the first day and copied everything he did, and by the end of the day I realized all there was to it was simply driving from one site to another, loading and unloading dirt—very easy work. That went on for about a week. My pop never mentioned to me what the pay rate was going to be, and since I was so young I never bothered to ask, feeling secure that he would make sure I was taken care of.

I had no idea the term "taken care of" would have a whole new meaning for me. Friday came and my pops called me into his office and handed me my first check. I thanked him and walked out the door, anxious to run to the bank to cash it. When I arrived at the bank, I immediately opened the envelope and signed the back without even checking the amount. As I waited for the teller to hand me my money, she paused and asked me if I wanted all large bills. I looked at her believing she was talking to the person behind me and didn't answer. She asked again, "Would you like large bills?"

Surprised I responded "Who me?"

She laughed and said "Yes you."

Not wanting to look suspicious I responded, "Yeah, that's fine," thinking if I took any more time they would swear the check wasn't mine and all the while dying to ask her what the amount was for. As she counted off the bills I followed her count and thought I was seeing things because I finished my count at $2,400.00 even. There was no way that could have been right. When she handed me the money I squirreled it into my pocket and rushed out the door as if I had just robbed the place.

My heart was beating so fast I felt like I had just hit the number. All I could think was my pop must have made a mistake and gave me his check. I went to the nearest pay phone and called him. He had hardly said hello before I started telling him he had made a mistake and gave me his check instead of mine, an easy mistake considering I was his junior. He laughed calmly and told me to relax and that there was no mistake. I could barely form my next word, and all I could think to say was, "What?!"

He said, "I told you the job pays well, and that's why I had wanted you to get your commercial license when you turned eighteen so that I could bring you in."

I said, "Why didn't you tell me it paid like this before? I would have come down here and got on."

He responded by saying, "When you came I wanted it to be a surprise to you, and I didn't want you coming into the business for the money only. I wanted you to appreciate what goes into this business along with what comes out."

Chapter Thirty-Seven
Allen & Allen

Ever since I received my first paycheck from working with my pop, I knew that hauling dirt was going to end up being a good thing for me. The absence of glamour and glitz didn't mean a thing to me. The money I was making meant I could easily make up for all of the glory my profession lacked—and I made damn sure I would compensate for the difference. I spent a little more than a year and a half working for my pop's company, Allen & Allen Trucking.

During that time things went from good to spectacular. Right around my second year of trucking, my pop managed to secure a large portion of a major contract to begin the H.O.V. lane expansion of I-75. I had learned the ropes well enough for him to feel secure in letting me manage the day-to-day operations for various other contracts we worked throughout the greater Atlanta metropolitan area. I had even purchased two additional trucks and had drivers of my own. As good as things were going, nothing could've prepared me for the magnificent surprise that came my way after the lane expansion contract materialized.

"Malik, how much money you got saved up?"

I wasn't sure why my pop asked me that question. I knew it wasn't because he wanted anything from me. Instead of wasting time trying to analyze why he asked, I decided to simply answer the question. "I got about $76,000. Why?"

He paused and I noticed he frowned slightly and nodded his head at the same time—the way people do when they are pleasantly surprised. I was still unsure what his purpose was until he spoke. "I'm glad to see you've been saving your money. How are things working out with your drivers?"

I was surprised when he asked me that question because I never told him I had secured a few additional trucks or that I had subcontracted work of my own. He noticed I was hesitant and quelled my uneasiness by saying, "You don't have to be nervous. I knew about your little business venture the day after you got the trucks. Jack called me the minute you left his lot." I had bought the trucks from Jack, and now that I think about it, he was very friendly and gave me a real good interest rate on the purchase. Both of the trucks were used and about five years old, but in the trucking business a truck ain't cut its teeth until it's had least a good fifteen years on the road.

"I thought you'd remember, but I guess you didn't. You met Jack back when you were about twelve years old—the first summer you came down to visit. He and I used to be partners. He told me you stopped at his lot a week or so before you came and made the purchase. But don't worry. I didn't interfere with your deal. Watever it is, I let you cut your teeth on it." I was glad to hear that. I was equally glad to see he wasn't offended by my bold move. I had planned to tell him once I had gotten things flowing strong. I wanted to show him that was on my square. The truth was from the time I got my first check I never looked back.

Relieved he wasn't angry with me, I felt comfortable asking him his reason for inquiring. "If you knew all of that, why you just asking me about everything now?"

Pop laughed because he could see that he'd made me uncomfortable by the way he probed into my personal business. After he finished chuckling at me he said, "I chose not to say anything for a few months so I could see how well you did on your own. I've been watching you since then, and I am glad to see you haven't let me down. The reason I chose today to ask you about it was because I have a surprise for you."

He paused briefly, reached in his back pocket, and pulled out a folded piece of paper. As he unfolded it, he looked at me with a twinkle in his eyes. He knew he had made good, and what was good for him was especially good for me. "I know that ain't what I think it is, is it?!" Me and my pop had just had a conversation about how nice it would be if we could get in on the new lane expansion contract. The way he was looking at me and smiling, I knew that had to be it. I also knew it was paying big money that was expected to last a few years.

"Son, this is it, and I ain't talking about no barbeque either. With the kind of money this contract is going to bring in, we can both live life on the high side. I'd been thinking about retiring and now I will be able to do it." My pop was only forty-six, and as far as I could tell, he loved the trucking business. Announcing his plan for retirement came as a shock to me because I knew his business was thriving. Suddenly his reason for sitting back and quietly watching me do business became evident. Although he mentioned something about me taking over his business one day, I had no idea he was thinking one day soon.

When I first came onboard I could hardly stomach this business, but I quickly discovered if you stick with a plan everything falls right into place. In the midst of all the excitement and flights of fancy, my happiness subsided as the realization of Allen & Allen's operating capacity became apparent. Most of the contracts we maintained were relatively small, many of which typically lasted no more than four to six months and only required ten to fifteen trucks, a number we maintained comfortably.

I had heard scattered rumors about the big H.O.V. expansion contract the city of Atlanta was planning to issue to get the ball rolling. The rumor was that it was going to take a minimum of one hundred trucks to move all of the dirt that would be lifted from the site. Although Allen & Allen wouldn't be the only trucking company at the site, most of the other companies came with a compliment of at least twenty-five to thirty trucks in their fleets.

Compared to them, we had a fraction of the trucks they had, not to mention all of our pre-existing contractual obligations. If we weren't careful, we stood to lose money just from the perceived notion of breach of contract, something that could potentially cost us all of the few million we stood poised to earn. Still we couldn't miss an opportunity as big as this. The lane expansion was Mayor Bill Campbell's baby. Construction companies and haulers had been jockeying for a piece of it since it was first proposed. Rumor was the mayor was looking to get kickbacks from whichever company he selected to participate.

Well, I don't know what he expected from us, but one thing was for certain: Allen & Allen Trucking had gotten a piece of it. "Pop, how we gon get the machines to accommodate the contract?"

"I'm way ahead of you son. Once I found out we were approved for the contract, I leased twenty additional trucks. That was all I could do legitimately through Allen & Allen, but I want you to lease seven more under your own operation."

Confused, I put my hand on my head because I had barely made the deal with Jack to get the two I had already. "Pop, how in the hell am I going to be able to do that? My credit ain't like that, and besides I don't even have an actual company. Everything I do, I do under Allen & Allen."

My pop looked at me, shook his head, and said, "Boy, you worry too much. You don't think I thought that through? I already talked to Jack, and he said he wouldn't have a problem leasing the vehicles to you, but he wanted a $50,000 deposit before doing so. That's why I asked you what you had saved. I already spent my cash reserves leasing the twenty Tandems I just got. I know once you get the machines, the work would be nothing to handle. I even spoke to Marsha over at M.A.R. trucking just to make sure there would be work for the trucks if the highway contract slacked up. She assured me she would keep you afloat because she liked the way you handled your business."

It had been about four months since I made the purchase of my two trucks and about three months since I had gotten a contract of my own with M.A.R., an independent trucking company that subcontracted work regularly. I met the owner, Marsha, one day while hauling dirt from a M.A.R.T.A. project. She had come to the site after she had gotten word one of her drivers hadn't shown up after picking up his first load and had been missing for the better part of five hours.

At a rate of $50.00 an hour that meant he had just cost her $250.00. After watching her rant and rave over her numerous unsuccessful attempts to reach him on his two-way radio, I saw an opportunity presenting itself and decided I was going to grab it. "I got two trucks and two drivers I can have here in twenty minutes, and all your problems will be solved."

She looked at me, smiled, and said, "What's your name?"

I returned the smile and said, "Malik."

She said, "Nice to meet you Malik. I like your proposition, but I only got need for one driver at this site. I like the way you approached me; you are definitely about your business. Send your other driver to my office, and I'll give him directions to another site, and we can do business."

She wrote down the directions along with her name, and that was all it took. My shit started in overdrive after that. I wasn't surprised that my pop knew Marsha. It seemed as if everybody in the trucking business in Atlanta knew each other or at least heard of the other. But what did surprise me was how he continued to know down to the detail who I interacted with and how I did business. As we wrapped up our conversation, I began to realize instead of being concerned about how he came to know my business dealings, I should have been grateful knowing that he approved of them and that I was making him proud. Making him proud all but guaranteed me being cut in for my piece of I-75 under my new business—Rok Solid Trucking.

Chapter Thirty-Eight
Temporary Happiness

"Leek, you ain't got no more ice brotha. You want me to grab a bag from the gas station." Jay was cool and I appreciated him asking to make the run for me, but he was a guest at my barbeque, and it was my responsibility to make sure everybody was accommodated, even for something as simple as getting another bag of ice.

"Naw, Jay. I got it man. Just chill and make sure everybody's cool while I run to the store."

Jay said, "Alright but look, get a bottle of Hipnotic while you up there 'cause I don't really like Smirnoff, and that's all you got left."

I laughed thinking, "Niggas can't ever be simple." Jay knew damn well that wasn't no reasonable request, especially for one nigga. As I walked out of my new house I paused for a minute to turn and look at it for what had to be the tenth time that day.

I was proud and happy being only twenty-three years old and already owning my own home. It was an all-brick, two-story, three-bedroom, three-bathroom, two-car garage home. I took my time driving to the store because those Dekalb County dick-heads was always somewhere, hiding in the cut waiting to pull over any black man they saw in a nice car with the same bullshit seatbelt excuse. For as nice as Georgia was, the cops are what left a bad taste in my mouth 'cause they never cut you a break.

That's what I missed about Philly. You could be leaving Pat's Steaks at 3 am after a nice grub. The police might stop you but only to tell you, "Nice car, man." I managed to make it safely from my house to the liquor store at the intersection of Covington and Panola. I went in and bought what I came for, including the twenty-five dollar bottle of Hipnotic. I popped the trunk and put the ice inside and jumped back in the car and rolled the windows down to catch what was left of the breeze I felt walking into the store.

As I pulled from the spot I noticed a familiar face sitting in a silver Range Rover in the parking space next to me. It was Glenn. He didn't see me right away until I said, "Whassup, old head?"

His face lit up as he smiled, pleasantly surprised to see me. "Damn, young Leek, I guess the big body wasn't good enough for you I see."

I laughed before saying, "I had to step it up and change wit the times. Yah-mean?" After I got the house I decided it was time to get a new car, too. So I bought the new Lexus GS-400.

Glenn smiled and said, "I feel you."

I said, "I know you do. I see you made the change to that platinum Range!" We both laughed afterward 'cause the rhyme was unintended.

Glenn looked the car over and commented, "I know the note on that jawn is crazy."

I smiled as I said, "I ain't got one of those. This thing paid for."

Surprised again, Glenn said, "I see you really doing the damn thing, huh?" I tilted my head slightly, half nodding and said, "Naw, nigga, you know how I am when it come to these cars; you know that first hand."

Glenn said, "You right, you right."

It was good to see him and the rap was cool, but I had to get back to the house and cater to my guests. Before pulling off I asked, "Yo, what you doing right now?"

Glenn responded, "Nothing. I was just about to grab a bag of chips and a soda before going to my mom's crib. Why?"

I said, "Follow me. I'm having a cookout. My crib is around the corner."

Glenn said, "Alright" and pulled out behind me.

When we pulled up to the house a few female guests were standing on the front lawn talking and sipping wine. I instructed Glenn to park his truck in the only open space there was about twenty feet from the house. By the time he walked up, I had already been in the house, dropped the ice and drink on the counter, and returned to meet him at the front door. I opened it just as he was about to ring the bell. "Come on in, man. Are you thirsty? If you wanna grub, it's plenty of food too." Glenn looked around at the house and shook his head in an approving manner and said, "I see you keep it coming Leek. You talking 'bout you stepped it up; nigga, you knocked it out the park!"

I was glad Glenn was impressed. It meant a lot coming from him. In the midst of my thoughts Glenn said, Iit seem like ain't nothing but females at this jawn."

I smiled before saying, "The barbeque is kind of like a housewarming party too. One of my female friends put it together for me, plus I don't really deal wit a lot of dudes."

Glenn said, "Yeah, I feel you on that. I ain't got no rap for a lot of these cats either. They get too caught up asking you about your personal business and how can they get down."

Glenn and I paused silently after that. I knew why he felt that way. Ceez had mentioned that Glenn had been setup once years earlier by a couple of cats that he thought were cool with him. By the time he realized they weren't, he had been stuck up for twenty thousand dollars! "Glenn, I know Ceez must have told you all I really know is women. So if you see one you like, let me know and I'll put you on her."

I must've sounded like a pimp when I said it, but that's not how I meant it. Glenn understood and said, "You ain't got to worry about that young buck. I been in this game a long time and don't need no assist."

A few more friends showed up and I had to play host. I asked a close female friend who was there to fix Glenn a plate and make sure he was cool. I was surprised to see she was all too eager to wait on him, and before I walked away she asked, "Does he have a girlfriend?"

I laughed and said, "That's something you got to ask him." After my new arrivals settled in, I went back over to Glenn, who was now holding a conversation with Ashley and she seemed to be enjoying every minute of it.

"You alright, old-head?" I was smiling as I said it because I knew Glenn was alright. The smile on his face confirmed it.

"Oh, yeah, I'm cool, real cool now that Ashley here took care of me." I looked at Ashley and winked at her. She correctly read the sign and excused herself but not before promising Glenn that she would return later to finish their conversation. Glenn sat up in the chair and said, "How's the trucking business?"

I said, It's good and getting better and better every day."

Out of the blue Glenn said, "What you doing later tonight 'cause you need to get wit me."

I laughed to myself because that was Glenn's subtle way of showing his approval of my success. I was cool with Glenn's evaluation of me and thought to myself, "We could definitely hangout." I got with Glenn later that night and he took me to a classy house party in Alpharetta that was filled with nothing but beautiful women. We represented well and realized that we shined good together. From that point on we started hanging out regularly.

Chapter Thirty-Nine
First Friday's

"I don't feel right. Glenn, you sure this shit look i-ight?"

"Leek, I told you you was cool. The shit is tight!"

"I know it's thearl, but you know dudes might be on some bull-shit." No sooner had I finished my statement and was becoming comfortable with Glenn's assurances than some corny-ass nigga wearing pointy toe shoes and a muscle shirt chuckled as we passed. I heard him say, "Look at that gay nigga wearing capri pants!" My night was ruined!

The only saving grace was we were headed to the V.I.P. entrance, and I didn't have to stand there to be scrutinized by hundreds of (non-fashion conscious) hard-legs. What that corny nigga didn't know was I had just come off of a bangin' ass weekend in Miami South Beach and grabbed the latest linen designs by Ermenegildo Zegna and those capri pants his corny ass referred to were actually 1940s styled, classically tailored white linen knickers.

I decided to wear them that night along with a midnight black, short sleeve, potato-sack linen shirt also by Zegna. I had spent the better part of the night deciding on whether to wear some Prada sandals versus a crisp, black pair of classic slip-on Gucci loafers with the ensemble. The loafers won. By the time we got to the Swiss Hotel, I had a strange feeling people weren't going to be able to appreciate the outfit, and the dude with gay comment confirmed it.

Glenn for some reason continued to assure me my shit was hot. He had always been known for his taste in clothes and had even schooled me on the importance of a custom-tailored suit. He would always remind me to make sure all of my slacks be tailored with a two-inch French cuff. I used to wonder why it was such a big deal to him until he explained, "It distinguishes between clothing bought off the rack from clothing custom tailored for you." He would always point out the difference in the way one's slacks would drape over shoes with a two-inch cuff versus the customary one-inch.

Two inches gave the slacks depth where a one-inch cuff reminded you of the suit you had to wear going to church when you were twelve—short and stiff. That knowledge has become embedded in my mind and is confirmed every time he and I go out or I see a classic movie from the forties with well-dressed men in suits.

As we entered the doorway to the party we were immediately greeted by one of the sponsors. He was a friend of Glenn and he ushered us in past the admissions counter. Glenn and I had gone out plenty of times before. Whenever we entered the scene, it always seemed as though everything stopped and all eyes would be on us. We lived for that and would confidently walk by the gawking eyes with a self-assured look on our faces.

That night Glenn was the only one with a self assured look, while I on the other hand was trying as hard as I could to conceal the uneasy feeling that was tearing my stomach apart. It was as if someone made me swallow a thousand butterflies, and they were all flittering around with each step I took.

Glenn noticed I was still bothered by the faggot statement made by the guy outside and told me again, "Listen ock, I'm telling you you cool. That shit is gone get 'em. Stop worrying about what the dude said and focus on these broads!" I began to think maybe Glenn was right. After all, I know if my lay wasn't cool he wouldn't have been caught dead with me. He was particular like that; it wasn't unusual for him to suggest I change an outfit if he felt it didn't accurately project the image he wanted us to collectively display—although that rarely happened.

Routinely, whenever we entered any party, we would always seek out the best vantage point where we could easily see and be seen by all of the potentially qualified prospects for the night. After casing the central area of the party, we decided it would be best to post up near the open bar located ten feet from the entranceway. It was generating a large amount of traffic and was well lit. There was an open wall directly adjacent to the bar that held a large colorful picture, which was attracting a large number of oohs and ahs. We decided that's where we would stand.

That night was a little nicer than most. It was the beginning of August and the summer was in full swing. All of the women seemed to be dressed in skimpy little sun-dresses that accentuated their bodies. As we stood there, Glenn and I both silently wished a light breeze would come along and reveal all of the treasures they each were hiding. As I stood there in my lustful daze I was reminded of the classic pose Marilynn Monroe struck over the subway vent in the movie the Seven Year Itch.

"Hey Glenn, don't act like you don't see me over standing here." It was Lex. She was known throughout Atlanta circles as one of the flyest girls in the city. Her reputation was well deserved because on any given day it was nothing to see her carrying the latest patent leather handbag by Cartier. She also had a major fetish for high-end designer shoes, Jimmy-Choo to be specific. If you asked her the time, you had better pull out a pair of sunglasses otherwise you would be blinded by the diamond bezel resting atop of the ladies presidential Rolex wrapped around her wrist.

For as fly as she was, she unfortunately had a lot of miles on her. Glenn pointed her out to me once, and I realized that I had seen her around Atlanta for years and already knew who she was. She was one of those women who go all out trying to project a quality image, but the minute you get her alone that shit goes out the window.

Her and Glenn had met a while back at a club, and whenever she saw him she always felt compelled to make her presence known. Probably because after knowing her less than five hours Glenn had scored, screwed, and forgotten about her without backwards glance. As she continued to pester him he turned to me sighed and said, "Here she go."

"Glenn, you ain't shit. You know you did me dirty," she began.

Glenn turned to me with a smirk on his face before turning back to Lex and saying, "Lex, you know it ain't even like that. You know you my baby; so how you been anyway?"

She answered him as if she were waiting for the starting pistol to go off at the Penn Relays. "I'm getting married," she said, smiling ear to ear as she proudly flashed a dull yellowish stone in his face.

Glenn grabbed her hand examined the ring and blandly commented, "That's nice; I'm happy for you."

Lex, disappointed by Glenn's lack of enthusiasm over her news started to speak, but I tapped Glenn on his arm before she could open her mouth and pretended I needed his attention on something. The slight was obvious to Lex and she played it off by saying, "I just wanted to say hi, and let you know the good news."

As she walked away Glenn turned to me and said, "Good looking out, but how you know I wanted you to bail me out?"

I said, "I could tell you wanted her oucha face, and besides we in here for new ass. You already hit dat." Glenn agreed with me, nodding as I continued, "And didn't I hear her say she getting married or something?"

Glenn responded, "Yeah, and how 'bout whoever the nigga is is either broke or obviously don't give a fuck about her 'cause that ring looked like somebody dipped it in some pissy toilet water! Personally, I feel sorry for the dude 'cause I know he don't know her background. She came at me like that too when we first started messing around, but I told her I wasn't feeling her like that."

I was sipping on a drink and spilled my last sip as my jaw dropped. "What?! She asked you to marry her?" Glenn chuckled briefly before saying, "no, she asked could we start seeing more of each other. The sex was good, but she was too needy, and was always asking for money. Plus my man Vic told me she used to dance at Magic City back in the day. I asked her about it and the dumb-bitch admitted it, and still had the nerve to think we had a shot."

I shook my head and commented, "And the crazy part about all of it is if she getting married, then why in the hell is she up in here?" After the episode with Lex, I loosened up a bit, and with the help of a few drinks had actually forgotten my anxiety about my outfit. The flow of female traffic was good. Standing there was like being a celebrity. Virtually every one we reached for stopped to listen to what we had to say and gave phone numbers. The attention we were getting put me in a joking mood, and I started busting on Glenn about Lex stopping.

I teased him about the way she looked. She was wearing a tight-fitting skirt that seemed to be just a tad bit too small and open-toed Gucci sandals with a few really-noticeable corns on her feet. I guess she figured her sandals being from Gucci would compensate for her ugly ass toes. Glenn mentioned he'd heard she put foundation on them because one of the corns looked so ugly. After the conversation Lex walked away switching really hard, as if she'd hoped Glenn was watching.

I looked and laughed saying, "Tell the truth, nigga. You was really thinking about making her your girl, wasn't you?"

Glenn laughed as I finished busting on him, and as the last word rolled out of my mouth I felt a tap on my shoulder and heard a small voice say, "Hey Keith."

I stood there momentarily wondering who in the hell Keith was, and then I remembered it was me. Keith was an alias I created to give to broads who weren't worthy of knowing my real handle, especially loud mouth, gossiping street broads who name-dropped any thearl cat they met to gain credibility with their friends, and this was one of them.

I couldn't remember her name right off, and Glenn could tell. He seized the opportunity to get back at me for teasing him about Lex and said, "Damn Malik, who your friend? You could have introduced me."

I widened my eyes and tried to speak through my teeth saying, "Call me Keith." Glenn deliberately ignored me and repeated himself again, "Whassup Malik? Introduce me to your friend." Seeing that I didn't have a choice other than to stall for time, I responded in an unnecessarily long manner, trying to remember her name. Meanwhile, the as yet un-named girl looked at me saying, "Who's Malik?"

I ignored her and responded to Glenn's question saying, "Come on man, you know I was going to introduce you. You ain't give me a chance to. Why wouldn't I want you to meet my friend?"

At that point it became obvious to her that I didn't know who in the hell she was, and she interjected by saying, "Hi, I'm Heather."

While she was talking I briefly looked up to the ceiling and played it off by interrupting her at precisely the same moment she'd finished saying her name saying, "My fault. Heather, this my man Glenn."

Glenn chuckled as he extended his hand and greeted Heather, and I asked, "So what's up? How you been?" I really didn't care what she had been doing or how she really felt. I was just trying to be polite and speed the conversation along so she could get the hell out of my face. Naturally, that didn't happen. Instead she perceived my fake attempt at politeness as an opportunity to prolong a meaningless, dead end conversation. After asking a barrage of questions about my current goings on, she paused and looked me up and down before complimenting my appearance.

As she did so she circled around me, stopped dead center in front of me, and pressed her ass directly up against my crotch. Not

217

wanting to draw more attention to what she had just done, I discreetly leaned into her ear and asked, "What are you doing?" She half turned, looked up at me and responded, "Marking my territory!" Glenn erupted into uncontrollable laughter at what was obviously this broad playing herself and embarrassing me. She had no idea I not only hadn't remembered her name, but also wanted her gone.

Thankfully, her overactive bladder allowed us to salvage what was left of the night. It was 1:30 am by this time and the night was ending soon. Aside from a bunch of old, familiar faces, I had yet to come across someone who made my appearance at that First Friday's worthwhile. I leaned over to Glenn and tapped him on his arm to tell him I was ready to roll out. He ignored me and continued his conversation with some chick he had stopped in passing. From the time she stopped all I could hear was constant giggling at Glenn's bullshit lines of how nice she looked and how pretty she was.

I sighed in utter disgust, mostly because I hadn't found anyone I wanted to engage in conversation, and Glenn seemed to be having a ball. Just as I was about to nudge him again, and tell him I was out, I noticed a petite, light-skinned sista breezing through the crowd. All of sudden I couldn't hear the music anymore; I couldn't hear the silly giggles of the annoying female attached to Glenn's every word anymore. All I could see was this incredibly attractive sista walking directly toward me.

My focus became acute as I made out every detail of her being. She stood about 5'5" tall; her hair was full and flowed down to her shoulders, and I could tell it was hers because it lacked the stiff, lifeless hang that hair weaves reveal. Her skin was honey brown and accompanied by hazel eyes that appeared to be locked in a gaze on mine. I had noticed her early on that night, but I chose not to acknowledge her, and now she appeared to be headed straight toward me. My mind raced to figure out what she wanted or who she must have thought I was. By the time my thoughts had rested she was standing right in front of me, and she was beautiful.

Her first words were, "It takes a brave man to wear that outfit."

I laughed nervously, not knowing if she was trying to poke fun at me or truly appreciated my style. I held my composure and played my part and responded, "The fact that you're standing here proves bravery has its rewards."

She blushed, and I could tell she was impressed by my confidence. She extended her right hand and said, "Hi, my name is Tracey. I wanted to tell you your outfit is really nice. I noticed you earlier tonight and told my girlfriend to look at how nicely you were dressed. You look so distinguished standing over here I just had to come and tell you personally."

Before I could return the compliment she hit me with a, "Thank you and good night" and turned to walk away. If I didn't know any better, I would've sworn she was Russell Simmons. I had zoned out so long that I didn't notice Glenn had been standing there, watching and listening to every word Tracey and I exchanged. I was reminded by his presence when he jabbed me in my ribs telling me to grab her before she got too far away.

I reached out and said, "Whoa, whoa. Pump your brakes, baby. Where you going? I was just about to tell you the same. I saw you earlier tonight too but figured you was stuck up." What I was really thinking was, "I wasn't going to give none of the women in that party the satisfaction of shooting me down." But Tracey changed the game and approached me. So that made it all okay.

As I continued with my campaign I followed up by saying, "You're a brave girl too. It took a lot of heart to cross a room just to compliment me. Beautiful black women don't normally do that. That tells me everything I need to know about your confidence and character. Personally, I think we both should take advantage of this opportunity." As I spoke I knew she wanted the same thing but for whatever reason continued to play her little game.

Her response was, "Well, I really just wanted to tell you that you looked nice, and that's all." That was bullshit and she knew it. What woman, let alone a black woman, would go out of her way to compliment a man from across the room who she has absolutely no interest in whatsoever?

Just as I was beginning to become frustrated by her pointless charade, Glenn leaned over and I heard him softly say, "You crossed the room for a reason and playing hard to get wasn't it. At this point, sis, it ain't no need to overplay your hand." After Glenn's comment Tracey was immediately more receptive; realizing that if she pulled away a second time I would let her go. So instead she asked, "Do you have a card or something?"

I wasn't no card-carrying nigga, and I didn't fake it like I had just ran out. I said "Naw, baby, I don't have a card, but I got my cell phone and we can program in each other's number.

She said, "That's cool," and pulled her cell phone out of her purse and programmed my number into hers.

Chapter Forty
Food for Thought

I rarely got the chance to come to Philly anymore after moving to Atlanta and was only in town for a funeral. My childhood friend's father had died of liver failure. Kash—as we all called him—seemed to handle it better than expected. It was as if he was okay with his fathers passing after having watched him suffer through his illness. I guess death in that instance was more like a homecoming, a kind of peace that allowed the family to bring closure to a man whose life represented happiness and stability.

I saw a lot of Kash's father's traits in him and was proud to see that he had followed in his footsteps. It's a good thing when a black man takes a wife and resolves to live a positive life with one woman. Kash had a thousand paths he could've chosen but chose wisely when he decided to settle down and marry Tiffany and pursue a career in acting. Tiffany gave him a son, and I knew Kash was proud because he brooded over the boy, the same way his father used to brood over him.

Being around Kash and his family had a bittersweet effect on me. Although I was there for a sad occasion, I found myself at peace, enjoying the love and happiness his family was expressing despite the tragic loss of his father. Not being too familiar with myself, I discovered after a while that I didn't know how to handle the emotions I was experiencing, and said my goodbyes to Kash and his family and made my way through the streets of Philadelphia. I ended up taking a walk on South Street lost in deep thought.

I couldn't help thinking about life and how short it can be. One minute you're here and the next minute you're gone. I wondered if Kash accomplished all that he wanted before his loss and if his father was proud of him because of it. I wondered if his father left this earth feeling sure his son would make it. Hell, I had begun to wonder if I was ever going to make it.

Halfway through my reflections, my thoughts were interrupted when I heard a friendly and familiar voice. "Malik, come here buddy." It was Neve, the owner of Milan. The word on South Street was he had become Philadelphia's answer to New York's Jacob. Whenever I came into Milan, Neve always made me feel at home. He was young like me but worth millions. I respected and admired Neve because, like me, he came from nothing, and although I had yet to find true success. I knew I was on the right path.

I had been a customer for a few years, having bought my first Rolex from him. From the beginning I appreciated the way Neve treated me. It took me a while to buy my first watch, and Neve allowed me to take my time with him, not once rushing me. His patience and mutual respect paid off. When I decided to buy my next watch–a diamond bezel Breitling Chronograph—I chose Milan Jewelers. "Where have you been buddy? I have not seen you in a long time." I liked listening to Neve's accent; it reminded me of the many cool, foreign characters from spy movies. Neve was smiling as he spoke to me, and I felt bad not returning his gesture.

"It's good to see you too, man but I been busy. I'm in town for a funeral. My friend's father died and I'm not in the best mood today." I hated not being able to return Neve's enthusiasm but was glad he understood it wasn't personal.

Neve nodded his head in an accepting way and came from around the counter and patted me on the back and asked, "How much time you got today?" Before I could answer he had already motioned to one of his employees to bring a couple of stools from behind the counter.

He sat them side-by-side, sitting in one and patting the other. I sat down and we began to talk. "You know Malik, from the moment I met you I liked you. Not because you spend money with me, but because you are humble. Many young black men come into my store, and because they're rich they have attitude. Like the world owes them something. Not you. You keep your word and are an honorable man. In my country such things are revered.

"Do you see this place?" Neve stopped talking briefly, allowing me time to look around. I nodded, unsure as to where he was going by asking what he did. He picked up where he left off, "I started from nothing. When I came to America from Israel, I had nothing. I didn't even have a place to sleep! But my belief in God and myself is what got me through my struggle." I wasn't sure, but it seemed as if Neve had read my mind. I didn't recall telling him I was troubled by my life and my lack of accomplishment, and yet he seemed to detect that my melancholy mood was the result of exactly that—my troubled life.

There had been many setbacks in my life, luckily none of them had to do with any family tragedies, but I felt I should have been a lot further in life than I was. I spent a lot of time judging others for their shortcomings but had yet to truly examine the true extent of my own. Without knowing it, Neve had found an inroad to my own personal struggle and was graciously sharing his strategy for beating it. "Malik look at me. How old do you think I am?" I looked at Neve and tried to discern his age from his looks.

His hair was black and curly with no signs of gray, his face youthful and vibrant, and his build tight and healthy. I was sure he was in his late twenties, or early thirties, I answered him hesitantly, saying, "Twenty-eight?"

Neve smiled at me, laughed, grabbed my leg, and said, "I am only twenty-three years old my friend." I felt a rush and the top of my head became tingly.

I knew he was young but would never have guessed he was that young. I was immediately more impressed than I had been originally and found myself thinking "How, with what, and whose help did this man come to have all he had?"

Again, as if reading my mind Neve said, "Self determination and discipline are what kept me working Malik, and God did the rest!" I had never been one to share my innermost thoughts with anyone. I always believed people tended to take advantage of secrets and shortcomings, but I somehow felt comfortable with Neve.

I felt privileged he chose me to share his secrets with, and it compelled me to do the same. "Neve, I been trying to get them M's for a long time."

Neve looked at me in a puzzled sort of way and asked, "What does M's mean?"

I laughed and said, "Millions."

Neve leaned back in his chair as we both laughed. I think he thought that's what I meant but wasn't sure. Neve had dealt with more street niggas than most street niggas deal with and had a handle on all of the latest from the streets.

He was very subtle, but I noticed on numerous occasions where he would reveal his awareness of the streets and the effect it had on his business saying, "Shit is really fucked up out there. The streets are dry right now, but I don't let that stop me from continuing to invest in my business. I will be ready when the floodgates open again. The customer won't have to wait for me to say, 'I can get that for you, but I have to order it.' No, buddy, I will have it in the store."

I listened and didn't interrupt. I detected Neve's conviction as he spoke of his discipline and realized that is what it takes to succeed in this life. I thought of what I was about to say to him, half ashamed of the content, but followed through and said, "Neve, I got a problem man. I spend too much time chasing women. I think I would have been rich a long time ago if I could just get these broads out of my head."

When I bought my first watch from him, Neve asked me what I did for a living. I told him I was in the trucking business and that I had several contracts with the city of Atlanta. By all rights I should have been well on my way to wealth and stability if it weren't for all the time and energy I spent cavorting with women.

"Malik, don't worry about what you do not have. What you must do is begin to separate yourself from the negative energy your thirst for sex brings to you. You must also remember discipline can only come through self-control. Before you can control conditions, you must first control yourself, which maybe the hardest thing you ever do. Sometimes we can be our own worst enemy because if we can't learn to conquer self, then we defeat ourselves!"

"I know, Neve, and that has been my hardest battle so far—self control." I looked at my watch and noticed two hours had passed like it was nothing. I got off the stool, stood up, and stretched. I extended my hand.

Neve grabbed it and pulled me into him and gave me a hug and said, "Listen Malik. Don't worry. Everything is going to be alright." I looked in his eyes and felt what he was saying was true. I also felt I had made a real friend that day.

Just as I was about to walk out the door Neve said, "Oh yeah, I knew there was something I forgot. I wanted to show you a new set I made."

I put my hands up and said, "Neve, I ain't bring no money up here with me, and I don't want to see nothing. Shit, I'm just now getting over paying for this fucking watch!" "Malik, don't worry about it. Just take a look at it and tell me if you like it."

Neve went in the back and reappeared with a large black box. He laid a swatch of cloth down on the display case and set a bracelet and ring on top of it. I took one look at the jewelry and my jaw dropped. That shit was hot! Both the ring and bracelet were set in platinum and looked like something out of a magazine. I immediately asked, "What's the total weight?"

Neve looked at me and smiled; the salesman in him had reappeared. "The bracelet is five karats and the ring is two karats."

I nodded at him and said, "The shit is nice, but I ain't holding like that right now."

Neve interrupted me and asked, "Do you like it?"

I responded, "Damn right. The shit is hot. Both pieces."

Neve looked at me and smiled and said, "Take them, wear them for a while, and if you like them then we will work out a price." I noticed each item was marked with a small tag. The ring listed for $3,500 and the bracelet for $4,500. I knew that was the price for retail, and I also knew if I decided to buy the set, Neve would give it to me for a little below cost.

I had had a credit of about seven hundred dollars with him from an overpayment on the diamond bezel he custom made for my Breitling. I had almost forgotten about it and was only reminded of it after Neve himself spoke it up. I think my lack of pressure and willingness to pay upfront for all of the jewelry I purchased with him made him comfortable with letting me take such prized pieces with me without payment. Whatever the reason, I was happy and looked forward to returning to Atlanta with my shiny new trinkets.

Chapter Forty-One
Rendezvous

"G, you know my man Dame, right?" I didn't have a chance to answer before Malik continued saying, "I got him on the line, on three way."

Damon chimed in, "What's up, Glenn? How you been man?"

I replied, "What's up, young buck?" I'd met Damon a few years back. We attended Temple University together—I got a late start—and would often speak to each other in passing.

When we met I discovered he was the mutual friend who'd originally introduced my brother Ceez to Malik. I responded to Malik's question with a smile, "Yeah, I know Dame-dash." That's what I called Damon whenever I saw him.

Malik, satisfied that Damon and I were familiar, asked, "G, what you doing later around 7pm?" I didn't know why Malik asked me what my plans were later and wondered briefly why it mattered, knowing it was probably because he needed a favor. I said, "I ain't doing nothing. Why?"

Malik said, "Dame coming in town around seven, and I was supposed to pick him up from the airport, but my flight don't get in until nine o'clock. I would've let him take my car since it's parked at the airport, but I got the keys with me. If you can, I want you to go grab him for me."

I didn't mind doing the favor for Malik. I knew he went to Philly for a funeral and stayed longer as a way to express his personal condolences. I knew the stress of the funeral was still heavy on his mind and offset some of it by saying, "Don't worry about it man. I got you; Dame, what time your flight get in for sure?" I wanted to make sure he knew so I wouldn't have to drive all the way down to Atlanta Hartsfield International Airport and be forced to wait because of misinformation. My plan was to get the arrival time and get there ten minutes after, giving Damon time to collect his bags from baggage claim.

I was glad Malik caught me before I had the chance to get lost in the hustle and bustle of the street. It had been a while since I last hung out and felt it was time for me to get out and recruit a new bed warmer, and I knew just where to find one—the Shark Bar. I liked the place because you didn't have to be dressed to go, and it didn't take much to pull something up out of there if your shit was right. "Dame, what you got planned when you get here?"

Dame laughed before saying, "I'm wit-choo playboy, ya mean." I laughed slightly at Damon's response, mostly because I enjoyed hearing Philly slang and rarely got the chance to use it since coming to Atlanta.

"Oh, okay. If you with me, then we hanging tonight. Malik, what time are you getting in? Cause if you get here on time then you can meet us at the Shark Bar." Damon had planned his trip to Atlanta some months back. He was an investment planner for American Express and was in town for a rarely scheduled weekend meeting. Unfortunately, the funeral in Philly put a damper on things, pulling Malik away on short notice and forcing all of their original plans to change. Unsure as to how Damon felt I checked with him to be sure he was okay with the events for the night. "Dame, you cool with rolling out?"

Dame paused before saying, "Yeah, man. I'm good. I was supposed to meet with a client later for dinner, but I'll just cancel and tell 'em that my flight got in late."

Malik interrupted Damon's confirmation saying, "If y'all going to be there for sure, then I'll just go straight there from the airport." I was happy the plan was already laid out and was looking forward to having a relaxing drink and hunting for new prospects.

Chapter Forty-Two
Sharks in the Shark Bar

Friday nights in Atlanta are reserved strictly for the Shark Bar. Whether you're a somebody out doing the town for the night or a wannabe hoping to be noticed, the Shark Bar is the place to be.

For the men it is a place to come to flaunt and flex their platinum jewelry, frosted out wrist wear, throwback jerseys, fitted caps, braids, or baldheads. And the sole purpose is to attract the women. The whole place is like a scene out of a Jay-Z video. Everywhere you turn you see young brothas and sistas dressed in the latest urban wear, drinking belvedere and Alize. In the dining area you may find a few bottles of champagne, Moet mostly.

The fabled Cristal is only seen when a local celebrity or pro athlete feels like he got to prove that he got dough, seemingly unaware that being a celebrity or athlete means you ain't got to prove shit. But whenever it's brought into view, the women get whipped into a frenzy. Doing any and everything they can to see and be seen by whoever the purchaser of that treasured nectar is.

In Atlanta, it's common knowledge the Shark Bar is top draw for all of the town's who's who. Translation: paid niggas and beautiful black women! Only this crowd is not like the traditional group of well-to-do characters chronicled in so many other books on black America. These folks are the real mix—the rowdy, unruly, ruthless bunch that go out in search of blood each and every weekend, and those are just the females. They are the sharks that truly rule the shark bar.

Girls Gone Wild ain't got nothing on those broads, many of whom can be seen circling the parking lot before going in, eyeing whatever nigga they see in a late model foreign car and then zeroing in on his unsuspecting ass once he's spotted inside the club. The way they do it is like poetry in motion. Typically, some unsuspecting playa catches their eye and then is enticed by a friendly smile and an intense stare that convinces him he has been chosen because of his looks when in reality it was his S-class Mercedes Benz parked in the valet or the quarter to eight (BMW 745il) he was seen pulling up in.

It's amazing how those females weed out and separate the true ballers from the frontin' ass niggas. It's as if they have special radar that detects how thearl you are. A lot of the men fool themselves by thinking it has to do with the amount of shine they wear. Sometimes they even go as far as to order Moet, hoping to crystallize the paid image they so desperately want to project.

But these sistas today are a new breed 'cause they know. Don't ask me how, they just do! Pulling these bitches is just like recruiting for the top pick in an NBA draft 'cause they come in expecting a signing bonus and long term contracts for sponsorship. Once you have been chosen, one of two things is going to happen. First, you will be pleasured and primed by small gestures designed to win your confidence, like buying towels for your bathroom, making breakfast, or even picking you up from the dentist after having two teeth pulled!

Second, if they haven't scored a big payoff by then, they intensify the level of passion with sexual indulgences all but guaranteeing a financial come up! The second part only happens to niggas who are a little more reluctant to share the wealth—niggas like me. Shark attack is the number one reason a lot of people are scared to go to the beach, and it is the same reason I will never go back to the Shark Bar.

The last time I went I arrived late. I was supposed to be meeting Damon and Glenn who were already there. By the time I got there they were already seated, which was a miracle 'cause the reservation list was always full on Friday nights, and if you wasn't ready to grease Anna's palm, then you could fuckin' forget about it. As I walked in the door and made my way through the crowd of wall-to-wall women, I couldn't help but feel a little nervous.

I hated walking through crowds, especially those full of broads who sized you up with every step you took. I saw a lot of familiar faces and knew a lot of the dudes in there from passing in the streets, niggas that didn't really have it like that but who lived for Friday nights when they could put on their best street wear and try their hardest to get noticed. What those niggas didn't know was that they never stood a chance! Cause like I said before, these women was Atlanta's number one heat seekers, and the only thing that could shut down a heat seeker is a 100% thoroughbred.

As I continued to breeze through the crowd, I passed a table full of broads who seemed to like my stride. I reached the table Glenn had reserved, and my food was being brought out as I sat down. I'd called Glenn and asked him to order for me on my way there. "G, I see your spot is doin' it tonight."

"Yeah, Nigga., I told you this shit be poppin'."

I looked around and said, "Yeah, but these broads bought dat change." As I spoke I was looking around at all of the tables filled with bad-ass sistas, each accompanied by an expensive handbag prominently displayed—some real, some fake. They all seemed to be sporting the latest eyewear by Chole, Fred, or Gucci, not to mention the thirty to forty sporting the classic Farrah Faucet flip hair-style. They all seemed to be desperately trying to project that bourgeois, high-maintenance image you see in all the videos.

"What's up, Dame?"

Damon stuck out his fist and gave me a pound before saying, "You see what it is." He smiled afterward, lifting his hands, palms raised just slightly in an inviting manner, prompting me to look around at all of the women surrounding us. I turned back to ask Glenn another question but was too late. He'd finished his meal and was now in hunting mode, hoping to bag a new prospect to take home for the night. He'd rolled out so fast I thought maybe he was ducking somebody and disappeared to keep a low profile.

Dame saw me looking around for him and said, "He saw some jawn earlier he knew from Philly and got up to holla at her. He over there by the bar." I looked to see if I could find him but gave up because the crowd was so thick. The whole place was abuzz, and I could tell from the outside valet that there were some heavyweight cats inside. It didn't scare me because we blended well.

I had ordered catfish, macaroni and cheese, greens, and candied yams. Halfway into my meal I had a strong desire for some hot sauce, and our waitress hadn't made her way back to our table to take any further requests. I looked around hoping to find some on another table before I finished my meal. The table behind ours had a bottle, and the women sitting there were finished with their meal.

I turned around and asked if I could take it, and they all paused as if I had a different reason for asking. Sistas are good for thinking brothas are trying to holla even if they have a good reason for interrupting them. By the time they responded to my request I had said excuse me twice. One of the girls at the table said, "Nicole, I think that guy behind you wants you for something."

As she turned around she had an arrogant look on her face as if she was being bothered. I excused myself again and said, "Could we get the hot sauce?"

She passed me the hot sauce and I thanked her, and turned back around and finished my meal. Glenn reappeared in time to see the exchange and tapped me saying, "That bitch think she the shit.

I spoke to her earlier and she straight ignored me." I listened to Glenn complain about the chick mistreating him, and although she was attractive her attitude made her ugly.

I didn't let that stop me from coming at her though. I have always had a thing for challenging situations and got off on conquering women who felt they couldn't be conquered. The night went by rather quickly, and after we finished our meal we all got up and mingled in the bar area, bought a few drinks, flirted, and did a little flossing too. By the time we were leaving, I noticed the women who had given us the hot sauce were leaving at the same time.

As we walked through the parking lot we ended up behind them, and I noticed Nicole's ass was perfect and round and protruded in a lovely way out of her jeans that must have been painted on. I walked up to her and tapped her on her elbow and said the classic line "Excuse me, miss."

She turned, surprised it was me, and said, "What's up?"

I said, "You ain't appear to be too friendly in the restaurant, and I wanted to know why?"

She responded by saying, "I was tired of everybody grabbing me all night."

I could barely prevent myself from gritting my teeth before I responded, "Don't you know when properly addressed by anyone, you have a responsibility to respond politely, and you can't always assume somebody is trying to talk you."

My first thought was to close the statement with "bitch!" but I didn't and instead waited for her response, which was nothing, but then I didn't expect anything else from her type. She was more sexy than cute, and I could tell she knew her banging-ass body compensated for everything her face didn't. Not to mention all the designer clothing she wore; Frankie V jeans, Chloe tee shirt, high-heeled stiletto boots, and Louis Vuitton belt with backpack to match. And all of that would have been cool had she not been fumbling with the keys to a 1992 Dodge Neon.

After a brief silence she finally replied asking, "So what's your name anyway?"

I replied, "Malik."

She smiled and said, "That's cute. My name is Nicole and I'm from Richmond." I said, "That's a nice place. I went there for black college weekend at Kings Dominion."

She asked, "Did you like it?"

I responded saying, "It was cool, but the crowd was too young for me." The Valet wheeled around and pulled up right behind Nicole's Dodge Neon just as I finished my statement, and asked, "sir would you like me to put the top down for you?" I nodded in approval as Nicole replied to my statement saying,

"I'm sorry to hear you didn't have a better time Malik, but what's on your agenda for the rest of the night? Maybe I can make up for it?"

I said "Nothing really, but I'm not tired."

She interrupted me and asked, "Have you ever been to Café Intermezzo?"

I smiled and said, "That's my spot. I especially like the chocolate walnut cheesecake."

Nicole nodded and said, "Well, why don't you follow me there?" That was perfect, especially since I always drove my car alone wherever I went, specifically so I wouldn't have to drop off anyone at the end of the night.

I ended up selling the Lexus and copped a 2000 convertible Jaguar XK8. although She didn't show it, I knew my drop-jag was the reason Nicole suddenly became so receptive, in inviting me to Café Intermezzo. It was only about two miles away going into the Buckhead side of town. Café Intermezzo; it was a down low, mellow spot that had an intimate atmosphere where everybody went when they wanted to get personal. I had converted many in that spot, mostly sistas who wasn't sure if they wanted to close out the night with me, but after an espresso and pastry they would literally be eating out of my hands. Nicole was no different.

I convinced her to stay with me, only she didn't want to come all the way to Lithonia, which is where I lived. So I went against my rule and decided to go to her house. Now, let it be known I ain't never been one for slippin, but that night my man downstairs was dictating policy. Before I had a chance to even think about what I was about to do or come to my senses about where I was, I was already eight inches deep into danger, ecstasy, and regret.

The next morning I woke up from the previous night's joy ride to a phone call. One of my drivers had been in an accident and I needed to get there ASAP. As I rushed to put on my clothes, I forgot I had separated my jewelry and was wearing the brand new 5-karat diamond bracelet and 2-karat pinky ring I had just bought from Neve! I was used to only wearing my watch and had taken it off and put it with my cell phone on the dresser. My ring and bracelet I put on the nightstand next to the bed.

After I finished getting dressed I went in the bathroom, washed my face and came out, headed straight to the dresser, grabbed my watch and cell phone and bolted out the door. I jumped into my car and got right on to I-285, trying to get to the scene of the accident 'cause my driver's CDL license was suspended and the Georgia Department of Transportation would be on my ass if I wasn't there to represent my business, not to mention the $250 tow fee that would be immediately applied to that 17,000 lbs dump truck.

As I got closer to the scene I put my hand right hand on the steering wheel so I could call a second driver to come and drive the wrecked truck from the scene. It was then I noticed that my shit was not on my fucking wrist! Worse than that, I was stuck in a position that didn't allow me to turn around, go back, and get my shit.

I immediately called Nicole, "Yo, I left my jewelry on your nightstand. I got to go handle this emergency right quick, but I'll call you later before I come back and get it."

Nicole acknowledged me by saying, "Yeah, I see it. Just call me when you're ready to come get it."

Cool. I was relieved and felt as long as the bitch knew I knew it was there then she couldn't get fly with my shit or so I thought! A day or so passed, and I got caught up with dealing with some major issues. The dude who was driving my truck got charged with a DUI, and since he was contracted through my company, I was directly responsible. Turns out he had run into a woman with a kid in a car seat.

The hit was hard enough to make the air bags deploy, but thankfully she had her seat belt on and the kid was in the back seat facing the rear. Still I was looking down the barrel of a major lawsuit and raised insurance premiums. All for giving some washed up ass alcoholic a break.

It never fails. You just can't put your faith in niggas. They'll shit on you every time. The nigga even had the nerve to call and ask if I could bail him out of jail. By the time I had got my thoughts back in order long enough for me to refocus on my business with Nicole, a day had passed and I realized that although I hadn't called her, she hadn't called me either. It wasn't a big deal until I called her the following day and got no answer. I assumed she must have been busy and I would wait a day or so more and call again, each time leaving a message letting her know why I was calling.

Chapter Forty-Three
One of the Good Ones

It had been two weeks since I last talked to Tracey and a month since we met at First Friday's. We had gotten to know each other in the immediate two weeks that passed since that time, and things were good. We did lunch and dinner a few times, and she was proving to be a true quality sista. She even offered to pay for dinner several times, and although I didn't let her I could tell she meant it.

The harmony was interrupted when I had to go out of town for Kash's father's funeral. I returned a week and a half later, still feeling remorseful over the loss and remained withdrawn from everyone. I thought hanging out with Glenn and Dame Friday night would have cheered me up, but when I woke up Saturday morning to the news of the accident with my truck, I was sure I was in for one more blow 'cause bad luck comes in threes.

It was midway through the following week and I still hadn't heard from Nicole. By now I realized she was dodging my phone calls. Frustrated and depressed, I decided to pick up where I left off before I went out of town and called Tracey. "What's up, baby? You busy?"

She paused curiously before saying, "Malik?"

I said "Yeah, did I catch you at a bad time?"

My question went ignored as Tracey started asking concerned questions about my trip to Philly. She knew I had gone to a funeral and immediately asked, "Are you okay? Do you need anything? Because I can come over if you want and fix something to eat." Tracey's concern was real, and I appreciated the sincerity of her offer. Without thinking I responded, "Yeah, some dinner would be nice, but I don't have any groceries."

On cue she responded, "Boy, leave that to me. You know you my baby, and I am going to make sure you are all right. What do you want from the store?"

I felt like seafood and said, "I could go for some fish, some salmon or something with a baked potato and broccoli." Jokingly I asked, "Can you make that?"

Tracey couldn't tell I was joking, and her response proved it. "I am a true blue southern belle, and a real man would be able to see that. Cause honey, there ain't nothing I can't make."

I started laughing and she realized I was just joking around,. She calmed herself and followed up by saying, "Boy, you so crazy; I'm on my way. I'm going to stop and get a bottle of wine too so we can light a fire and relax." I acknowledged her and hung up hurriedly so I would have time to straighten up the house before she got there. About forty minutes later the doorbell rang. I opened the door and said, "Please don't comment on my mess. You got here faster than I thought you would, and I was trying to clean up 'cause I left in a hurry when I went to Philly."

She looked at me curiously before asking, "Cleaning up for who? Me? No, you go sit down on the sofa. I'll pour you a glass of wine, and you just relax while I tend to the house."

Tracey's attentiveness to me left me feeling satisfied and well cared for. I had known many women in my life, but none had ever been as attentive to me as she was being. They were all self-absorbed beauty queens who were more concerned with breaking a nail than pleasing a man! Just like at the party, Tracey proved once again she was indeed a rare breed. The wine she gave me seemed like an aphrodisiac and caused me to drift into thoughts of a sexual nature. All throughout dinner I could barely keep my mind off of her alluring beauty.

After eating her incredible meal I was ready to show my appreciation by returning all of the attention that Tracey so graciously extended to me. I put on Moods by Will Downing, and we sat on the floor in front of the fireplace with the flames set low so as not to cause a sweat. The central air was on and provided the perfect balance to an otherwise warm summer night.

As we sat there I wondered if Tracey could be the one. After all, she was damn sure treating me as if I was. The night was passing by slowly, and we were just sitting together, me on the floor leaning back into her lap while she stroked the back of my head and neck. All of a sudden I heard her say, "Baby, I could do this; I can see me here with you, making sure you're alright and us just being happy together."

I silently listened to her and thought, "Maybe that isn't such a bad idea." I was twenty-three and had only been in love twice. I had been single for seven years now and was getting real tired of the dating game.

While the thought was still floating around in my mind, Tracey got up and went upstairs. After being there for about five minutes she came to the stairwell and beckoned me to come up. "Malik, turn off the lights and fire and come upstairs."

I did as she asked and made my way to the bedroom. As I did so, I realized I was following her orders in my house, and I liked it. By the time I got to the bedroom, I was so turned on I noticed a slight wetness in my boxers.

As I entered my bedroom I looked and expected her to be lying on the bed, but she wasn't. Instead, I noticed there were lit candles leading from the nightstand to the dresser and on into the master bathroom. I followed the candles into the bathroom doorway and found her there. Nothing could have prepared me for the beautiful sight that was now before my eyes. It was dark with a faint glimmer of light but enough for me to see her pecan bronze skin disappear into a sea of bubbles. She had put candles all around the rim of the tub and Will Downing could still be heard through the newly wired surround sound I had almost opted not to install.

Tracey motioned for me to come to her, and my legs didn't wait for the command from my brain. Before I knew it I was standing over her as she looked up at me. Her hair was pinned up and held in place with two wooden pins looking much like an oriental princess, and I was her king. She was smiling as she stood up, and I watched the water run down the length of her body. The glow of the candles made her look like a statue—only she was real.

Meanwhile, the bubbles seemed to be playing hide and seek, revealing certain parts of her anatomy while hiding others. She reached out and grabbed the bottom of my shirt and lifted it above my head as if was a child. I stood there motionless; impressed by her sensitivity and sensuality. She unbuckled my pants, letting them drop to the floor. I stepped out of them as she slid back into the tub. I finished the job by quickly pulling off my boxers. Tracey chuckled looking at me and said, "I see you're happy to see me." I laughed too, unconcerned by my physical display of eagerness but more ready to return the satisfaction I had gotten from the ambiance she had taken the time to establish.

I was feeling her, and somehow I felt I would soon discover there was much more to her than I had perceived. As I climbed into the tub she stood up to turn so she could be in my lap, and we both slid back down into the warm soapy water. I was at peace. We washed each other thoroughly, and afterwards made our way back into the bedroom.

"I love your sleigh bed." I didn't respond to her comment about the bed; I was deep in thought about whether or not I was going give her oral pleasure. Truthfully, I felt she deserved it, and although I didn't have doubts about my sexual ability, I wanted to ensure her complete and total satisfaction. I gently laid her down and began to kiss her from head to toe. I wasn't used to paying attention to or appreciating a woman's body, but Tracey made me want to. Funny, not two nights before, I was lying in bed with a nothing ass bitch who proved she was nothing by taking me home with her on the first night. Now I was with a real woman, a woman who took the time to cater and caress me, and I desperately wanted to do the same for her.

Tracey was feeling my efforts, and I was happy to see I hadn't lost my touch. As she moaned and writhed on the bed, I became more and more confident. I finished my mission and rolled onto my back staring up at the ceiling. Not wanting to be outdone, Tracey gently lifted my head and kissed me passionately, seemingly eager to taste her own juices. Again I found myself lost in a hypnotic sexual trance. The feeling was so overwhelming that I started to plunge myself inside of her. Tracey sensed my anticipation and knew that I was ready and anxious.

Tracey was feeling me too but wasn't ready; unbeknownst to me she had a plan of her own. She laid me down, not quite as gently as I had done her, and with a controlled force thrust my legs apart, exposing my manhood as if it were a telephone pole standing alone in the middle of a field. I closed my eyes and soon afterwards the warmth of her mouth surrounded my erection. As she pleasured me I looked up to the ceiling thinking to myself, "This girl is the truth!" After about twenty minutes of touching, tasting, and feeling, we were both finally ready to experience each other's most treasured parts, and what followed was something I have yet to figure out how to put into words.

The next day I awoke to the smell bacon and eggs and wasn't surprised to see Tracey walk through the bedroom door with a tray full of food. She sat the food in my lap and placed my drink on the nightstand. I expected her to crawl back into bed, but instead she asked, "Where are all of your dirty clothes and cleaning supplies?"

I looked up from my plate with a mouth full of food and

silently thought, "Whoa, I ain't about to let her wash my clothes. The next thing I know she going to be cracking for some dough." I finished chewing my food and said, "Don't worry 'bout it baby. You ain't got to do all that."

She quipped sarcastically, "I am aware of what I don't have to do; now if you don't mind, please tell me where your dirty clothes are." Attitude had always been a main attraction for me, and Tracey had it to spare. I didn't hesitate after her demand and told her where she could find everything. She gathered them together, separating the whites from the colors, and loaded them into the washer. Her assertiveness appealed to me in ways I didn't think possible, and I was reminded of the night when she approached me.

Until now I had wondered how much I could actually like this girl and truthfully was beginning to see that the boundaries were limitless. I watched her as she finished gathering all of my things, even going as far as to get the hand towels I used to wash my car from the garage. She came back into the house and proceeded to clean it from top to bottom. I had gone back upstairs and stretched out across the bed trying to doze off while my body digested the breakfast I'd just ate. That hope was dashed as Tracey forced me out of bed so she could remove the sheets from the mattress.

I was okay with it and decided to go handle a few errands and got showered and dressed. I felt comfortable leaving her there alone because I sensed she was stand up sista. I needed to get at Nicole, to see what was up with my jewelry. I waited until I left my house before calling her. I didn't want to disrespect Tracey by talking to another woman in her presence. At the rate Nicole and me were going, ain't no telling where that argument would've led.

The phone rang twice before Nicole answered it. I knew the voice on the other end was hers, but I asked for her anyway. "Hello, can I speak to Nicole?"

She responded, "Dis me."

I casually asked, "Whas going on, stranger? I been trying to get with you for a minute."

She said, "I'm sorry. I had gone out of town to Richmond to see my mom. I was gone for about a week, but I'm back now so whas-sup wit-choo?"

I replied, "Ain't nuffin up with me. I been trying to get at you so I could get my jewelry. When you going be home so I can come through?"

Nicole paused before saying, "I'll be here later. I'm on my way to work right now. The salon is packed and I ain't been there in a week. Call me about nine o'clock. I'll be home by then. But damn, that's all you called for; no hi Nicole or nothing, huh?" I thought to myself, "Bitch, you must be kidding! You been MIA for a whole week with over eight thousand dollars worth of jewelry." In my mind there wasn't anything else to talk about, but I humored her by saying, "My fault. How was Richmond?" My response came out scripted and lacked sincerity.

Nicole sucked her teeth hurriedly and said, "It's was cool. Just call me at nine o'clock."

She hung up the phone immediately afterwards, not allowing me to say anything more. I wondered why she didn't just have me meet her at the salon, but I guess that would have been too much like right. Now that I had mapped out my plan for retrieving my jewelry, I went and took care of a few other errands I had on my agenda for the day. Three hours had passed by the time I had finished and returned home to a spotlessly clean house. The smell of Pine-Sol and Downy permeated the entire house. Tracey had outdone herself.

I am a true bachelor, and my house hadn't been that clean since it was first constructed when I moved in. As I entered I could hear the faint sound of my stereo playing. The tune was new to me, but I liked it and wondered who it was. Curious, I walked over to the receiver and noticed an open CD case on top of it. I picked it up and read the cover. The artist was Michael Franks and the album was called Barefoot on the Beach. Track 3 was playing and the name of it was *"Now Love Has No End"*—and the shit was hot! I smiled thinking, "How appropriate."

Without even knowing it Tracey had done it again, exposed me to something new and thereby elevated my perception of taste. I put the CD case down and smiled, thinking she was definitely a classy sista. I looked around downstairs and assumed she must have been upstairs because the washroom was empty and all of my dirty clothes were gone. I walked upstairs and entered the master bedroom. Tracey was lying on the bed, and just like the night before, the sight of her put me in awe, only this time she was asleep and there were no bubbles to tease my view.

For some reason she was lying there in only her panties and bra and her body barely indented the freshly made bed. I stood there gazing at her as if for the first time for what seemed like an eternity. I found myself wondering what she would think if she knew I was so captivated by her. I forgot myself even more and slipped even deeper into fantasy thinking, "If I were to ever take a girlfriend, maybe Tracey could be her."

Everything about her was perfection, especially her bronze skin, velvety smooth legs, even down to the meticulous pedicure on her toes. I realized my fascination had nothing to do with lust but rather the appreciation for the natural beauty of a flawless black woman. My gaze was interrupted as Tracey moaned and turned to see me standing there. Her eyes met mine and she smiled saying, "Hey, baby, when you get back?" I was relieved she didn't know I had been standing there watching her for the last five minutes, thinking all sorts of thoughts I had no business thinking.

I had only been in love twice and had never met another woman who made me want consider loving again, but somehow Tracey was able to elicit those thoughts and it scared me. "I been back for about twenty minutes. I see you handled your business, though, so what's my tab?"

She looked at me half smiling and said, "Something light?"

I laughed and asked, "Yeah, what's that?"

She walked over, kissed me, and whispered in my ear "Dinner and a movie." Then, she left the room and headed downstairs to get something to drink. I stood there thinking that wasn't such a bad bargain after all she had put in work on both fronts.

I was more surprised at myself because I had never let one woman get two consecutive days unless it was someone I had imported from out of town. The day passed and before long I noticed it had gotten dark out. Tracey went home to freshen up and get dressed. Before she left I said, "Be ready at 10:30 pm. I'll call you if I come before then." It was quarter after nine by then, and I had gotten so consumed with my thoughts of Tracey that I had almost forgotten to call Nicole.

I picked up the phone and dialed her number, and she answered on the third ring, "Nigga, you cutting it close. I told you nine o'clock!"

I could barely respond for wondering why in the hell she appeared to be so angry. I kept my cool and said, "Naw, I just lost track of time, but I'm on my way."

She responded, "Just try to get here before ten-thirty 'cause my girlfriends and me are going to a dinner party."

I said, "Alright, that's cool. I'll be there in thirty minutes." As I hung up the phone I began to realize that Nicole seemed as if she was trying to dictate policy and use my jewelry as leverage to puppeteer my movements. I had already waited the entire day to get my shit, and now I had to get dressed, drive to Riverdale and back to Stone Mountain to pick up Tracey, a round trip of at least sixty miles and all within the span of one hour.

I called Tracey to tell her I might be running a little late, but I would be there no later than eleven o'clock. She was okay with it, allowing me a little more time to do all of that extra running around. By the time I got to Nicole's complex it was 10:23 pm. I parked my car, got out, and knocked on her door. There was no answer. I knocked again but this time a little harder, believing she may have been in the shower and just didn't hear me the first time.

I stood there for about three more minutes, knocked again, and looked around the parking lot to see if her beat up little Dodge Neon was anywhere in sight. It wasn't and I realized that she wasn't there either. I couldn't fucking believe it! I looked up into the moonlight sky mumbling, "This bitch is really trying me!" and afterward cursed myself for ever dealing with a broad like her in the first place. I immediately pulled out my cell phone and dialed her number. I couldn't wait to hear her excuse this time.

She left without telling me. She could've called but didn't and didn't even bother to tell me where I could meet her, not to mention the fact I had driven all the way to fucking Riverdale from Lithonia to her house. As the phone rang I didn't expect her to answer. She knew I would blast her for making me drive all the way to that side of town for nothing!

I was really tired of playing games with her, and the whole thing was starting to give me butterflies! I couldn't control my thoughts as my imagination began to run wild, and the thought of losing eight thousand dollars in jewelry was enough to make me sick to my stomach. I dialed Nicole a few more times and on the last call I left a message, "Yo, I'm out here like we agreed and it ain't even 10:30 yet. Whas fucked up is that you ain't have the decency to call me and say you was leaving out early. Look, how 'bout we just try it again tomorrow early, and at least that way no one should be inconvenienced."

I hung up the phone in disgust and called Tracey to see if she was dressed and to tell her I was on my way. "Whassup? Are you dressed?"

She responded, "Yeah, I'm dressed and hungry but I guess dinner's out 'cause it's already 10:45 and you just now calling me." Tracey was trying her best to be subtle, but I could tell she was irritated and I didn't blame her. I felt bad and decided to do something nice for her since she had shown me so much love. By the time I pulled up to her house she was standing in the door waiting.

When she came out I was blown away once again. Her hair was out and it draped over her exposed shoulders that were left bare by a strapless, form-fitting black Ci-Ci Hunter dress. She also wore a pair of high-heeled, tie-up Prada sandals. She looked so good I decided to get out and open the door for her, some shit I had never initiated on my own. As I closed her door I thought to myself, "Tonight she going on display."

I pulled out my cell phone and called Glenn. "What's up, old head? What you getting into tonight?"

Glenn laughed and responded, "It's your call, young buck. What you got in mind?"

I said, "Well, Ima be with Tracey tonight, and I figured you could grab one of your jawns and meet us at Taboo or something."

Glenn said, "Yeah, that sounds like a good idea. I'll call Sharon and make sure she at the door so if y'all get there before me she'll let y'all in." Sharon was a friend of Glenn's and had been the hostess for Café Echelon in Stone Mountain before the Dekalb County School District bought the property. She was probably the most attractive older woman I had ever seen. Rumor had it she was Japanese and black. Whatever it was it was enough to have Glenn ranting and raving about this woman every time he saw her. She was now the hostess for Taboo and always showed Glenn strong love whenever he came out. She would even bless his friends with the same love if he requested it.

I didn't notice it at first, but Tracey had been looking and listening to me make plans for the night. After I got off the phone she leaned over and kissed me on the cheek. Surprised I asked, "What was that for?"

She said, "For being a gentleman and for thinking enough of me to take me out clubbing with you and your friend." She was right because I was never the nigga to take a broad with me to a club, but like I said she looked incredible that night and I wanted the world to know it.

She didn't know it, but I had one more surprise up my sleeve. I decided to take her to a nice little intimate spot called Sambuca's. Their menu consisted of a light fare and they served dinner thru midnight. I liked the atmosphere. It was classy and the dress code was strictly enforced! I called ahead and made reservations. When we got there we were seated next to the stage. Sambuca's had a nightly jazz ensemble, and it contributed to the romantic ambiance it was famous for. By the time Tracey and I finished our meal, we were acting like two teenage kids who had crushes on one another, holding hands and hugging.

Secretly I couldn't wait to get to Taboo because I wanted Glenn to see just how beautiful she looked. When we arrived I called Glenn, and he met us at the front and pointed to us in the line, and Sharon told us to come to the front, and when we got there she ushered us straight to where Glenn had a table and a couple bottles of Moet waiting. Glenn was sitting at the table with a tall, attractive woman, one I had never seen before, which was surprising considering I had seen virtually all of the women he had frequented with in Atlanta.

"Tracey, this is Monica; Monica this is Tracey." They each said hello to one another and sat back down. Glenn seemed to be enjoying his companion, and I was definitely enjoying mine. The night was fun and after a bunch of dancing, mingling, and sipping champagne, we all converged back at our table. We'd finished both bottles of Moet and were waiting for our server to return to our table. I noticed she was at the rear of the dining area waiting on another table.

As she leaned up and removed the plates and glasses from the table, I saw a familiar face sitting directly in my line of sight—it was that bitch Nicole! My first thought was to go over to her table and blast her for that bull shit earlier, but then I remembered I had Tracey with me and that would have been a definite scene.

Chapter Forty-Four
Tracey's Let Down

I usually slept in on Sunday mornings, but after seeing Nicole at Taboo the night before I was anxious as hell to call her. I'd spent the night with Tracey and rolled out of bed early, hoping not to disturb her and catch Nicole while it was still early. The phone rang its usual three rings, and at the start of the fourth one I was beginning to think she wasn't going to answer. I'd blocked my number this time so I knew it wasn't because she was ducking me. To my surprise she answered the phone sounding wide awake. She said, "Hello."

I said, "Morning, Nicole."

Surprised, Nicole responded, "Who dis?"

She knew who it was and was probably mad that I blocked my number and got through, but I played along as usual and said, "It's Malik."

Disappointedly she responded, "Oh, whassup?"

Sensing the tension and not wanting to create more I said, "Damn, it's like dat. Did I do something wrong?"

She snapped back, "No, you ain't do nothing wrong, but you keep calling me 'bout this fucking jewelry."

That was it. I couldn't take anymore and blasted her saying, "Whoa, whoa, whoa, who the fuck you talking to like dat? Maybe if you wasn't playing cat and mouse, you wouldn't have to fucking hear from me no more."

Nicole paused, obviously surprised by my sudden outburst and responded, "Well, my rent was due."

I turned the music down on the radio unsure if I'd heard her correctly, and said, "Whachoo say?" Nicole remained silent after that, and all I could think was, "This bitch done put some shit in the game!"

I'd heard her originally and only wanted to hear it again for confirmation but quickly departed from that objective and said, "What the fuck do your rent got to do wit my jewelry."

She responded, "Well, I'm just saying ain't nobody helping me, and I'm down here by myself and my family is back in Richmond so I got to do what I got to do!"

I felt like my head was about to explode from anger and said, "First of all, what the fuck are you doing in Atlanta if you can't take care of yourself anyway? Cause it's the wrong place to be trying to find yourself. You bitches kill me coming down here thinking it's sweet and thinking y'all gon catch some rich dick-head willing to take care of y'all asses when y'all ain't bringing shit to the table! Yeah, and it may work for a few of y'all, but I ain't the one!"

I could hear Nicole's breathing coming through the phone. The bitch was hot! "Who the fuck you think you calling bitch, bitch? That's why I pawned your shit! You a cheap-ass Philly-nigga, and the shit wasn't even platinum, it was white gold! You think you the shit, nigga. You ain't the shit. I know real niggas das getting it! You broke bitch!"

I had laughed when she said that because she showed she had the typical ghetto mentality, thinking since my jewelry wasn't platinum that it somehow reduced the level of quality and value it held. I fell back thinking, "How in the hell did I let myself deal with this nothing-ass bitch in the first place" before responding, "Let me tell you something dummy, you watch too many fucking videos and listen to too much rap music. My shit still cost eight thousand dollars, and I don't care who wearing platinum, I bought white gold! And whatever it was I see you thought enough of it to pawn it, you broke bitch!"

All Nicole could think to say after that was "Whateva." She obviously felt the impact of what I'd said. Meanwhile I was still wondering why I always seemed to let my dick make my decisions for me. After all, everything I was going through was my own fault. This is what I lived for: beautiful women, one nighters, and no attachments. The shit normally worked out fine. This time I wasn't so lucky because this bitch was beginning to look more and more like Regan from the Exorcist, all that was left for her to do was vomit and piss on the floor!

I had had enough of going back and forth with Nicole and paused long and hard before saying, "I can't believe you pawned my jewelry." Nicole tried to comment, but I cut her off saying, "That's cool. Bitch Ima holla at-choo!" and hung up the phone.

I decided that I was going show that bitch who I was, I grabbed my keys, got in my car, and headed straight to her house with every intention of knocking her fucking head off. As I drove I kept replaying the shit repeatedly in my head in disbelief. It was all so unbelievable and crazy that I had to tell somebody and called G. "Old head, remember that nothing-ass bitch from the Shark Bar parking lot?"

G responded, "Yeah, the one with phat-ass, right?"

I said, "Yeah, how 'bout I left my jewelry over at the bitch's crib by accident and she pawned it, and when I asked about it the bitch got fly and disrespected me even more saying that I wasn't no real nigga, and I was broke because my jewelry was white gold instead of platinum."

G laughingly asked, "Where you at now?"

I responded, "I'm on my way to her fucking crib to knock her head off!"

G laughed again before saying, "No, no, you don't want to do that. If I'm correct you told me she live in Riverdale right? That's Clayton County, and excuse my French, but them dick-heads will cut ya fucking balls off and hand em to ya pahtna!"

As I sat there listening to G, I realized he was right and I became more frustrated than I was before and said, "What am I supposed to do G 'cause I ain't 'bout to lose to this bitch!"

G took a deep breadth and ran it down, "First of all, what she did was stealing. Think about it. If you drop your cell phone in McDonald's and someone sees you drop it and deliberately prevents you from noticing it or picks it up and pockets it, that's theft. The fact that she acknowledged it was your shit and pawned it anyway without your permission means she stole it. All you need to do is produce paperwork proving it belonged to you and with that you can go to Clayton County and get a warrant for her arrest."

I shifted in my seat as I pondered G's advice and said, "This is street shit and street shit should stay in the street."

G chuckled and said, "Yeah, but you ain't in Philly nigga. This is Georgia, and you ain't got no win down here putting your hands on a female. So if you wanna win, then do it the way I tell you to, starting with calling her back and apologizing."

I responded, "Nigga, you crazy. I ain't 'bout to apologize to her for stealing my shit."

G, very coolly and calmly, said, "Yeah, you are, and I'll tell you why. She has the receipt from the pawn shop, and without that you won't ever get your shit back, and if you get the receipt you'll have proof by way of her signature that she actually pawned it. So call her back now, turn on the charm, and hit me back when you finish to let me know how it went."

I called Nicole as G instructed and she went for it. I guess she was all too happy to be relieved of a debt that would now be in my lap. Her giving me the receipt was all I needed, and the next day I went down to Clayton County and got a court date for the case to be heard.

A few days after the fall out with Nicole, I got a phone call from Tracey. Several days had passed since we last spoke, and after my run in with Nicole I didn't have no rap for none of them Atlanta broads. "Hey, Malik. I haven't heard from you in a few days. What's up with that?"

I responded, "I'm just chillin, takin' a break, you know. Just trying do me das all."

Tracey's tone switched from pleasant to hostile as she said, "Huh? What does that mean? I need you to elaborate."

I hesitated because I didn't expect her to be so adamant in demanding an explanation and said, "Like I said, I'm just falling back ya-mean? I ain't doing nuffin."Tracey responded, "No, I don't know what you mean, but I tell you what. Don't let me stop you from doing you now that you're finished doing me. But that's cool. Bye!" I knew I fucked up, but that shield that'd always protected my heart popped right back up after Nicole did what she did. Truth was, I was scared to love and didn't really know how to deal with a real black woman so I did what came natural to me, crawled back into my shell and shut everybody out.

Two weeks had passed since I filed charges against Nicole. Although Clayton County Police department allowed me to file them, they couldn't automatically issue a warrant without a judges approval. I was advised that I would receive notice of a warrant hearing in the mail at which point I would be required to appear and argue the reason I believed the charges were justified. When the day finally came I couldn't wait to see how things were going to play out. , I was the first to arrive in the courtroom and was surprised to see Nicole and a girlfriend enter smiling and laughing. I couldn't help thinking, "If I get played out and lose this silly-assed case, this bitch gon really think ima joke."

Shortly after that the judge came to the bench, and I was glad to see it was a woman. I thought at least by her being a woman I felt there would be no sympathy for the opposite sex, and she would represent for positive independent women. Boy was I ever right. By the time she was through with Nicole the baliff was placing handcuffs on her, and her girlfriend who shared the laughs with her was asking her for the car keys so she could get home. I left the courtroom feeling good, not so much because I got my jewelry back but because of the principle. What made me laugh the most was that

Nicole had no reason to be in court that day; the hearing was for me. She came thinking it was all a joke, but when the judge found her guilty that smile left Nicole's face quicker than roaches scatter once the lights are turned on! And since she was already in the courtroom Clayton County didn't even have to go and find her.

I knew after that Nicole would definitely think twice before she did it to somebody else, and I was cool with that. But for real, for real, the way it all went down still had my head spinning, and I couldn't believe she even tried me like that. Thank God, G stopped me before I did something stupid. I never really believed a person could learn from someone else's experience. I guess all the shit he and Tina had gone through was enough to make him rethink all of his future actions when it came to dealing with women.

Weeks had gone by before I realized I hadn't spoken to him, and I decided to give him a call to let him know I appreciated the advice he gave me. "G, what's up, man? I just wanted to hit you up and tell you good looking out. Cause Clayton County hammered her ass! After I flashed those receipts and she stupidly admitted she pawned my stuff, the judge looked at her and gave her 10 days in jail, three hundred hours of community service, ordered her to pay court costs, and fined her an additional one thousand dollars for pawning stolen merchandise!"

G could barely contain his laughter as I finished telling him the story and said, "Ain't that some shit? These broads will try you, but I bet she respect you now though." I interrupted G in mid-sentence and said, "Speaking of respect, how 'bout she called to apologize two days ago for the whole thing. It fucked me up when she called 'cause she had talked so greasy to me during the entire ordeal. I didn't even know how to take it in. But I listened and could tell she regretted what she'd done."

G said, "She probably figured she could get away with it and that you would respond in a typical way by putting your hands on her. If you had, then the stolen jewelry would've ceased to be the issue, and yo' ass would be fighting an assault charge—in Clayton County no less." G was right. I am so glad I put a little strategy behind my actions this time. "So what's up with the nice girl you took to Taboo that night? You probably got her on wifey status by now the way you was acting."

I tried to ignore G's question because I knew I was going to catch it once he found out I cut her off. I ended up responding, "Man,

I fell back 'cause I'm just tired of this shit man."

G paused before saying, "Tired of what? What she do?" Before I could respond G said, "Tell me you didn't cut that girl off." He sat on the other side of the phone silently in disbelief until finally saying, "Know what man, this is making me physically sick." He repeated it again, "I mean physically sick. Here I am, out here looking for love and can't find it, loving a bitch who don't deserve it and left one who did; and you cut off one of the best ones to step foot in our circle since I don't know when and all because of your disappointment over another female. Malik, you a real fucking dick head."

The phone went dead after that. G had hung up on me. I didn't care, though, because it seemed like most of the sistas I had met since I had been in this town seemed to be on some bullshit anyway, and I was tired of it. I felt I should just walk away from 'em all because nothing seemed real; I couldn't be appreciated for being me. It seemed like everything was face value with highly attractive black women. And the only reason Tracey hadn't shown her ass yet was because we rarely dealt with each other.

As for the rest of them, if you wasn't pulling up in a highline foreign car or coming at 'em with various industry-related tales—I'm a producer, a rapper, etc.—then you didn't have a shot! I knew that first hand because on many days, handling business required I drive my second vehicle, which was a 96' Chevy Caprice. In the midst of working or running errands I would occasionally stumble across various women whom I would approach. Although I did find limited success with some, even with them I noticed it was harder than it was whenever I drove the jag. The thought and reality of it made me sick! I thought about all of my homies who chose the drug game all because they wanted street fame, easy money, but mostly to be recognized and desired by attractive black women, the majority of whom don't have a pot to piss in or window to throw it out, but don't have no problem proclaiming: "If a Nigga ain't got no money, he better not say shit to me."

Face value is a mutha-fucka! Woman can be so stupid 'cause they think if a dude is driving a nice car then it must be his. There were plenty of times when G and I would swap seats and chauffer each other in either his car or mine. It was always funny to watch women run to the driver side to holla at whichever one of us was driving whatever car that day, never knowing the passenger was the owner; and that's what made me physically sick!.

Chapter Forty-Five
Peasey

My hands were full of residue as I walked out of the house. I had just finished cooking up. I don't know why I didn't wash my hands. My man and I had just finished breaking down a whole brick. I promised to front him four and half ounces for helping me cook it up. After I passed off, I packed up my shit and rolled out.

Shit had gotten hot on the block, and I had been reduced to contracting with niggas who wasn't really on top of their game. You know the kind: niggas who are always begging you to put 'em on and then front like they had it all along. This particular dude was always asking me to front him something on consignment. Everybody had been telling me not to fuck with him 'cause it was rumored he was down with the Feds. I didn't really believe it 'cause niggas on the block was always shitting on a nigga's reputation, especially if he was getting money.

Duce had been locked up once and mysteriously got released from jail after being caught with a large amount of weight. Everybody on the street thought he was snitching, but I knew the case had been thrown out by the state 'cause they didn't have no probable cause. I was never too quick to judge the next man by what niggas on the street said about him, mainly 'cause those same street niggas spent a lot of time hating on my brothers and me. All of us had been getting money for years. From the oldest on down to the youngest, we were all connected up and down the east coast, from Philly to Delaware and D.C. to Georgia.

You got to watch yourself around street niggas who ain't got shit 'cause it ain't nothing for them to set you up, stick you up, or take your life, thinking they can cash in on the ultimate jackpot. When Duce and I first pulled up to his apartment, I noticed there were a few strange looking white dudes sitting around in different cars. I didn't think nothing of it 'cause he lived in a predominantly white suburban neighborhood, but by the time we were leaving I had a real strange feeling walking to my car. As I drove out of the complex I noticed one of the white men I had seen earlier started to drive off too.

Duce had left out the same time as me, and when he got to the intersection he turned right and I turned left. All of a sudden a red flashing light appeared on the dashboard of the same car I saw the strange white man I saw sitting in the parking lot earlier. Duce's ass was fucked 'cause he had put those four ounces I gave him in the trunk of the car when we left his apartment. I thought for sure the nigga wouldn't have been stupid enough to pull over—but he did! Just as the undercover was getting out of his car to approach Duce, I drove past a county K-9 unit parked about three hundred yards facing the opposite direction. Then it hit me. Those mufuckas had been waiting on us—we had been setup!

I knew because a county police K-9 unit was a strange sight in that part of town. I hadn't gotten more than ten feet past him when I looked in my rearview mirror and saw him u-turn and pull out right behind me. I knew what the deal was from that point and waited to see the flashing lights and hear the tell-tale whoop-whoop of the siren. No sooner had the thought crossed my mind than I heard the siren; I couldn't believe they were pulling me over! Stopping was not an option for me 'cause I had a little over a half a brick in the truck, a fully loaded nine millimeter Desert Eagle with a 16 shot clip sitting in my lap, and coke residue all over my hands and steering wheel!

Luckily, I was less than a mile from the interstate and only three miles from the Pennsylvania state line. I figured if I could just make it to the highway I would be cool. By this time the police could tell I had no intention of stopping. Out of nowhere three more police cruisers appeared, but they were all behind the original vehicle tailing me. I maintained my composure as if I didn't know I was the person they intended to stop. Just as I hit the overpass connecting Namaan's Road to the onramp of I-95 north, I hit the gas, sped through the red light, and hit the freeway!

I had about three miles to go before I saw the "Welcome to Pennsylvania" sign that sits on the right side of the northbound freeway, marking the divide between Delaware and Pennsylvania. I was doing about eighty miles per hour by this time and was right on the state line when I looked into my rearview mirror and saw what looked like a scene from Smokey and the Bandit. Delaware cops were everywhere! As I crossed the state line I wasn't sure whether the Pennsylvania authorities would try to intercept me, or if the Delaware cops could even pursue me from that point.

They stopped a little ways past the line and were actually already within the Pennsylvania state boundary. As I sped along the highway headed north, I began to see a whole slew of Pennsylvania state and township police getting onto the freeway from all directions. They were even crossing the grass median that separated the northbound side and the southbound side of I-95. I guessed they were going after me.

Luckily, I knew the area like the back of my hand, and now that that Delaware K-9 unit was out of the picture, I figured if I jumped out I wouldn't have to worry about no fucking dog tracking me down and eating my ass when it caught up with me! All of the coke was sitting in the front passenger seat. I carried it that way for just such possibilities so that I could easily dispose of it if need be. I wasn't about to get caught crossing state lines with a kilo of crack and a loaded gun. If that happened, I knew I would never see beyond prison walls again.

I called my brother younger brother Ceez on his cell phone and told him what was happening. "Man, you ain't gon believe this. The fucking police is on my ass and I am dirty as a mufucka!"

The first thing Ceez said was "Where you at?"

I replied, "I'm on 95 north passing through Chester right now, and the Pennsylvania state boys are on my ass!"

Ceez's main girl Nicky lived in Chester, right off of the Highland Avenue exit, which I was coming up on fast. I said, "I'm by Nicky's exit. Call her and tell her to unlock her door so I can run in. I'm 'bout to ditch this fucking truck!"

The thought of ditching my truck turned my stomach. I had just bought it. It was a 2001 green Mercedes M55 with chrome 22-inch wheels. I hadn't had it a month, and now I didn't have no choice but to get rid of it.

Excitedly Ceez asked, "What you got on you?"

I responded, "Man, I got half a brick in the car and my nine!"

Ceez immediately said what I had already planned to do, "Nigga break that shit up and let it crumble out the window. They won't never find that shit!"

He was right and I grabbed the bag and started banging it on the dashboard to break it apart. Luckily, it was still kind of moist since it had just been cooked up. It fell apart like nothing. The PA State boys were closing in fast and seemed to be having no problem finding my truck, which stood out like a sore thumb in the crowd of all the other SUVs. Thankfully, they were still about a quarter mile behind me.

I calmly slowed my speed just a little and exited onto Highland Avenue, sprinkling the cocaine as I entered Chester. Chester is a small suburb township located about 10 miles outside of Philly. Ceez had made good and called Nicky. He hit me back and told me she was home, and the door was unlocked. I was going to need a place to duck out in after I ditched my truck! I felt like I was in the Twilight Zone. I had just got that pack and now it was gone! The worst part was that I had got it on consignment. Now not only did I not have a way to hustle the forty thousand I owed, but if I wasn't careful I would be in police custody.

The truth was I ain't really give a fuck about the police. I knew once I disposed of the coke and the gun it, was nothing they could really do to me. I was more afraid of not being able to pay my debt I had with my connect. I was already in the hole with him for ten grand, and now it had become fifty! A million thoughts were entering my head at once, but the one that kept coming back to the front was, "What in the fuck was I thinking when I decided to deal with that nigga Duce?!"

The law of the street is real simple—never deal with a nigga who has been in contact with the law. Even if he wasn't snitching, common sense should have told me that he was definitely still hot. When the state was forced to drop the charges against him, they got petty and turned it over to the Feds. And them fuckers ain't got nothing, but time and money to wait on yo ass to fuck up. And that is exactly what I had just done—fucked up!

The unmarked car that pulled Duce over had to be DEA and the county cop posted down the road was their back up. Duce swore nobody knew where he lived. I guess a little bird told them—stool pigeon or canary, somebody dropped dime on that nigga and got me all caught up in his mix!

Chapter Forty-Six
Midnight Train to Georgia

"Yo, did he make it?"

"Yeah, he's here now." Nicky was looking at me as she responded to Ceez's question.

"Let me talk to him."

Nicky said, "Your brother wants to talk to you."

"What's up, nigga? You cool?"

"Yeah, man, I'm alright, just a little out of breath, that's all."

I played it off as much as I could because I wasn't cool, nor was I alright. That shit was crazy and I was scared to death. I was already on my last leg, and without that last pack I was crippled.

Ceez could tell I was frontin' and said, "Don't worry 'bout that shit man. Ima hold you down. The only thing that we have to do at this point is get you somewhere so you can be on the D-L." He was right, but I wasn't about to go back out onto the street. The police were everywhere, like a swarm of killer bees looking for someone to attack. I visualized what would have happened to me had I gotten caught; that Rodney king shit would have been nothing compared to what those fuckers would have done to me, especially after I took 'em on a high-speed chase and all.

"PeasyPeasey, are you listening to me? Nigga, you need to get your head straight man so we can get a plan together."

I couldn't think about anything at that point and said, "Man, Ima go lay down for a while and get my thoughts together. I'll hit you back later." I handed the phone back to Nicky and went and sat on the couch.

I couldn't believe it. My life was over. I was wanted by the police, the Feds, and I owed my connect fifty grand. I didn't have any place I could go and no way to get there—and it was all good just a week ago. I was that dude in Delaware. All my brothers and me had been getting much paper in that town for years, and now it was over for me—forever. Nicky was always cool with me and I treated her like a sister. She was almost blood because her and Ceez had been together for like five years and had been through a lot of shit. It felt good being someplace safe with someone I could trust.

Nicky came over to the couch and sat next to me and put her hand on my back. She patted it gently before saying, "Don't worry. I know your brothers' are going to make sure you will be okay." She was right. As stressed as I was, I knew that between the three of them; shit would be worked out. No sooner had she said that than my cell phone rang. It was Dax. He was the second oldest. "Peasey, you alright?" I started to respond to him, but he interrupted me and said, "Listen, I got a bitch on her way up there to get you, and she going to call you when she get to the Crozier Medical Center right off of the Highland Avenue exit. I want you to catch a cab to Crozier, and from there she is going to drive you down to D.C. to Ceez's crib. You got any dough on you?"

I said, "I got a couple hundred on me, but that shit ain't gon get me far."

Dax replied, "Don't worry about it. I gave the bitch a stack, and Ceez going to have some more for you when you get to D.C. Do G know what happened yet?" I hoped he didn't because I knew I was going to catch if he did. He was the oldest and was the glue that held us all together. He was always telling us to get out of the game and that if we wasn't rich by now, then it was time to walk away. We weren't rich, but life had been good to us. Now, though, I could see what he meant because this shit wasn't worth it.

I had always heard life on the run was a bitch, and now I was about to find out firsthand what it was really like. Dax mentioned that the word on the street was out that I was wanted, and the police had put out a wide dragnet for me. Wilmington, Delaware is a small town, but the drug trade there is huge. The city had established a Task Force comprised of federal, state, and local law enforcement to combat Wilmington's drug culture when crack selling was in its infancy.

The task force had been in place so long that all of my brothers, from the oldest to the youngest, had fallen at some point or another under investigation by it. Detective Lee Solomon was the lead investigator in the Task Force, and he had had a hard dick for my brothers and me for years. He knew each of us by name and would regularly harass us whenever any of us were spotted. I was the last of us to get in the game and the only one who had never been caught. Now that that was no longer the case, I knew he would be happier than a faggot in Boys' Town at the news I had slipped up.

Thankfully, they didn't know where Nicky lived and had no idea of what my next move would be. Hell, I didn't know either. But one thing was certain: Solomon was trying to find out bad as hell 'cause my cell phone was ringing off the hook. I found out he had gone to my sister's house and all of my known girlfriend's houses, too. After he left my sister's house, she got on the phone and immediately called Dax, and he called Ceez. Both Ceez, and Dax downplayed what happened because they knew she would call our mother, who didn't need to be worried unnecessarily.

All of her sons had been in the game for the better part of their lives, and I know that was stress enough. The news of the high-speed chase, and an all points bulletin would've probably given her a heart attack. Even if she found out, I knew I could spin the situation. I just didn't want G to know; the thought of that didn't sit well. I knew it was inevitable, but I just wanted a little time so I could get my thoughts and my story together.

I knew once he got to me, he would question me mercilessly about what, when, where, why and how. I could hear him asking me, "What in the fuck was I thinking fucking with a nigga I knew had been knocked already!" I guess that's just what big brothers do. All day the thoughts in my head kept me on edge, "What was I going to do, and how was I going to live, and then the call came. I was both relieved and nervous at the same time.

"What's up, young buck? I see them niggas finally got you by the balls, huh?" I started to respond, but I could tell G wasn't done talking and that his question was rhetorical. I was right and he continued, "Listen, I don't care who you been talking to or who you think is cool with you, but get that shit out of your head right now. Say your goodbyes and get ready to detach 'cause this shit is done and over with. You got to start living for you now, and that is the only way you will be able to stay out here. Your family is your backbone now, and your friends ain't shit!"

G knew what he was talking about. He had been on the run once for five years and didn't get caught. Fortunately, he only did it to avoid a bunch of traffic offenses and a possible probation violation, but he pulled it off. He came in from the cold after an amicable negotiation between his attorney and the prosecution. What resulted was an in-depth knowledge of the do's and don'ts of life on the run.

He had books on identity changing and how to be a fugitive as well as one called How to Disappear Completely and Never be Found. I'd remembered reading that one for pleasure once when I was visiting him at his apartment. I enjoyed it and never thought there would have ever been a time when I would need to put any of what I read into practice. G didn't know the details of my situation and never asked. I could tell he knew that if he did know he would be violating some law. So he kept his concerns centered on my safety. He knew I had owed a few cats, and they wanted to holla at me about they dough. And by the time our conversation was finished, he had constructed a plan on how to get me out of Washington, D.C. and down south to Atlanta, Georgia.

✱✱

"All aboard. Please have your tickets ready when boarding the train." I was hoping to get lost in the crowd of people on the platform. The fact that I managed to get to Washington, D.C. from Chester, PA was nothing short of a miracle. The police presence was visible at every state line crossing from Pennsylvania on down to Maryland. They also had lookouts at every train and bus station in the area. As I boarded the train the anxiety I felt was almost unbearable.

It was as if I was a paranoid schizophrenic. I was hearing voices and thought every white man I saw was after me. The ride to Atlanta took an eternity. I found myself drifting in and out of thought about my life and the lives of all those I loved. Life as I once knew it was over. I had always wanted to get out of the game; I just thought I would have been able to do it a little more gracefully than it went down. Sitting on that train, riding into midnight and headed to Georgia felt strange; I wanted to sleep, but the thought of being watched and ultimately captured prevented me from relaxing.

I slumped down into the seat and leaned my head on the window. A tear rolled down my cheek as I wrestled with the thought

258

of my new reality. The uncertainty of my tomorrow toyed with my sanity and kept me from entertaining hope in any form. By the time the train pulled into Atlanta the next morning I was exhausted. I got out of my seat and cautiously made my way to the rear of the train to exit.

I went to the baggage car and waited until the porter unloaded all of the remaining baggage, and when I saw my bag I snatched it as quick as I could and disappeared into the shadows of the station. Ceez had already called G and let him know what my status was and to let him know I had made it. I had tossed my cell phone shortly after the chase because I knew the Feds can sometimes trace your whereabouts by isolating the signal to a space of a few city blocks. I didn't want to run the risk of them finding out I was in Georgia.

G was on point as was his usual, showed up as planned, and covertly picked me up. I was glad to see him. His presence had a kind of calming effect, the kind you get when you know everything is going to be alright. "Young Peasey, whassup wit-choo? You alright?" My real name is Sean but Peasey was a nickname G had given me when I was little because my hair used to be really beady and unmanageable. He used it so much over the years that it stuck.

I didn't want to rain on his enthusiasm, but his loud reception made me uneasy and forced me to whisper, "Chill G, I don't want to bring any unnecessary attention to what's going on with me." I was blessed to have a brother like G. He always knew exactly what to do no matter the situation. After we finished securing my things, we took a moment to hug each other and get personal.

"How was the trip down?"

I laughed sarcastically and said, "Nigga, that shit was the worst. I thought every white man I saw was 5-0. Shit was so bad I couldn't go to sleep."

G laughed and said, "Trust me when I tell you that if they was the Feds you wouldn't be standing here now 'cause they would not have hesitated to snatch yo ass the minute they saw you." That's what I loved about my older brother, his brutal honesty. I don't know if he was that way purposely or it just came naturally, but he had this way of putting things into perspective. It was sometimes hard to accept but always beneficial.

After we got everything packed in the car we briefly scanned the parking lot to make sure no one was watching. Satisfied we were unnoticed we calmly pulled away and headed toward downtown Atlanta.

Chapter Forty-Seven
1660 Peachtree

"Just put your stuff in the room on the left. Don't worry about hanging it up. I don't have any hangers." The apartment was nice; it was a two bedroom with a fireplace overlooking I-85, ironically less than two blocks from the train station. G took the long way to get there and drove through downtown Atlanta as he was unsure if we had been noticed. Like I said, he was thorough.

We drove for about twenty minutes and ended up back where we started, westbound on Peachtree, As we crossed the overpass I noticed G had flipped on his turn signal to make a right turn into a gated community that looked like a fortress. We drove four levels in an upward spiral, arriving on the fourth floor. I unloaded all of my things from the car, carried them into the apartment, and put them into the second bedroom.

G said, "Listen, I'm 'bout to run out for a minute, but I will be back in a few hours. If you need anything just call me." G gave me his number and instructed me not to call anybody from up top because the Feds would very likely be monitoring everyone who I was known to associate with, especially family. "Listen Sean, don't fuck around. The shit they trying to get you on is major. If you want to enjoy your freedom, then you had better do what I tell you. Otherwise you will find yourself sitting behind bars saying 'Damn' and asking yourself, 'Why in the hell didn't I just do what he told me to do?'"

I listened to G tell me what to do and knew it was in my best interest to do what he said. After all, he knew the game having been through it himself. Before leaving he said, "If you get hungry, there's food in the freezer or you can order some Chinese. If you ain't got no dough, there's some money in the top dresser drawer."

I watched him make his way to the door and leave out. I walked up and made sure it was closed and checked the locks, even though I had just heard the tumblers clicking as he put his key in from the outside and locked it himself. I was becoming cautiously optimistic about being with him because he never seemed to worry about anything. He was the go-to guy in the family and always had shit under control. I made my way to his bedroom after that and flopped down on his bed. I laid there staring at the ceiling, dazed and confused about what had just happened to me. My heart was still aflutter, and my stomach seemed like it had a million butterflies flittering around inside it. I wanted to reach out and call someone—anyone—but I knew I couldn't. Not just because G told me not to, but because I had to let go of my past and never look back.

****

I was knocked out when G came back in the house and was only awakened when the door slammed behind him as it closed. I looked at the clock and saw six hours had passed, and I was still sleepy. I heard a few voices in the living room and crawled out of the bed and walked in to see who G was talking to. I was surprised to see it was Malik. Ceez and I had known him for about three years; we used to hang out in Philly way before G met him.

He smiled and did an impression of Tommy Lee Jones saying, "Your fugitive's name is Dr. Richard Kimble. Go get him!" Although I wasn't in the best of moods, I had to laugh at Malik's reference to The Fugitive. Dr. Kimble was the lead character played by Harrison Ford and Tommy Lee Jones was the U.S. Marshall who was hunting him. It felt good to laugh, and I appreciated Leek's attempt at making me feel better. I grabbed his hand and pulled him in close, hugging him, and said, "Whassup wit-choo, nigga? I ain't know you was still down here."

Ceez mentioned that Malik had been considering moving up to D.C., and I thought that he had already rolled out. I was happy to see him because he and I were basically the same age, and I wasn't looking forward to trying to create a new relationship with G, who still treated me like as his little brother.

"What's up, man? I know you got to be hungry. You wanna go get a grub?" Malik could see I was still a little on edge after having escaped from Pennsylvania, and he was trying to find a way to ease some of my anxiety.

I looked over to G, who was on the phone talking with a female. I saw right away he wasn't going to allow my presence to affect his day-to-day practices. He heard Malik and paused long enough from his conversation to acknowledge Malik's inquiry and nodded to me, letting me know it was cool. He finished his conversation in time enough to say, "Look, whatever you do, don't drive and make sure you don't carry any identification with you. Malik, is your license good?"

Malik looked at him and said, "Yeah, nigga, you know my shit has always been straight. It's how I make my living."

G responded, "Good, 'cause if the police pull y'all over, they won't ask Sean anything as long as the driver has a valid license." G had read a lot of books, but I knew his information didn't come from research, it was from genuine experience. He knew the driver of any vehicle, if licensed, could vouch for the identity of his passenger without arousing suspicion. He also knew that in Georgia, if you were stopped and didn't have any legitimate identification on you, the police had the right to arrest you and hold you for seventy-two hours. G found that out the hard way years ago while scalping Braves tickets down at the old Fulton county baseball stadium when he was detained because of not having any identification.

They kept him because there was no one with him to validate his identity. I always remembered him complaining about the incident. He questioned its legality and lambasted the state of Georgia for even having the desire to deal in such pettiness. He was released two days later, after they'd run his name and fingerprints through NCIC—the National Crime Information Center—and it came back with no holds.

It was cool being in Malik's presence. For just a moment, it felt as if nothing had happened, and I was instead just visiting a friend and out enjoying the scenery of downtown Atlanta while driving down Peachtree Street. The illusion ended when Malik asked, "How much shit did you have in the wheel?"

I was looking out the window when he asked the question and continued to do so as I answered him. "I had a half a brick in the car and a fully loaded Desert Eagle, too." Malik shook his head and sighed, "Whew," and then asked, "What was you doing with a gat anyway, nigga? You don't get down like?"

He was right. I was never violent and was cool with everybody in Delaware. Me carrying a gun was totally out of character. I had started doing so because of an incident involving some chick I was screwing. "Man, remember the bitch I was fucking with named Kiana? We fell out a month ago 'cause I found out she was fucking the nigga L-B from the eastside. The broad tried to play me thinking I ain't know. Ceez was cool with a lot of them niggas, but I ain't really fuck with 'em all like that. Anyway, after I confronted her about the shit, she said something real slick about how them niggas was playing stronger than west-side niggas. I laughed and said, 'Them niggas be getting they shit from us.' The next thing I know, I hear she went back and told them cats I said they work for us! Shortly after that, the word on the street was they was trying to see me about it."

Malik looked at me and said, "I know you ain't talking about that dusty ass bitch you used to bring to Philly with you?"

I hesitated, because I didn't want to acknowledge it, but knew I couldn't put it off on anybody else. Reluctantly I said, "Yeah, that's the same one." I paused because I knew I was about to hear it from Malik, and then it came.

"When y'all niggas gon get enough of taking these street bitches personal? Ceez is the only one out of all of y'all that don't give a fuck 'bout these bitches. Pillow talking with that broad got you caught up in some shit that didn't even happen the way she said it did." Malik paused, and then looked at me again. This time his eyes lit up as if he just saw a ghost. "Wait. is that L-B nigga the same cat that put a gun to Ceez's head and took fifty stacks from him?"

I paused 'cause I didn't know Malik had heard about that, and because I didn't want to confirm it, knowing it all happened because of me. Instead of responding verbally, I tried to offset the effect by hunching my shoulders and tilting my head to the side in reluctant acknowledgement. Malik said, "God-damn, so that bitch is the reason Ceez got stung for fifty grand and part of the reason you in Georgia, huh?"

I didn't respond to that but said, "Look man, I don't even want to talk about all that shit, and G don't know nothing about it either so keep that shit to yourself."

Malik dug himself and remembered I was already stressed out, and his riding me about the past wasn't going to change it. "Yo, my fault man. I just can't help getting mad about the shit 'cause these black bitches is treacherous."

Malik's statement seemed to be rooted in something deeper

264

than our conversation justified. The contempt he expressed resonated in every word he spoke and culminated finally when he said, "I can't stand these broke, nothing ass bitches."

We were pulling into Houston's parking lot as Malik finished his statement. The valet opened his door and said, "Welcome to Houston's." Malik didn't acknowledge him and met me at the entrance to the restaurant and we walked in. "Hello and welcome to Houston's. How many in your party?"

Malik said, "Two." The hostess grabbed two menus and showed us to our seats. We had barely been seated when we looked up and saw two females sitting across from us. One was waving and smiling frantically.

After about ten seconds they both got up and walked over to our booth. "Hey, Malik."

Malik smiled and answered, "Hey, what's up, Tina? I ain't seen you in a minute. What you doing in here?"

Tina responded, "Me and Stephanie waiting for our girlfriends to show up so we can plan Stephanie's bridal shower." Tina turned to Stephanie and asked, "You know Malik, don't you Steph?"

She responded "Yeah, I met him and Glenn's little brother about a year ago." Malik looked at her and said, "Oh yeah, that's right. I remember you."

Stephanie had played herself when she first met Malik, She had seen him and Ceez at Lenux mall. She didn't know Malik was a friend of Glenn's or that Ceez was our brother. They were standing at the valet, and when she saw the valet bring up Malik's new Jaguar XK8 she immediately asked him the time and boldly lifted his sleeve to reveal the diamond bezel presidential Rolex he was wearing.

When she did that, Ceez recognized her by her voice and said, "You used to fuck with my man Brian didn't you? You don't remember me, do you? I'm Glenn's brother." Stephanie, embarrassed she had been caught on the hunt acknowledged him by abruptly saying, "Yeah," and played it off by opening her phone and making a call. Malik and Ceez told Glenn about it, and he laughed, calling her a gold digging bitch.

"Who's your friend, Malik?" Tina was looking and smiling, waiting for Malik to introduce her to me.

"Oh, this is my man Sean, Glenn's other brother."

Tina's smile sagged just a little and she paused before saying, "Damn, how many of y'all is it?"

Stephanie nudged Tina before chiming in saying, "You the cutest one out of all of y'all though. Ain't he, Tina?" I could tell Stephanie's comment was made mostly out of contempt for Glenn's dislike for her and Ceez's similar attitude.

Tina said, "If you wasn't Glenn's brother, I could see me giving you some."

I knew G, and if he had heard her say some shit like that, he probably would have snapped her neck. I had heard stories about the infamous Tina, but I'd always figured them to be exaggerated manifestations of my brother's shattered ego. But I should have known better 'cause G ain't never lied when it came to these broads. We all laughed and joked around a little after breaking the ice.

Tina offered to join us asking, "Do ya'll want to share a table?"

Malik said, "Naw, y'all go head; we'll get back later."

Malik knew Tina's offer was a thinly veiled tactic to get their meal paid for, and he wasn't having it. I wasn't feeling too comfortable with the idea either since I knew G and Tina had been on and off for the last year, and I didn't want him blasting me for fraternizing with the enemy.

Chapter Forty-Eight
Peace of Mind

"Yo, how you like this piece?" G said smiling.

I responded, "It's nice. When you get it?"

G responded, "I bought it a while back, but it was in the shop. I let Tina drive it one weekend and she got in an accident."

I remembered Ceez telling me G had bought a new Range, but when I got down here I didn't see it. There was so much going on with me that I never thought to mention it. I figured if he did have it, maybe he put it up and was trying to keep a low profile. I remembered he mentioned wanting one a while back when he was trying to sell his Benz, but I thought he was just bullshitting. He'd ended up buying a 2000 Cadillac Deville after selling the Benz to Malik and seemed happy with it until he went to holla at some chick coming out of club Vegas Nights" one night, and she said, "I know he ain't trying to talk to me driving his grandfather's car."

After that all he talked about was buying another set of hot wheels. I was still up top when he bought it and was disappointed when the family mentioned that he'd gone ahead and done it—all because of the comments of some know-nothing, simple-minded young street broad. The Cadillac retailed for $52,000 and was immaculate. Granted it didn't have much street credibility with younger women, but it was still a damn good car. No matter, now that G had gotten the Range out of the shop, I relished the idea of being able to make the switch from the hoopdy I was driving to a late model car, even if I did end up looking like somebody's grand-pop.

When I got here G went and copped a '94 Ford Taurus for me to get around in. It was a good car, but in this town if you ain't driving around in something hot, then the women won't even look at you. I was used to having nice shit and hated driving around in Atlanta appearing as if I didn't know what life was like on the high side, but that was me, and I was still in my twenties.

The revelation that G was still trying to maintain a street image had a bitter-sweet effect on me in that it confirmed he too was as shallow as all the people he complained about, yet his being that way provided me the opportunity to bounce-back and tool around town in a classy, modern car. "So what you gon do with the Caddy now that you got the truck back?" G knew my reason for asking was because I wanted to upgrade and try my hand in attracting some of Atlanta's black beauties. The only time I really had it good was when I would hang out with Malik, and even then it was hard 'cause I was the passenger.

Malik was doing his thing. He had bought G's Benz, got rid of it, and jumped into a new royal blue Lexus GS400. I thought he would have been cool with that, but he ended up flipping out of that into a Jaguar XK8 convertible and was killing 'em! Whenever we drove down Peachtree, it seemed like everything stopped and we were the only ones on the street. The chrome wheels sparkled under the streetlights and made us look as if we were superstars.

Hanging with Malik was cool, but the minute the night ended he would drop me back off to the '94 Taurus and back to my new reality. Although I hated my situation, I had begun to develop peace of mind, especially since I was no longer faced with the pressure of maintaining my former street image. Here in Atlanta I was free from the baller image I had been cultivating for the last ten years of my life. The only problem was I wasn't too sure I was happy about it.

G's phone had rung at exactly the same moment I'd asked him about the Caddy, and he didn't have a chance to respond to me. He hung up the phone and looked at me and smiled. "So you want to stem the piece now that I got the double R back?" I looked at him and laughed. He used to set us up when we were younger, and the way he said that I knew a set up was definitely in the works.

I hesitated before answering him because I knew the joke was coming. "Yeah, nigga, what you think I want to keep driving this nut-ass Taurus around town? These bitches ain't got no holla. I don't even be coming at 'em cause I know Ima get shot out the sky!"

G laughed and said, "Well, nigga, I guess you better go get a parachute 'cause they gon keep shooting at yo ass. I'm giving the Caddy to Mom."

I looked at him half mad and half okay. Our mother needed a new car, and what would be more fitting for her to drive than a brand new Cadillac? Maybe it was just as well for me, though. I ain't have no business trying to get out in these streets again. I needed to maintain a low profile and driving a 2000 Caddy wasn't going to help me do it.

I can't even bullshit y'all! I wanted out of that Ford Taurus so bad that I would almost rather catch MARTA than ride in it! "You mad?" G asked me the question as if somehow expecting me to say yeah and that he should give me the car instead of mom. I held my composure saying, "Naw, man. Mom need the jawn more than me, and she look good in it. I'm glad you gave it to her."

I meant what I said and was only irritated by the thought of me being the only one in the crew without a nice car. G could be very serious when he wanted, which was why I had no idea he had been toying with me the entire time. "Take a ride with me, young buck. I need you to do something for me."

"I don't know man. I'm kind of tired. I was about to take a nap." G looked at me and could see I was a little disheartened by my current situation. He knew what I was going through. Back in the day he had fell off, after being under investigation by the Feds. They seized everything he had. It took him no less than a year to recover from that shit.

"Man, you know I understand, but listen. Shit ain't always as bad as it seems. Just take this ride with me. You know I got you, young buck."

I climbed in the truck and was instantly reminded of my former life. Riding with G made me feel good, but that was his life and not mine. I wanted my life back and if I couldn't have it back, I wanted to at least pretend I was living it again. As we drove I noticed G had made several phone calls and was in the process of confirming some information on the whereabouts of something.

I didn't know what it was, but I knew it was something that was supposed to be delivered someplace out in Marietta, Georgia. "Yeah, is Woody available?"

I heard a voice on the other end of the phone say, "This is woody. Who am I speaking to?"

G responded, "Hey, Woody, this is Glenn. I was calling to see if we were still on schedule for today?" I knew that whatever the schedule was for it was still on 'cause G said, "Okay. That's great. I'm on my way now." He hung up the phone and looked at me smiling and said, "You never know when the sun is going to start shining."

As he said that he turned into a large parking lot that contained scores of highline cars. I looked at the name of the business and it read "Magnum Auto Body and Collision." As we pulled up I asked, "Why we out here?"

G looked at me and said, "You ask too many questions. Just hold tight I'll be right back." He got out the truck and walked inside the establishment. When he came out, an older white man, who was also smiling, followed closely behind him. I watched as they shook hands, and I noticed the white man patted G on his back in a friendly manner and pointed over to a corner on the lot. My eyes followed the direction of his finger, and I watched G walk in the same direction. When he got there he disappeared between several cars, and I wondered where he'd gone.

No sooner had my thoughts began to drift than I saw him pull up next to the truck in a 2001 BMW M5 wagon with twenty-inch Lowenhart rims! It was Ceez's joint! G got out the car, walked over to the passenger side door of the truck, and beckoned me to get out. I climbed out the truck not knowing what was going on and confused about how Ceez's car got down to Georgia.

"Yo, how Ceez's joint get all the way down here? I thought it was in storage up in D.C." Just three weeks prior, Ceez had recently gotten sentenced to two and a half years in the Fed for a case he picked up the year before. An informant signed a criminal complaint and was Ceez was charged with criminal conspiracy during a drug operation. The drug amount in question was insubstantial, and because of his lawyer he was sentenced to only five years—half in and half out. The whole family had known about the situation, and it wasn't a big deal to us because Ceez knew the extent of the game he was involved in. We were all just happy the judge didn't bury his ass. I was surprised to see his car down here in Atlanta because I thought Nicky was going to keep it for him until he came home. Excitedly I asked, "Yo G, what's going on?"

G said, "The car was sitting in a parking garage and somebody had hit it and run. Nicky called me and said she didn't feel comfortable with it up there anymore, especially since she was living in Maryland and the car was forty minutes away in D.C. She told Ceez about the accident, and he called me and asked me to bring it down here with me so I could keep my eye on it. I had it shipped down and put it in the shop to get fixed."

The big question I was waiting to ask was, "Who is going to drive it?" G didn't give me a chance to ask, and I knew the reason he brought me with him today was that he felt me slipping just a little, and my peace of mind was getting away from me.

"When I talked to Ceez, I asked him if he had a problem with you driving it and he said it was cool. Just make sure that you took care of it."

G handed me the keys and I grabbed them eagerly. I had driven the car before and knew it to be a hell of a machine. It was silver with a dark black tint on all the windows and the wheels that were on it gave it a beefy look, like it was made for the streets. I got in it and immediately felt as if I was in a space ship. The tint on the windows was so dark that it made interior of the car look like night, and the darkness was only interrupted by the soft orange glow of the dash-board, and the navigation that illuminated the remaining areas of the car. I adjusted the seat to fit my contours and set the radio to C-103. I was mildly agitated because I wished I knew we were coming to pick it up, that way I would have grabbed some of my CDs from the Taurus so that I could breeze home listening to the sound of the custom stereo Ceez had had installed.

The bass was so strong that it made you cough when you turned it on. The entire rear of the wagon was filled with a custom designed woofer system by Larry Perzan in Philadelphia. As I prepared the car for its transition to new ownership, G pulled up on the side of me saying, "Look, just because you in some hot shit now, it don't mean you should forget your situation. Don't be doing nothing stupid with Ceez's license."

Ceez was the youngest of us, and when he got arrested G, came up with the brilliant idea for me to use his information since he had a legitimate driver's license and was close to my age and size. I even went as far as to transfer it to Georgia so as not to arouse any suspicions if pulled over. Since Ceez was incarcerated there were no warrants or holds on his name, and he was definitely not wanted in Georgia. So I was cool, and now that I was driving a beast, I couldn't wait to get out and meet my share of Atlanta's black beauties!

Chapter Forty-Nine
My Share

Six months had passed since I came to Atlanta. Six months of endless street running, women chasing, and late night sexcapades. Malik and I had become a partnership, almost like a tag team, and every night he and I would ride throughout the metro Atlanta area in search of stragglers. We didn't do the club scene; that was G's thing, we instead chose to cruise Peachtree mainly and play the parking lot after the clubs let out.

We would always find a spot to strategically park our cars in such a way that any woman coming or going was sure to see us. I was never one to do a whole lot of talking, and Malik wasn't either. Whenever someone passed us that we liked, the first thing we'd do is determine which of us was going to go at her, and once that was established, the other would fall back unless there were two of them. Most of the time there was, and we'd sell them on going to breakfast and end up back at 1660 Peachtree.

G didn't mind us chilling there and rarely awoke, considering we only came in after 3:00 or sometimes 4:00 am. By the time he woke up the next day, our fun for the night had already showered and left. Malik liked the fact that G's apartment was downtown. It made things convenient, saving him from having to shuttle all the way to and from Lithonia when he was through with his temporary guests.

Keeping up with him was something of a marathon though. His drive for pulling women bordered on insane. He needed to have a different female in his bed every night, and if he wasn't able to pull any new pussy, he would act as if the world were coming to an end. It was funny to listen to him say, "Man, I ain't got no bitches." Whenever I would hear him say that, I wanted to go knock him on the side of his head to remind him of the last twenty or thirty he'd just run through in the last two months. I on the other hand wasn't posting numbers like Malik.

I got my share, but my activities were severely limited by my cash flow. G had been looking out for me the entire time I had been in Atlanta, which included gas money, food, clothes, and my bitch bill. Whenever I wanted to go out on a date, I hit him up for dough. If I wanted to fly someone in, G made it happen. If I wanted to sit home and cook dinner or have one of my new friends come and cook for me, G paid for the groceries.

He never said anything about it because he had it like that, but I knew he was becoming irritated by my conduct. I slept most of the day and complained about being bored with the lack of activity Atlanta had to offer during daylight hours. G mentioned I should get a job so I wouldn't be so bored, but somehow I knew he also wanted me to work so I wouldn't become complacent and dependent on him. I agreed and felt that although he was looking out for me, it didn't make sense for me to sit around and wait for him to make everything okay when I could be doing my share. His overhead was tremendous, and if it weren't for my knowledge of his financial ability, I would have been hard pressed to know how he did it.

Throughout our travels, Malik and I would run into Tina and Stephanie quite often. They both did the party scene religiously. Whenever we would see them, I would always mention it to G, who would dismiss the information as if it was beneath him. In a strange way, I felt his doing so was his method of ridding his mind of someone he cared about but knew he couldn't deal with. If that was the case, I understood. No man wants a woman who runs the street more than he does or knows more men than he does.

Every time I saw Tina and Stephanie they were hanging in the window of somebody's Benz or Range Rover, smiling and being receptive to just about any guy who looked like he had it going on. The last time I mentioned what I'd seen, G said, "Peasey, stop telling me what you see that girl doing. I don't want to hear that shit." That's when I realized the information must have been too hard for him to accept. Realizing I had irritated him with unnecessary information, I followed up by telling him Stephanie had offered me a job at MCI, and it was automatic if I wanted it.

When he heard me say that his tone changed, and the first question he asked was, "Do they do background checks? Because if they do then we have to come up with some kind of way for you to get hired without your criminal history coming up." I didn't know how the shit worked, but I was confident G would figure it out and put together the best possible scenario for me in order for me to get the job.

"So when did she say she could do it?" He asked that question almost immediately after I'd mentioned the conversation, and I almost felt like he had been waiting for me to get my shit in gear.

"She said whenever I call her she'll let me know when to come out there and set everything up."

G looked at me and nodded his head and said, "Cool. Call her right now and let me talk to her."

I dialed Stephanie's number. When she answered the phone she was happy to hear from me. "Hey, Sean! You gon be ma boyfriend?" Stephanie started laughing after she'd said that. I don't know if it was because she wanted to deflect the possibility of me taking her seriously, or she meant it and didn't want me to know she was serious. Whatever the reason I responded favorably saying, "All you have to do is say the word and I'm yours."

She laughed and I could tell she was smiling as she asked, "What's up?"

I said, "Nuffin. I was just calling about the gig you was telling me about last night. G told me to call you so he could ask you a couple of questions about it."

I handed G the phone, and he and Stephanie started talking, "What's up, Steph? How you been?" I knew G didn't give a damn how she was doing and only said it as a matter of protocol. Stephanie knew it too and responded similarly. I listened to G get the gist of what the position entailed as if he was my father and I was his sixteen-year-old son. I was okay with him handling everything, though, because he was good at it. That was what he did.

By the end of their conversation he had ascertained every aspect of the job: the location, position, rate of pay, and criteria for hiring. I didn't know whether Stephanie knew what my situation was, and I was surprised when G alluded to it saying, "Sean don't need nobody pulling his name and bringing attention to him, especially for some bullshit job!" He might as well have said, "Cause the police are looking for him and he's hiding out with me right now."

Either way I was sure that Stephanie now knew the scoop. G said his phony, friendly goodbyes and handed me the phone, but not before Stephanie got the chance to say, "Tina is here. She's standing right next to me."

G said, "That's nice," and handed me the phone. When I put the receiver to my ear Stephanie said, "Who is he? Your father or something? You ain't have to let him talk to me. I would have told you everything you needed to know about the job." I was kind of relieved to hear Stephanie say what she did. It was obvious she didn't catch on to the scope of G's questioning.

She looked at it as if he was just being intrusive, and that's all. Dealing with her in passing I did get the idea that she was a bit flighty, but I'd figured that was only because she was usually drinking and having fun. Now I could see that it was a genuine part of her character. It fascinated me to know that someone could be as dingy as she was and still hold a position of authority. If I took the job at MCI, she was going to be my immediate supervisor. I was comforted knowing we liked each other and didn't anticipate any problems once I came on board.

After I hung up the phone with Stephanie I turned to G and said, "So what you think?"

He looked at me seriously and said, "If you take the gig, you can't be up there telling people your situation. I don't care how cool mufucka's seem to be or how cool you think they are, they ain't your friends. And the minute you go up there acting all jo-jo and shit you gon find out real quick!"

I sat there thinking, "Damn, I wasn't expecting all that," and all of a sudden wasn't so sure if I even wanted to go forward with it. G's critical response was only because he knew the seriousness of my situation, a situation I had all but dismissed as real. I was living good and riding good too. It almost seemed as if nothing had ever happened, and I hated being reminded of it when he spoke it up. Still I knew it was all good. He was just protecting me.

"Listen, when you go to fill out the application make sure you transpose the last two numbers of your social security number in case they do run a background check on you. It should come back as a no match, and if it does have a match, then you can always just say you made a mistake trying to remember your number. That way you won't be found out, and if you slip through the cracks, then MCI won't be paying taxes on you."

Listening to G talk reminded me of the books I'd seen at his place, and I knew he knew what he was talking about. I was curious as to why my social security number mattered so much on the application and asked, "Why do that shit matter anyway, G?" He broke it down with the precision of a neurologist performing brain surgery. "The government uses your social security number to track your movements. A lot of people confuse themselves, believing it is just something that was created as a means of registration for census purposes and such. That's true, but the most prevalent use is the government tracking how you're paid, when you're paid, and who is paying you. The tracking potential derived from those uses is limitless.

"Whenever you're hired someplace and fill out a job application, you are also required to fill out an I-9 form. That form goes straight to the Immigration and Naturalization Administration, which then processes the information to see if you are a legitimate citizen or someone posing as one. In criminal situations, law enforcement agencies use it to pull credit checks to see if you've used your credit card, applied for credit cards, loans, or apartments. Sometimes they even check to see if you have a utility bill in your name somewhere. That enables them to track you down by the last known address listed on a recent application or go to the address the utility bill has you registered under, and bingo, they got you!"

I never thought of it that way. I'd always believed if you committed a crime, they either caught you in the act or somebody snitched on you or they pull you over and run your license and registration. The shit G had just broke down put shit in a whole new perspective and made me realize why he was so adamant about the information I provided on my paperwork. The part about the I-9 kind of bothered me. I wondered if they send the paper work straight to Immigration, then wouldn't they would find out if I put down a bogus number, and I asked him to clarify. "So if I switch the last two numbers of my social, won't immigration find out?"

Again he broke it down for me saying, "Not immediately, by the time they'd get wind of the discrepancy, you should be long gone from the job. If you're on the run, you should never stay at any one place for more than a few months if you can help it. But don't worry. Even if immigration did notice the problem, it wouldn't be classified as a criminal matter. Instead they would view it as a typo and would request verification from your employer, at which time they would come to you and you would know that it is time for you to go."

"Wow, nigga, how you learn all of that shit?" G wasn't interest-ed in all the accolades I fed him and ignored the opportunity to bask in my praises. He was more concerned with keeping me from going to jail; the shit they'd accused me of was enough to put me in jail for more than twenty years. Listening to him made me feel like the Karate Kid when he had to wax the cars, not knowing the lesson in following the instruction, because it seemed like I would never understand the importance of all he was trying to teach me.

I went into the kitchen to get something to drink and yelled, "Can I get you anything, Mr. Miyagi?"

G chuckled briefly before saying, "You can take this shit for a joke if you want, but everything I know came from experience and deductive reasoning." His response was stern as he followed up saying, "Play if you want, but you gon be the one sitting up in there doing fifteen plus, wishing you had paid attention and listened!" He didn't say another word after that, and neither did I. I wasn't worried because he was taking care of everything for me. I didn't even have to think for myself.

Chapter Fifty
My Boss and Me

Working for Stephanie wasn't such a bad thing—it was the commute that was the bitch! Every morning at 6:30 am I rolled out of bed, showered, got dressed, and took my place in the slow moving back-to-back Atlanta rush hour traffic. I had to be at work by 8 am, and it took all of one hour to drive from downtown Atlanta to Holcomb Bridge Road. Every so often, I was forced to roll up my windows, turn up my music and scream at the top of my lungs at the stupidity that seemed to be all around me.

As long as I live I will never understand how a four-lane highway can be jammed with traffic every morning without it being caused by an accident. And don't let it rain; that's when shit got really bad. People put on their hazard lights and creep along as if they're caught in a blizzard. The whole scene is like something out of the Twilight Zone. On the days I didn't scream, I thanked the Lord above I didn't have a gun in the car. If I did, I would've been all too happy to blow my brains out.

I had lived the better part of my life believing workingmen were suckers, and now I was one of them. Truth was it wasn't all bad. Putting in an honest day's work for an honest day's pay felt good. Being a hustler was never a good thing, but it was all I knew, and now that I was working for a living I had to rethink all I had come to believe. One thing was sure: working customer service was a bitch!

The people I dealt with on daily basis were like something out of an insane asylum. They cursed you, screamed at you, threatened you, and after all of that hung up on you. MCI claimed our leads were never cold calls, but the way those people complained, I couldn't tell. One guy went as far as to politely ask me for my home number. When I asked him why he said, "So I can wait until your in the middle of dinner and bug the shit out of you, asshole!" before slamming the phone down. I almost split my side laughing so hard. I couldn't believe people let stuff like that bug them.

All in all life was good. I was the star attraction working at MCI. Every morning when I pulled up in the parking lot, there always seemed to be a group of young girls lingering around the entranceway drinking coffee and a few smoking before going in. They would speak almost in unison when I passed. A few made it known that I was on their hot list, but I never acknowledged them. I wasn't interested in dealing with anyone at work; it was almost like being in high school. People were always talking about who went to lunch with whom and speculating on who was screwing whom, and I didn't want any part of it.

My goal was to keep a low profile; and I barely managed to do that now that I was driving the BMW. Every day Stephanie would come to my cubicle to tell me of some young girl who thought I was cute. Then Tina would show up bringing similar news, mostly after she'd ask how Glenn was doing. I don't know why she bothered asking; their time had long since passed, and he'd given me strict instructions not to tell him anything more about her, messages of hello or otherwise.

He'd even cautioned me not to become too familiar with her, saying that she was trouble. I saw that for myself; she was making her way at MCI—fast. Rumor was she had already slept with five guys and counting, including her supervisor, his boss, Carnegie, and the director of the facility. There was a big controversy over the rumor that prompted MCI to circulate a memo on sexual harassment and employee fraternization.

Showing up for work at MCI required a certain state of mind. I had a song I played every morning as I pulled into the lot, kind of like a theme song. "Can't Knock the Hustle" by Jay-Z put me in a zone. It reminded me of who I used to be and made me realize I had to do whatever I could to survive at this point. I needed it to help me deal with my new reality. A reality that had me questioning myself almost every morning: "You can't be serious?!"

I was never one to judge other people, but the people at that place seemed like a bunch of rejects. Granted there were some who didn't fall into that category, but the vast majority were losers who couldn't catch a break anywhere else and migrated to MCI the same way the people gathered at the Sea of Galilee seeking a blessing from Jesus. I didn't pay much mind to what other people did. I was busy making plan and focusing on winning bonuses.

I was one of Stephanie's star performers, and she would regularly take me to lunch or look the other way whenever I came back a little late. She was a bitch to everybody else, and they hated her for it. Almost every day she would launch into one of her trademark tirades. "Y'all need step it up in here. I don't know where y'all think y'all at, but you won't be up in here if these numbers fall like they did last week. Try me if you want. I'll send all of y'all home!" Every time she went on one of her rants, she always came over to my cubicle the minute she finished, laughing and ridiculing the members of the team whose numbers had fallen.

She took pride in telling me of the names of people she would be removing from the team: a daily occurrence. "Sean, see that boy over there." Stephanie never bothered about being discreet and pointed blatantly to her left. "I'm 'bout to tell him to close up shop. He hasn't made plan in two weeks. He must think this is a joke or something, but I ain't having it on my team." Stephanie always laughed whenever she mentioned sending someone home. As if the thought of somebody losing his or her job was humorous. She got away with it because she was engaged to one of the senior managers at the site.

She walked around place like she was untouchable, and for a time she was. I had been there for about four months, and she treated me better than she did all the others, but every now and again she would get beside herself and come at me sideways, too. I never took it personally and hardly ever said anything about it. The last time it happened, she went off on me so bad I mentioned it to G when I got home that day.

"Yo, man, I think Stephanie going through something. She seem like she manic or something. One minute she smiling and joking around, and the next minute she screaming on me like I'm her son." Don't ask me what I was thinking mentioning that to G because after he finished lecturing me on why I shouldn't let anyone talk to me that way, much less a female, he then explained what he knew of Stephanie's psychological state.

"She going through it. B tore up all her shit and rolled out! When he left she didn't think it would've mattered, but when she never heard from him again, it fucked her head up 'cause he did it cold turkey. Not to mention the fact that dude she ended engaged to ain't what she thought he was."

I was a little confused by what G was telling me and asked, "How you know all that?"

He answered, "Before me and Tina broke up, she used to tell me everything that she and Stephanie talked about, and she told me that Stephanie ain't happy with that dude. The only reason she with him is because he is the senior manager up there, and he got good ass credit."

Listening to G break everything down to me made me realize that maybe he was right. Stephanie would always seek reassurance whenever Stephon's name was mentioned over the loud speaker or his picture flashed across the monitors. I got tired of her asking, "Sean, you think Stephon is nice looking?" I always responded favorably but would remind her that she shouldn't care what the public thought of him, especially if she loved him and was happy with her choice. Even with that kind of advice, it was evident that she was completely at odds about him because she continued to seek public approval.

G laughed at the thought of Stephanie's misery and then dropped a bombshell. "You know, Tina told me that after B rolled out, Stephanie started seeing a psychiatrist. Stephanie had stopped being mad at Brian for about a year and wanted to talk to him, but she didn't have any way of contacting him and it put her into a major depression."

I couldn't believe Stephanie went through all of that and asked, "If she was going through all of that, then why did she get engaged to Stephon?"

G chuckled again before answering me. "After Brian tore up all her shit, she didn't have any more clothes and couldn't afford to repurchase all that shit on her own, so she got wit the dude, and he been sponsoring her ever since. I told you neither one of them bitches ain't shit. It's all about money with them. I even heard Stephanie on the phone once telling Tina she didn't really want to marry the dude and privately joked that she didn't want to have his children. She was even using birth control and the dude ain't know nothing about it."

I didn't know what to think about all of what G was telling me. I usually wasn't one for listening to gossip, but since it was coming from the horse's mouth, I soaked up every word. I couldn't help feeling sorry for Stephon but also felt he had a responsibility to himself to find out what the real deal was with Stephanie.

Being stupid hurts, and I believe being stupid should be painful when you ignore the signs, especially when they are right in front of you. I thought G was finished giving me the run down on Stephanie and Stephon, but he wasn't.

"Did you see the ring she wearing?" Tina said the dude spent fifteen thousand on that piece." I shook my head in disgust because I knew the ring and all the money in the world wouldn't change the fact that Stephanie didn't love him. I knew early on she didn't by the way she flirted with me and everybody else she thought was cute.

Plus, she would always ask about Brian. I had to admire B though. He played that shit right; she disrespected him, and he rolled out without looking back. The way Stephanie asked about him, you would swear nothing bad happened between them, but I guess it just goes to show that the only thing women truly respect is power whether it's demonstrated through resolve, indifference, or whatever. I have come to learn they actually prefer a little disdain to too much consideration. I don't think Stephanie will ever get over how easily Brian walked away from her, and Stephon would never get the love and respect he deserved because he loved a woman loved someone else.

Chapter Fifty-One
Yeast

"So what's up, man? How you like working out there?"

"It's cool, but cats be dick riding hard ever since they seen me driving the BMW. The broads be going crazy too, especially when I drive the Range up there. Plus, they always be grabbing on my gear, asking where I got it from and how come I come up there so sharp."

G laughed at my description of life at MCI before acknowledging my new spending habits. "I see you been buying a lot of new shit. I hope you stacking your dough now that you got a little yeast up in you. Don't forget you still on the D-L." I hated it when he would remind of my situation. It wasn't that it made me angry or anything, but it made me remember something I had managed to put behind me. I guess I had started living like I had no worries. I had even started dating again. Running the streets with Malik was cool, but I wasn't really feeling it all like that and was happy when I met Monique. She was a cute little dark-skinned girl. She stood about 5'3" tall and had deep brown eyes that complimented her chocolate skin. Her smile had a way of making me forget I was in the trouble I was in.

When we met I never bothered telling her about my situation. I figured she didn't need to know about it, especially since I couldn't tell if we were going to last. I hated not being able to tell her everything about me and almost slipped up a few times, but I remembered all too well the dangers of pillow talk. It has brought many a man down and damn near got me killed.

When I brought Monique home for the first time, G hit me with a barrage of questions about who she was, what I told her, and how I felt about her. I didn't have the heart to tell him I was feeling her and that we had already talked of finding a place and moving in together. I still hadn't figured out just how I was going to do it, but it was definitely time for me to find my own way. I was making good money at the gig and continued to rise through the ranks with Stephanie's help.

They were even talking of making me a supervisor. I wasn't sure if I was going to accept the position if they offered. The pay was only a dollar or two more than the base pay for regular phone reps.

The only good thing about it was if your team did well, then the bonus you received was based on the collective efforts of the team instead of individual compensation, which equated to much larger rewards. G noticed I was making more money than I had been originally. I had been at MCI going on a year, and aside from few bad cycles, I was killing 'em! A lot of my old habits resurfaced ,too.

When I was hustling it was nothing for me to go out and spend thousands on the fleet of women I was seeing. Driving a fancy car kind of made me feel as if I was still living like I used to, and now that my money was on the rise, I started acting like I was the man again. "G, me and Malik 'bout to go to Magic City. You coming?"

G replied, "Naw, man. I'm cool. Ima chill. I see you doing the damn thing, though, huh?" I started to respond to G's inquiry, but he didn't let me. "Listen, man. I told you you have to remember your situation. Every penny you spend on bullshit is a penny you should be saving. You never know how shit is going to fall, and you don't want to get caught out there on a limb. Actually, you need to start thinking about leaving MCI. You been there too long already. When you get with Malik, talk to him about getting a CDL and you can probably drive one of his trucks. I think he pays his drivers twenty dollars an hour."

I don't know what G was thinking, but I wasn't about to start driving no truck. I didn't care how much the shit paid. I was dat dude up at MCI and the shit felt good. I had a squad of females up there and one main jawn, and they were all on call whenever I wanted to have fun, no matter what it was. I was getting tired of listening to G's advice, and after listening to his last suggestion about leaving MCI, I decided it would be better if I left 1660 Peachtree instead.

Chapter Fifty-Two
Disgusted

"Sir, what would you like to drink?" I paused 'cause I had zoned out from the moment we were seated in the restaurant. Benny fucking Hanna's, these Atlanta bitches make me sick. I didn't even know why I was there. Looking out for G and Sean and trying to be a good sport was the reason I guess. I told G from the start these bitches had a hidden agenda, but as usual he ain't want to hear that shit.

Now we sitting here at the fucking restaurant, and these bitches done ordered the whole fucking menu. And to top it off, their cell phones had been ringing back to back from the time we sat down. One of them even had the nerve to invite some nigga they knew to come and sit down with us when she saw him walk through the door. He knew the game, though, and decided to get seated at his own table. I guess he knew we wouldn't have been cool with him joining us.

I watched how it went down and noticed the broad's cell phone rang right after the dude got seated. I looked over to G, wondering if he had seen the exchange. He did but motioned to me to chill saying, "Fall back, man, it's cool. I seen it but I'm just trying smash."

I responded, "Nigga, these bitches ain't trying do nothing but get a grub and get wit the next nigga! And if you don't believe me, peep how she still on the phone with the dude! You and Sean can do what y'all want, but I'm 'bout to be out!"

One of the girls had heard me and G talking and asked me if I was okay. I responded and said, "Yeah, I'm cool."

Then she asked, "Why you ain't order nothing?"

I said, "Because I'm about to be out. That's why." No sooner had I finished my sentence than I scooted my chair from the table, stood up, dropped a fifty-dollar bill on the table, and walked out the door.

Sean was the first to come out to the parking lot. When he came out he said, "Whassup, nigga? Why you leave like dat? I thought you was going to at least try and smash the broad." Sean had been walking behind me as he was talking. As I turned to respond to his question, he saw a tear had rolled down my cheek. His concern switched immediately to me and he asked, "Leek, whassup? Whass wrong?"

I took a deep breath and ran it. "Man, the very fucking reason we up in here ain't got shit to do with us. If you ask any one of them bitches what my name is, they couldn't tell you. I knew from when they approached us that it wasn't about us, and they proved it at the liquor store when you and Glenn offered to buy them coolers, and instead they grabbed two bottles of Belvedere and orange juice.

"See, Sean, those bitches is used to niggas with nice shit who don't value themselves. Niggas who think it's ballin' to take broads out and spend money, not knowing a fucking thing about 'em." I didn't bother to wipe the tear from my cheek 'cause I didn't give a fuck. I was at the point where I was tired of doing shit I didn't want to do all for the sake of getting air time. To me none of that shit should matter if you truly wanted to get to know someone. What was supposed to be a simple day at the park now threatened to become an unexpected four hundred dollar dinner tab.

It wouldn't be so bad if it was a rare occurrence, but unfortunately it wasn't. In Atlanta, having a nice car is a gift and a curse because the women assume money ain't a thing. To some cats it ain't, but it was about principle with me. Just two hours before we were all in the parking lot of the tabernacle across from the CNN center. The day was supposed to be for us guys sitting around rapping about business, and this new book G was writing. We were all sitting in the parking lot in our cars. G was in his silver range, I was in my drop jag, and Sean was in his kitted up M5 BMW wagon. I saw them when they pulled into the lot where we were sitting.

I'd noticed them drive past ten minutes earlier and watched as they circled the block and pulled into the lot where we were sitting as if they had planned it all along. I didn't say anything 'cause I was trying to handle business for the day despite the informal surroundings we chose. Sean had asked me about getting a commercial CDL and getting into one of my dump trucks. G was telling us about the latest chapter in his book Ghetto America: A Personal Review. And the vibe was good. "Yo, I'm 'bout to read this chapter from my book to y'all, and I want y'all to tell me what y'all really think, and don't front on me either. It's called "Fly Girls of the Past."

Fly Girls of the Past

Back in the day, Biz Markie, a well-known rapper during the mid-eighties, had a song out called The Vapors. It was a song directed toward all the people who used to diss him before he made it big. I remember watching the video and seeing the various types of people he referred to in his song: previous school teachers who said he was a loser, record store owners who refused to play or sell his demo, and girls who paid him no mind until he started making money.

The most popular verse in the song was, "Nigga please, you work for UPS." That verse summed up all of the anguish so many legitimate young black men felt and still feel because it was the typical response one would receive whenever he would try to approach a sista he was attracted to. It also confirms much of what I have been saying throughout my previous chapters— the prevailing attitude of high maintenance black women, ghetto and professional alike, was that anyone with a regular, blue-collar job was lame and inadequate.

Well, times are a little different now. Actually, a lot different. It seems that all those s- called less fortunate corny guys, who had the foresight and discipline to steer clear of criminal activities and instead chose to focus on education and hard work, are now in hot demand. In fact, many of those guys are now considered the real men that so many sistas yearn to have, especially now that their own glow is gone and they are no longer on the sunny side of thirty.

Lately, it seems for many single black women that the ultimate goal is to find a man, get married, and be treated properly, but there is one problem, they are no longer the hot commodities they once were. Many are quickly approaching thirty and others are thirty plus. They've been married previously, or not ,but in either case they now come with a package of one or more children. The man they originally chose over the corny guy is dead or in jail, most often resulting from a life on the street, or he revealed himself to be a total loser.

Other beautiful black jewels knowingly chose doggish men they thought they could change only to discover they were wrong. This revelation coming only after giving birth to several children, wasting numerous years chasing him, and demanding that he do right, only to be ignored time and again. They've gained ten to twenty extra pounds and the relationship has ended. The man has moved on to a new, younger, and child-free woman without a backward glance, and she is left with a gang of kids, wondering why she can't find a man, *or better yet why she can't find a good man. I'll tell you why, but first we must start at the beginning.*

I'll begin with the women who possess the ghetto mentality. The majority of them have spent their peak value years being chased by every kind of black man there is from blue-collar to well-off professionals. Unfortunately, these women did not have the presence of mind or foresight to appreciate a good thing when it came calling. The only kind of man to tickle their fancies were the thugs and street hustler types. This man was typically involved in some type of criminal enterprise, drug dealing, hustling, etc., and for a time did quite well in his chosen profession. He provided all of the creature comforts any woman would wan—fine cars, expensive jewelry, opulently furnished, lavish homes or apartments along with fur coats, vacations, and cash to spare.

He also had many risks and problems that accompanied dealing with him. The first being his life and the lives of all he associated with, being under constant threat of danger; second, the constant harassment and investigations at the hands of law enforcement, local and federal. Lastly, she had to contend with his insatiable appetite for different women. The money and power that was at his command dictated his personality be of similar makeup— arrogant. Because of dealing with so many undesirable people, it became increasingly difficult for him to differentiate between the improper treatment of them versus proper treatment of her. His inability to distinguish between proper and improper treatment often blurred the line and very likely caused him to react violently whenever she failed to respond properly to whatever his request or command happened to be.

As for the professional woman, she too had black men of all kinds pulling on her coat tails, but she preferred those who seemed to epitomize success. Time and again she chose to overlook those individuals she considered beneath her: the construction worker who spoke to her every morning as she walked by, the contractor she hired to repair the faulty plumbing in her house, or basically anyone who worked in a manual labor capacity. Instead, she set her sights on cats who she felt had made it—men who were able to wine and dine her on a level that rivaled the lifestyles of the rich and famous without the risks of the street hustler. Her men of choice were ball players, rappers, and successful businessmen (preferably in that order).

Even with all of the apparent enjoyment she received from this, she was still unfulfilled because those guys knew they indeed were a rare find and, subsequently, had their way with any and all of the sistas they chose. They not only refused to commit, they also had grown accustomed to treating even the most sophisticated women with a banal lack of appreciation. This was due in large part to the massive amount of attention they received on a daily basis as well as their over-inflated sense of self-worth. No matter how beautiful the professional woman was to these cats, she was just another fine piece of ass.

Very rarely did these guys choose to have a wife, because life is good when you are at the top of the food chain. In some instances, a few of those sistas managed to hook that type of man, marrying him only to discover their careers made it an impossibility for them to thrive. The original relationship was predicated on mutual success and/or bragging rights and lacked the benefit of real love. She never really got the kind of attention she longed for because they both were too busy, and now she is forced back out into the meat market. Only this time she vows to do it better.

The irony in this apparent shift in preference is a large number of the black women of whom I speak have exhausted all of their original value. Their beauty has begun to fade, they have one or two fatherless children, and they no longer want to play hard to get because they know they won't get got. They have entered in and out of failed relationships because of their inability to recognize their need for change and, for many, because of an insatiable thirst for the next man's money. They have also chosen to continually involve themselves in similar relationships with different men, where the behavior patterns are just the same. No matter they still somehow expected a different outcome and the one they got was insanity. I read the definition of insanity is "doing the same thing over and over again, and each time expecting a different result." It's like pulling a different pickle from the same barrel. They're all going to taste the same.

Since many round-the-way sistas' relationships evolved from neighborhood romances with local thugs and hustlers. Any successive involvement with different men is viewed in an entirely negative light because of the visibility of it. Facts have no bearing in ghetto communities. If she is seen with an abundance of different men, she is automatically labeled as community property or a ho. Oftentimes, this distinction comes from the mouths of men who were unsuccessful in their bid to win her affections. In the case of the professional woman, she has it only marginally better than her ghetto counterpart. She has to contend with the consequences of her choices because she has staked her fantasy on meeting Prince Charming, only she feels Prince Charming must come with a seven-figure salary, a microphone, or a basketball. With each successive fling inflicting more wear and tear on her body, she begins to discover she has become the laughing stock among her coupled-up or married peers. They pretend to be concerned with her social life for her sake but privately ridicule her for being the only one left without a seat when the music stops.

In either case, that kind of behavior causes irreparable damage to one's reputation. Knowing this, these lackluster, former fly girls have now sought refuge with the kind of man they should have been with originally. They often sit and reflect on the error of their ways and frequently reminisce about the one who got away—the good guy, the one who appreciated them, and expressed his yearning to marry and treat her right. He was not given the opportunity then. Time passed and he persevered, maintained a good job, and now has a reasonably successful career. But more important, he is a safe and secure option, and working for UPS is no longer considered a joke. Only now it she who must prove herself worthy.

Sean and me stood there in awe! I had always known G was a smart dude, but nothing about his past could have prepared me for what he had displayed at that moment. The shit he said was so relevant to what I had been feeling for years, only I didn't know how to express it. In one chapter, G brought me back to the days where I could remember being embarrassed because I worked for a living, instead of opting to project the image of a street hustler when asked by females, "What you into?"

I never really paid any attention to the idea of G writing a book 'cause I know niggas typically don't like to read. Now I wasn't so sure. "God damn, G. That shit was hot. Nigga, how in the fuck did you come up with that shit?"

Sean barely let me finish talking before he interrupted me by saying, "G, when that shit hits the press, niggas are gon be on your dick! Cause you speak for all of the cats who got shitted on by bougie high society bitches.

It was one of those rare occasions where men have no concern about a woman or women for that matter. Until they came: Gretchen, Lisa, and Charlene. "Hi, whatchall doing sitting here in the parking lot like this." I started to blast them bitches for even interrupting us like that.

G looked at me and saw I was on path and responded before I got the chance to launch my rude response. "We just out here shining with the sun. What y'all up to?""Nothing. We about to go to the park across the street and chill out for a minute and look in the water and smoke a blunt. Y'all want to come?"

G and Sean looked up and responded, "Yeah, that's whassup," in an enthusiastic but composed manner and looked over at me.

I wasn't feeling them broads. G and Sean hadn't seen what I had seen. They didn't know they had circled the block and zeroed in on us. I also knew they wouldn't have paid us no mind if we hadn't been sitting there in our whips. The thought of that turned me off before they even got to the lot.

I didn't really know what was happening to me, but I had been feeling very uneasy with Atlanta and was growing real sick of the whole flow of the city. Back in the day I would've embraced the situation, but now it just didn't do it for any more. Besides, they were a bunch of college girls. I was surprised G entertained any of the shit they were talking about. Number one, neither him, Sean, or me for that matter, smoked weed. Not two weeks prior to that he and I had gotten into a heated argument about the types of girls we each dated, and he tried to discredit my achievements by telling me my success rate was only good 'cause I went at silly college girls or young broads who didn't require any real conversational skills.

Shit. When I first came to Atlanta I was fucking non-stop. In the first three months alone I had fucked over forty bitches, and that was when I was driving my father's beat up ass Jeep. Glenn's problem was that he compared his style to mine, which is something that couldn't be done fairly and accurately. The bottom line is that we attracted different types of women. The truth is I like all kinds of women—light, dark, white, black, Spanish, and even Chinese as long as she looks good. And I ain't afraid to approach any broad. The older the better—those are the ones I enjoy most because I always end up shattering their perception about younger guys.

Younger women, on the other hand, don't waste time frontin'

like they all sophisticated and shit. The girls at Benny Hanna's with us were just as young as the ones G claimed I had been dealing with all along, and now all of a sudden since he wanted to try his hand, it was cool. How 'bout dat shit?

I decided to fuck with him about it and said, "Damn, Nigga. I thought you ain't have no patience for 'silly assed young girls.' What happened to all that rap you had? You a funny dude!" G gritted his teeth and looked at me sideways as if to cue me to keep quiet, but I didn't give a damn 'cause I ain't want to fuck with 'em anyway. So I continued and followed up by saying, "And none of us smoke weed so what the fuck we gon do when we go over there with 'em?"

Gretchen, the cutest of the bunch, happened to hear what I was saying and chimed in saying, "Y'all at least drink, though, right?"

Sean responded, "Yeah. Lets go get some coolers or something. Then we can all chill in the park." After the save by Gretchen I left the issue alone with G. I had made my point, and he knew it that was enough for me.

The chicks represented the typical story about three girlfriends. One was cute and sexy as hell' another was ugly, but had an incredible body; and the last was chubby and had the nicest personality, and of course she chose me. Gretchen, the prettiest of them, tried to be distant, but Sean decided she was the one he would go after. G was left with the ugly one, Charlene. He didn't really seem to care 'cause all he wanted to do was smash anyway, and that bitch's body was incredible. Lisa, the fat one, and Gretchen were sisters and were attending classes at the AU center. The ugly one, Charlene, said she was sitting out a semester. I overheard G asking her what she was doing while she was sitting out her classes. Her response was, "That's not important right now." The funny thing was that wasn't the first time I had heard that line.

I was discovering more and more in Atlanta that the statement, "That's not important," when given by a female in connection to the question of current employment, usually meant she was pursuing a career stripping. Personally, I could care less about what anyone does for a living, but why be ashamed of it? I mean if you decided to do it in the first place, then have enough dignity to not be embarrassed about it.

I was beginning to hate ever being a part of the Atlanta scene.

There was a lot of shit that bothered me about it, specifically all of the constant frontin' and faking. Women chasing dudes for the kinds of cars they drove, dudes playing up to 'em, pro-athletes and industry cats going at the same broads regular guys be comin' at; making the dime-pieces believe they're too good to deal with an average, middle-class working black man because they dated a millionaire, which forces that average black man to attempt to do above average things just for the opportunity to establish an interest, only for his hopes to be dashed and the date canceled because he came to pick her up in a Toyota Camry.

The flip side to that is watching paid niggas idolize strippers as if they were queens, even going as far as choosing them over quality, working class women, and as if that wasn't enough to get on your nerves, then you have the dudes who want to walk on both sides of the fence, gay and bisexual cats that get off on sleeping with women and each other. I didn't go to church much, but Atlanta seems like it is the new Sodom and Gomorrah; they even have a Gay Pride weekend.

I remember one Saturday G, Sean, their nephew and me went to Lenux mall to do some shopping and girl watching. None of us seemed to notice the unusual number of niggas walking together throughout the mall until one of G's female friends saw us walking by the store she worked in. She rushed out and confronted him like he was guilty of something and asked him "Whachoo doing in here?"

G looked at her, frowned, and said "Out here with my nephew to pick up some new sneakers. Why?"

She stared at him with a relieved look and said, "Because it is gay weekend up in here. That's why, and you and your boys better get the hell out of here if y'all don't want nobody to think y'all a bunch of turd burglars. Nigga, you ain't know it, but I was two seconds from slapping the shit out of you."

One of the biggest fears of black women in Atlanta is the thought of hooking up with a nigga who goes both ways. I never really had a problem with gay dudes, mostly 'cause I figure people are free to do what they want and shouldn't be judged for it, but a lot of them cats be fucking up the game! And that takes the fairness out of the dating arena. I have been asked the same question repeatedly by different women I have met, "Are you gay or bi-sexual?"

Personally, I am tired of it and have become afraid to deal with the sistas because I know of so many of them who are careless and will fuck a nigga raw the minute he spends a few dollars on 'em and takes them to a nice place to eat. Ain't too many niggas out here that don't like going up in some new cock raw, only now the shit is a death sentence, especially in Atlanta.

Chapter Fifty-Three
A Place to Call Ours

"Sean, did you see this one? It has two bedrooms and two and a half bathrooms and a fireplace."

"Let me see it; yeah, it looks nice. Where's it at?"

"It's off of Georgia 400 and only five miles from your exit to the job."

I liked the fact that Monique had considered my commute and picked an apartment that would eliminate my now daily foray into the twilight zone. The apartments she found were called Dewberry Glenn. They were located just off of Glenn Ridge Road nestled between Roswell Road and Johnson's Ferry Road. I liked it because whether I turned right or left when leaving the complex, I had access to the interstate.

"I think this is the one we should get, baby. Plus, I'm tired of looking. We been at it now for a whole week, and everybody wants eight to nine hundred dollars, and I ain't trying to pay that."

I didn't know what Monique was talking about saying what she "ain't trying to pay," knowing damn well I was going to be the one who was going to be paying for everything. I was cool with it, though, because I loved her, and now that she was having my baby there was nothing I wouldn't do for her. It had been months since I moved away from G at 1660 Peachtree. We'd had a big argument about my choices, lifestyle, and decision to take on girlfriend.

He had become fanatical about me living my life the way a fugitive does and started quoting Robert Dinero from the movie Heat saying, "Allow nothing to be in your life you can't walk away from in five seconds flat!" I understood his intentions, but I had a life of my own to live. I was grateful for all he had tried to do for me. I wasn't sure if he knew that, but unfortunately now that we'd fallen out I wouldn't get the opportunity to tell him.

I had kept Monique's pregnancy a secret. I knew if word got out it would have just complicated things further, and besides it was nobody's business. I had also kept my circumstances a secret, and as I watched her stomach grow larger, my guilt grew with it. Everything was going so perfect for us I didn't have the heart to rain on her parade. Besides, it didn't matter because I was going to make everything alright. I was taking care of business.

"Monique, are you sure you like the place? Cause if you do then Ima go get an application today and fill it out." Monique came out from her bedroom smiling. Her face was round and chocolate. Looking at her always made me smile; her look was wholesome and pure. I liked that about her. She wasn't caught up by all of the trends and passing fads that seemed to affect everybody else. Hers was a simple beauty that didn't require any enhancements. Her attitude was equally pleasing. She rarely raised her voice and was always asking me if I was okay or if I needed her to do anything, a welcomed change from all of the selfish gimme-gimme broads I'd known for the better part of my life.

She made me want to do more for her, and now that she was carrying my child, that is what I was going to do. She had been living with a roommate when we met, and although they got along, she had expressed her desire to have a place of her own, a place where she could cook, clean, and tend to our soon-to-be-created family, and it was my job to make it happen.

"Hello, Dewberry Glenn Apartments. Come join us."

"Hi, I was calling to find out your availability for two bedroom units. I saw a listing stating they came with two and a half bathrooms and a fireplace; is that correct?"

"Yes, sir, it is correct. We also have a special running this month. $99 dollars moves you in, and we waive the security deposit and give the first month rent free." Atlanta was like that. There were so many new apartment complexes springing up all around that the market was quickly becoming saturated, and the properties were in fierce competition with one another. They were offering so many perks I expected hear her say, "The unit is yours. Just come and get the keys."

It was a Saturday, and the office was going to be open until 5 pm. I looked at the clock and noticed it was only 11:30 am and said, "Do I need to have an appointment to come and view the unit?"

The rep seemed instantly pleased at my question and responded enthusiastically, "No, sir, you don't. All that's required is to bring a valid form of identification and you're all set." I hung up the phone, threw on some sweats, and yelled to Monique to get dressed. She put on a similar outfit, and when we walked out the door, we looked like twins.

"What they say when you called them?" Monique's face was all aglow as she waited for my response. She was anxious because she had been hoping to get a new apartment and would've gotten one on her own, but her credit wasn't in the best shape. I knew mine was cool. I hadn't used it in years, and since I was always a cash and carry dude from my days as a hustler, I didn't have any blemishes on it either.

I never mentioned to Monique I had good credit. It wasn't because I was keeping it secret but rather I had gotten so accustomed to withholding information that it became a force of habit. Now that she was having my kid, I figured it would be best if I kept her mind at ease and told her so she could stop stressing and worrying about whether or not we would get the place.

"They said the unit we saw was available, and we needed to have valid identification to see it." As I repeated the criterion to Monique, I realized that the only identification I had was Ceez's driver's license. I also realized that although his credit was cool, I didn't have a job or pay stubs I could present with his name. As we neared the complex I remembered I always kept my MCI badge in the car. Luckily, it was a well known company, and I reasoned that no one would care if I used my work badge as a form of identification. I didn't want Monique to use hers because then they would automatically list her on the intake visitor's card and be on the lookout for her as an occupant later, requiring her to put her information on the application. As bad as her credit was, it would probably be the nail in the coffin for both of us.

"Sean, it looks so nice, and I like the way it's tucked away." I liked it too. Living with G gave me a much-needed outlook on how things should be done, and I liked the way he kept to himself. I, too, planned on being rarely seen and seldom heard from, and Glenn Ridge was built just so. Nosy neighbors were always a sore spot when I was on the street, and I hated the way they paid attention to my comings and goings.

Now that I worked for a living, things weren't going to be as bad. Still, you always had to be careful around white people. They all seemed to have deep rooted suspicions of black men in nice cars, and the BMW was definitely that. My going to work every day didn't change the fact that I was still a bona fide fugitive.

"Welcome to Dewberry Glenn. I'm Terry. How are you?" Terry was a tall blonde with a nice ass for a white girl. She was wearing a tight cardigan sweater that barely covered the double C cup implants her too-small tee shirt struggled to keep in place. She stuck out her hand and I shook it. Her grip was firm and I could see she took her job seriously.

"My name is Sean, Sean Starks."

Terry responded smiling, "Well, hello Sean Starks. I gather you're the gentleman I spoke with earlier this morning on the phone?"

I smiled using my best anal white man smile and responded, "Yes, that was me," raising one finger in the air the way people do when they've heard their name during roll call. Terry began her pitch on Dewberry Glenn and asked a whole slew of questions regarding who I was, what I did, and when I planned on moving in. I answered all of her questions and presented my MCI badge, hoping she wouldn't refuse it.

Luckily she didn't, and I searched my mind hoping I didn't give her any contradicting information that I wouldn't remember later when I filled out the application. I believe that's why they ask you all those questions in the first place—so they can try and trip you up later. After she finished subtly interrogating me, she turned to Monique and asked, "Will you be moving in as well?" Before Monique could open her mouth, I interjected and answered for her saying, "No, I'll be occupying the unit alone."

Terry looked at me with a half smile on her face. She knew it was a lie, but there was nothing she could do about it. I don't know why they go through all they do trying to squeeze people for an extra application fee. I wasn't trying to be there all day and let out a deep sigh signifying that she needed to hurry up. She got the picture and wrapped up the question and answer session she was reading from her clipboard.

She got up and retrieved the keys and walked us over to the model unit. When we walked in, I heard Monique gasp. The place was all that! It had vaulted ceilings, a fireplace, a patio, a sunroom, and a washer and a dryer—the works! I almost expressed the same sentiment, but I didn't want to seem too anxious. We went through the usual walk-through of the unit. Monique and I walked behind Terry, who had drifted into a self-rehearsed zone as she explained all of the features and amenities of the apartment and even demonstrated the gas stove and fireplace.

By the time she finished, she turned to me with a look on her face that appeared to be one of hope. She didn't know my mind was made up when we arrived at the gate. I smiled and commented, "This is a really nice unit. I think it is what I need. Now, does the special apply to this unit as well?"

Terry replied, "Yes, it does." I figured it did and only said what I said trying to sound more studious and to eat up some of the time before I sat down to fill out the application because I had to decide what I was going to write down.

"Mr. Starks, here is the application. You can take it home or fill it out here. Upon acceptance we will require copies of your last two pay stubs." I remembered thinking, "This is going to be the shit!" I knew I wasn't going to be rejected because of credit issues, and it was close to my job, and most importantly, Monique was now going to be able to have my baby and relax in her own place.

****

The move went as planned. Monique and I got the place as expected, and from the time we got the keys, she started decorating like she was on the payroll for Better Homes and Gardens. I'd followed G's advice and saved a few bucks from a few bonuses I'd received from MCI. I gave Monique a budget of three thousand dollars to do whatever she could with it. Back in the day I would've wanted to be there and monitor how and what she spent my money on—if I would've given up the dough in the first place; but the time for that had passed.

Monique was my girl and future mother of my child. She had to know any slick shit on her part would affect her in the long run. Living a legitimate life was surprisingly good for me. I slowed down long enough to appreciate all the good things that normal, God-fearing people had been enjoying for years. Truthfully, I was overjoyed by the thought of having my first child. Out of all us boys, my brother Dax and my sister Tiffany were the only ones with children.

Everybody thought G was going to be the first one to have kids, but that cat was real particular about who he wanted to have his kid. Whenever he did discuss it, he'd always refer back to Tamika saying, "She is the prettiest girl I've ever dated, and the most wholesome woman I have ever known, and I know she would raise my kids the right way." When I thought of how strongly he felt about her, I wondered how he and Tina ever ended up together in the first place.

At any rate, I was about to start my own family and wanted to do it right. I wasn't sure about how I would go about it, but I figured a good way to start was by making the woman I was to be with happy. I started working more hours at the job, and before long I was bringing home in excess of three thousand a month—more than enough to cover our monthly bills and facilitate a stress-free life of leisure. Monique was happy and that meant our kid would be happy.

She was six months along now. Her stomach looked like a basketball, and I enjoyed watching her waddle around the house every day and ease in and out of chairs like she was an old woman. Since she was short, she looked like a big belly with legs. I don't know how, but somehow word got back to G that Monique was pregnant, and I got a call from him out of the blue after about three months without contact. "I see you 'bout to be a dad, huh, main man?"

I was reluctant to answer him. He knew the answer and I wondered why he even asked. "Yeah, how you know?" G didn't answer, and I figured Malik must've said something to him about it. It bothered me that he didn't express any congratulatory sentiments. He seemed more intent on leading me into a setup so he could justify reprimanding me about Monique being my girlfriend. I wasn't about to get pulled into that. Malik already tried to give me his opinion about my choice to be with Monique, and I cut him off before he had a chance to get started good and that was about a month ago. I haven't heard from him since, but I guess we're still friends.

I was fascinated by the way he only chose to speak on my decision and Monique's pregnancy after I refused to hang out with him and run the streets hunting for stragglers. It seemed like no matter how hard I tried to live my life like a normal person, everybody had something to say about it. If I ran the streets aimlessly, that wasn't good enough either. I was fed up with all of it and decided that when it came to my personal life I wasn't going to listen to anybody, especially if it involved Monique.

At that point it didn't matter what was best for me. I had a child on the way and Monique was depending on me. G and I talked for awhile, and he even suggested the possibility of abortion to me. I didn't get angry with him. Up until now he didn't know how important Monique was to me. Initially, I had convinced him she was just something to do, but now there was no need to pretend. I loved her and that was that.

"G, listen. I appreciate everything you've done for me, but I have to make my own choices in life at this point, man, and I'm tired of living on the edge."

He interrupted me saying, "Sean, I know what you saying, but you can't do it this way man. What good is it going to do you if you get locked up? I know the girl don't mean you no harm, but you got to realize you don't need to have anything in your life you aren't prepared to walk away from."

I understood, but I had to make him understand that it was too late at that point. The damage was done and I was okay with it. I just wanted everybody to leave me alone and let me do me and said, "I know, but now that she pregnant I ain't got no choice."

G responded coldly, "You always have a choice, and you have to put yourself first. Don't get me wrong. I don't have anything against Monique, but you have to remember your situation man. Trust me when I tell you that the minute the Feds scoop you up— heaven forbid—she going to be doing her thing, and all you going to be doing for the next fifteen years is kicking yourself in the ass thinking, 'Damn, why didn't I walk away when I could?'

I don't know if it was because I knew what he said to be true or because I wanted to believe otherwise, but I didn't want to hear anymore about it. "Listen, G. I feel you man, but Ima just take my chances and let the chips fall where they fall."

G didn't say another word after that. Instead he just sighed before closing the conversation with, "Alright, but just remember what I said. Whatever happens at this point is on you."

Chapter Fifty-Four
Whoopdedo

"Guess what, Sean?!"

I didn't feel like guessing. I didn't feel like talking. But I pretended to be interested in what Tina had to say as long as she said it quickly. I was on my lunch break, and Stephanie had been going through one of her mood swings, bitching at everybody for the smallest things like coming back from lunch two minutes late.

"What's the deal?" I said with a half smile on my face.

Tina either didn't notice or was so consumed with joy she didn't care. "Stephanie is getting married tomorrow!" Now I understood why Stephanie was so bitchy and why she had suddenly started flaking out on everybody. She must've been getting cold feet! She'd been asking about Brian an awful lot too in the last month. Out of curiosity, I asked G when was the last time he'd spoken to him, and he said B had disappeared and nobody knew where he was or what he was doing.

Now that it was show time, Stephanie was forced to finally go through with it because calling it off was out of the question. Besides, Stephon was too good a catch to let go, even if she didn't love him. The dough he was making was enough for him to lease all the affection money could buy. I turned to walk outside to my car, and Tina interrupted me again to say, "And they're getting a house built from the ground up!" I stood there thinking, "How else does a house get built?", and I chuckled as I remembered G setting me straight when I mentioned something similar to him about someone I knew once who said the same thing.

He said, "Black people are always misrepresenting and overplaying regular shit, knowing damn well the house is going to be built whether it's sold or not and picking a floor plan is not the same as designing one!" He called it monkey shit; and hearing Tina say it the way she did, I reluctantly agreed with him. By now we were ten minutes into my lunch break, and I cut her off saying, "Listen, I'm 'bout to go to Chick-fil-A up the street, so if ya mouf ain't hurten you can ride wit me and finish your story, but I got to get a grub."

Tina laughed and said, "You got jokes, huh? You just like your crazy brother." She paused and seemed to be waiting for me to respond with some news about G, but I wasn't about to walk down that road. After a brief moment she realized I wasn't going to bite the bait she'd thrown out and went back to her original story.

"Stephanie told me her and Stephon got a good deal on their house and that I should look into buying one, too." Right before we fell out, Malik and I had just had a long conversation about how Atlanta is full of black women living in houses alone, wishing for a man. The majority of them come home every day and bypass the living room and go from the garage directly to the bedroom because there's no reason to stop anywhere else in the house.

Malik said, "It's like they all come here and immediately buy a house for the sake of buying it or bragging rights and are quick to say, 'I don't need no man for nothing. I pay my own bills!' As if paying your own bills is something to be rewarded for. Yeah, sure there are a few who don't ask, but they ain't got no problem revealing the hardship they're currently enduring, hoping to catch a sucka who'll be more than willing to rescue 'em from a situation they claim don't exist."

Malik went on to say, "And they all do it thinking we can't see through it, not realizing that that's the reason why half of 'em can't keep a man and end up spending most of their time clustered up over their girlfriends' houses to keep from being lonely. The other half work such long hours that by the time they get home they go straight to sleep, too tired to notice they're alone. If you notice, you don't see no single white women in these new developments, do you? That's 'cause they know that you don't buy a house until you're married or getting married, and that's something you and your husband do together!"

For as ditsy as Stephanie was, at least she had enough common sense to buy a condo and wait until she was proposed to before choosing to a house. That's how me and Monique were going to do it. Tina and me had been to Chick-fil-A and back and were now sitting in the parking lot as I tried to stuff my chicken sandwich down my throat. Tina meanwhile was still running her mouth about Stephanie's wedding plans while I sat there thinking, "Whoopdedo."

Chapter Fifty-Five
The Good Life

Life is good when you have a roof over your head, food in the refrigerator, and a good girl by your side. It had been a year and some months since I showed up on G's doorstep, and I still couldn't believe the way I had changed my life. I never thought it was possible; all I knew was hustling.

My life didn't have a purpose then, and I never considered doing anything else with it other than making as much money as I could as quick as I could so that I could live the good life. Working and loving Monique made me realize my original idea of the good life was backwards. All I did was wake up thinking how nice life can be when you do things the right way. Our bills were paid and Monique respected me as a man.

"What you making for dinner tonight?" Monique peeked out from behind the kitchen cabinets where she had been standing preparing my breakfast. She always got up to make sure I had something to eat before going to work.

"I was going to make some fried chicken, spinach, and macaroni and cheese."

I nodded my head and jokingly said, "Dass whassup. I'm glad to see you trying it again."

She laughed and handed me a bacon and egg sandwich as I made my way to the door. I laughed as she barely made her way over to where I was standing, wobbling the whole way. I kissed her on her forehead and rubbed her stomach and walked out to the car to go to work. She was standing in the doorway looking at me. She'd never done that before and I waved and said, "Bye-bye. And make sure you don't burn up the chicken this time."

Monique's cooking skills were a little suspect, and I rarely teased her about it. But messing up the fried chicken was something that wasn't to be played with, and I wanted her to be extra careful as I was looking forward to coming home and kicking back and getting my grub on!

I got to work a little late that morning, and by the time I walked into the building and onto my floor, Stephanie was already in full swing, riding everybody about getting their numbers up. She looked at me as I made my way to my cubicle. I had barely logged in before noticing Stephanie walk off the floor to take a phone call in her office. She reemerged less than a minute later and looked at me strangely, making me wonder what in the hell was she mad at me for this time?

After she finished cracking the whip and getting the team started for the day, she came over to my cubicle and said, "Whass your problem today? I got two calls for you this morning; the first time they asked if you worked here, and the second one just now they asked were you at work today. I know you ain't been trying to find another job 'cause if you think Ima give you a good reference you crazy. If you leave my team, you might as well stop speaking to me."

I didn't know what the hell Stephanie was talking about and wondered who in the hell would be calling me at work, not to mention how they even knew to call Stephanie to inquire concerning my whereabouts. I knew it wasn't Monique because she knew the number to my cell phone. Although I didn't know what in the hell Stephanie was talking about, I decided to allay her worries and put her mind at ease.

"I don't know what that call was about 'cause I ain't trying to work nowhere else, and everybody I know got my cell number so I'm just as confused as you are." Stephanie's suspicions subsided after that and she went into her office and tended to business for the day. My day was going well and by lunchtime I had sold 12 long distance packages.

"Listen up, all y'all. Sean has already made twelve for the day out of the team projected 50 for the day. After lunch, if he does twelve more, then I guess I'll be sending a few of y'all home since it will be obvious that he's doing the work of several people!" I laughed at Stephanie's veiled threat, knowing no one else took her seriously. I was headed to Chick-fil-A and decided to go and come right back.

As I crossed the parking lot toward my car, I heard a voice from behind call out to me. "Sean. Wait up, man. Ima ride with you." It was Travis. Travis was a good dude who appeared to be just like me in that he liked nice things and was always popping up to New York and coming back with the latest styles of everything. Whenever he would go I always gave him dough to grab something hot for me. "Yo, son, check this shit out. I just got the new Prada sneakers. They ain't even get down here yet, son."

I smiled and said, "They hot, but why you ain't tell me you was going up there so I could've passed off some dough for you to cop me a pair."

Travis looked at me, smiled and said, "Yo, son, you know I ain't forget about you. I grabbed another pair in blue in case you wanted 'em. If you don't like 'em, Ima just sell the jawns."

I liked Travis for that and didn't mind him hanging out with me from time to time because he knew how to have a good time. We had gotten to my car and were pulling out of the parking lot when Travis said, "Yo, son, why the dude sitting in the blue Impala looking at us like he crazy?" I looked to see what Travis was looking at but couldn't see what he saw. I didn't bother asking him what he was talking about because he was always gossiping about something. In fact, that was the only thing about him I didn't like.

We were on our way back down the road from Chick-fil-A, and I noticed my cell phone had started ringing. When I reached for it I noticed it was Tina. Just as I opened the flip to answer it the call was lost. The phone rang again immediately, and the second time it was Stephanie. It happened a few more times, and I became frustrated and decided not to answer. I figured they were both playing games. The two of them would often do shit like that as they had in the past, and I was going to blast both of 'em when I got back to the building.

As we pulled up the parking lot, Travis said again, "Yo, look at that dude looking at us all funny." This time I was able to see what Travis was talking about. I turned in the direction he was looking in and noticed a strange white man sitting in the no parking area. The security people at MCI are sticklers for the parking regulations there, and I wondered how and why dude was able to sit there unbothered as he'd obviously been there since we'd left for lunch some thirty minutes before.

We sat in the car listening to a new house music CD Travis had brought back from New York that he claimed was exclusive and ate our chicken sandwiches while we talked of how fly the new Prada shoes were. "Travis, them jawns you got on are like dat! I like the white, and I don't know why you ain't just get two pairs in the same color 'cause I ain't really feeling them blue jawns 'cause you can't really play 'em with anything that ain't coordinated right."

Travis acknowledged me saying, "No doubt, but it's cool son. I told you I had a couple of dudes who wanted to buy them jawns." I was cool with that and figured the next time I went up top to Philly, I'd grab some shit on my own and not have to settle for colors I didn't want.

I finished my sandwich and said, "Yo, I'm 'bout to go back into the building." Travis cleared his throat. The Sprite he was sipping burned his throat and prevented him from responding immediately. "Um-umm. Damn. My fault. Hold up, son, I'm coming too."

We walked back into the building and made our way past the usual dick-riders and fans. When we got to our floor, Travis went in a separate direction as I walked the straight line to my cubicle. As I walked I noticed there were several strange people standing near my cubicle. I was about twenty feet away from them when Tina appeared out of nowhere, grabbed my arm, pulled me into an empty cubicle, and said, "Sean, that's the FBI down there. They got here right after you left to go to lunch. Steph and I were calling you non-stop but you wasn't answering your phone."

All I could think to say was, "Damn! I thought y'all was playing around again like y'all usually do." At that moment I realized they must've been the people who'd been calling all morning and the strangers parked outside in the secured area. My mind raced as I pondered an escape route.

Tina interrupted my thoughts asking, "What they looking for you for?"

Before I could answer I heard unfamiliar voices approaching from the other side of the cubicle and told Tina to leave because I hadn't figured out what I was going to do or how I was going to do it, and I didn't want her getting caught up if I ended up doing something drastic.

She did what I asked and gave me a hug and dipped off without being seen. I took a deep breath and walked out the cubicle in the opposite direction from where the agents were standing. I made it all the way to the elevator and was about to get on, and then stopped dead in my tracks when I heard Travis call my name. "Sean, I left my CD in your car, man. Make sure you don't leave without giving it back to me."

Just as he finished broadcasting my presence to what seemed like everybody on the floor, I heard a deep male voice say, "Sean Starks, I am Special Agent Tucker, and I need you to put your hands up and stay where you are." Unbeknownst to me there had been an agent posted in the stairwell next to the elevators in case I tried to fly the coop; I was caught! I saw no need in making a break for it and didn't want to create a bigger spectacle than the one their presence already caused.

I stood there thinking about Monique, the baby, and how I wasn't going to be there when she gave birth. A feeling of hopelessness was beginning to overwhelm me, and I contemplated doing something crazy, but remembered I did have something to live for now. By this time the whole department was watching, and I felt like dying!

"Mr. Starks, kneel down and put your hands behind your head."

I did as Agent Tucker instructed while everybody on the floor watched in awe. A few of the females let loose a few tears and I heard one or two people say, "Let him go" and "Leave him alone." I knew that wasn't going to happen. The jig was up and it was time to pay the piper. Agent Tucker pulled up a chair, sat it next to the elevator, and instructed me to take a seat while he waited for the other agents to arrive to assist him.

While sitting there I found myself dazed and confused, and I wondered how they were able to track me down. Stephanie and Tina appeared by the elevator doorway as it opened, both saying in unison, "Don't worry, Sean. Ima call Glenn." The thought was comforting, but even he couldn't do anything for me now. The shit was finally over and Agent Tucker, now joined by other nameless agents, led me into the elevator. I turned in time to see the doors slowly close on what was to be my future.

Chapter Fifty-Six
Bad News

I sat there wondering what Glenn was going to say once he heard the news. I knew him well and that meant there was no way of telling how he would react. I'd been planning on reaching out to him but didn't want to do it bearing bad news. On the other hand, I thought who better that he hear it from me. Sean and I were friends, and I owed it to him to call his brother immediately, and I did.

"Hi Glenn."

He paused as he tried to determine who I was. I had called from inside the building and all of the phones at MCI came up as unavailable on caller ID.

"Who's this?"

His response was somewhat harsh, and I started to express all of how I felt, knowing I might not get the chance to again, but that would've been selfish. The Feds probably had Sean in some unmarked car and were probably taking him to some cold, dark jail somewhere. I thought of how nice Sean was and how even though I knew Glenn had dragged my name through the dirt, Sean never judged me for what he'd heard despite what his brother probably said about me.

"It's me. Tina." Glenn paused again as I waited for his response. I knew he was still angry with me for all that'd happened between us, and I expected him to hang up on me. He promised he would if I ever called him again after our last conversation. Seems he got wind of more news about my past indiscretions and discovered many of 'em happened during our time together. "Before you hang up on me, I was only calling you to tell you the FBI came and locked your brother up today."

"What?! Awe wow! How the fuck did they get him?" I wasn't sure if Glenn was asking me directly or just thinking out loud.

I heard him sigh deeply before he said, "Was it hard on him? Did they rough him up or something?"

I responded, "I was there when it happened and he seemed alright. He was sad, though, and I could tell he wanted to cry, but he didn't."

Glenn said, "I don't know why that boy ain't leave that fucking job like I told him to. I told him not to stay there 'cause I knew they was going to find out sooner or later and come and snatch him up!"

Although Glenn's response was a concerned one, it contained a little bitterness too, almost as if he was more concerned with being right than thinking of all the problems Sean was now going to face. I forgot myself momentarily and said, "Glenn, you should really be worrying about how we can get Sean out of trouble."

Glenn chuckled cynically before saying, "You really don't get it and neither did Sean. Once the Feds get you, ain't nothing nobody can do, and the shit they got him on, it don't matter if he was guilty or innocent. He got to sit for at least a year before anybody pays any attention to his situation."

I didn't really know what Glenn meant when he said "anybody." I guess he meant lawyers and the prosecutors and how long they would take to bring Sean's case in front of the judge. Midway through my thoughts I noticed that Glenn was silent on the other side of the phone and I asked, "Glenn, are you okay?"

He responded slowly as if his thoughts had consumed him, eating away the portion of his brain that controlled speech. "Yea…Yeah, I'm cool, My fault. I zoned out thinking about how I was going to tell my mother that her second baby boy was now incarcerated."

I had forgotten that Glenn's other brother Carlton was locked up and wondered how their mother would take the news of Sean's situation. I wanted to suggest to Glenn that maybe he shouldn't tell her and instead just keep it from her, but then I remembered how Miss Helen always got the news no matter if it wasn't meant for her. She also had a right to know what was going on no matter how she would take it.

I only hoped the news of it wouldn't cause her to slip into a depression or something. It had been a few hours since Sean had been arrested. I wanted call immediately, but I was afraid Glenn wouldn't understand the nature of my call. I suppose it was because, in truth, part of my reason for calling was to tell him about his brother and to find an inroad to rebuild our shattered relationship.

"So what are you going to do? I know you going to come up with something." I was curious to know what Glenn was thinking and what he planned to do. He always had an answer for things and always came through whenever there was a crisis. This time he remained silent, and his silence seemed to confirm this time he wasn't going to be able to come through for Sean.

He finally broke the silence and confirmed it, "You must not have heard me the first time. The Feds are too powerful, and all the creativity in the world can't even come close to resolving Sean's problem, unless he was sitting on a million dollars." There was a finality in Glenn's words. I'd only heard him sound that way when he last told me not to call him again. He paused after expressing his last thought and an awkward silence floated over the phone line.

He seemed to be waiting for me to say whatever it was I was obviously lingering on the phone to say. Finally he said, "I appreciate you calling me and telling me what happened, but Ima go. I got to call my mom and tell her what happened."

Glenn politely waited for my response, and as badly as I wanted to talk about our past, I knew it would've been inappropriate at that time so I just let it go, saying, "You're welcome, and I want you to know that I love you, Glenn."

He let out a big sigh before responding, "You know, Tina, maybe that's true, but I just don't like the way you show it."

Chapter Fifty-Seven
The Letter

It was Saturday when I got the letter. It was the first I'd heard from Sean since the Feds grabbed him. As I opened it, I wondered what it would say and how I would take it.

(Actual letter)

Dear G,

What's up, ock? I hope this letter reaches you in good health and spirit Me, I'm cool. Just waiting things out. What's up with Tina? I hope she's fine. I wish things could workout between 'y'll. I've been heavy into those books you sent me. Man, I can't express enough how they help my mental state, especially The Forty-Eight Laws of Power. I should have been into those books when they were right in my lap. I know, I know. You told me to adopt your theories, but I didn't. I can't lie to you and tell you that I want to go ahead and get this situation over with. I'd much rather be out there with y'all enjoying life. Man, it seems as though I'm a twilight zone in this place. It's seems it was only yesterday that we were in Atlanta safely nestled away. Oh, well. I must press on and get through this ordeal. I pray that one day we will all be united again. I remember you telling me that damn is all I would say. I was in a comfort zone at work and basically brought all of this on myself, but still I pray for a good outcome. Niggas be all over me for how I carry myself and my mannerisms. It behooves me to have a brother like you. I really need you to be around when this thing is over simply because you are like a guiding light. We may squabble and the like, but it's always resolved. Man, all I ask of you is to hold Mom down and the rest of the family. We are a small unit so all shit and differences aside, handle that! One thing is for sure, in here your time kind of flies, especially if you stay busy. What's up with Mom? Kids? The same I'm sure. Listen, the saga must continue; as you said about the Starks clan, you have too much brain capacity to be reckoned with. In other words, we all have to draw from it. We are not ignorant dudes. Sometimes—well, most of the time—I look around and say to myself, "Our people need to be more progressive—CO's and inmates alike—pitiful! Can't expand on it a great deal. Let's just be in observation of law 38. Basically, I can't spread my ideology to common thinking folks nor do I want to even take the time to entertain the thought. It's been four months, and I know I am in for a nice stint, but Lord willing I will make it okay. So pray for me and Ceez. I see from my own experience and others' that people tend to move on and forget about people in jail. So make sure that doesn't happen to anyone of us. So for now I'm out.

P.S. Monique should have the baby sometime soon. At least, that's one thing on the radar that's positive. Wish me luck and send me some dough when you get a chance. Peace, man and I love you.

Chapter Fifty-Eight
Half & Half

I was just turning over after getting up to take a piss. It was 7:00 am. I'd just managed to fall back into a deep sleep when the phone rang. I wasn't going to answer it and let it ring, hoping whoever it was would just leave me alone. I was trying to catch up on my rest after a long night prowling Buckhead in search of sexual pleasures.

The straggler I picked up was a cute college girl who had gotten a little tipsy. She and her friends were walking to their car after having what appeared to be a banging ass night at Cream. I had the top down on my jag as I pulled up to her. She took one look and asked, "Can I ride with you?" My response didn't require words, and I just nodded and hit the power locks, and she hopped in.

After stopping at a gas station to grab a box of condoms, I did my usual and took her back to my place. In a stroke of luck, I discovered that she lived less than a few miles from me, and when she awoke the next morning I gave her cab money to get home. She performed so well that I didn't even have the strength to walk her to the door and told her not to worry about it being unlocked when she left.

When the phone starting ringing I thought it might have been my recently departed guest calling because she was a little short on cab fare, and I dreaded the thought of getting out of bed just to bring her more money. Truthfully, I felt our business was done. Looking at the caller ID I was relieved to see it was G and groggily answered, "Hello."

G responded, "Get rid of whoever you got over there and get dressed 'cause we going to church."

His tone was serious, which was unusual for him. I figured it was probably because his brother Sean had just gotten locked up a few days before. To tell you the truth, I had been feeling a little strange after it happened too. Sean was my man and a real good dude. I couldn't help thinking life must truly be a bitch for something like that to happen to a cat like him. But then, I guess it was his own fault because he knew the risks of being a hustla.

In the middle of my thoughts, G chimed in again saying, "I heard about this church called New Life." I could hear church music playing in the background and could tell G was feeling whatever he was going through that morning. I sympathized with him briefly before looking over at the clock, noticing it was now 7:05 am and snapped out of it saying, "Dog, I'm still sleep. Ima holla at-choo. Just hit me back in an hour or something, and I'll let you know."

G laughed before saying, "I guess you ain't heard about New Life, huh? If you get there ten minutes too late, then you'll be parking at least ten blocks away from the church. Plus, my mom told me I should check it out 'cause the pastor is supposed to be all that."

Before G could say anymore, I interrupted him and said, "Man, I'm cool on that big ass church. Plus, I heard the dude got Bentleys and air planes and shit. How we gon get the Word from him. He seem like he into the same shit we into."

G for some reason was unaffected by my remarks and was determined to go but obviously didn't want to go alone and said, "I ain't want to say this, but my mom also told me that that church is always packed with wall-to-wall women."

I sat up and thought to myself, "Nigga, that's all you had to say in the first place." It was funny that G knew exactly what to say to motivate me, and I wondered if my lifestyle was truly that transparent. I decided to go but not because I thought it'd make any difference, but more so to support my man in whateva he was going through—and to sneak a few peeps at some eye candy. "Alright, nigga. Just come through. I'll be ready in about thirty minutes."

By the time we got to the church it was already overflowing with members. I had never seen anything like it before in my life. Everywhere I looked there were women: to my left, to my right, in front of me, and behind me. They were tall, short, dark, light, skinny, and fat. Whatever you liked, New Life had it all. As we walked through the doors we were handed programs with a picture of a young black man who looked to be in his mid forties, and the name beneath the photo read Bishop Freddie Strong.

We arrived just as services were about to begin. Walking between the pews was like trying to navigate through an obstacle course because I couldn't help bumping my knees every time

I looked up to see a pretty face. The choir began to sing We Worship, and the whole place seemed to resonate with love and spirituality.

Soon afterward the music subsided and the pastor appeared at the pulpit. I looked down at the program to see what the sermon for the day was to be and it read: Proverbs 31, "Give Not Thy Strength Unto Women, Nor Thy Ways To that Which Destroyeth Kings." From the time the Bishop began preaching the Word, it seemed as if he was directing sermon to G and me both.

Halfway into his fiery diatribe I was hit with a feeling of anxiety and guilt. Because the main reason I was at church that day was because I knew it would be filled with women. I slumped down in the pew feeling ashamed at not having enough respect for the Lord's house because from the time I entered the place half of me was on the prowl and hoping to see the finest honeys the church had to offer.

The other half of me was hoping salvation would find its way to me and save me from the life of foolishness the Bishop had just exposed. "Malik, how 'bout it seem like the dude is talking about you and me." Without knowing it G had tapped into my exact thoughts and continued on, as was his way, to break down his interpretation of Proverbs 31.

"Yo, Proverbs is deep, but what it should really say is, "Do not give your money to women or waste your time and energy in pursuit of gratuitous sex and foolishness. I think it would reach a lot more dudes if it was written that way."

I was always surprised when G came up with his unique observations. I couldn't help wondering, "If he had so much insight, then why in the hell did he not follow his own logic and wisdom." I guess that's just the way it is with some people. When it comes to giving advice, everyone is an authority, but when it comes to following it, most act as if they ain't got the sense God gave a goat. On the other hand, G had plenty of sense, but somehow when it came to women his mind switched to a different mode, a mode that was almost too accommodating, whereas my attitude toward women had always been to treat them as objects.

Either way, G and I both needed to rethink what it was exactly we wanted to do with our lives and do it! I only hoped he was sitting thinking the same. In the last few months, a change had taken hold of G. It appeared almost instantly after he'd left Tina's trifling ass alone. When he called me this morning, I would never have guessed he would have wanted to go to church or that I would have even gone with him.

He knew the deciding factor for me was the women. That didn't seem to matter much to him. I looked at him a few times during the sermon and saw he was completely enraptured by Bishop Strong's commentary. Admittedly, I was too. I had heard many stories about New Life and had come to believe it was nothing more than an establishment that catered to fashion and money more so than to the word of God.

That Sunday I discovered I was wrong. Sitting in church that day, I realized that no matter what people in the street have to say about anything, it is always better to get your own answers. That way you won't have to rely on other people's opinions, which are all too often slanted by personal dislikes that typically have no basis in truth.

All the mansions, Bentleys, and jets in the world wouldn't have made what the Bishop preached that day any less true, and I was happy and blessed to have been there to hear it for myself. When services ended G asked, "You going to holla at any of the sistas?"

He was shocked when he heard me say, "Naw, man. I don't even have that kind of feeling right now. I'm feeling something, though. I can't really say I know what it is, but it feels good. I like it and I don't want to cheapen it." I went silent afterwards; in truth, there was nothing else to say. I came to church that morning with a different agenda, and now was about to leave with a changed outlook. I was humbled and wanted to know more about the power of God, the same God who had the power to change my mind.

Chapter Fifty-Nine
Up Top

"Whassup, G? Come take this ride wit me."

I was a little curious when Malik asked me to roll with him. For starters it was still daylight and he rarely prowled the streets before dark. "What's up, young buck? You seem like you got something on your mind."

Malik was sitting slumped down in the seat of his car with a blank look on his face. The radio was playing *"This Can't Be Life"* by Jay-Z, Beanie Siegle, and Scarface and Malik's face seemed to fit the theme of the song. I knew something was bothering him because of how long it took him to respond to my question.

He responded finally by saying, "Man, I got a lot of shit on my mind. I need your advice on something." I heard the locks click on the car. I opened the door and climbed in. The sun was just starting to set as we pulled off from his driveway. The top was down and the wind in my face was refreshing as we zoomed down I-20.

I had no idea where we were headed and only stopped over there to pick up a new valour Sean-John warm-up suit I'd asked him to grab for me the last time he went to Philly. It had been awhile since Malik and I hung out. We were still cool and all, but the energy he expended roaming the streets of Atlanta and chasing women was more than I could handle. Now that Sean was gone, Malik was rolling solo. He and Sean had been tag teaming heavy while I had been quietly doing my own thing, chasing one here, two there, but still in moderation.

I never really could keep up with "young Leek" and was happy when he and Sean started hanging out, allowing me to silently fade off to be the thirty-something cat I was. I knew whatever Malik was going through centered on his insatiable lust for different women. For a time I attempted—unsuccessfully—to wean myself from my dependency on sex, too, and was still going through my own private hell when it came to my vice.

We were well into downtown before Malik turned the music down and started talking. "Yo, man. I'm thinking about selling my crib and getting the fuck out of Atlanta."

Malik's statement caught me totally off guard. Although I knew what he was going through it; I didn't know Sean's arrest had gotten to him to that extent. I guess everything, combined with the loss of his "Roady," had begun to overwhelm him. Realizing it was a delicate situation, I crafted my response carefully so as not to seem unconcerned and said, "Naw, man, you need to just cool out for a while and don't make no decisions right now 'cause your mind ain't right, and if you make a move when your mind ain't right, you end up worse off than you were to begin with."

Malik responded, "G, I don't know whas going on wit me; I can't seem to make up my mind. One week I'm cool, breezing through and sweeping the streets and pulling broads. The next week I feel all guilty and shit because they don't know that I don't give a fuck about 'em; and the worst part is it seems like that's all I do."

I didn't have the heart to tell Malik that that was all he did, but I was glad to see he had become aware of it for himself. Malik and I both were responsible for causing a great deal of heartache and pain to others as well as ourselves. I used to wonder how he felt or if he even knew he was responsible for his own unhappiness.

Hell, I'd still believed some of my actions were justified and had only recently begun to rethink the validity of my behavior after that Sunday in church. As a result, I started saying a new prayer, one I hoped would help me find my out of the chaos that was my life in Atlanta.

After a long pause an idea hit me and I said, "You know what, man? We going up top to Philly. Take me back to my car and meet me at the airport by 6 o'clock, and we'll catch the 8:30 flight."

Malik responded, "That's probably just what I need 'cause Atlanta got my head spinning."

It was only 2 o'clock and we had plenty of time to go home and pack our things. We each did so and met back up at Hartsfield International at 6 o'clock as planned. When I arrived, I called Malik and discovered he was already there.

"Yo, I'm over here in Houston's getting a grub. You know where it is?"

I responded, "Yeah, I'll be over there in a minute. I see this shirt in Bernini's window I want to grab. By the time I made it over to Houston's, Malik was already sitting there eating. I joined him as the waitress came to ask what I was having. I wasn't hungry and decided to order something light. "Just give me some chicken fingers and a ginger ale, and that'll be it." My food came back quickly, and I satisfied myself on it and washed it down with my soda while watching Sports Center on ESPN. Malik was on his cell phone the whole time. I tipped the waitress, and we made our way to the gate and got there just in time to make our flight.

Chapter Sixty
Life's Lessons

It had been two days since I last spoke to G and four days since I had been in Philly, and I was bored as hell. When we arrived initially the excitement was at a premium, seeing old friends, meeting new faces, and visiting family members kept me busy for a time, but after while it all seemed to fizzle out, leaving me to realize that being there didn't make happy either. The more I thought about it, the more I realized I was just running from myself and coming to Philly didn't change the fact that I had brought myself with me because no matter where I went there I was.

I was about to make call, but my cell phone rang at the same moment I lifted the lid. I was surprised to see a Philly number on the display because I hadn't given my number out to anyone during my visit. I answered hesitantly and was pleasantly surprised to hear the voice of my aunt Sandra on the line. "Hey boy, your mother told me you was in town, and you ain't even call your aunt Sandra."

I responded, "Naw, Aunt Sonj. I just been running around. You know I love you. How you been anyway?"

I could tell she was smiling as she said, "I'm fine and everybody's okay, except for your grandfather."

I paused for a second, wanting clarification on what she meant about my grandfather's health. "What you mean? What's the matter with Big Charles?"

Aunt Sonj replied, "Well, he's very sick and he's been in the hospital for the last few days. Ironically, he asked for you yesterday without knowing you were here. The doctors say he only has about a month before he's expected to pass. And that's why I called your mother and found out you were up here."

My heart dropped once I heard the news that Big Charles wasn't expected to make it. He wasn't my grandfather by blood. He had married my grandmother after my mother was born, but he was the only grandfather I had ever known. He would always brag on me as if I was his grandson, and although there were no blood ties, he never made me feel as if there wasn't. I loved him for that, and he was the first person to give me a shot at driving a car, even though I was only eight years old at the time. I'll always remember that.

The news of his illness came as shock because I had always known him to be a strong, outgoing, and otherwise gentle man. I couldn't and didn't want to picture him lying in a hospital bed waiting for his time to come but realized that this would probably be my last opportunity to see him. So much strange shit had been happening lately; and after seeing how fate handled Sean, I wasn't about to gamble with it by taking chances by thinking tomorrow could be a better day.

"Aunt Sonj, what hospital is he in?"

She replied, "He's in Temple University Hospital in North Philly on Broad and Ontario, and he's in room number 712." I knew Temple University Hospital well. Their trauma center was world renowned for treating gunshot victims. And the Streets of Philadelphia ain't have no problem keeping them beds full, a few of which played host to friends of mine a time or two.

I drove to North Philly as soon as I finished my conversation with Aunt Sonj. It normally took twenty minutes coming from South Philly, but that day virtually all the lights were green, and after I crossed Spring Garden Street headed north, I got there in fifteen minutes flat.

As I walked in the hospital I was greeted with smiles from the numerous female nurses, medical assistants, and orderlies employed there, each enticing me in her own personal way and inviting me to engage them. As hard as it was, I ignored the temptation and remained focused on the reason I was there—to see my grandfather.

As I walked the corridor intermittingly passing pretty, smiling faces and voluptuous bottoms, I wondered if my ability to attract women was a curse or a blessing. I got off the elevator and neared my grandfather's room. When I got there a nurse was coming out and closed the door behind her. As she passed I asked, "Is that Charles White's room?"

The nurse smiled passively before softly saying, "Yes, it is, but he's asleep right now. Are you an immediate family member?"

I responded, "Yes, I'm his grandson."

The nurse responded, "You can go in and visit with him, but you may want to wait until later because he's just been sedated and he may not be coherent."

I thanked her as I softly pushed the door to his room open.

I walked in and he was lying there peacefully asleep. I turned to walk back out, deciding to take the nurse's advice and come back later but was stopped as I reached the door, when I heard him say, "Where you going Malik?"

I walked back in the room smiling, mostly because his voice came through clear and strong just as I remembered it. "I ain't going nowhere Big Charles. How 'bout you?" He laughed, and I could tell it was a struggle to do so. Still it felt good to see him in good spirits.

He responded by saying, "They say my time is up, but I ain't worried about all that. And as for where I'm going, if you count the last twenty years of my life, I know Ima be alright, but if you count the first half, then I got to tell you I ain't so sure."

We both laughed after that, but the pain of it wasn't funny. There was a short pause before he picked up the conversation again saying, "So I hear you been doing real well for yourself down south and I'm proud of you. We all are. But I see something in you right now that ain't settin' too well; am I right?"

I stood there thinking, "Damn, is my stress that clear to everybody? And how could this old man who hadn't been around me in over ten years detect something was wrong with me." I tried to shift the attention from me off to something else, by asking, "So what day they gon let you outta here?"

Big Charles ignored me and went right back to his original question. "Boy, I asked you if I was right?"

If he didn't have much time left, I sure as hell couldn't tell because his voice boomed with the same intensity I'd remembered it having back when I was kid, and it intimidated me in just the same way. It was obvious that I wasn't going to be able to get away from the topic so I took a deep breath and answered him by saying, "Yeah, you know how life can be sometimes, but I'm alright. I'm just worried about you right now."

Big Charles struggled as he sat up and said, "Malik, I know I never gave you much in your life, but the words Ima give you right now are worth their weight in gold. The one thing I am most happy about is the time I took in choosing my wife and raising my children. Yeah, sure when I was younger I had my share of chasing skirts, but I too remember coming to a point in my life as a single man when I decided that it was time for me stop wasting my time and energy on short term pleasures, and I'm glad I did because had I not you wouldn't even be standing here by my side right now.

"Basically, son, any man can get out here and chase some skirts and have a good time with 'em, but it's a real man who knows that true happiness lies in choosing one woman and settling down to raise a family, and if you got somebody in your life that loves you and cares for you, then you need to treat 'em right and stop fighting what's good for you."

My mind was in a thousand places at once. I couldn't believe my grandfather was able to see straight through me and my struggles. Miraculously, I didn't feel as badly as I had before, and even though he was lying there in a hospital bed, the wisdom in his words made him appear to be as strong and vibrant as he had ever been. He was staring at me as he spoke, and his eyes seemed to be focused on everything I thought was hidden. Now that he was finished speaking I didn't know what to say.

Big Charles must've sensed I was at a loss for words and removed the burden by saying, "Come here, boy, and give me a hug, and let me go back to sleep, but you make sure you give me a call later on, you understand?" I did as he asked and afterwards helped him settle back down into the bed. As I turned to walk out the door I stopped and thanked him for giving me what I'd needed to move forward, and told him I loved him.

It's funny, though. Here he was in what was supposed to be his last days on earth, yet he still found the time to make me feel like I mattered, just like he'd done when I was a kid. I owed Big Charles a lot and decided to start paying him back immediately by heeding his advice and calling Tracey the minute I walked out of the hospital.

****

"Hello, can I speak to Tracey?" She paused, pretending not to know who I was, like most women do when you're on their shit list.

After about five seconds she responded, "Who's this?"

I responded, "It's Malik. How you been?"

She said, "I'm fine, but I'm busy right now. Can I call you back?"

I knew that wasn't going to happen and didn't let her get off the line saying, "Tracey, please just hear me out. I know I been an asshole and I hurt you, but I want you to know that it was never personal. I knew all along you were a quality woman; I just didn't know how to embrace your qualities or you. The thought of us being together scared me because I was afraid if I let you get close maybe I would get hurt in the end, and that was something I wasn't prepared to deal with.

"The reason I called you was because my eyes have been opened, and I am aware of what I need in my life right now—and it's you." Tracey sat silently for a long time, making me wonder if she was still on the line. The silence was interrupted when I heard a faint sniffle as Tracey chimed in, trying to catch her breath and form words between the sporadic breathing caused by her crying.

"Malik, I tried so hard to make you happy and show you I could be a good woman. I spent a lot of nights trying to figure out why you played me like that, and I still don't know why. Malik, I'm thirty-one years old and I'm tired of walking down this road so if this is another one of your confused plots to get me back in your rotation, then I'm begging you—please spare me."

I sat there thinking, "How could I have done her wrong? She must really love me" and that was all the confirmation I needed. "Tracey, I'm in Philly now, but I'm on my way back to Atlanta tonight and I need to see you as soon as I get back. Is that okay with you?"

Tracey composed herself long enough to respond, "We'll see when you get here." I didn't blame her for that and knew I deserved worse. She had every right to be unsure of my intentions, and it was going to be up to me to show her that this time they were good. Tracey didn't know it, but she was all I had left and, more importantly, all I wanted. I promised myself I wasn't going to lose her again.

****

I was already at the airport when I called G, "Old head, what's up? I ain't heard from you in a couple days. Whachoo been doing?"

G responded, "I been chillin.'You know, making my rounds. Right now I'm down on South Street with this broad I been trying to get at for the last six years, but damn, young Leek, you sound real happy over there. What brought dat on?"

What made me happy was too much to go into at that moment and I just sufficed by saying, "G, I'll tell you when it's official, but I do want to thank you for bringing me up here to Philly for these few days. I'm going back to Atlanta tonight. I'm catching the first thing smoking. As soon as you get back give me a call. Maybe we can go to church or something."

Me and G both laughed at my comment as he said, "Yeah, how bout dat!"

Chapter Sixty-One
What a Fool Believes

"Come here, baby. I like the way your body feels against mine." I had been in the hotel room for three hours, completed two sessions, and Tonya still wanted more. She didn't know it but not only was she not getting another rise out of me, I also wanted her gone. I was stressed and the emotions I had been secretly experiencing lately had put me in a trance-like state. When I spoke to Malik earlier that day, I pretended to be happy, but in truth I wasn't. It seemed everything was going wrong in my life and all was instantly made worse after hearing the news of Sean's arrest.

"Glenn, why are just laying there looking up at the ceiling like that? Didn't you hear me ask you to come closer?"

I heard Tonya, but getting close was something I was beginning to realize I might not ever be able to do. I had known her for six years, and I had been waiting equally as long to get the chance to lay her down. Mission accomplished. I discovered it didn't quite bring me the satisfaction I'd always fantasized it would, not that she wasn't fulfilling; in fact, she ranked with the best of 'em! My discontent had a much deeper origin—me.

I'd spent the last year relentlessly pursuing pleasure, making foolish decisions, and yet still somehow expecting fulfillment. I lay there thinking, "I should be smiling by now." After all, I was in bed with a new beautiful conquest. Isn't that the way things are supposed to be? I followed the blueprint, moved on, and didn't look back. What I couldn't figure out was why I was still unhappy. Who was I kidding? I knew why, and my subconscious was tired of the game I was playing. Something inside me was fighting its way out and had been ever since going to church with Malik that day.

I wondered what it meant, and if I allowed it to manifest itself, would it make my life better? Whatever the outcome, I realized God was forcing me to see the truth for what it was. I had to become accountable for my own actions and face the reality of my misery as being self-inflicted. I had let scores of good girls slip through my fingers; first because of immaturity, and then because of anger, but overall because I was a fool. When I thought of my weaknesses, I wanted to scream. Because of them I was half the man I could be.

Sex for me was like food, and my quest for it led me to women who gave me indigestion. Although I knew better, I kept doing the same thing over and over again, expecting a different result each time and was actually beginning to wonder if I was insane. Although I'd written about it, somehow I just couldn't seem to follow my own advice because here I was again, lying next to someone whose companionship made not an ounce of difference to me.

"Baby, come here. I want you."

Tonya gently pulled my arm, but I didn't budge. The thoughts I was having had begun to overwhelm me. The realization that sex would never equate to happiness created an awkward feeling inside me, and I rolled over onto my side to keep her from groping at my crotch. I was facing the window now, and the curtains were pulled back, and I was staring out into the night sky. It had been awhile since I had been back and Philly looked beautiful to me.

I don't know if it was because I had experienced so much misfortune in Atlanta, or I'd just really missed that old city. Whatever it was, I was glad see it hadn't lost any of its charm. Looking out the window felt as if I was looking out into my past, and the night sky swallowed my thoughts. As my eyes roamed the clear, moonlit sky, I noticed it was littered with stars, each seemingly representing all of the people I had encountered throughout my life. The spaces between them seemed to represent my lack of closeness, trust, and compassion. Still, they all seemed to be foolishly drawn to the moon, which I likened to myself. It sat in the center of them all, shinning like the gigantic, unreachable, desolate, and lonely place it is.

When we got to the hotel room, I had turned on the radio. Sunday was oldies night in the city and WDAS 105.3 had been living up to its reputation by playing a non-stop barrage of classic oldies by Tina Marie, Donnie Hathaway, and the Isley Brothers. I got up to relieve myself and noticed Tonya had fallen asleep.

I guess she got tired of nagging me about giving her another round. After I came out of the bathroom, I got down on my knees and began saying my prayers, asking the Lord to forgive my vanity because had Tonya not been asleep I would've ignored my obligation to Him. I had this funny way about me and truthfully didn't like myself and often wondered if God felt the same. I was on my knees so long they started to get sore, but I refused to get up as I clutched my hands together in repentance, asking what seemed like a thousand requests for wisdom, forgiveness, strength, and understanding.

I was tired of being a fool, basing my happiness on the whimsical nature of women and not having enough common sense and discipline to know that what you want ain't always what you need. I felt tears rolling down my cheek as I finished my prayer with a promise: from that point on, as much as was in my power, I would always do the right thing and would never again be the cause of someone else's unhappiness. How could I when I was currently enduring the aftereffects of my own.

I opened my eyes and lifted my head, looking first at Tonya. I had gotten so immersed in my prayer that I had forgotten she was in the room with me. Satisfied she hadn't eavesdropped, I turned and sat on floor where I had been kneeling and faced the window, looking back out into the now empty sky. All of the stars had disappeared and all that could be seen was the moon, isolated and more alone than before. I thought of Sean and the turn his life had taken, Ceez and his plight, and ultimately my self-created reality as evidenced by the truckload of failed relationships and one-nighters peppered throughout my life.

In the midst of my reflections the D.J. announced, "Up next: "Love Won't Love Nobody" by the Circles." It seemed like ten years had passed since I had last heard that song and just like then, the effect was still bittersweet. I hadn't wiped the tears from my face and noticed they increased as I turned up the volume on the radio. I'd always liked the way the piano subtly began to play at the advent of the song, as if it were preparing you for a sad story, but you knew you had to be strong when you heard it because the lesson it contained was more enduring than the pain of listening to it. I folded my knees up close to my chest as the first chords of the piano began to play and crossed my arms over them and rested my head similar to the way kindergarteners do on their desks and listened silently for the vocals to begin:

> Sometimes a woman will come and go
>
> You hope for love but it won't let you know
>
> In the end you'll still be feeling her,
>
> But then she's gone; and you're all alone
>
> I never learned to love myself, I've been a fool but right now I need someone else yeah yeah yeah
>
> And Just like Boy Blue, I'd blow my horn so you could find your way home
>
> girl, I should have known: it takes a fool to learn that love won't love nobody...

Proverbs 31:10

"Who Can Find A Virtuous Woman? For Her Price Is Far Above Rubies."

Black Reality Publishing
"Lost In Atlanta"

Please send me_____copies ($19.80 each; this price includes 7% sales tax,

for shipping and handling of Lost In Atlanta.

Method of Payment ____cash ____check# ____MasterCard ____Visa

Card #_____Exp. Date _____

Signature_____

Please allow a minimum of two weeks for delivery

For future orders please list your name, phone number, mailing address and E-mail for upcoming promotions. Thank you.

Name_____

Address_____

E-mail_____

Phone number_____

Please make checks payable to: Black Reality Publishing

For more information mail or call

Black Reality Publishing
4195 Panola Lake Circle, Lithonia Georgia 30038

Phone number 1-866-250-8880

Info@LostInAtlanta.com

www.LostInAtlanta.com